WILD WESTERN PASSION

Zac saw Prudence standing amongst the shadows of the trees, off the brick path and away from the flowering plants.

"If you looked at a man like that out west, you'd be flat on your back in minutes," he said.

"My back?" She flushed as his meaning sank in. "Oh!"

"Unless you knew how to protect yourself—with a gun. Do you own a gun, Prudence?"

"No," she whispered as he stepped toward her, slow, sure, and easy.

"Then what would you do if he reached out for you?" he asked, and his hand shot out, circling her neck.

"I'd tell him to take his hand off me," she said firmly.

He drew her toward him. "And if he didn't?"

"I'd scream," she said, more calmly than she felt.

"He'd silence you first." Zac brought his mouth down on hers. He tasted her, all her sweetness and innocence. And she tasted good, too good.

Prudence felt her legs grow weak and her heart hammer wildly. She took a deep breath before she spoke. "So that is what a woman can expect out west?" The thought sent a flood of excitement racing through her.

DANA RANSOM'S RED-HOT HEARTFIRES!

ALEXANDRA'S ECSTASY   (2773, $3.75)

Alexandra had known Tucker for all her seventeen years, but all at once she realized her childhood friend was the man capable of tempting her to leave innocence behind!

LIAR'S PROMISE   (2881, $4.25)

Kathryn Mallory's sincere questions about her father's ship to the disreputable Captain Brady Rogan were met with mocking indifference. Then he noticed her trim waist, angelic face and Kathryn won the wrong kind of attention!

LOVE'S GLORIOUS GAMBLE   (2497, $3.75)

Nothing could match the true thrill that coursed through Gloria Daniels when she first spotted the gambler, Sterling Caulder. Experiencing his embrace, feeling his lips against hers would be a risk, but she was willing to chance it all!

WILD, SAVAGE LOVE   (3055, $4.25)

Evangeline, set free from Indians, discovered liberty had its price to pay when her uncle sold her into marriage to Royce Tanner. Dreaming of her return to the people she loved, she vowed never to submit to her husband's caress.

WILD WYOMING LOVE   (3427, $4.25)

Lucille Blessing had no time for the new marshal Sam Zachary. His mocking and arrogant manner grated her nerves, yet she longed to ease the tension she knew he held inside. She knew that if he wanted her, she could never say no!

DONNA FLETCHER
Tame My Wild Touch

ZEBRA BOOKS
KENSINGTON PUBLISHING CORP.

To my son Marc,
"The Keeper of the Faith."

ZEBRA BOOKS

are published by

Kensington Publishing Corp.
475 Park Avenue South
New York, NY 10016

Copyright © 1992 by Donna Fletcher

First printing: September, 1992

Printed in the United States of America

Chapter One

"Ladies, take your petticoats and corsets off. What you need now is a gun and courage." Zac Stewart didn't smile when he made the strange announcement to the Boston Ladies Social Club. He was serious. Dead serious.

The thirty-five women attending the meeting sat staring at the handsome man, their mouths opened in shock, their faces paled to an off-white.

Zac continued with a telltale shake of his head. Not one of them had actually heard what he had said. The only thing on their empty-headed minds was that he had had the audacity to mention their undergarments.

"The West is far different from the East. There are towns where law and order is the gun you wear strapped to your side. Where weather conditions can prove fatal and food supplies can run so low that you eat one meal a day, or perhaps none at all."

Zac gripped the podium in front of him. His long fingers tightened on the sides of the polished wood as he looked out at the sea of intent and shocked faces.

"Snake meat is good when nothing else can be found. You learn to kill it, strip it, and stew it."

Several of the women groaned, while others raised their hands to their mouths and ran hastily from the room.

Zac caught the eye of one woman near the back. She hadn't flinched since the beginning of his speech. She sat stiff and straight, so stiff that he was positive her corset ran the entire length of her back, forcing her to retain her rigid posture.

Even her lips were puckered tightly shut, and the crazy thought of how difficult it would be to kiss her flashed through his mind, bringing a smile to his face.

Heavy silence descended over the room, and Zac cursed his straying imagination. He'd been told time and time again how devastating his smile could be on the female species, and he wasn't the least bit interested in becoming involved with a specimen from Boston. They were too stuffy and proper for his sinful taste.

"Think wisely about your decision to go west. There are hardships to endure, unpredictable weather, illnesses, and much more."

"You mean the savages, Mr. Stewart?" a young woman in the front row questioned.

"The Indians," Zac corrected, "have proven to be difficult at times."

"Difficult?" another soft, yet stern voice asked.

Zac had no doubt who the staunch voice belonged to. His eyes abruptly settled on the young woman with the puckered lips.

"Difficult is not a word I would use to describe savages who horribly torture decent white people."

"Prudence Agatha Winthrop, really," Caroline Davis admonished. "This is neither the time nor the place to discuss such things. As president of this club, I extended an invitation to Mr. Stewart to speak of the West—"

"And what one could expect if one traveled there," Prudence finished. "He isn't being fair to those who in-

6

tend to journey there if he doesn't properly explain all the hazards one will face."

"Prudence, you are being obstinate as usual," Caroline scolded with a shake of her finger.

"I only wish to hear the truth," Prudence said, her chin tilted just a fraction, a clear sign of her tenaciousness.

"In full detail, Miss Winthrop?" Zac asked, thinking her name *Prudence* fit her prudish nature perfectly.

"If it will help those preparing to make the trek west, then yes."

Zac couldn't help but smile once again. Of course, it wasn't Prudence Agatha Winthrop's face that brought the curl to his lips. She was too plain. Her features were too common to stand out and make a man take notice. No, it was her proper posture and speech that rattled him. She obviously thought herself better than others and perhaps more intelligent.

"Very well, Miss Winthrop, details it is. Let's see, shall I begin with how the Indians strip the women bare, burn various parts of their body, gorge chunks of flesh—"

"Mr. Stewart!" Caroline Davis screeched, standing on shaky legs and covering her full chest with her hand as though her aging heart could take no more.

"Excuse me, Mrs. Davis, but Miss Winthrop did request details. I apologize if I offended anyone."

"Nonsense, Mr. Stewart," Caroline responded sharply, then turned to glare at Prudence. "It is Miss Winthrop who should apologize."

The twenty remaining women focused their attention on Prudence and waited. Each face spoke clearly of their disdain for her improper behavior.

Prudence folded her white glove-covered hands primly in her lap. She held her head erect, looked straight at Mr. Stewart, and spoke. "Please accept my

7

apologies. You have made it quite clear this is not a topic for the Boston Ladies Social Club."

"It's not a topic for any decent woman to discuss," Caroline chided, then turned with a distinct flourish to face the eager faces of the other women. "Ladies, I'm certain Mr. Stewart would be glad to answer *appropriate* questions."

"My pleasure," Zac said with a polite bow, stepping in front of the podium.

There was a chorus of chatter and smiles while the women took a moment to admire Zac. His dark unruly hair fit his handsome features perfectly. It accented his rich brown eyes, defined his strong jawline, and added character to his slender nose. And if his striking looks didn't catch a woman's breath, there was his splendid form to consider. Standing in a smoky gray waistcoat and matching trousers, with a pale gray vest and white shirt, he looked the respectable Bostonian gentleman. But beneath his false facade lurked a far different man. A dangerous one.

"Mr. Stewart," Glenda Butterfield said, waving her hand excitedly. "Is it true you were at one time a gunslinger?" Zac hated that word *gunslinger*. The term sounded wicked, dangerous. And although both elements were part of the lifestyle to a degree, the tabloids had painted a far different and unrealistic picture. Zac hid his musing well and spoke to Mrs. Butterfield with the tone of a patient adult tired of correcting a child.

"Yes, ma'am. I was a gunslinger."

"And you cleaned up the notorious town of Devil City, Kansas, the Sodom of the West," Margaret Dutton announced with a sharp nod.

"Single-handedly," Mary Brisbane added.

There was a quick round of applause.

Zac could see these women weren't interested in the West. The real West in all its raw beauty and horror.

8

They were only interested in his exploits as the infamous gunslinger, Zac Stewart.

"I was hired by the good citizens of Devil City to do a job."

"And a good job you did," Caroline said. "Throwing out the trash and making room for God-fearing, honest citizens."

The questions came rapidly then, like a round of gunfire. Zac felt unprotected, yet his six-shooters wouldn't do him any good here.

"How long did it take you?"

"How many villains were wounded?"

"How many gunfights have you faced?"

No one, not even Prudence, dared to ask the one question that was on every one of their lips: *How many men have you killed?*

Caroline soon brought the question and answer session to an end and invited all to partake of the delicious cakes the ladies had baked for this special occasion.

The women ignored the tempting cakes that ordinarily drew them like bees to a hive, rushing instead toward Zac to question him further.

He didn't back away from them, but stood steady and tall. His six-foot-three-inch height and broad width were intimidating, but his enticing smile and pleasant personality kept them humming around him.

Prudence stood, smoothing the wrinkles from her claret faille skirt.

"That was quite rude," Caroline admonished, walking up to her.

"I think not," Prudence said in defense of herself. "Mr. Stewart was here to inform us of what one could expect if traveling west. I only sought the information promised."

"Oh, for heaven's sake, Prudence. What do you care about the West? Your life is here in Boston and always will be."

"As well as all the other women in the room, Caroline. Now tell me. Why did you really have Mr. Stewart speak to our club?"

Caroline's full face flushed to a bright red. "To-to-to expand our knowledge."

"Of gunslingers?" Prudence questioned tartly.

"You don't care for gunslingers?" Zac asked.

Caroline jumped and turned quickly at the sound of his voice. Prudence turned slowly as though his presence had not the slightest effect on her.

"They have their purpose, Mr. Stewart," she answered calmly.

Zac's dark eyes scrutinized her as he spoke. "And what purpose is that, *Miss Winthrop?*"

Prudence didn't care for the way he emphasized her name. Nor did she like the way his eyes assessed her in one sweep.

He was waiting for an answer and Prudence didn't fail to give it.

"They do away with each other, thereby leaving the streets free of crime for decent citizens."

Caroline's gasp could be heard clear across the room.

Zac couldn't help but grin. This proper Bostonian miss with green eyes that lacked luster and a mouth that was pinched and probably had never been kissed by a real man had the audacity of a saloon hall floozy.

"I suppose, then, my time is numbered," he said calmly, enjoying her brash nature.

"In the end, Mr. Stewart, our past always comes back to haunt us."

"And what in your past, Miss Winthrop, will come back to haunt you?" Zac had meant his words only in jest, but from the way her body tensed in response, he was certain he had hit a nerve . . . and a very raw one at that. *So Miss Winthrop has a skeleton in her closet. How interesting.*

10

Caroline broke the tense silence. "Prudence's past is immaculate. She is from an old Boston family. Her upbringing has been proper as it should be. She has no past to haunt her."

Touch the Bostonians where it hurt the most, their lineage, and they will attack in full force. Even if they didn't care for each other, and it seemed to Zac there was no love lost between Mrs. Davis and Miss Winthrop.

"I meant no disrespect," he said.

To his surprise, Prudence issued the same apology. "I meant none, either."

"Good, good," Caroline said. "Now please enjoy the cakes. They are absolutely delicious. And the ladies worked so hard to please you, Mr. Stewart."

"If Miss Winthrop will join me?" he said, and held out his arm to her.

Proper etiquette would not allow her to refuse his gallant invitation. She took his arm with the slightest of touches as though she were adverse to his nearness. "I'd be delighted, Mr. Stewart."

"I'm happy to hear that, Miss Winthrop," he said, walking with her toward the long table arranged artfully with a white linen tablecloth, sparkling china, polished silverware, and a variety of cakes dripping with sweet icing.

"And why is that, Mr. Stewart?"

Zac placed his hand over her arm and exerted a possessive pressure.

A display of his strength, Prudence thought idly. Men did so love to display their power over women. She smiled pleasantly, especially since she was talented at forced smiles during forced situations, and awaited his answer.

Zac was caught off guard by her expression. Her features were plain and her looks common. Her hair so neatly tucked beneath her hat was a nondescript reddish brown. Her eyes were a soft green. And he concluded from the shape of her dress that she was full in figure, with a large bosom, not that narrow a waist, and full hips.

The type, Zac reminded himself, that a man could grab hold of comfortably and know he's got a woman full in flesh and spirit . . . a real spitfire.

"Did you forget my question, Mr. Stewart?" Prudence asked after his eyes had wandered a bit too assessingly up and down her. She was certain he was ascertaining that she wasn't his type, but then he wasn't hers, either.

Zac shook the crazy thoughts from his head. "I felt you had a distinct aversion toward gunslingers."

Prudence easily slipped her hand from beneath his. "I have no feelings toward gunslingers one way or the other. They are of no concern to me."

"Then why did you attend my lecture?"

"The West, Mr. Stewart. I am interested in the West."

"Why?"

"Knowledge of the unknown."

"No intentions of traveling there?"

"Why? Do you think me incapable of surviving the so-called vigor of the wild?"

Zac gave his head a shake. "You've got that right, ma'am."

Prudence stiffened. "I am quite capable of taking care of myself."

"Here in Boston, where you know what is expected of you. Where the weather conditions are not unpredictable. Where food is in abundance. And where your father's wealth keeps you properly entertained."

"I'm adaptable, Mr. Stewart, and can survive on far less if needed," she retaliated with a decisive lift of her brow.

"That's easy to say when one has everything and is familiar with her surroundings."

"In other words, take me out of my predictable environment and I'd crumble."

"As fast as a slice of this delicious cake, honey," he finished with a smug smile.

Affronted by his use of the endearing word when he meant otherwise, Prudence managed to retain her composure. "Tell me, Mr. Stewart, where did the women who now live out west come from?"

She was quick-witted, Zac noted. "From various parts of the country and some from foreign lands. Most are accustomed to hard work. Their dress is simple and suited to the area. They don't worry about fancy hats and clean white gloves. It's an entirely different way of life, Miss Winthrop. One, I'm certain, you would find repulsive."

Prudence held her head up and stared straight into Zac Stewart's dark eyes. "Your remarks have been most informative. I shall remember them. Good day."

Prudence turned, and with a quick acknowledgment to Caroline for a lovely time, she left.

Zac found a teacup shoved into his hand and dozens of questions being tossed at him once again. What he really wished he had was a strong whiskey and a willing woman. But they would wait. It was only a matter of days and he'd be on his way home, to a life he loved and the land he adored.

Prudence stood on the brick steps of Caroline Davis's house and took a deep breath. She was angry. And anger annoyed her. It was such a wasted emotion. One always lost control of oneself when anger took hold. Several more deep breaths followed, and Prudence once again found herself calm.

"He's a gunslinger," she said softly, as though it were explanation enough for his rude behavior.

She walked down the three remaining steps, turning right at the row of waist-high hedges at the end of the brick walkway. It was a beautiful spring day and she would walk the short distance home. She needed the solitary time to think.

She was determined to follow through with her plan. It was most necessary that she do so. Her steps were sure and quick, as was her mind. This journey west was no hasty decision. She had thought long and hard. She had taken books from the library and studied what was available on the area. And then when Caroline had announced that a gentleman from the West would be speaking at their monthly club meeting, she was thrilled. Her prayers had been answered . . . until she met Zac Stewart.

He thought her spoiled and pampered and, of course, unattractive. Prudence was no fool. She knew herself to be plain, and some referred to her as plump. She had never thought herself *plump*. She just refused to wear a corset. Its confining restraints made breathing next to impossible.

She laughed to herself and wondered how a man would react when he discovered on his wedding night that his wife's waist wasn't as slim as he had been led to believe.

Zac Stewart probably liked his women slim, petite, and perfect.

She hastily covered her left hand with her right as she walked. It was bad enough being plain, but the deformity . . . how she detested it.

Tears of bitterness stung her eyes. Her grandmother had tried so hard to help her. But society could be cruel to those they felt were different.

After several episodes of being laughed at and joked about, her grandmother had stitched her the prettiest gloves to wear all the time.

"If no one can view them, no one can make fun of you," her grandmother had said.

So Prudence wore gloves wherever she went. And no one made fun of her any longer. The two end fingers on her left hand, which had been crooked and useless since birth, were tucked away so as not to offend anyone. And when propriety insisted her gloves be removed, she learned to keep her afflicted fingers from everyone's view.

It was at her grandmother's death bed six months ago that Prudence discovered just how much her plain features and deformity had cost her.

Her grandmother, whom she had loved beyond reason, had whispered the shocking truth to her. *Your mother is alive.* She hadn't believed her, attributing her raving to her illness. After all, her mother had died twelve years ago, a fever having taken her while she was away tending to a sick relative.

Her grandmother had seen Prudence through her grief, her father having been too lost in his own. It had taken years to accept her mother's death. She had been such a vibrant part of Prudence's life.

Now her grandmother was asking her to believe that her mother had left her and even worse she was insisting Prudence go find her.

"The truth. Go find the truth," she had urged.

What truth? Prudence had thought. The truth that her mother had never loved her. That she was ashamed of her only child and had run away. Was this the truth she was to search for? To find a mother who didn't want her then and most certainly wouldn't want her now.

Still, her grandmother's words haunted her. She had been so adamant.

"You must go. You must find her."

Prudence hadn't considered it at first, but then it became a driving force within her. She wanted desperately

15

to find her mother, Lenore Winthrop, and hear her reason for leaving. Hear her tell Prudence herself that she didn't love her.

Her plan had been made then. Nothing, absolutely nothing, would stop her. Not even Mr. Stewart's prediction that she wasn't capable of surviving out west. She had survived a mother's desertion; she could survive worse.

A private detective Prudence had hired discovered that a woman fitting her mother's description had last been seen in a town called Wells City, Kansas, several years ago. She had been in the company of a woman named Sadie, who still resided there. And Wells City was where Prudence intended to go.

She stopped in front of her house and stared at its immense size. It bespoke wealth — three stories, lace curtains, a house staff of fifteen, an outside staff of ten. Yes, she was certainly accustomed to the best.

Prudence entered through the black iron gate and walked up the brick path. She would miss her home and her father, but she would return when her task was complete.

Her plans were final. There would be no change. She would inform her father now, not exactly the truth but a tale he would find believable. He would rave and rant and forbid her to go. She would submit to his command as a proper daughter should. Then tomorrow at dawn, she would slip away and begin her journey. And she wouldn't return until she had found her mother and the truth.

Chapter Two

"You what?" James Allen Winthrop yelled.

"I wish to go west and help educate the heathens," Prudence repeated calmly, having expected this outburst and prepared for it.

James Winthrop shook his head, not actually believing his daughter's words. "That is the most ridiculous notion I've ever heard."

Prudence sat primly on the edge of the green velvet chair opposite her father's mahogany desk. "Not at all, Father. The heathens need culture as well as anyone."

"But *you* won't be teaching it to them," he said sternly.

"And why is that?" she asked softly, ignoring his parental insistence.

"Because I refuse to allow it, Prudence," he said, smashing his hand down hard on the desk and rattling the ink bottle in its silver holder.

He didn't like the way his daughter's eyes glared at him. She was determined. He could see it clearly. Well, this was one time she wasn't going to get her way. "I've been lenient with you to a fault. I have allowed you too much freedom to do as you've wished.

But this . . . this crazy idea is beyond consideration."

Prudence listened like a dutiful daughter. She focused on the familiar way her father, when irritated, would rub his large hands together as he spoke. The way his brow would crinkle in thought. How the few wrinkles around his green eyes would deepen. He was still so handsome at forty-eight. His body still retained its well-defined lines, and his almost six foot height was straight and tall, not hunched over like so many men his age. Even his rich brown hair showed no signs of aging, not a streak of gray touching it.

She had often wondered why he had never taken another wife. Now she knew. He was still married and, therefore, not free to love again. A deep resentment raced through her. How could her mother have hurt him so?

"Are you listening, Prudence?" he demanded.

Prudence nodded. "Of course, Father."

James Winthrop stood and walked around to the front of his desk, facing his daughter. He slipped his gold pocket watch from his dark brown vest and checked the time. He really wasn't interested that it was four in the afternoon. He just wanted some time to formulate his little speech. He had been planning to have this talk with her for the past week, but quite frankly he hadn't had the nerve to approach her.

"Prudence," he started, clearing his voice while giving thought to his words.

"Yes, Father?"

"I've been thinking about your future."

Prudence braced herself. She realized instantly what was coming and she was prepared. She was always prepared.

"In five months you'll be twenty—"

"Four and a half months," she corrected.

18

"Yes, yes, four and a half. I think now is a good time to make arrangements for your engagement."

"To whom, Father?" she asked, having already determined marriage would not fit into her immediate plans.

Her father's eyes widened. "Why, Granger Madison, of course. You have been seeing him, haven't you? He's led me to believe it so."

"I see him on occasion, but I didn't think him serious in his quest for me." She was well aware of Granger's intentions, and love had nothing to do with them.

"And pray tell why not? You have many qualities a man would find endearing."

"Endearing, Father, but not attractive." She intended to get straight to the issue, to face it head-on.

"Endearing is much more important, when marriage is being considered, than attraction," James said seriously. "A marriage that is to last must be based on trust and consideration for one another."

And love, Prudence thought, which was why she couldn't prevent herself from asking the question, "Is that what yours and Mama's marriage was based on?"

As soon as she witnessed how her inconsiderate words affected him, she was sorry she had asked. Pain tore across her father's face. Prudence could almost feel his anguish, for she was filled with it, too.

"Your mother's and my marriage was based on love. We were lucky to have found each other. I would wish the same for you and would gladly agree to any marriage you desire if you but tell me you love the man."

His love for Lenore Winthrop had not diminished over the years, and Prudence realized hers hadn't, either. "No matter who he was, Father?"

James smiled then. "No matter, Prudence. Boston stock or not, he would be yours, with my heartiest approval."

Prudence stood and balanced herself on her toes to reach up and plant a light kiss on her father's cheek. She did love him so, which made her plans all the more difficult. "Thank you."

James Winthrop blushed and brushed his thoughtfulness aside. "Nonsense. I only wish your happiness."

Prudence returned to her seat. "I don't know if I'd be happy married to Granger Madison."

"He is a good young man, intelligent as well as wealthy. He holds an excellent position in his father's bank and could provide for you the things you are accustomed to."

That word again, *accustom*. Did everyone think she could live only one way?

"He assures me he would treat you well. He cares for you. I think it a wise choice to make."

"Especially since he is the only man who has ever offered to marry me. After all, the chance may never come again. I'd be left a spinster, an old maid." The idea actually frightened her, but she refused to voice that fear openly to anyone.

"Nonsense, Prudence," her father scolded. "There could be others."

"Could be, Father? Not will be?" *Never will be,* she thought. There would be no man to love her. No hero to sweep her away as she had fantasized since childhood.

James Winthrop ran his hand through the side of his hair and down his neck in frustration. "I didn't mean it that way, Prudence. Granger is a nice young man . . . thoughtful, considerate."

"And interested in establishing one of the strongest banking empires in Boston. A marriage to me would unite the two largest banking families and give him

20

exactly what he wishes. Of course, he's willing to make the sacrifice of marrying the plain Miss Winthrop in the interest of his future."

"Many marriages are based on such an interest and they have prospered nicely."

Prudence didn't answer. She couldn't, since what she would say would only shock her father. She knew of such marriages and she knew what they harvested. A husband who spends his night at the *club* and a wife who fulfills her social obligations and does charity work appropriately. Neither spending time with each other until the proper time that a child should be produced.

"Will you at least give the proposal consideration?" he asked.

"Very well, Father, I shall think on it," she agreed, knowing full well she had no intention of agreeing to such an odious proposal.

"Good," her father said. "I'm happy to hear that."

"And will you give my proposal thought?" She was well aware of his answer, but her obstinate nature forced her to press the issue.

James Winthrop shook his head. "I thought I made myself clear on that, Prudence. You will not now, or ever, go west to educate the heathens. My God, child, you wouldn't survive a day out there on your own."

Prudence stood, her chin up, her eyes narrowed, and her look determined. "As you wish, Father." She roughly grabbed the side of her skirt, lifting it as her steps took her toward the door.

"Prudence, I only wish to protect, not hurt," he said with a sad smile.

"I understand, Father." And she truly did. He was doing what he thought best. What was expected.

"I look forward to the Butterfields' ball this evening."

21

He was attempting to make peace with her. He was not one for harsh or hurtful words, and he always made certain that they never parted angry with each other. She loved that about him, his sensitivity and caring.

"I look forward to it as well," she said sincerely.

"You will save your *old* father a dance?"

Prudence laughed then, her face lighting up with pleasure. "I will always save a dance for you, Papa."

She had called him Papa when she was small, and when she did so now, it touched his heart, for it held the telltale hint of the little girl who had thought him her hero.

"Good, good," he said with a hint of a tear in his eye.

Prudence walked to the door and stopped. She braced her hand on the cherry wood frame and turned her head. "And you are far from old. As a matter of fact, you are the handsomest man in all of Boston. And the women know it."

James Winthrop smiled and bowed graciously to his daughter.

"I'll be ready at eight. See you then, Father."

"You look lovely, Prudence," Glenda Butterfield said, squeezing her hand.

Prudence delivered her usual complacent smile. After all, Glenda had expressed the standard compliment, even though she had barely glanced over Prudence's attire.

The woman was too busy ogling James Winthrop with her doe-eyed expression. Prudence was certain that any minute Glenda would throw herself at the man.

"Father, I see Charles Dutton. Didn't you wish to speak to him?" she asked, feeling a hasty retreat was best.

"Yes. Yes, I did. Please excuse me, Glenda," he said, and carefully pried his hand from her grasp.

Prudence slipped her arm around her father's as he carefully maneuvered them through the crowded ballroom.

"Thank you. That woman makes me feel uncomfortable," he whispered as they approached a short, rotund man, puffing madly on a cigar.

"I told you you were handsome," she teased softly, causing a faint blush to race to her father's cheeks.

They stopped before the Duttons, who were engulfed in a haze of cigar smoke.

"Hot in here, isn't it, James?" Charles Dutton asked between puffs.

"Yes, most uncomfortable at times," James agreed.

"Prudence, dear, did you see that Mr. Stewart is in attendance?" Margaret Dutton asked, waving her hand in the air to chase the offending smoke away. "Really, Charles, it isn't proper to smoke in here."

"I don't care," Charles said. "I'll enjoy my cigars when and where I please."

Prudence ignored the arguing couple and cast her eyes about casually, catching no sign of the gunslinger.

"Perhaps some air, Charles," James suggested, motioning toward the open doors to the garden.

"Good idea. I've been wanting to talk to you about some stocks, anyway," Charles said, walking away with the cigar smoke trailing after him.

The two men were soon out of sight.

"Your dress is lovely, dear," Margaret said, chasing the last of the offensive odor with another wave of her hand. "Have you seen Mary Brisbane's dress? It's ab-

23

solutely gorgeous. Mr. Stewart's been by her side since his arrival. I believe the man is quite taken by her. But then, she is beautiful."

"Excuse me, Margaret. I must speak to someone," Prudence said, and walked away. She knew she was being rude, but she couldn't bear listening to that blabbing woman another minute. Everyone was well aware of Mary Brisbane's beauty. Blond hair, petite form, gracious manners, soft speech, she was the perfect woman and many men sought her attention.

She spotted the gunslinger then, his height and confident manner causing him to stand out in the crowd. As Margaret had informed her, he was by Mary's side. Several other women stood nearby, and why not? He looked even more handsome in his dark formal dinner attire. He wasn't stuffed into it like so many men who appeared to be inflated from the neck up by their white starched collars. No, his collar hugged his neck perfectly. And where the other men's vests stretched the limits of their buttons, Zac Stewart's vest lay flat against his firm midriff. His dark brown hair defied style by falling in an unruly fashion along the top of his collar, around his ears, and sinfully curling on his forehead.

But it wasn't only his appearance that drew women to him. It was the air of mystery surrounding Zac. It was assumed he had done wicked and unspeakable things. And each and every woman there wanted to be near him. They wanted to sense and perhaps sample the danger that lurked within him.

"Prudence."

Though her name was spoken softly, she jumped, her hand flying to her chest. "Granger, you startled me."

"I'm so sorry, my dear," he apologized, holding his

arm out to her. "Shall we have a glass of champagne?"

Prudence accepted with a gracious nod. Granger was an attractive man, not handsome, although his features were strong. He was just shy of six feet and his body was firm, though Prudence suspected it wouldn't stay that way with his love of food. His hair color was common brown and it was worn in the familiar style of bankers, neat and combed back straight.

"You look lovely," he said, selecting two glasses from a silver serving tray.

"Thank you," she answered automatically. *Lovely*. Was there no other word to describe her? But of course there was. *Plain*. Only no one wished to insult her. The cream-colored faille dress she wore was simple and unadorned. It rose high over her chest and hugged her neck. The sleeves caught at her elbow where her long gloves of the same color met them.

Mary Brisbane, on the other hand, showed quite a bit of bosom, with bows and lace accenting her apricot and yellow dress.

"Prudence, dear, do pay attention," Granger ordered firmly.

"Sorry," she said, hiding her annoyance at his commanding tone. "My thoughts are elsewhere this evening."

"The West, my dear?"

Prudence gripped the slim handle of the crystal glass tightly. "What do you mean?"

"Your father was at the club early this evening and mentioned you were interested in the West."

"It intrigues me," she said, hoping her father hadn't felt it necessary to enlist Granger's assistance in preventing her from pursuing the idea of traveling west.

25

"Yes, the tabloids paint a most interesting picture. But you can't believe all you read or even all you hear."

Prudence noticed he had directed his annoyed glance toward Zac Stewart.

"Glenda informed me of Mr. Stewart's lecture this afternoon. I daresay the gentleman was intent on entertaining you ladies."

"You don't believe what he had to tell us was the truth?"

"Oh, come now, Prudence. You believe the word of a notorious gunslinger?"

"I truly know nothing of Mr. Stewart's exploits as a gunslinger. I was but interested in his knowledge of the West."

"Most of those gunslingers' exploits are fairy tales, anyway. And besides, there's no reason for you to find any interest in the West. Your life is here in Boston, and I hope," he said, stopping to take her hand, "I'm included in your long-term plans."

Prudence forced a smile. "Time will tell."

Her reply pleased him. "Perhaps you will join me for a carriage ride tomorrow afternoon?"

She wasn't going to be in Boston tomorrow afternoon, and the thought brightened her face. "I'll let you know."

"Shall we dance?" he asked, directing her toward the dance floor without waiting for a reply.

Prudence danced several dances with Granger and one with her father. Her dance card was never full. It had disturbed her when she was younger, but now there were more important things to worry about.

The evening moved along uneventfully. Prudence mingled appropriately, keeping her distance from Mr.

26

Stewart. She had no desire to match wits with him again. Besides, the other women, single and married, kept him entertained enough.

She wandered toward the open door and the sweet, rich smell of the spring flowers. Granger was deep in conversation with her father and Charles Dutton. She was certain she wouldn't be missed.

Zac watched Prudence disappear out the open doors. He had actually been watching her all evening. He didn't know why, although he had to admit those full hips of hers were awfully inviting. They swayed with just the right motion, left to right, left to right. And her lips weren't as pinched and puckered as the last time he had seen her. They were narrow and soft. The type a man could run his tongue over and cover in one sweep. The suggestive thought startled him.

"Damn," he muttered, and without a moment's hesitation headed toward the open doors.

The moon wasn't completely full, but it was still bright enough to cast a glow on the brick path that circled the garden.

Zac saw Prudence standing amongst the shadows of the trees, off the brick path and away from the flowering plants. He approached her. His steps were quiet, his stride confident.

"Out west you'd be dead right now."

Prudence jumped and turned in a flash. "There are no gentlemen out west?"

Zac laughed and shook his head. "Very few."

"Then I thank you for the lesson, Mr. Stewart."

"Zac, my name is Zac." He hated when she called him *Mr. Stewart*.

"Short for Zachariah?" she asked.

"Heaven forbid. No, it's just Zac."

Prudence liked his smile. Truth be told, it wasn't the

smile as much as his face. He was so handsome it was hard not to stare at him. His features were sharp and striking. A narrow nose, firm chin, sensual eyes, and tempting lips far removed him from the common man. He was a man women could die over.

"That's a dangerous way to look at a man," he said. His voice was low, his tone testy.

"I—I—I don't know what you mean," she stammered, embarrassed by her blatant perusal of him.

"You look hungry."

"I've eaten."

"I'm not talking about food," he said, and stepped closer.

Prudence took a step back.

"If you looked at a man like that out west, you'd be flat on your back in minutes."

"My back?"

"Yes, your back."

She flushed as his meaning sank in. "Oh!"

"And your protests would make no difference."

"The man would force himself on me?" Prudence asked, assuming he meant to frighten her.

"Unless you knew how to protect yourself."

"And how does a woman out west protect herself?"

"With a gun. Do you own a gun, Prudence?"

"No," she whispered, her eyes focused wide on the way he stepped toward her. Slow, sure, and easy.

"Then what would you do if he reached out for you?" he asked, and his hand shot out like a speeding bullet, circling her neck so fast Prudence hardly saw it move.

"I'd tell him to take his hand off me," she said firmly, though she doubted his compliance.

He drew her toward him. His grip was tight, his intentions obvious. "And if he didn't?"

"I'd scream," she said more calmly than she felt.

He moved in closer, his hand still strong on her neck. "He'd silence you first."

"How?"

"Easy," he whispered, and brought his mouth down on hers.

Prudence wasn't prepared for his kiss. Her experience with a man's lips extended as far as a peck on the cheek. And this was far from a peck.

His lips covered hers, enveloped them, swallowed them. His tongue lazily outlined her mouth, while his hand sneaked around her waist and urged her toward him inch by inch until their bodies were almost touching. His tongue ran across the seal of her closed lips, but they remained firmly locked. He played and teased, wetting them until they were moist with pleasure. But still they remained pinched together.

Her resistance not only angered him but also heightened his desire.

Playtime was over.

He yanked her hard against him. His hand, firm around her neck, slipped to her hair and pulled her head back.

"Open!" he demanded. "Now!"

Prudence looked into his determined eyes, then at his mouth, hungry and waiting. She could scream. She could push him away. She opened her mouth.

He took it. He tasted her, all her sweetness and innocence. And she tasted good, too good. His tongue left no place untouched. He wanted to brand her, every sweet inch of her. He eased his hunger when he realized she wasn't accustomed to such rough play. Her hands gripped his arms lightly. And her tongue seemed to dart and hide from his.

His tongue found hers and gently teased it into acquiescence. It was obvious she was inexperienced, and his body was more than ready for her innocence. A warning signal went off in his head, and he abruptly pushed her away and took a step back.

Prudence felt her legs grow weak, as though ready to give way, and her heart hammer wildly. She took a deep breath before she spoke. "So that is what a woman can expect out west?"

"No, by now you'd be stripped naked and beneath the man."

The thought sent a flood of excitement racing through her and she shuddered. She wasn't thinking of lying naked beneath a stranger. She was thinking of lying naked beneath Zac Stewart. That thought and the strange sensations that accompanied it aroused in her a combination of fright and pleasure.

"Protests would do no good unless you had a gun. Then you could shoot him."

She spoke, although she wondered where her calm control came from. "Then I would get a gun if I traveled west, since it is obvious there are no gentlemen in that part of the country."

"A wise choice, Miss Winthrop, but a better choice would be not to go west at all." Zac turned to leave, the night shadows too tempting and inviting for what he had in mind.

"Mr. Stewart?"

Zac cringed at the proper form of address. He turned again, his dark eyes still sensually blatant.

"Are you a gentleman?"

Zac's grin was wicked. "Not by a long shot, honey."

Dawn was another hour away. Prudence looked out her window into the darkness. Everything was

30

going according to plan. Her letters were all written, her bags all packed. She only had to leave.

Her stomach protested with a flutter. She would miss her father terribly. And she would miss all that was familiar to her, but this journey was necessary.

Even Zac Stewart's warning of how dangerous the West could be didn't sway her decision. Although his kiss last night had troubled her. She had never been kissed like that before. Granger had only offered kisses on the cheek. She had not been aware of how a man, experienced in such matters, could make a woman feel. And Zac Stewart made her feel . . . much too much. It was necessary that she keep her virginal feelings under control. This was no time to lose control over a gunslinger . . . or anyone else for that matter. And besides, she would probably never lay eyes on Zac Stewart again, which was just fine with her.

Prudence checked her satchel one more time. She had taken only a minimum of clothing, recalling that one should travel light. Sensible skirts and blouses as well as two pairs of ladies' walking boots had been packed. Naturally, her undergarments, her nightgowns, and her linen duster were also included. Her traveling bag contained her personal toiletries as well as her extra pairs of gloves. She had taken three just in case. And of course, there was the money she had withdrawn from her personal account at the bank. It was more than enough to see her through her journey and any emergency that might arise. She was all ready.

Prudence placed her bonnet on her head. It was the only one she was taking and it fit comfortably, turning up at the sides and down in the front and back, with a white silk ribbon tied loosely beneath her chin. She slipped on her gray gloves that matched her gray day suit and hung her traveling bag on her shoulder, checking once more to make certain her train tickets were inside.

She lifted her satchel from the bed and didn't dare glance around the room again, fearing she would dissolve into tears. She quickly walked out.

Quietly, she made her way down the steps, realizing the servants would be up and about by now. She left the note for her father on his desk and one for Granger on the hall receiving table.

Prudence opened the front door, glanced back over her shoulder one last time at her home, and then walked out, closing the door softly behind her.

Chapter Three

"What do you mean your daughter's gone west?" Zac yelled, jumping out of his seat.

James Winthrop's hand trembled as he held it up, directing Mr. Stewart to take his seat. "Please, sit and let me finish."

Zac wasn't accustomed to taking orders. He walked around the large leather chair and stood behind it, bracing his hands on the top edge. When Winthrop had sent an urgent summons to his hotel room he had come immediately, never expecting this. "Do you realize what you've just told me?"

James ran his still-trembling hand through his hair. "Believe me, Mr. Stewart, I realize more than you think. My daughter has gone off, alone, thinking she can bring culture to savages."

"Savages come in all colors, shapes, and sizes," Zac warned, annoyed at Winthrop's ignorance of the West. "People assume that the Indians are their only worry when traveling through the different territories."

"If you think to frighten me, you're doing an excellent job."

Frighten him? Zac was frightened himself, a foreign feeling to him. He had learned to disengage his emotions. It was necessary for a gunslinger. But now thinking of Prudence and her obstinate nature out there alone, he shook his head. "Good. But it's a little late, since Prudence has already left. Is it that difficult keeping her in tow, Mr. Winthrop?"

"Difficult, Mr. Stewart, doesn't begin to describe handling Prudence."

Zac couldn't help but smile. So a spitfire did actually lie beneath that proper Bostonian surface. His smile quickly faded. She was bound to get herself into trouble. It was inevitable.

"I need your help."

"What you need is more control over your daughter's actions," Zac argued.

"I agree," James admitted freely. "I have spoiled Prudence terribly. Her mother's death left me numb, then I found myself lavishing my young daughter with everything. I felt guilty that her mother was gone and—"

Zac waited, sensing exactly what the man was about to say and disturbed that he thought such of his daughter.

"—that Prudence was . . . plain. She had much to deal with as a child. Losing a loved one was difficult enough, but having to cope with only being asked to social functions because of her father's business standing in the community was another difficulty."

"So you felt spoiling her was the answer to her problems?"

"My only fault, Mr. Stewart," James said firmly, "was that I loved my daughter too much."

34

Zac couldn't argue that point. He could tell the man was hurting, worried. And rightfully so, since he felt the same way, though he was completely puzzled as to why.

"As I said, I need your help."

"Let me guess," Zac said, walking around to the front of the chair to sit, having already surmised Winthrop's intentions. "You want me to go after Prudence, find her, and bring her back to you safe and sound."

James released a heavy sigh, as though by the words being spoken the deed was done. "Yes, Mr. Stewart, that's exactly what I want from you."

Zac's response was edged with hostility. "And I suppose you will offer me a fee to secure her return?"

"Yes, yes, by all means. I will pay you a substantial sum."

Zac stared at the man, and James had no doubt that his intense look was the one he wore just before he drew his gun on an opponent.

"Do you assume all gunslingers hire for a fee?" His voice was clear, steady, and in control.

James had a feeling he was treading on dangerous ground. He proceeded with caution, fearful of losing his only chance of having his daughter returned safely. "I must admit, Mr. Stewart, I am ignorant of the ways of a gunslinger. And if I have insulted you, I apologize."

Zac had to hand it to the man. He was intelligent. He had sized up the situation immediately and acted accordingly. No wonder he owned the largest banking firm in Boston.

"This proves my point," James continued. "If I

am ignorant of the ways of the West, then Prudence most certainly is and I fear for her safety."

Zac hated to admit feeling likewise. Ever since Winthrop had announced that Prudence was gone, Zac had felt edgy, annoyed, angry. She was a fool to think she could survive such a trek.

"Please, consider before you refuse me," James begged. "I know this may seem a preposterous proposition. After all, you have dealt with much more difficult tasks and this must seem a petty annoyance. But I ask you to consider her fate. A young woman, alone, incapable of protecting herself, ignorant of her surroundings. She may be in danger this very minute. Please, help me."

Winthrop's impassioned speech disturbed Zac, mainly because the picture he had painted was so true. It also brought to mind the previous night in the garden and the kiss. She had tasted fresh and innocent and much too good. No doubt someone would force his intentions on her, and then what would she do? Shoo them away with her glove-covered hand?

"You, of all people, should be able to control her, Mr. Stewart. She wouldn't dare give you trouble," James said.

Zac didn't agree. Prudence would probably find his intrusion inappropriate. "You mean she wouldn't refuse my suggestion to return to Boston?"

James hesitated a moment. A moment too long to Zac's way of thinking.

"If she entertained a different notion, I'm certain you'd be able to persuade her."

Zac leaned forward in his seat. "What you're saying is she can be stubborn at times?"

James found it impossible to contain his smile. "When Prudence is convinced she's doing the right thing, she'll go to great lengths to see it through to completion."

Zac entertained the notion of how interesting it would be to force Prudence Agatha Winthrop to comply with his directions. The idea did hold promise. "Then I assume you wish me to do whatever is necessary to see to her return?"

James wasn't certain he should agree to such a limitless proposal, but he did want Prudence back. And from the determined look on Stewart's face, he wasn't about to agree to any other terms. "I trust your expertise, Mr. Stewart," James said, but quickly added, "And I trust you will return my daughter to me safely."

Safely? He wondered if it was Prudence's virtue or stubborn nature Winthrop worried more about. "If—and I say if, since I'm still considering taking on this task—I accept, then the fee shall be determined by me."

James had expected this but it didn't matter, since there was no price too high to pay for his daughter's safe return. "As you wish."

"I won't take money, Mr. Winthrop," Zac said sitting back in his chair.

James looked at him oddly. "I don't understand."

"I came to Boston for two reasons. One was to order more furnishings for the home that I recently built for myself in the Dakota Territory. The second was to invest money and in return secure the future of my ranch."

"I didn't know you were a rancher."

"Not many people do. My skill with a gun enabled me to save the money to fulfill a longtime dream. My ranch has prospered and my guns are no longer necessary for my support."

"I'm impressed, Mr. Stewart, and I'd be happy to help you choose the best investments for return on your money."

Zac wanted to make certain he wasn't in for any surprises. "Before I make my decision, you are telling me everything? Prudence's reason for going west is to teach? There is no other reason?"

"What other possible reason could there be?"

Zac shrugged his broad shoulders. "She hasn't recently been jilted, has she?"

"No, no," James insisted. "Actually, I had been trying to convince her to marry Granger Madison. He had made his intentions clear to me. I thought the marriage a good idea, but—"

"Prudence thought differently?"

James shook his head. "She wasn't certain. She was giving the idea thought. I can imagine how upset Granger will be when he discovers this."

"He loves her?" Zac asked sternly.

James chose his words carefully. "He cares for her."

"You weren't forcing this marriage on her? Causing her to run away?"

"Heavens, no," James said. "Quite the opposite. I told her that if she found someone she truly loved, I would give my approval with great pleasure. I want to see my daughter happy, Mr. Stewart. And Prudence would never be happy in a forced marriage."

Zac stood. "Very well, Mr. Winthrop. I accept your proposal."

James stood and hurried around his desk. He grabbed Zac's hand and shook it vigorously. "Thank you, Mr. Stewart."

"Zac," he corrected.

"Zac," James repeated with a smile. "And please, my friends call me James."

Zac nodded. "All right, James, now let's get down to business. Prudence has several hours start, but I assume her destination to be Philadelphia. There she should be able to get a train to several destinations. Have you any idea where she could be headed?"

"No, but we could question some of her friends. Perhaps she spoke to them about her intentions. But isn't it dangerous to wait too long to pursue her?"

"It's more dangerous for me to go off without some idea as to where she's headed. If I can determine that, I can probably have her returned within a few days."

"A few days, that's wonderful," James said, feeling more relieved with each word Zac spoke.

"Now let's see . . ."

The commotion from outside the study door interrupted Zac's words.

"I don't care who he's with, Mr. Winthrop will see me now!"

The door burst open and Granger Madison stormed into the room. "How witless could she be? Didn't you see this coming? All this talk of the West. Why didn't you do something? By God, when she's my wife, she'll do exactly as I order."

"Calm down, Granger," James said firmly. "This isn't the time to lose one's control."

"Not lose my control?" he repeated indignantly. "This will be a full-blown scandal by this evening. Everyone will be discussing her unladylike behavior. She must be found and returned immediately before this goes too far."

"And how far is that?" Zac asked in a threateningly dangerous tone.

Granger looked at Zac but addressed James Winthrop. "What is he doing here?"

"I've hired Mr. Stewart to find Prudence and bring her home safely."

"You what?" Granger yelled. "Have you lost your mind? Sending a notorious gunslinger to return your daughter? What will people say?"

"Actually," James began, "I don't care what they say. My only concern at the moment is Prudence."

"What about her reputation? People will talk . . . and viciously."

"As I said, at the moment it doesn't concern me."

"Well, it concerns me. I will hire a private agency to find her and return her."

"That isn't necessary, Granger. Mr. Stewart has certain skills I feel would be more helpful in finding and returning Prudence."

"And I'd feel more comfortable knowing someone is watching him, since his *skills* extend to many areas."

"Really, Granger, you are being rude even to suggest Mr. Stewart would take advantage of Prudence."

"Am I? Prudence is plain to look upon, but her wealth is another matter."

"Granger! That is enough," James ordered.

Zac wished he had his gun. He wanted nothing

more than to shoot the lousy bastard. He remained silent, fearing what he would say if he spoke. He'd allow James Winthrop to handle Granger Madison for now. Anyway, he'd always found silence and a look to be more intimidating than words.

James could see that Granger had become uneasy with Zac's refusal to participate in a verbal altercation. He was glad Zac had a level head. It made him feel all the more comfortable with his decision.

"I still feel it in mine and Prudence's best interest that I hire an investigator who will report directly to me."

James shook his head. "You do what you feel you must. But I warn you, Granger. If the man you hire interferes in any way with Mr. Stewart, you will never be welcome in this house again."

Granger began to perspire. "I will inform the man to work closely with Mr. Stewart and offer any help he can."

"And not to interfere," James added.

Granger nodded his agreement.

"Good," James concluded. "Now if you will excuse us, we have business to discuss."

James knew his curt dismissal of Granger was not to the man's liking, but he reacted as he knew he must and left.

"Now, Zac, we've wasted enough time. I want my daughter back as soon as possible and with as little scandal as possible."

"Believe me, James, I want the same thing. I can't wait to have this task over and done with."

Prudence felt relieved as she stepped off the

stagecoach in Wells City, Kansas. Her body ached from the rough ride. She was certain the driver had intentionally hit every rut and rock on their journey here. Her linen duster was covered with a film of dust and her dry mouth longed for a cool, quenching drink.

Her traveling experience had started out rather well, but the further west she journeyed the less she saw of civilization. At least civilization as she was accustomed to it. The land itself possessed a raw, untouched beauty. She admired the changing landscape, and the cultural differences fascinated her.

Her first sight of a savage took her by surprise. She hadn't expected to see an Indian amongst white people or dressed in white man's clothes. Prudence had thought all the heathens were restricted to the reservations, but she learned quickly from her traveling companions and her own insights that there were those who worked for the U.S. Army as scouts and were free to come and go as they pleased. Then there were the Indian women who were married to white men. Prudence found that they were not always accepted by polite society, and she kept her distance until she could ascertain for herself their status in the Western culture.

She didn't think it was possible to feel as fatigued as she did. Her traveling bag was placed on the ground with the others and Prudence eyed it woefully. She wasn't certain her arms could lift it, but experience had taught her to retrieve her bag as soon as possible, since at the last coach stop one of the passengers had been lax in securing his bag and

42

someone had walked off with it. She reached for her satchel and picked it up. Her sore arm muscles protested in pain.

"Don't complain, Prudence Agatha," she scolded herself in a whisper. "This is what you wanted."

She stepped up on the wooden boardwalk that ran the length of the buildings down the street. Not that there were many. Six in all, Prudence got from a fast count.

She brushed the dust from her linen duster as best she could, coughing from the particles of dry dirt that floated around her. She adjusted her bonnet, which had tipped to the side, and secured the white silk ribbon beneath her chin. Clapping the dust from her gray gloves, she walked into the coach station office.

The office was small, and the shadows of the late afternoon sun were not dispelled by the small amount of light that came through the open door. Two benches sat against one wall, while the other wall was occupied by the usual ticket counter and cage. Prudence approached, ready with her query.

The man behind the iron bars, where the tickets could be purchased, smiled at her question. Then his face split into a wide grin. "Sadie? You here to see Sadie?"

"Yes, that's correct," she answered, thinking the man slow-witted. "I don't know her last name, but I was told to ask for Sadie. Someone would know her."

"Everyone knows Sadie, miss," the man grinned. "You here to work for her?"

Prudence, fearing her reply might make a difference, said, "Possibly."

43

The man's face brightened even further. He ran his hand back over his unkempt brown hair and across his mouth. "Sadie's place is the fourth building down on your right."

"Thank you, sir," Prudence said with a pleasant smile, and turned to leave.

"Miss?"

Prudence turned around. "Yes?"

"I'll see you at Sadie's."

Prudence nodded, still thinking the man witless, and walked out of the office.

She counted the buildings as she passed them and came to a stop at the fourth, a bit puzzled.

"A saloon?" she whispered. Had the man given her the wrong directions? She glanced up at the sign. The Devil's Den.

Prudence shook her head. Could her mother have possibly known a woman of such ill repute? Or worse, could her mother have turned into such a woman herself?

Fear never entered her mind, only curiosity. With no thought as to her actions, she pushed on the swinging doors of the Devil's Den and marched inside.

It took a moment for her eyes to adjust. The late afternoon sun streamed through the front windows, casting a glare across parts of the room and leaving the rest in the shadows.

There weren't many customers about. Two men sat at one of the round tables near the rear while three others stood at the bar, drinking. The other tables, about eight in all, were empty and a piano stood silent against the far wall.

The barkeep looked her over quickly, then walked

to the end of the bar, leaning on the scarred top. "What'd ya want?"

"I'd like to see Sadie," Prudence said in her most snooty tone.

The man shrugged. "Sit yourself and I'll get her."

He walked over to where the other men stood drinking, whispered something, then disappeared through a door to the left at the end of the bar.

The three men all turned and stared at Prudence. Their intent looks made her feel uneasy and she wondered just what the barkeep had said to them.

When she thought she could take their strange stares no longer, a short, rotund woman with raving red hair emerged from the doorway.

She stared at Prudence from the end of the bar. Then she held her hand up and stuck a thin cigar between two chubby fingers. The barkeep lit it for her and she took a deep puff, sending the smoke swirling into the air.

"Drinks on me, fellahs," she announced to all, then walked toward Prudence.

Prudence stood, although she wasn't certain why.

"You wanted to see me, honey?" the woman asked.

"You're Sadie?"

"None other," she laughed. "Sit and we'll talk."

Prudence smiled. Sadie was far different from the women she knew back in Boston. Her aging face was thick with powder and her lips heavy with rouge. Her heavy bosoms bulged like twin peaks from her purple silk dress, and she puffed on her cigar with all the skill and desire of a man.

"What do you want?"

"Some help."

Sadie grinned. "On your own, are you?"

"Yes, is it that obvious?" Prudence asked, hoping she didn't look too out of place.

"Well, I'll say one thing for you, honey. You don't look like the usual ones that come around here."

"Oh, I'm not from here."

"No, you don't sound it. East somewhere?"

"Boston."

"They're awfully proper and prudish back there, ain't they?" Sadie asked, sizing her up in a quick glance.

"Proper etiquette is not synonymous with prudish behavior," Prudence corrected, affronted by the woman's besmirching remark.

Sadie raised her brow, surprised by the young woman's spirited nature. "And you? Are you proper but not prudish?"

"I believe so."

Sadie waved her hand. "It don't matter. Proper or prudish, you'll get used to it soon enough. Not much choice out here."

Prudence assumed she was speaking of the different lifestyle. "Oh, I adapt easily."

"Good," Sadie said with a satisfied smile. "I like to hear that."

Prudence was pleased with the way this was going. Sadie seemed pleasant enough and more than happy to help her.

"Thirsty?"

"Terribly," Prudence said, her throat even more parched than before.

"Love that accent. Yes sir. That'll do real fine

here," Sadie said. "Jake, two glasses and a bottle."

"Oh, dear."

"Problem?"

"I don't drink," Prudence whispered, as though the admittance in such a place was sacrilegious.

"That's all right, honey. Actually it's even better. Jake, one cider."

Prudence remained silent until the cider was placed in front of her. She was so thirsty. She reached for the tall glass and drank, finishing almost all the cider before putting it down. "I'm so glad you've agreed to help me."

"Honey, I'll help any girl."

"New merchandise, Sadie?"

Prudence looked up at the man standing next to Sadie. He was a good five inches taller than herself and heavy, with a combination of fat and muscle, the muscle being in his arms and the fat being around his protruding belly. His clothes didn't look dirty, but then they didn't smell too clean, either.

"Like what you see, Ned?" Sadie asked. "You know the new ones are more money."

"Got paid today," Ned said pulling a roll of bills from his pocket.

"Well, darling, we just might be able to do business." Sadie patted his hand. "You just go back over to the bar and have a drink on me while I discuss some business with the little lady."

"Okay, Sadie, but I'm first. Bill says he wants to be first, but remember I asked you first and I got more money."

"You'll be first, Ned. Don't worry."

Ned wasn't worried, but Prudence was. She was foolish, so very foolish, not to have realized what

47

the woman had been alluding to. She should have been more attentive. She should have questioned Sadie about her mother immediately. But she was so tired and thirsty that she hadn't paid proper attention. "I think there's been a misunderstanding."

Sadie grabbed her wrist. "Now, don't go getting cold feet. One time and you'll be fine. After Ned you'll service Bill. This way you won't have a chance to get sore. The more you do it, the easier it'll get."

"I'm not here to *service* anybody," Prudence insisted, and pulled her wrist free.

"You said you wanted help," Sadie argued.

"I should have been more direct. It's information I seek. I'm looking for someone who was a friend of yours several years ago."

Sadie spied Ned and Bill getting anxious. She didn't want to lose the money they were willing to spend.

"Information will cost you."

Prudence saw the way the woman's eyes darted back and forth between the men and her. "How much?"

"I'm a reasonable woman," Sadie said, leaning back against the wooden chair. "Let's say you entertain those two men, and I'll provide you with all the information you want."

Prudence became irritated. How dare the woman assume she'd do such a thing. "That isn't acceptable, Sadie."

"It's the only offer there is, honey."

Sadie was no match for Boston tenacity. "No, Sadie, it isn't. Whatever those men are willing to pay you for me, I'll match it." She could have doubled

48

it, tripled it, but she was no fool. Prudence didn't want anyone to know the large amount of money she carried with her. And she wouldn't give Sadie one more penny than was necessary.

"Come on, Sadie," Ned yelled. "I'm hurting waiting so long."

"Yeah, he's in a bad way," Bill added with a laugh. "I ain't gonna have to wait long for my turn. He'll be done in a flash."

The patrons in the saloon laughed.

Prudence didn't find it funny.

"The lady's changed her mind, fellahs," Sadie said, and in a lower tone added, "You better show me that money now, or you'll find yourself upstairs right quick."

Prudence produced a roll of bills that made Sadie's eyes widen in appreciation.

"She has other plans, fellahs. Sorry," Sadie announced. "Have a drink on me to ease the pain, and I'll give you Betty at a cheaper rate later this evening."

Ned pounded his whiskey glass down on the bar, splashing the contents. "I'm tired of Betty. I want someone different. This new one ain't bad to look at and under that garment she looks to be full-bodied, and I like them that way."

"Yeah," Bill said with a laugh. "Old Ned here loves to grab onto a woman's ass while he's ploughing her."

The men laughed. Prudence didn't find their talk funny. She found it repulsive.

"At least they know what they're getting," Ned joked. "I give them a good one for their money."

"Well, this little lady don't want your *good one*," Bill teased. "Maybe you should persuade her."

Prudence recalled Zac's warning. He had been right about the untamed nature of the West. She had to get out of here and fast. She moved to stand.

"Stay put," Sadie said sharply. "He'll just follow you."

Ned walked over to the table.

"She's not interested, Ned," Sadie said, attempting to chase the man with a wave of her hand.

"She don't know what she's missing."

"Yeah," Bill agreed, leaning over Ned's shoulder. "Show her what she's missing."

Bill was taller than Ned and definitely dirtier.

"It doesn't matter. I'm not interested," Prudence said firmly.

"Ain't that pretty, the way she talks," Ned said.

"Makes you want her even more, don't it?" asked Bill.

Ned jiggled his butt. "I'm hot and ready for her."

"Ain't gonna take you long," Bill joked. "She'll be wanting a slow one like me after quick draw gets done."

Sadie even laughed this time.

Prudence didn't. The men's remarks were too rude and repugnant. "I'm not interested," she repeated, trying to sound stern but hearing a slight quiver to her own tone.

"I can make you interested, sweetie," Ned said, moving closer. "Come on, touch me. See what you're missing."

Prudence felt trapped, cornered like an animal with nowhere to run. She quickly stood, pushing her chair back. "I don't intend to tell you again I'm not interested."

"Leave her be, fellahs," Sadie said more sternly.

"Aw, come on, Sadie. I got a hankering for her," Ned pleaded.

"Well, she ain't got a hankering for you," Bill said, laughing so hard he sounded like a snorting bull.

"Come on, sweetie, just feel how much I want you," Ned begged, "One feel, just one feel.

"No!" Prudence shouted, and reached for her satchel.

Ned grabbed her arm. "I'm gonna change your mind."

"Take your hand off me," Prudence demanded.

"Let her go, Ned," Sadie said. "A woman ain't fun if she ain't willing."

"And I'm definitely not willing," Prudence assured him.

"But I want you, sweetie. Bad, real bad. You smell pretty and talk pretty, and I got money. I'll pay whatever you want."

"It isn't enough."

The voice was so deep, harsh, and threatening that all the patrons turned their heads in quick succession to see who had spoken.

Ned released Prudence and turned around himself.

Prudence stepped away from him, rubbing her wrist as her eyes searched the room. The glare of the sun partially hid the man. He wore a dark hat low on his forehead, shading his face from full view. Even his dark outfit spoke of menace. He wore a black shirt and black trousers. A gun belt, holding two silver six-shooters, hugged his hips tightly and outlined his strength. There was no doubt he was a gunslinger. And from the startled gasps that circled the room, a dangerous one. But why was he interfering?

"Why ain't it enough?" Ned asked, attempting to sound brave.

The dark figure walked out of the glare and toward Ned. His stride was slow, sure, and steady. No doubt or fear was present in his approach.

"Because she belongs to me and she isn't for sale."

Prudence was shocked not only by his statement but also by his voice. She recognized it. She stared at him as he raised his head and gazed at her. His look told her that he would not be denied. The thought vexed her and excited her all at once.

Zac Stewart held out his hand to her. "Come here, Prudence. Now!"

Chapter Four

"Yes, dear," Prudence said with a controlled smile as she stepped around Ned. She didn't really want to submit to his command, but then she didn't want to remain in this precarious situation, either. "Sorry to have kept you waiting, but I was so thirsty and—"

"Shut up and come over here," Zac ordered. He had a feeling that quick wit of hers would land her and probably him in even more trouble before their return to Boston. The thought didn't improve his temper.

"Now hold on just a minute," Ned demanded, grabbing Prudence's arm and preventing her from moving. "The little lady and me were doing business."

"I gave you one warning, mister. I never give two. Now get your filthy hands off my woman." Zac's words were strong and restrained, while his right hand moved lazily toward the six-shooter in his holster.

"And if I don't?" Ned asked, puffing his chest out to intimidate and producing a smug grin.

"Yeah, and if he don't, what are ya gonna do?" Bill added bravely in defense of his friend.

Zac shook his head at the pair's dual stupidity. "Simple. I'll kill him."

The deliberate calmness of his voice brought a shocked gasp from Prudence. He wouldn't really kill these two harmless men, would he?

Sadie gave a hoot, slapped the table, and yelled to the barkeep, "Jake, order two coffins and charge them to Zac Stewart."

Ned released Prudence's arm with such a swiftness that she lost her balance and grabbed onto the back of a chair for support.

"No harm meant, Mr. Stewart," Ned said apologetically upon hearing the infamous gunslinger's name.

"Yeah, no harm," Bill agreed, urgently shoving Ned to move toward the saloon doors.

Ned took a careful step around one of the tables, with Bill close on his tail. Another step brought them within a few inches of Zac, and that's when he moved his hand to rest on the handle of his gun.

The two men shot out of the saloon so fast that the swinging doors flapped a multitude of times before coming to a stop.

Sadie laughed and walked over to Zac, throwing her arms around him. "You devil. You're going to ruin my business. I'll be lucky if they come back in here at all."

Zac hugged the woman and whispered in her ear. Sadie blushed, her already rouge-laced cheeks burning an even brighter red.

"Zac Stewart, you're a devil."

"But you love my evil ways, Sadie," he said with a wink.

"Damn right I do," she agreed, and punctuated it with a hearty laugh. "Now let me get you a drink."

"*Mr. Stewart!*"

Zac cringed at Prudence's formality. Her tone was clearly condemning.

"Make that a double, Sadie," he said as she turned toward the bar.

Zac walked over to Prudence. He wasn't exactly expecting an apology, but then he wasn't expecting indifference to his rescue of her, either. Hell, he didn't know what to expect of Prudence Agatha Winthrop.

"I assume my father sent you."

Not a thank you or a question, just a statement . . . and a correct one at that. The lady was quick. "You've got that right, honey. And just in time, too."

Prudence bristled over his assumption that she wasn't capable of handling herself in the West and his use of the endearment *honey*. He certainly didn't mean it endearingly.

With her dander up, her tongue struck sharply. "I suppose you're charging my father an exorbitant fee for my return? Especially since you had no trouble finding me."

"Actually, it took some convincing on his part to make me agree to this little rescue. And yes, the fee is quite favorable, thank you. As far as finding you? You left a trail an idiot could follow. A few questions asked to the right people at the right places, and I was on your trail in no time." Zac

55

caught the flash of pain that shot across her otherwise contained features. His words had hurt her considerably. He hadn't meant any harm, and he was suddenly stung with a twinge of guilt.

Prudence pushed aside his cutting remarks. Why else would he come after her other than for money? Love? A stupid, preposterous notion that irritated her all the more. "Then my announcement should cause you a share of relief and regret."

Zac's guilt instantly vanished as he waited for the announcement he expected.

"I have no intention of returning to Boston with you."

Zac pulled out one of the chairs from beneath the table and sat down in a negligent slouch. "I don't believe I gave you a choice."

Prudence refused to unleash her anger. The wasted emotion caused one to lose her senses, and she wasn't about to do anything improper. "And I don't believe I gave you the authority to dictate my actions."

"That's right, honey, you didn't, but your father did."

"He has no right."

"Not so. He has every right. A woman obeys her father and then her husband. A righteous law."

"Archaic and one I refuse to submit to." She hated being dictated to by anyone, especially Zac Stewart.

Zac removed his hat, placing it on the table, and ran his hand through his hair. The warm brown strands fell unrestricted along his collar and around his ears, highlighting his handsome features. "Your father warned me you might be stubborn and difficult."

Prudence raised her chin in defiance. "And I suppose you guaranteed my compliance."

His smile broadened. "You might say that."

Prudence's caustic response had to wait, since Sadie appeared with a whiskey for Zac.

"Prudence, is it?" Sadie asked, handing Zac the glass.

"Prudence Agatha Winthrop, to be exact," Zac said with a salute of the glass to Prudence, before he downed the contents in one gulp.

Prudence refused to look at him. She kept her eyes focused on Sadie.

"You know, Prudence, you're worth your weight in gold around here."

"Why's that?" she asked, ignoring the rumble of laughter coming from Zac.

"Hell, girl," Sadie said, "if you can please Zac in bed, you can please any man. His women better be good. Damn good. Yes sir, I'd have them lined up waiting for you. We could make a bundle."

"I don't share," Zac said. His tone was dead serious.

Sadie slapped him on the back. "Hell, I know that, but I can dream, can't I?"

"That you can, darling," Zac said with a smile, slipping his hand around her and patting her ample backside.

Prudence had had enough. She had no intention of going anywhere with Mr. Stewart, but she had every intention of returning to the saloon to speak with Sadie about her mother. Although it would have to be at another time, preferably when she was able to rid herself of her newly acquired baggage.

She picked up her satchel. "I'm sorry you made this trip for nothing, *Mr. Stewart.*"

Zac winced at her usual formality. Someday he was going to put an end to that *Mr. Stewart* once and for all. "I assure you, Prudence, my trip isn't in vain."

She stepped over his outstretched legs. "But it is, since you'll be returning to Boston alone." With that announcement she walked out the swinging doors, releasing them gently so they wouldn't flap too strongly.

Zac snatched his hat from the table. He placed it on his head, tugging it down firmly on his forehead. "I don't know why I agreed to this," he mumbled.

"What's that?" Sadie asked.

"Women," Zac said. "They ought to be outlawed." He reached in his pocket for some coins to pay for the whiskey.

Sadie stayed his hand with hers. "This one's on me. What you need is to get that woman of yours into bed. Fill her up some. Sounds to me like it's been a while for the both of you."

Zac shook his head. "Sadie, that's the last thing I need right now." He gave her a kiss on the cheek and walked toward the swinging doors. *Fill her up some.* Damn if that didn't sound inviting, despite what he'd said to Sadie. He gave the doors a mighty shove and walked out.

Prudence was halfway down the main street of town, which wasn't much of a distance since the dirt street was short though wide. She appeared

58

headed in the direction of the only hotel in town. He watched her steady and sure footsteps. She had been traveling long if the dusty condition of her linen coat was any indication, and she was probably tired if not exhausted. But she refused to show it.

"Stubborn," Zac said, and picked up his pace to catch up with her.

She heard the rapid approach of footsteps and hastened her own pace.

"Hold on," he said, reaching out, grabbing her arm and halting her progress.

Prudence stiffened against his touch. "We have nothing to discuss, Mr. Stewart. Now take your hand off me."

"You tried those words once before and they did little good."

Prudence recalled she'd used the same words just before he had kissed her in the garden. He was right. They did little good. "I think it would be best if we found a proper place to discuss this matter in a more civil manner."

"I assume your destination is the hotel. It has a small but adequate dining salon," he suggested.

"Perfect," she said, snatching her arm free from his grasp and continuing her walk.

Zac shook his head once again. Actually, he had the strangest feeling he'd be doing a lot of head shaking. "Let me take that," he said, walking beside her and reaching for her satchel.

Prudence swung it away from him. "That's not necessary. I've carried it this far on my own; I can continue to do so."

"Damn it, woman. I didn't ask your permission,"

he snapped, pulling it roughly out of her hand.

Prudence stopped dead in her tracks, her expression reproachful. "Mr. Stewart, you will not use profanity around me again."

"Then do as I say, or you'll hear words that will make your ears burn hot red."

"Mr. Stewart!"

Zac stopped, walked over to her, and looked down into her upturned face. "I'm going to tell you this one more time. Don't call me Mr. Stewart again."

"And if I do?" she persisted.

"You'll never finish the name," he said with a nasty grin.

"And how do you propose to prevent me — ?" She stopped suddenly when she realized his intentions. He would stop her with a kiss. He would capture his own name with his mouth and do unspeakable things with his lips and tongue. Again she recalled the kiss in the garden. Had his kiss been unspeakable or delightful? Perhaps a little of both.

"I see you understand me."

"Perfectly," she answered, purposely refraining from using any name.

"Good," he said, then walked away.

His "good" made her wonder if he had found kissing her repulsive. After all, he had only kissed her to prove a point, not because he desired her.

"Let's go, Prudence. I can't carry you and this satchel."

Prudence noticeably stiffened, walking toward him with her head erect and her body straight. He didn't have to insult her. At least she now knew he favored petite women and, of course, that answered her other question. About the kiss. He hadn't enjoyed it. She was certain of that now.

"I didn't ask for your assistance, nor do I need it," she said, and walked quickly past him.

"Damn," he muttered.

"Watch your profanity, *Mr. Stewart*, and I shall be more careful as to how I refer to you."

Zac was about to say *damn* again, but instead he smiled. Prudence Agatha Winthrop was one determined and smart lady. She had made sure she was a safe enough distance away before she called him Mr. Stewart, and she had bartered one irritating habit for another. Although he doubted he wouldn't say damn again around her, and he seriously doubted she wouldn't call him Mr. Stewart again. The thought made his smile grow. He was going to enjoy that kiss. Yes sir, he damn well was.

Prudence was already in the hotel when Zac entered. Now he could clearly see her fatigue in the way her shoulders drooped slightly. If he hadn't been familiar with her stiff posture, he wouldn't have noticed it. But having grown accustomed to the erect way she held herself, he now saw the slightest droop. Even her eyes had lost some of their luster and vitality. The girl definitely needed rest.

"Let me see about rooms and have them hold your bags until after we talk and have some food," he said, turning away from her before she could protest.

Prudence walked over to the well-worn Victorian chair near the lone window. Its red velvet material was faded and stained from years of use. She glanced down at the chair forlornly. It looked almost as weary as she felt. She wondered if she would be able to stand up again if she sat down.

Her tired body decided for her. She plopped down in a most unladylike fashion and sighed contentedly.

Prudence looked about the small quarters of the hotel. The furnishings were sparse, a few chairs grouped strategically for conversation, a large braided rug threadbare in spots, and a freshly polished smell that added a definite air of cleanliness. And the delicious, heavenly scent of spices and roasted beef drifting in from the dining salon made her mouth water.

Food and rest were two of the priorities on her list, but the top one was convincing Zac Stewart she couldn't return to Boston with him. And the only way she felt she might have a chance was if she confided in him and told him the truth.

"All set," Zac said, looking down at her.

It wasn't necessary for Prudence to force a pleasant smile. It came naturally this time, and the change it brought to her face was startling.

Zac took immediate notice. Her cheeks were warm with a gentle blush, her green eyes soft in their look, her lips loose and pliable, as though ready to be tasted and enjoyed.

"Let's eat!" he snapped and walked away from her, not even bothering to extend his hand in assistance as a proper gentleman should.

Prudence stood, a moan involuntarily escaping her lips in protest.

Zac turned quickly, shook his head, and walked back to her. "How much does it really hurt? And don't bother to deny it does. I hate martyrs."

"I'm not a martyr, nor do I wish to be. I assumed soreness would be part of my travels. And how much it really hurts is none of your concern," she said and, though it pained her to move as fast as she did, walked past him in quick strides toward the dining salon.

Zac smiled. He liked strong women. Soft and responsive to the touch, but strong-natured. And Prudence surely was that. He wondered if she would be responsive to his touch. He would love to wrap his arms around those full hips, bury his face in her soft breasts, and taste her.

Roasted beef, potatoes, turnip greens, and hot bread dripping with honey was the night's menu. Prudence sipped at the welcoming hot tea as they waited for their food.

Zac drank cider. The young woman serving them left not only a full pitcher for his use but also a smile that hinted interest.

"Mr. —" Prudence immediately amended the slip of her tongue when she caught the warning glare in his eyes. "Zac, I would like to discuss my reason for coming west. Perhaps then you will understand why I can't possibly return to Boston with you."

Zac nodded his consent as the food was brought and placed on the table. They helped themselves to generous portions from serving dishes and took several delicious bites. Prudence was about to continue when Zac interrupted with a question.

"Don't you ever take your gloves off?" he asked.

She had removed her linen duster and her hat, but the gloves remained. She glanced down at them, not allowing his query to upset her. She was accustomed to handling such situations, and she did so now with calm aplomb as she raised her eyes to meet his. "My hands are soiled and sweaty from the long trip. Until I can properly clean them, I prefer to eat with my gloves on."

"Look, Prudence," he said, leaning forward, "everything out here gets soiled and sweaty from time to time. Water isn't always conveniently located. We make do. It doesn't matter if your hands aren't perfect."

She thought about her two crooked and useless fingers and the way her friends had often made fun of them. Perfection in her branch of society was important. "Yes, it does," she said softly.

Zac found her Bostonian manners grating here in the West. He'd love to strip them away from her, along with that confining gray dress and the corset and undergarments beneath. Damn, but he couldn't stop thinking of her in a sexual manner. He'd been too long without a woman, that was the problem. And since she was here, his mind just naturally wandered in that direction. That was it, pure and simple. Her full breasts and hips had nothing to do with it. Absolutely nothing. Then why the hell did he want so badly to feel her naked beneath him?

"Zac?"

"Sorry, my thoughts were wandering."

"Pleasant wanderings, I hope," she said, her tone sincere.

"Very pleasant," he said, leaning back in his chair. "Now where were we?"

64

"I had hoped to explain my reason for traveling here."

"Which is?"

Prudence didn't falter in tone or response. "I am trying to locate my mother."

Zac sat staring at her for several silent moments. "Excuse me, I don't mean to appear insensitive, but your father informed me that your mother had died several years ago."

"Yes, which was what I was told and believed until my grandmother informed me of the truth."

"Your father knows your mother isn't dead and has kept it from you?" he asked doubtfully.

"Correct, and I wish to locate her. I hired a man to track down her whereabouts, and the last place he could trace her to was here in Wells City."

"And you didn't mention any of this to your father? Didn't confront him with the information? Ask questions?"

"No," she hesitated a moment. "I thought he would discourage my search for her."

For a minute, Zac thought she might be telling the truth. Then he recalled James Winthrop's description of his daughter's tenacity when she set out to do something. Was a lie beyond a means to an end for her? "I think it best if you return to Boston, confront your father with this, and allow him to help you."

Prudence could see his doubt. "You don't believe me?"

"It's a bit farfetched."

"I'm telling you the truth."

Her look was gentle, compelling, and trustworthy. Her tender expression was so opposite her usual resolute nature that it almost did him in. Almost, but not quite. "That's not for me to decide. We'll return to Boston and let your father settle this."

"I'm not going back to Boston until I find her," Prudence said, her tone cold, breaking her soft demeanor.

Zac tried to remain calm, but he was growing extremely tired of her dictating to him. "You're returning to Boston with me. We leave in the morning."

"You can't make me—"

"I can make you do anything, honey," he said gently, much too gently.

"I wish to go to my room," Prudence said. She needed distance from him so she could find a solution to this perplexing problem.

"Excellent idea. We both could do with a good night's sleep."

Prudence retrieved her linen duster and hat from the nearby chair and followed Zac to the front desk.

"Your key, Mr. Stewart," the thin gentleman behind the counter said. "Towels and water have been sent up."

"Thank you," Zac said, and turned to Prudence.

"Where's my key?" she asked a bit apprehensively.

Even if he had wanted to, which he didn't, he couldn't stop the sinful grin from surfacing. "Do you really think I would let you have a room all to yourself?"

Prudence's wild-eyed look conveyed a temper gone a degree too high. "I will not share a room with you."

His grin darkened his expression, as his lips curled sinfully and his eyes became molten with sensuality. "You don't have a choice."

A dank shiver ran through her, but she retained her composure. "It isn't proper and I will not allow it. If father knew what you—"

"Your father told me to do *whatever* was necessary to return you to him."

"Not ruin my reputation."

"And what *nasty* things do you expect me to do to you in that room, Prudence, that will ruin your immaculate reputation?" he asked, stepping closer to her.

"I—I—"

"I could do things that would drive you wild. You would have stories to tell at the Boston Ladies Social Club that would make them green with envy and moist between their legs."

Prudence gasped at his audacity and took a step away from him.

His hand reached out and firmly snatched her wrist. "Don't tell me those proper ladies didn't entertain the idea of what it would be like to crawl into bed with a gunslinger?"

"Mr.—"

"Careful, Prudence. I hold no qualms about kissing you right here in front of everyone, especially since they think you're my bride."

"What?" she said, trying to pull free but getting nowhere. His grip was iron strong.

"Bride. That would easily explain your reluctance to go upstairs with me."

"You are an unspeakable beast."

"That I am, Pru. That I am," he said with a

laugh and yanked her toward him, hoisted her up without a grunt or a groan, and flung her over his shoulder.

"Put me down," Prudence shouted, turning scarlet when she raised her head behind him and saw everyone watching her with a smile.

"Relax, dear. It will be over soon," an older woman offered with an understanding nod.

Zac patted her backside, turning her face an even deeper red. "I'll be gentle," he promised, loud enough for the room to hear before taking the carpeted stairs two at a time.

Chapter Five

"You're a despicable beast!" Prudence yelled after being dumped carelessly on the bed.

"Now, honey, is that any way to start a marriage?" Zac asked, each word dripping with false sweetness as he walked to the door, slamming it shut and turning the lock.

"I'd never marry you!" she shouted, gathering her duster and hat in hand from where they had fallen beside her on the bed.

"Likewise!" Zac shouted back.

Prudence scrambled off the bed and ran toward the door, not bothering to consider that Zac was blocking it. His determined stance and rough tone brought her to a halt only a few feet in front of him.

"Touch it and I'll tie you to the bed! *Naked!*"

Prudence was about to say "You wouldn't" but thought better of it. He would. Instead, she chose silence as her weapon, walking over to the wooden chair opposite the four-drawer bureau and sitting down, her duster over one arm and her hat in her hand. Her eyes settled on the lone brass bed that took up a good portion of the small room. A sizable lump formed in her throat.

"I can see you intend to remain stubborn," he said, noticing her stiff posture. "Well, suit yourself. I intend to wash up."

Zac didn't wait for a response, didn't expect one. He unbuckled his gun belt and carefully hooked it over the brass head post, placing his hat atop it. His fingers worked on the buttons of his black shirt, opening it wide and pulling it free from the snug confines of his trousers. He slipped it off, tossing it on the bed.

"Sure you don't want to join me?" he teased, facing her, arms spread wide, causing her to blush at the sight of his naked torso.

Prudence was too shocked—much too shocked—to say or do anything in objection to Zac Stewart's rude behavior.

"Offended your proper sensibilities again, have I? Well, pardon my common sense and my partial nakedness while I wash," he said. He walked over to the large white porcelain pitcher on the bureau and poured water into the matching bowl. He then proceeded to wash the traveling dust from himself, trying very hard to ignore the two bulging eyes glaring at his naked back.

Undressing in front of her! How dare he! The man had no morals, no convictions, no decency. He was an animal, probably a state brought on by his questionable lifestyle.

Her eyes stayed fixed, though, upon his back, broad and weighty with thick muscles. She wondered how he retained his rich muscle definition. The thought of hard manual labor crossed her mind, but then that type of work wasn't really part of a gunslinger's life. His back was smooth and unmarred, until it reached the top of his trousers.

There to the right, just above his waistband and firm cheek, peeked the tip of a thin scar. How far down did it travel? And how had he come by it?

She bristled over her improper thoughts. What difference did it make where the scar traveled, or that his looks could melt a woman's heart and his body could . . .

Good gracious! Whatever was she thinking? She didn't actually find this man attractive, did she? And if so, what would it matter? She wasn't his type. He wouldn't give her a second glance. Her shape was too full. The silly description brought a hint of a smile to her lips.

Full. Plain. Nice. She had heard those words many times over the years. Never beautiful, stunning, gorgeous. Those words just didn't fit her. But it would have been pleasing to hear them, if only once.

"Are you all right, Pru?"

Was that genuine concern she heard in his voice? She smiled, a tired smile, when she raised her face to look at him.

"You're exhausted," he said, noting the heavy droop of her eyelids, the way her shoulders sagged, and the weariness of her expression. "Let me take those things from you. Go wash up some. Then it's off to bed with you."

He took her duster and hat from her and hung them on the hook by the door

He was right. She was exhausted, partially from her journey and partially from the problems she faced. It was all too much for her right now. It had seemed so simple when she had planned it. She had unrealistically assumed she would find her mother in a matter of days. Her practical side had tried to warn her, to make her aware of the insurmountable odds of locating a woman who had disappeared years ago. It would take more than the few weeks she had been traveling, much more. And for the first time since her journey started, Prudence doubted the wisdom of the venture. She was about to slip off her gloves, lost in her musings, when she remembered Zac was in the room. Her movement was slow as she turned and looked at him. "May I have some privacy?"

She had never requested permission from him for anything and her doing so now startled him. Even her eyes appeared different. Their color was a softer green, giving her the appearance of being drugged with a lazy sensuality, as though if he reached out and touched her, she would melt in response.

"I have no desire to see you naked," he snapped. *A downright blatant lie.* "I'll sit here on the bed with my back to you."

Prudence was stunned and hurt by his forceful words. After all, like every woman, she wanted to feel desirable, actually needed to feel desirable. It was part of being a woman. Her response was an obligatory, "Thank you."

She stripped off her gloves and top, standing there in her chemise and skirt and all the undergarments she wished she could shed. But that wasn't possible. She couldn't sleep in her nightgown in the same room as Mr. Stewart. She shouldn't even be sleeping in the same room with him at all.

He had replaced his water with fresh, and she hastily washed up. She was grateful to get what traveling dust she could off herself. She removed a clean white blouse from her satchel and slipped into it.

"I'm finished," she said as she unpinned her hair.

Zac turned and watched from the bed, having removed his boots and stretched out.

Prudence brushed her waist-length reddish brown hair until it sparkled to a coppery shine. She then plaited it and allowed it to rest over her shoulder. Finished, she hid her two useless fingers in the folds of her skirt and walked toward Zac. "It isn't proper for us to share this bed."

"Are you always proper, Prudence?" His question was posed in a strange tone.

"Always," she emphasized.

His voice was smooth and rich, like the thickness of sweet honey that promised a rewarding taste and didn't fail to deliver. "Wouldn't you like to be improper just once?"

She couldn't find her voice. It was there somewhere caught in her throat. He was contemptible, teasing her as such. A gentleman would never express such a crude thought. But then Zac Stewart was no gentleman. He was a gunslinger. He was accustomed to willing women, whiskey . . . and killing.

"Since you haven't answered immediately, I can only assume you are giving my idea thought," Zac said, adding a slow smile.

Prudence ignored the erratic beat of her heart and his suggestive smile. "You are contemptible!"

Zac patted the spot on the bed beside him. "Despicable. Contemptible. Those words excite the devil in me, Miss Winthrop. Do join me."

"Mr. —"

"Careful, Prudence, or you'll get more than you bargained for," he said with no trace of a smile, only sheer determination.

Prudence's dander was up considerably. "Perhaps,

73

Zac," she emphasized, "you would get more than *you* ever bargained for."

Zac leaned across the bed, keeping his eyes steady upon hers. His hand reached out slowly, so slowly that Prudence didn't think it would ever connect with her. But it did. He laid it upon her hip, and then with a dare-tell-me-to-remove-it look in his eyes, he ran it down her thigh, pressing the material of her skirt roughly against her leg. Causing friction, causing heat, and causing a warm moisture between her legs to embarrassingly appear, thankfully only to her knowledge.

Her eyes fluttered and her breath came in rapid spurts, but as soon as he spoke, her control returned full force.

"Is that a promise, honey?"

Prudence stepped back. "You are—"

"Remember, you've already used *despicable* and *contemptible*. How about something original?"

"Scurrilous!"

Zac braced himself back against the headboard. "Showing off your education, Pru. That won't do around here. No one would understand you. I, myself, would have chosen *depraved*."

"A perfect choice," she agreed. "And meaning just the same."

"Only more common. And you aren't common, are you?"

Prudence was struck by his statement. Was he referring to her social standing or her looks? She wasn't certain, but either way she was sure he meant it as an insult.

She raised her chin and gripped her skirt as best she could with her three good fingers. "I am who I am, and I make no apologies for it."

74

"Well, there must be something beneath that proper demeanor. Especially since you made it this far on your own." An amazing feat to Zac.

"I told you I could survive out here."

Zac laughed and shook his head. "Honey, you haven't begun to taste the West yet."

"Then give me time," she pleaded, taking a step closer to the bed. "Give me a few days . . . just a few to make some inquiries about my mother."

Zac hesitated. He was tempted, very tempted, to keep her with him for a few days. To show her the real West and perhaps learn if it was a truth or a tale she was telling him. And to learn just how responsive she could be to his touch. But his senses returned with a sharp sting. "No!" he snapped.

Prudence stepped away from the force of his word. "I'm only asking for a few days."

"And I said no. The subject is closed. You can discuss it with your father when you return. Now get in this bed and get some sleep. We're leaving early tomorrow."

"I cannot share a bed with you."

Zac sprung forward, grabbing Prudence by the wrist and tugging her down on top of him. Her breasts were plastered flat against his naked chest and her legs were caught snugly between his two large ones.

Prudence didn't know what to do. She raised her head and her lips were only a breath away from his. If she spoke, she would probably touch them, graze them with her own. Their gazes met and held for several seconds. She almost thought he waited for her to respond, to give him permission to do as he wished—or perhaps as they both wished. Could he possibly want her? Desire her?

"You aren't exactly light." Zac's words were meant to tease, not to hurt.

Prudence scurried off him like a wounded animal ready for flight, the moment destroyed by the reality of his words.

"Hold it," he yelled, yanking by her wrist. "You aren't going anyplace."

"I will not sleep with you!"

He pulled her down upon the bed once again. This time he went for her feet.

"What are you doing?" she demanded, trying to pull her foot, snugly secured in her walking boot, away from him.

"I intend to take your boots off," he explained, successful in forcing open her boot ties.

"You shall do no such thing!"

Zac held her ankle firmly in his one hand while he spoke slowly and clearly. "I am tired, very tired. And I want to get some sleep. I can't get any sleep if I have to worry about you running away from me. So I intend to make certain you can't escape me. And since I don't want bruised ankles, your boots come off.

"You are going to tie me like a common prisoner?" she asked indignantly.

"Correct," he said, trying to remove her other boot.

Prudence began to struggle in earnest. "Stop! Don't dare remove my boots!"

"Why? Do you have big feet you want to keep hidden?" he asked, laughing while holding her ankle and trying desperately to rid her foot of its boot.

"You are not my husband. You have no business seeing my stocking feet."

"The hell with your stocking feet and proper sensibilities. All I want to do is sleep. Now be still!" he shouted, and with that demand her boot fell to the floor.

Prudence remained still upon the bed. Her arms folded across her midsection, with her hands tucked beneath each arm. He was an animal. Uncivilized. Uncouth. She hated him.

"Your feet aren't *too* big."

She definitely hated him!

He finished tying her ankle to his with the black silk tie he pulled from his pocket. If she attempted flight during the night, a tug would now warn him. Then he stretched out beside her.

"Stiff in bed, too?" he asked, another laugh accenting his words.

"You have no manners." Her words were stern, like a staunch schoolteacher.

They irritated Zac. He turned, bending his elbow and bracing his head on his hand. His other hand captured her chin and roughly turned her face to meet his. "We both know I'm far from a gentleman. Would you like me to prove it?"

Her answer was a quick and decisive "No!"

"Then go to sleep and don't open your mouth again."

Prudence's lips moved to speak.

"I warn you. Try it and you'll be sorry, or perhaps you won't be," he said, a carnal grin spreading across his face.

Prudence shut her mouth and pulled her face free.

Zac lay back down, punching his pillow several times in annoyance before he did. Let her lie there and stare at the ceiling all night. He was going to get some sleep. He was tired. Damn tired. He wanted to sleep. Sleep was what he needed. He'd close his eyes and ignore her and sleep. Yes sir, sleep.

Her breathing was soft and steady, her chest rising and falling in soothing rhythm with every beat. Zac should know; he'd been watching her for the last two hours.

He couldn't sleep. No matter how hard he tried, he just couldn't slip into that blissful nocturnal slumber. Prudence, on the other hand, had not found it elusive. She had dozed off almost as soon as her eyes had closed.

He had become more agitated as the minutes slowly ticked by. At first he thought he was overtired, had gone too long without sleep and his body was protesting. But as he thought more on it, he realized it was Prudence who was keeping him awake.

Actually, it was his thoughts of Prudence that kept him wide-eyed. As soon as she had mentioned that he had no business seeing her feet, his eyes had focused on the area that was intended solely for a husband's viewing.

The dark stockings hid much from him, but her feet's narrow width and perfectly proportioned toes caught his attention. They were far from too big. In fact, they were just the right size for her full frame. And it was that full frame that kept his mind active with thoughts that were far from gentlemanly.

Zac rested his arms beneath his head and grinned. She'd probably faint if he touched her breast. A quick touch, soft and promising against her nipples, just enough to harden those brown areolas to gems that would taste deliciously sinful upon his tongue.

"Damn," he muttered, snapping his head sharply to the right to see if she had heard him. She was sound asleep.

He shifted his buttocks in the bed, the tightness in his pants annoying, especially since he had brought it upon himself. He had no business thinking of her in such a sexual way. She was proper and played by the rules. He, on the other hand, had never played by the rules. He had learned at a young age it didn't pay and was dangerous.

Just as it would be dangerous at this moment to reach over and touch her. He could satisfy—or more likely intensify—his curiosity while she slept. But she wasn't a saloon hall floozy. She was a young *lady* from Boston. Someday she would make a proper wife. She would submit to her husband at his will and probably suffer his inadequate fumbling until the sexual act was complete. She would experience no pleasure, at least not the type of pleasure he could give her.

The type where she would call out his name in sweet agony and cling to him in desperate want of more. And she *would* want more. He could feel it. Her sensuous, ample body was designed for passion, a raging fiery passion, not the simple grunt and groan and aah type.

"Damn!" he repeated again as he adjusted the bulge in his pants as best he could, reminding himself he couldn't get involved with Miss Winthrop. They didn't travel in the same "social circles." Marriage to her would mean a house in Boston, not a cabin in the wilderness of the Dakota Territory. Her husband would meet suitable standards. Ones he couldn't even come close to. He wasn't her type, and she wasn't his. They were the perfect mismatch. He would deposit her with her father and leave. He warned himself over and over that that was what he would do, and nothing—absolutely nothing—would stop him.

Zac's closed eyelids couldn't keep out the morning sun as it filtered into the room through the lace curtains. He moaned, knowing he had probably slept later than he'd intended.

He kept his eyes shut, stretching his arms above his head, then extending the exhilarating movement throughout his body until it reached his legs. That's when he felt the tug. He was no longer tied to Prudence's ankle.

His eyes flashed open and he sat up all in one swift motion. His bare ankle was neatly tied to the brass rung of the footpost. She had even added her feminine touch by tying a bow.

"Son of a . . ." He didn't bother to finish.

It took him several minutes to undo the intricate knots. He mumbled and swore the whole time, promising himself she would pay for this one. Definitely, without a doubt, she would pay.

Chapter Six

Prudence knew Sadie hadn't expected her to return to the saloon. She could tell by the surprised lift of the older woman's brow as she walked in.

She didn't have much time. She needed the information she sought directly. The sun would soon be rising and so would Zac. She could only imagine his expression when he found his foot tied to the post and his reaction when he attempted to disentangle the sailor's knot. A delighted smile reached her lips. She was so glad she had listened when her uncle, a sea captain, had shared his skill at seaman's knots with her. He had taught her much, and she was certain Zac would have difficulty untying the one she had secured upon him.

Now it was time to get the information and leave. She never wanted to set eyes on Zac Stewart again, if she could help it. At least now that she was aware he was following her, she'd be cautious.

"Changed your mind, honey, or ain't Zac as good in the bed as he used to be?" Sadie asked, sauntering up to her.

Prudence stood erect with a slight uplift of her

head, the perfect carriage of a well-bred lady. "I can assure you, my experience in bed with Mr. Stewart was most uneventful."

Sadie laughed and slapped her leg. "Wait till he hears that."

"I need information," she said, ignoring Sadie's remark. "And I need it *now*."

Sadie placed her hands on her hips and smirked. "And what if I don't want to give it?"

"Will one hundred dollars change your mind?" Prudence had no time to squabble. Money talked to Sadie. Actually, money would make Sadie talk.

"Jake, a cider and a whiskey," she called to the barkeep. "And see that no one disturbs us."

She directed Prudence to a table off in the corner. "So what can I do for you?" Sadie asked, tucking the bills Prudence had handed her into the crack of her large bosoms.

Prudence wasted no time. "Did you know a Lenore Winthrop?"

Sadie's eyes squinted in thought. "Name don't sound familiar."

"Perhaps a description will help," Prudence suggested and, with a nod from Sadie, continued. "She is a little shorter than myself. Has long dark hair. Dark eyes and complexion deeper than mine, but clear and unmarred. Actually, her features are quite striking." She recalled her father saying that once to her mother. Her mother had kissed him on the cheek and had led him by the hand into his study. Prudence could still hear the click of the lock.

"Not as endowed as you?" Sadie asked.

"Correct," Prudence said, having often wondered why she couldn't have inherited her mother's slim form.

"That description fits at least a dozen women I

know. Anything specific you can recall about her?"

Prudence reflected, drawing on the few memories she had of her mother. She remembered how often she had stood on the kitchen chair by the table as her mother baked. Her mother would tuck a large apron around her, so that she could scoop up, with her small fingers, the sweet mixture in the bowl. One particular recipe was her mother's favorite and she baked it on special occasions. "She loved to cook, especially rum cake."

"Lee." Sadie didn't hesitate in her response. "Lee's the only woman I know that could bake a rum cake that had you licking your fingers long after you had finished it."

"Lee?"

"The woman who helped me start this saloon. She fits the description. Nice woman . . . too nice for this business."

"She helped you start this place?" Prudence was surprised. Her mother running a saloon?

Sadie laughed and shook her head after downing the last of her whiskey. "She cooked in the back, good food, too, that's what brought the men in besides the whiskey. She wouldn't have anything to do with the men. Took a knife to one or two on occasion. After the saloon got on its feet financially, she asked for her share. Explained it was time to be on her way."

"When did she leave?" Prudence asked, finding it hard to believe she had a lead to her mother's whereabouts.

"Let's see . . . five, six, maybe eight years ago. I don't really recall. Didn't think she'd stay. She looked the wandering type, as though she were searching for something she had lost."

"Do you have any idea where she went?"

"Plattsmouth, Nebraska, last I heard," Sadie said,

motioning to the barkeep for another drink. "What do you want with her, anyway?"

"She's my mother," Prudence said, before realizing the information was best kept to herself.

Sadie looked shocked, very shocked. Her eyes were wide, her mouth dropped open, and she leaned back in her chair. "You sure about that?"

"Well, I think she is. I mean, I am looking for my mother, and the woman you spoke of could be her. I'll just have to track her down and find out for myself. How would I get to Plattsmouth?"

Sadie swallowed half the whiskey in her glass before answering. "That's a tricky one. You need to get to Alexandria, Nebraska first, and from there you can get a train that will take you to Hastings and then to Plattsmouth."

Prudence nodded, repeating the directions over and over in her mind for later reference. "How do I get to Alexandria?"

"I suppose you're in a hurry?"

"Yes, I am," Prudence admitted. "And I prefer to travel without a certain male companion, who I suspect will be waking soon."

"I understand, but what I don't get is why Zac is trailing you?"

Prudence decided honesty would be best under the circumstances. "My father hired him to return me to Boston and I imagine offered him a price too tempting to refuse."

"Then you better get your tail moving, girl, 'cause once Zac wakes up and finds you gone, he's going to blow his top. He doesn't like not finishing a job. When he's hired to do something, he sees that it gets done."

"I realize that. So where do I get my tail going?"

"That could prove a problem unless . . ."

"Unless what?" Prudence asked. "I'm willing to try anything."

"Anything?" Sadie asked, a questioning rise of her brow expressing doubt about the extent of Prudence's willingness.

"Almost," Prudence amended.

"How about telling a tall tale? Would that go against your convictions?"

"Not if it would get me out of here this morning."

"Then luck might just be with you," Sadie nodded slowly. "Yup, you might just pull it off."

"What do I have to do?"

Sadie leaned forward and lowered her voice. "There's a preacher, his wife, and six children leaving by wagon for Alexandria this morning. He might be persuaded to take you along if he felt it was urgent enough."

"I could pay him," Prudence offered.

Sadie shook her had. "Not a preacher. Better if he thinks he's helping one of God's lost flock."

"How do I convince him I'm lost?" Prudence asked, not certain what Sadie was getting at.

"The one thing that makes a man of the cloth want to help a lone woman is to discover she's been led astray into temptress ways and wishes to repent. Do you wish to repent, Miss Winthrop?"

Prudence smiled before changing her expression to one of soulful repentance. "Yes, Miss Sadie, I surely do wish to mend my sinful thoughts and ways."

Sadie stood. "Then you best hurry, child, 'cause that wagon is due to leave within the hour."

Prudence stood and reached into her purse, taking out a few bills. "Sadie, it is important that Zac doesn't learn my destination or about my mother."

Sadie pushed the offered money back to Prudence. This one's on me. It will be well worth it to see Zac's face when he finds out you left Wells City."

"I suppose he'll be mad?"

"Mad ain't the word. And I warn you, he'll probably find out where you're headed, though not from me, but he has ways. Don't ask me what they are; I don't want to know. But when he wants something, believe me he gets it."

"Yes, he does seem determined to have his way," Prudence agreed, recalling that his tenacity seemed to match hers. "But then I have a determined nature myself."

"What a mixture . . . pure explosive," Sadie said with a wide smile, then added in a more serious tone. "Be careful."

"I will, and thank you for your help," Prudence said, picking up her traveling case.

"Say hello to Lee if you find her, and if she turns out to be your mama, remember one thing: You're a lucky girl to have such a wonderful person for a mother."

It didn't take Prudence long to locate the preacher's wagon. She stood quiet and somber before Preacher Jacob Hyatt, an easy task. His six foot height and heavy yet solid bulk was intimidating, not to mention the long gray beard that grew down into a point and rested upon his chest.

Prudence was certain he preached his sermons with a fire and brimstone flair, frightening his congregation into obedience.

"So you fell into evil ways," his deep voice boomed in condemnation.

"I was led astray," she offered meekly. "I thought . . ." She paused to add a sigh for dramatic affect, then continued. "I thought he loved me. He told me he loved me and would marry me."

Preacher Jacob shook his head. His large eyes displayed his disappointment. "Women must be strong and resist temptation. What other temptations did you fall prey to?"

Prudence felt the blush start under her high-neck collar and creep up to stain her cheeks in flaming red patches. She had not succumbed to the "evils of the flesh," as he implied, but just the thought of herself standing naked before Zac Stewart was enough to deepen the color in her cheeks and give the wrong impression to the preacher.

Preacher Jacob squeezed his eyes shut a moment and folded his hands in prayer. "Dear Lord, help this lost child of your flock to repent and cleanse her tarnished soul."

Prudence bit on her lower lip, reminding herself why she stood before this man in a cowering manner. It was necessary because it would bring her a step closer to finding her mother.

Preacher Jacob's eyes shot open, glaring at Prudence like an avenging warrior of the Lord.

She spoke before he could. "I need to get to Alexandria. From there I can reach my older sister, who will take me in and help me."

"And why didn't you turn to her for help before instead of running off with this man?" His look was condemning and his tone disapproving.

"I was foolish," she said slowly, uncomfortable with admitting to something so out of character. Then she quickly added the one reason she thought so many women did foolish things. "I trusted his word, his love."

"It was lust he felt," the preacher admonished. "And you were unwise to think otherwise. Were you not taught the sin of succumbing to wantonness? Was the significance of the name given you at birth lost upon you?"

"My love blinded me," she defended, knowing full well her name stood for *intelligence*, which she was certain she possessed more of than the preacher.

"Your love for the Lord should transcend all other love, and it is His laws that must be obeyed. If I agree to take you along, will you pray with me for the salvation of your sinful soul and repent your evil ways?"

Prudence hesitated a moment, wondering if it was a wise choice to accompany a preacher who was so condemning and unforgiving. But the thought of Zac waking to find himself tied to the brass bed like a horse to a post moved her to speak. "Yes, Preacher Jacob, I will pray."

The preacher nodded, satisfied. "Then I shall take you with me and mine. And you will do well to learn from my dutiful wife, Ellie, the ways for a proper woman to act. When you reach your sister, you will confess your sins to her so she may help find you a suitable husband who should use a heavy hand to keep you in line."

Prudence found his last remark hard to swallow. No husband would "keep her in line." She would never entertain such a ridiculous notion, but she had to remember that he was a preacher and held a heavy belief in a woman's subservient role in life. Thanks to her father's lenient upbringing, Prudence thought such behavior nonsense. She would play along to reach her destination, and then she would be rid of him.

"Ellie!" his voice boomed like sharp thunder, causing his wife to jump to his command.

Prudence felt a pang of sympathy for the woman who hurried over to them. She was medium in height and weight, her features sharp to the point of making her appear unattractive. Her brown hair was pulled severely back into a bun. A well-rounded belly proved that Preacher Jacob had succumbed to the "sins of the flesh" about seven months ago.

"Yes, Jacob?" Ellie responded, her voice low and her tone obedient.

"Prudence will be joining us on our journey. You will teach her the Lord's way."

"Yes, Jacob," she answered.

"Go, Prudence, and assist my wife in preparations to leave. Later we will pray together and begin to cleanse your soul."

"Thank you," Prudence said softly.

"It is the Lord you owe thanks to for directing you to me. Now go, and, Ellie, pray with Prudence as you work."

"Yes, Jacob," Ellie said, motioning for Prudence to follow.

"Say that again, Sadie," Zac said, his expression murderous.

"She's gone," Sadie repeated, her voice a nervous quiver.

"Where?" he asked, standing away from the bar, ready to leave as soon as Sadie informed him of Prudence's destination.

"Don't know," Sadie answered sharply and with a rapid shake of her head.

Zac couldn't help but laugh, although the sound was more like an angry growl. "Sadie," he said, dragging her name out. "You know better than to lie to me."

Sadie downed the whiskey in her glass for courage. "Gave my word and I ain't goin' back on it."

"Your mothering instincts exerting themselves?"

Sadie shrugged. "Maybe, but that girl sure don't

need mothering. She's one willful gal."

"You don't have to tell me that," Zac said, disturbed by the fact that Prudence had outwitted him. He reached for his half-filled whiskey glass.

Sadie laughed and slapped the bar, sending a vibrating rumble throughout the saloon. "Don't know why you're chasing her, anyway. She said sharing your bed was *uneventful*."

"She said what?" Zac bellowed, smashing the empty glass down on the bar.

"Uneventful. Yes sir, that's the word she used. Uneventful," Sadie repeated once again.

Zac's jawline tightened and his eyes narrowed. "Uneventful," he said slowly, tasting the irritating word. "Wait until I get my hands on her."

"I think that's exactly what she found disappointing—your hands . . . or should I say what you did or didn't do with them," Sadie said, a hearty laugh bouncing her large bosoms.

The barkeep joined in, and Zac shot him a warning look that immediately turned the man's head in the opposite direction. He then focused his attention on Sadie. "Where did she go?"

His stony look chilled her. She shrugged her shoulders, not trusting her voice, especially since it was stuck somewhere in her throat.

Zac moved toward her. "I'm in no mood for games. Prudence Agatha Winthrop is a spoiled young lady who needs to be taught a lesson."

"You gonna be her teacher?" Sadie asked, a sly grin turning up the corners of her red-painted lips.

"I'm going to teach her things she never dreamed of learning," Zac said with the undaunted look of a gunfighter ready to face his foe. "Now where is she?"

"Hooked up with a preacher and his family on their way to Alexandria by wagon."

Sadie and Zac both turned their heads in unison to stare at Jake, the barkeep.

He grinned, his red moustache spreading wide. "Heard the ladies talking, Mr. Stewart, and I didn't give anyone my word."

Sadie raised a pointed finger to Jake and opened her mouth, but Zac cut her off.

"Don't you dare fire Jake," he warned.

"It's my place and I'll do—"

"As I say," Zac finished, grabbing Sadie and planting a big kiss on her cheek.

Sadie shook him off, fending annoyance, but the blush warming her cheeks spoke otherwise. "You're the devil himself, Zac Stewart."

"No, Sadie," Zac said in a dangerously controlled voice. "I'm worse than the devil, and that's what Miss Winthrop is about to discover."

A lump lodged in Sadie's throat once again, but she managed a small warning. "Don't be too harsh on her."

Zac took his black hat from the bar and put it on casually, tugging it down. "She'll get what she deserves."

"Which is?"

"More than she bargained for," Zac said with a smile that would chill the fires of hell.

"Oh, Father, this lost child begs your forgiveness," Preacher Jacob solemnly prayed in the darkness.

Prudence's knees had long since lost their feeling, for which she was grateful. She and the preacher had been kneeling on the hard ground and praying for an hour now, or perhaps for more than an hour. She had lost track of time. His words were a monotonous drone in her ears, going on for what seemed like forever.

She had been grateful when the wagon had finally been stopped for the night, more so for Ellie than for herself. Prudence was finding the West to her liking. Its stark, raw beauty appealed to her, as did the simplicity and hard work of everyday life. The people carved out a special existence for themselves against all odds and elements. Not an easy feat, but a challenging one.

Although she doubted Ellie was up to the challenge, through no fault of her own. Her condition and the hardships of wagon travel had completely exhausted her. Prudence had spotted it miles back. Still, the woman drove the team on, as well as cared for the children and fed everyone the noonday meal, while her husband rode ahead, ignoring all as he prayed.

As soon as they had stopped, Prudence had pitched in to help with the children and to prepare the evening meal. Earlier, Ellie had refused her help when they had stopped at noon, whispering that a lady such as she shouldn't work. But this time Prudence didn't offer her help; she just gave it. And Ellie didn't refuse.

Prudence had just finished settling all six young ones for the night and was about to do the same with herself, when Preacher Jacob announced her repentance time was at hand.

His words hung like a dire warning in her mind as he led her to the edge of the camp, away from the others and the glow of the fire. The dark night seemed to swallow them up as he forced her to her knees, kneeling beside her, his hand heavy upon her shoulder. Then he began to pray. And pray and pray.

Prudence's eyes grew heavy with needed sleep, her

shoulders slumped, and her back throbbed. She mumbled her prayers, not wanting the preacher to know she prayed for a quick deliverance from *him*.

"Do you renounce the sins of the flesh?" he asked. His voice was low, and there was a strange shift in its monotonous cadence.

"Yes," Prudence answered quickly, wanting desperately for this ordeal to end.

"You will allow only your husband to lay his hands upon you?" His voice quivered in urgency with each word he spoke.

"Yes."

"Where did this defiler of pure womanhood touch you?" he asked in a chilling whisper.

Prudence's head snapped up and she stared wide-eyed at the preacher. His lips were wet and heavy with his own saliva, and his look was hungry.

"Don't be afraid to tell me, child. I walk with the Lord and am here to help you."

Prudence was certain he walked with someone, but she doubted it was with the Lord. She had withstood her first glimpse of an Indian without collapsing and had outwitted a gunslinger. She wasn't about to let a preacher—a charlatan, at that—best her.

"Did he suckle your plump breasts with his lips?"

Her mouth dropped open from the shock of his words.

"Did he feast on you like a vile beast?" The preacher's eyes grew wide and shiny. His mouth grew even more wet with spittle, some running from the corner.

"Did he sully you with his—?"

"Hallelujah! I feel cleansed," Prudence shouted, fumbling on her hands and knees as she scurried to stand. From the corner of her eye, she caught the preacher's hands reaching for her backside. She scrambled away, her knees finally losing their numbness and feeling the hard earth. She pushed herself up, unmindful of the dirt that stained her skirt and blouse or of the thousand tiny pinpricks that ran up her legs.

"Thank you. Thank you, preacher. I feel one with the Lord again," she said rapidly, and just as rapidly walked away in a wobble that looked anything but dignified.

Prudence hurried to the wagon and crawled beneath the blanket provided her, grateful she shared the children's sleeping area.

"Ellie!" Preacher Jacob's voice boomed. "Come, we pray."

Prudence watched the young woman slowly stand, rub her back, and walk toward her husband, unbuttoning her blouse with each step.

Chapter Seven

Zac spotted Prudence as soon as the wagon rolled into Alexandria. He had been waiting patiently for its arrival, having shown up several days ago himself, by horse.

Now seeing her sitting atop the wagon, prim and proper, her hat in place, her clothes perfect, her gloves . . .

His patience snapped like a dried twig. "Damn those gloves," he grumbled. "Doesn't she ever remove them?"

In bed. The odd notion flashed through his mind, conjuring up an image of Prudence wearing nothing but her gloves. Pure white gloves, her flesh naked, her copper-colored hair loose to her waist and highlighted with the fiery streaks of red that danced through the silky strands. That was how she would appear. And, of course, she would touch him with those gloves—no, stroke him, she would stroke him. Slow and sensual would be her touch.

"Damn!" he grumbled again. Zac thought he had successfully extinguished his sexual fantasies concerning Prudence Agatha Winthrop. Yet here he was, thinking . . . thinking the impossible. She would never stand in front of him naked, with only her gloves on. The suggestion alone would probably cause her to grasp her chest in fright and faint. He had to get her back to Boston fast, for the sake of his own sanity. These flights of fantasy concerning her had to stop. He was a grown man of thirty, not some kid hiding behind the barn enjoying dirty thoughts.

If he wanted a naked woman, wearing only gloves, he could visit the local saloon and get exactly that. He could get anything he wanted for the right price, except Prudence.

He shook the aggravating thoughts away and kept close to the buildings, following and watching the wagon as it meandered down the dirt street.

It rumbled along at a snail's pace, a cloud of dry dust following in its wake. It was headed to the far end of town, where there was room to set up camp.

Prudence could hardly contain her excitement. Soon she would be free of this sanctimonious "soldier of the Lord," as Preacher Jacob often referred to himself. On a mission, he was, to wipe out sinners and redeem their blemished souls. He felt Prudence's redemption would be complete upon deliverance of her to her sister. Prudence thought otherwise.

The wagon groaned to a halt, with the wheels squeaking, the children hollering, Ellie sighing in relief, and Prudence set and ready to carry on her adventure. She helped Ellie and her large brood down from the wagon. The children ran off screeching, delighted with their freedom even if it was only temporary.

"Sister Prudence!"

Prudence cringed at the preacher's booming voice.

He walked up to her, slipping his black waistcoat over his white, sweat-stained shirt. "I will see you safely to your sister as soon as I've seen to the horses."

Without a second's hesitation, Prudence reached for her satchel and traveling case. "Preacher Jacob, you've placed me on the path of the Lord. I can walk the rest of the way on my own. Do not burden yourself further with me. It isn't necessary."

"It is my duty—"

"You've performed your duty most amicably. Thank you for your help," Prudence said, backing away and ready to take flight.

"But—"

"I walk with the Lord, Preacher Jacob. Praise be to you!" she sang, turning and hurrying off. She was grateful the horses needed tending, or he probably would have followed her.

She walked sure in step and stride toward the town's end building, stopping just before the boardwalk that ran in front of the stores. She placed her cases at her feet and dusted herself off, coughing as the dry dirt particles wafted about her. Prudence had not worn her tan duster, the late spring weather being unusually warm. Even the gray day suit she wore felt sticky against her warm skin.

She had noticed the women in various towns she had passed through wore lighter cotton dresses or skirts and blouses. Prudence thought about removing her suit jacket, but she was about to travel by train and it didn't seem appropriate to do so half clothed. She would wait, and perhaps if there was time before the train left, she could see about purchasing some of the lighter, more comfortable dresses.

Prudence lifted her cases and, in her usual proper stride, walked toward the other end of town. She had seen the train station as they had entered Alexandria.

She hurried along, her chin up, her shoulders back, receiving a nod or a smile here and there from the respectable women of the town. She wore her proper breeding like a mantle for all to see and admire. Her looks might be plain, but her manner was impeccable, and of that she was proud.

Two portly gentleman tipped their beaver-skin hats and stepped back so she could proceed them to the train ticket window. She nodded with a curt smile, not wishing to encourage their acquaintance.

"When is the next train for Hastings?" Prudence inquired of the gentleman behind the barred window.

"She arrives in two hours, ma'am, and departs fifteen minutes later," the man informed her cordially.

"I'd like to purchase a ticket."

"Just one?"

Prudence took a quick peek around her. For a moment, his question and the way his eyes scanned beyond her had made her fear she had company. Panic had nearly set in, but to her relief the two gentlemen, busy in chatter, were the only ones about.

"Yes, just one," she answered, taking the money from her purse to pay for the ticket. "Is there a store nearby where I might purchase ready-made dresses?"

The man slipped the ticket beneath the bars. "Harry's Dry Goods, middle of the street, this side. You can leave your traveling cases in here with me if you'd like. Just set them by the door."

"Thank you," she said, taking the ticket and moving her cases to the door. There was plenty of time to spare. She could pick up the few things she needed before the train's arrival.

She clutched the ticket in her hand and to her breast, not realizing the desperation of her actions, as she stepped off the steps of the train station.

"Going somewhere, Prudence?"

Her feet froze, her legs buckled, and her heart beat wildly. She turned and her breath caught in her throat. Zac stood before her and looked exactly like a notorious gunslinger should. He wore black trousers, waist-coat, and vest over a white shirt, with silver six-shooters resting in a black leather holster that hugged his hips. His black hat with a circling silver band sat far enough up to allow her to see his eyes. Satisfaction and victory was evident in them. She finally found her voice. "Mr. Stewart!"

Zac shook his head and grinned. "I warned you about that, honey." His mouth swooped down over hers before she could object.

She was shocked at the gentle and teasing way his lips touched hers. His hands hugged her shoulders as his lips pressured hers, feeling supple, warm, and tempting.

The tip of his tongue traced the junction of her tightly clamped lips. Slow and steady, his tongue roamed back and forth, gently prodding for admittance.

Her body reacted most noticeably with a shiver. She thought she heard a chuckle deep in his throat, or perhaps it was a groan. His lips pressured hers while his tongue continued to play against her defenses. Her temperature climbed, the warmth flushing her cheeks to a soft pink.

His mouth slipped from hers with a bit of hesitation. He kissed her cheek near her ear, stopping to whisper, "I'll take that."

The ticket was snatched from her hand before she could protest.

"You have no right," Prudence demanded, her common sense rushing back.

"I have every right," he corrected. There was an air of warning in his stern words. "You're returning to Boston with me."

Prudence pulled away from him. "I'm not going back until I'm ready."

Zac grabbed her arm. "You're ready."

Prudence attempted to twist free, but his grasp was tight and firm. She only managed to irritate her skin.

"Hold still and behave!" he scolded. "It was easier cleaning up Devil City of gunslingers than keeping tabs on you."

"I have a mission," she announced, almost cringing at the words that sounded as though they came from Preacher Jacob's mouth.

"Lord help me, a woman with a mission," Zac said with a rough shake of his head.

"It's important, Zac." Prudence's tone was soft now. Her voice was low and his name sounded sweet on her lips.

Zac's dark brown eyes settled with a strange intensity upon her face. He took note once more of her fatigue and weariness, apparent in the gray half circles beneath her eyes and the gentle droop of her lids.

The West had a way of draining a new arrival, replacing whatever energy it had robbed with a quiet strength and leaving the individual changed forever. For the better, Zac had always felt.

He wished he could allow Prudence her "mission," even if it was a daydream. He would have enjoyed watching the woman who would materialize and grow in strength and beauty. She reminded him of a long-blooming flower left neglected on the vine. Given the proper attention and care, she would flourish and outshine all others.

I could provide what she needed. The crazy thought was a jolt to his senses. "You're going back."

"I won't!" she said emphatically.

"Your father said you didn't take orders well."

"My father knows me well enough, therefore he won't be disappointed when you return without me."

Zac pulled her closer to him. "You're going back."

100

Prudence hated those words and, at the moment, Zac Stewart. She was about to tell him just that when a male voice interrupted.

"Excuse me, ma'am. Is this *gentleman* bothering you?"

Prudence smiled at the portly man from the train station and his friend beside him.

Zac turned quickly, slipping his arm protectively around her waist and greeting the men with that captivating smile of his. "Gentlemen, how nice to see that a lady is so well protected in your town. Especially when that lady happens to be my *wife*."

His emphasis on the word *wife* caused the men to grin and shake their heads as though they understood. Their action irritated Prudence. She opened her mouth to correct the situation, but Zac's biting fingers at her waist instead brought a strange and most unladylike sound from her.

The two men tipped their hats and walked on.

Zac's hand remained firm on her waist as he urged her to walk. "You should clear your throat before you attempt to speak, dear."

"You should keep your hands where they belong."

Zac squeezed her waist. "But they are where they belong, around my loving wife."

Prudence tipped her head up and to the side to look at him. His shoulder caught the brim of her hat and knocked it askew. She tried to right it but only made it worse.

"Take it and those stupid gloves off," Zac ordered.

Prudence attempted to stop in mid-stride, but Zac's firm hold wouldn't permit it. They kept walking.

"A lady always wears her hat and gloves when out," Prudence said, sounding like a schoolteacher instructing a student.

"Not out west," Zac corrected. "Here a woman has

no use for a fancy bonnet except maybe for church services. And gloves . . . well, gloves are worn when tending the garden or driving a team. You'll find no use for your fancy wears and airs out here."

"Proper attire and manners have a place even in the *wild West*."

"That they do. In the ladies' journals the women receive from back east."

"You're impossible."

"No, practical."

"Where are you taking me?"

"To the hotel."

Prudence stopped dead still, forcing Zac to do the same.

She raised her finger, pointing it in his face. "I refuse, absolutely refuse, to share a room with you again." Her face turned scarlet as several women passing by stared in disapproval.

Zac hid his merriment well, only allowing himself a sly smile. "Did I ask you to share my room?"

Prudence eyed him suspiciously.

Zac squeezed her chin playfully. "I need to get my bag and settle my account there. Then we'll be off."

"Where?"

"The train station. We'll be taking that train, but once in Hastings, we'll be heading in a different direction."

She didn't comment. She was happy they were going to Hastings. At least she was headed in the right direction. She could always find a way to escape him. She had done so once, and she could do it again.

They entered the small hotel.

"Can I trust you to sit here while I see to things?" Zac asked. "Or must I keep my hands upon you?"

Prudence sat down in the chair, finally adjusting her hat to fit properly. "I intend to take that train with or without you. And most certainly without your hands on my person."

"You mean you won't give me any trouble until we get to Hastings?"

"Correct," she announced. "Now please hurry. We don't want to miss the train."

Zac walked away, shaking his head. He didn't understand why he felt as if his troubles were just beginning.

Preacher Jacob watched Prudence and the man disappear into the hotel. "Our sister Prudence walks the evil path once again."

Ellie watched her husband's eyes as they remained transfixed on the hotel.

"In her lust for the flesh, she has lied and used a man of the cloth to help her sin. She didn't come to Alexandria to meet her sister. She came to meet a man. The very man she has probably fornicated with time and again."

Ellie stayed silent as her husband's eyes grew wide and bright with a desire for revenge.

"We must save her tarnished soul. It isn't too late. She must be made to walk the path of the Lord, as must the man with whom she has chosen to sin."

Ellie nodded and followed her husband as he walked with quick strides back to the wagon.

"We will gather the soldiers of the Lord to do his work. By evening, these sinners will sin no more. They will be one with the Lord. Come, Ellie, we must hurry. There is much to do."

Prudence relaxed in the chair, grateful for its comfort after days of riding the wagon seat. Her body was worn but her spirit was high. She found she enjoyed the unpredictable. She didn't miss the mundane routine of Boston. Here she experienced the excitement of life. Of course, she hadn't counted on Zac Stewart's presence. She stole a glance to where he stood. Tall and commanding in his stance, he inspired respect and awe in other men. And the women . . . they couldn't take their eyes off him. Some tried to be casual, stealing a glance here and there, while the more outrageous ones openly smiled and flirted with him.

Prudence had to admit he was a fine specimen of a man. Handsome and determined to see his job done, if one could ignore his gunslinger past, he appeared prime husband material.

She didn't often give flight to her imagination, always thinking of the practical. But for a moment, she pictured him following her west because he loved her and feared for her safe return. The ridiculous thought snapped her back to her senses.

"Don't be a fool, Prudence," she scolded in a whisper as she stole one more peek at Zac.

His eyes caught hers and he smiled that utterly charming, beguiling smile. Her heart thumped wildly and then he winked at her, causing the thumping to cease entirely and her breath to catch.

She turned her head quickly away. "Devil," she mumbled. "He's an absolute devil of a man."

A shadow fell over her and she jumped, startled by its nearness.

Zac stood over her. "Ready?"

She nodded and he took her arm to help her stand.

"You need some rest," he said. "It takes time to accustom yourself to the West."

"I'm doing fine," she defended.

"I didn't say you weren't. Actually I'm a bit surprised at how well you've held up out here."

Prudence smiled. "Disappointed I didn't crumble?"

He laughed. "Actually, I am. It would have made my job much easier."

"You're right," she said, adding a nod of delight. "It would have."

They walked to the door a bit more relaxed in their newly found camaraderie.

"Well, at least we agree on one thing," Zac said, reaching for the handle.

"A pleasant change," Prudence agreed, certain it wouldn't last long.

"Damn!" Zac said beneath his breath, but loud enough for Prudence to hear as they walked out of the hotel.

"Mr. Stewart, I warned you . . ." Her words died on her lips.

Zac gently nudged Prudence behind him as they both stared down the barrels of over a dozen rifles pointed directly at them.

"Preacher Jacob," Prudence whispered, spying the man in the lead.

"The preacher you hooked a ride with?" Zac questioned in a whisper.

Preacher Jacob's booming voice allowed for no response. "Sister Prudence, I have come to save you from your sinning ways and free your soul."

"Damn," Zac repeated.

The dozen men stood silent around the preacher, each holding steady his rifle. The grave looks on their faces warned Zac of the seriousness of the situation.

"My son, you have committed a sin against the Lord," Preacher Jacob announced. "You must repent and do the honorable thing."

Zac didn't want to think about what this crazy man was about to suggest. He also doubted Prudence had any understanding of what she had gotten them into.

"You have fornicated with this woman without the benefit of marriage."

Prudence turned bright red, and the volume from the crowd that had begun gathering grew with his announcement.

"You must save her soul and yours," the preacher continued, growing louder in tone upon hearing the murmur of approving voices. "You must join her in the holiness of marriage before this day ends, or forever be condemned to the torments of hell."

"Hallelujah!" the crowd cheered.

Prudence stepped from behind Zac and opened her mouth.

Zac immediately slipped his arm around her waist and pulled her to him. "Shut up," he whispered harshly.

She tried to protest, but he stilled her with a sharp squeeze to her side. "The only thing worse than an angry gunslinger is a preacher who believes an innocent woman has been wronged," he whispered.

Prudence looked at him in disbelief.

"He'll pull that trigger without second thought and be praised for carrying out justice instead of murder."

Prudence listened carefully to his whispered words, then looked around at the sea of faces. They were grave and determined to see that the Lord's justice be done.

"Will you take sister Prudence as your wife and cleanse her soul?" the preacher asked, raising his rifle and focusing the barrel right between Zac's eyes.

Prudence stared at Zac. What choice did he have? And that was what she saw written in his intense look. What would it be? Death or marriage to her. Not much of a choice. But then he was smart. His trade had taught him how to get out of many a tough situation. Perhaps he would find a way out of this one.

"I have no objections to marrying Prudence."

She heard his loud, clear words but didn't believe them. Why shouldn't he answer thusly? He had over a dozen rifles fixed upon him, set and ready to fire. What man wouldn't agree to marry someone under those forced circumstances?

The choice wasn't hers or his. She would think of the consequences later. After all, her father was a wealthy man and could buy many things. He could probably have this farce of a marriage dissolved in no time.

"Sister Prudence, prepare yourself, for it is your wedding day," Preacher Jacob cheered.

"What if I don't wish to marry him?"

The crowd grew silent, all eyes focused on Prudence.

She realized her mistake immediately. She had no choice, couldn't even voice an objection if she wished. They were doing this to protect her and she was ungratefully protesting.

Zac let out a hearty laugh. "Gentlemen, see what you saddle me with? A woman who thinks she can decide for herself. A wedding it shall be. Her opinion doesn't matter."

"Come all to my wagon and watch as I unite this couple in holy union," the preacher announced, waving his rifle like a staff to direct his flock.

Cheers rang out and everyone moved forward, carrying Prudence and Zac along in a wave of excitement.

Prudence pressed close to Zac, and his arm clamped firmly around her. Her hand reached for his vest, grasping the material as the crowd squeezed around them.

"I have a plan," Zac whispered. "Trust me."

Chapter Eight

Prudence didn't have an inkling as to what Zac's plan was, though she hoped he would implement it soon. All was ready for the wedding. In minutes the preacher would begin, and what then? Would they be joined as husband and wife?

The crowd was thick with eager faces, all waiting to witness the marriage. Men and women strolled around, smiling and nodding at Prudence, some in understanding, others in condemnation. The dozen men with the rifles stood on the outskirts of the crowd, ready to guarantee the conclusion of the ceremony.

Ellie fussed over her, helping right her bonnet and suggesting the children pick flowers for a bridal bouquet. Prudence cringed at the thought, although the children found delight in it and scampered off to gather wildflowers.

Zac stood next to the preacher, chatting. Prudence was surprised to see that Zac dominated their talk, while the preacher continually nodded his response. She wondered over their exchange and hoped it related to his plan.

The children returned with a full bouquet of common dandelions, their thick flowering heads a starburst of bright yellow. Ellie handed them to Prudence, then signaled with a nod to her husband.

The preacher stepped forward, motioning to the lingering crowd with his large hands. "Let everyone gather to witness the holy union of this loving couple."

Zac had removed his holster and his hat. He walked over to Prudence and took her hand, directing her with a gentle nudge to stand in front of the preacher.

"The plan?" she whispered, doubtful as to its success.

"Going accordingly," he answered in a much too self-assured tone.

She shot him a reproving look.

He countered with a smile.

She had the distinct feeling his plan was to marry her.

The service began, the preacher's voice booming out the ceremonial words over the crowd.

Prudence tilted her head to look up into Zac's face. He winked and his smile broadened. She didn't smile back.

The service was fast and to the point. A shotgun wedding to be sure. In minutes, Preacher Jacob was pronouncing them husband and wife and reminding Prudence of her duties.

Her duties were all too obvious. The first one was to rid herself of her forced husband as quickly and painlessly as possible. She didn't want anyone in Boston to learn of this. The women would gossip over why her marriage was so short-lived. And of course, since they all thought so highly of Mr. Stewart, the blame would be placed on her. *Inadequate as a woman.* That would be the talk behind her back.

Annoyed over the situation, she intended to give

Zac a piece of her mind, when he grabbed her, yanked her to him, and placed a fat, mushy kiss on her lips. She accepted it with little enthusiasm, realizing too late his intention.

His tongue slipped easily into her mouth, her lips limp from the childish kiss. And while the crowd watched a husband bestow a chaste kiss, Zac tasted her honey moistness with his tongue.

He was quick, unable or perhaps unwilling to continue. But he left his taste on her, and Prudence found herself running her own tongue over the area he had sampled only moments before. Warmth and a hint of whiskey tingled her tongue and sent goosebumps down her arms.

No man had ever taken such liberties with her, but then he was no man. He was her husband. She looked at him then and saw a strange glow in his eyes. It caused her to smile despite herself, and he returned her smile with a gentle one of his own. He reached out and took her hand. His flesh was warm, his grip strong and protective. It suddenly felt so right.

Everyone offered their congratulations, and it wasn't until the train whistle blew that the crowd began to disperse.

"Hurry, we'll miss the train," Prudence said, tugging at Zac's coat sleeve. He took his time buckling his holster, making her certain they'd miss the train.

He finished tying the leather holster thongs to his thighs, then began walking slowly beside her. "It doesn't matter. We're not taking it."

"You said we would be taking the train to Hastings," Prudence said, upset by this sudden change of plans.

"That was before *our wedding*. Plans have changed."

"This farce of a wedding changes nothing. Do you

110

think I would marry a gunslinger? My father will arrange an annulment immediately." Her words were spoken from anger and pain. How could he want her as a wife? If her own mother couldn't love her, how could a man like Zac Stewart? She didn't want to feel the hurt and rejection again.

Zac contained the urge to strangle her. Her thoughtless words affected him more than he cared to admit. "You have much to learn, Prudence. I intend to wire your father concerning our marriage and suggest he come immediately so this matter may be settled properly. You're familiar with doing things properly. After all, that's what concerns you the most."

"I find no shame in my proper breeding," she said. Her chin was held high, her shoulders back, and her chest out.

"There is no shame in anyone's breeding. Whether blue blood or mixed, everyone is the same. Perhaps one day you will learn that."

"I do not look down on anyone."

"Then you better lower that chin an inch or two and take a good look. There's much to see, if you weren't so blind."

Prudence walked right past him, her posture as stiff as ever.

Zac shook his head. "Why, Lord? Why did you saddle me with her?" Then he thought about their kiss and the way she tasted. The way her full body felt when it brushed against his on occasion. He smiled and raised his eyes to the heavens. "Many thanks, Lord. Many thanks!"

"Will we be staying in Alexandria?" Prudence asked as they climbed the steps to the train station.

"No. I'll wire your father and tell him to come to my home."

"Your home? You have a home?"

"Yes, I have a home," he said, exasperated. "Where did you think I lived?"

"I don't know. Hotel rooms, perhaps." The idea that Zac had a permanent residence, an actual home, puzzled her. It didn't fit his gunslinger image.

"I stopped living in hotel rooms a long time ago. I always look forward to returning home. A home that is now yours, since you're my wife."

Prudence thought about that as Zac wired her father and purchased two tickets for the morning train to Hastings. Why would he take her to his home? Why not return her to Boston and have her father dissolve the marriage? What was he up to?

"My father just can't take off and leave his business," Prudence informed him as he lifted both her traveling cases in one hand. His were still at the hotel.

"I told him there was no rush. You were safely in my possession and would remain so."

She didn't care for the staunch reassurance in his tone. "When he learns of our marriage, he'll insist on making arrangements to come here as soon as possible."

Zac stood looking down at her. She suddenly seemed more vulnerable, almost frightened of the present situation. "Perhaps. But until then, you're my responsibility."

"You take your husbandly duties seriously," she said, bewildered by his odd reaction to this ridiculous situation.

"I do," he said even more seriously.

She leaned over, reaching for her cases. He moved them from her grasp.

"It isn't necessary," she said.

Zac looked perturbed. "I don't expect you to carry

your cases. You're tired and need rest."

"I didn't mean my cases," she corrected. "I meant it isn't necessary to take this marriage seriously. I am well aware of why you married me."

Zac's brow went up and his eyes widened. "You are?"

"Of course," she said, absentmindedly fussing with the white silk ribbon tied beneath her chin. "Any man staring down the barrel of a dozen rifles would marry me."

Zac shook his head in disgust and walked past her. "You have a lot to learn about me, *Prudence Agatha Stewart.*"

Prudence followed, bewildered over his attitude and her name change.

They reached the hotel in minutes.

"Don't dare open your mouth to object," Zac warned her as they entered the hotel for the second time that day. "You are now legally my wife and will share my room."

"Did I say anything?" she answered defensively.

"You always have something to say," he said, dropping her cases at her feet before proceeding to the front desk.

He was back in minutes with key in hand. "I've ordered supper to be sent to our room."

"I haven't eaten all day," Prudence said, just realizing the growl in her stomach had persisted since noon.

Zac picked up her cases and his saddlebags. "Food and rest, in that order. Now follow me."

After the events of this strange day, Prudence was too tired to argue. She trailed behind Zac all the way to the second floor.

The room wasn't large, but it was clean and the bed soft and comfortable. A small square table sat by the window, the pane covered with lace curtains. There was an oil lamp in the center of the table and one on the bureau next to the large pitcher and washbowl. A wardrobe stood open and empty.

She removed her bonnet and jacket, hanging them in the wardrobe where Zac had placed his waistcoat.

"Why don't you wash up first?" he offered, unbuttoning his vest.

"Will you turn your back?" she asked.

He walked up to her and took her chin between his fingers. "Do you forget you're *Mrs.* Stewart?"

His eyes were much too dark and cunning. She didn't trust him. "In name only," she reminded him.

He brought his face down nearer to hers. "I can rectify that. Quick and easy, or slow and exhausting."

Exhausting. Is that how his lovemaking would be? The thought was spine-tingling and shockingly tempting.

"Interested, Mrs. Stewart?" he asked in a dangerously suggestive whisper.

He was teasing her. He wasn't interested in making love to her. He was playing a cruel game with her emotions.

"No. It wouldn't be proper," she said, refusing to let him know how much she was attracted to him.

A flash of resentment sparked Zac's brown's eyes. "I forget. A gunslinger isn't acceptable in Boston society." He released her chin with a gentle shove.

The slight dismissal irritated Prudence. *"Gentlemen* are always accepted in Boston society."

Zac was about to turn away, when her words stopped him. "Are you telling me I'm no gentleman?"

"Precisely. You have much to learn before you can earn that title."

Zac pulled off his vest and threw it on the bed. "Your name fits you well."

"At least I have morals and convictions," she said. Her eyes focused on his hands as they unbuttoned his shirt. They were large, yet slim and lean. And clean, with no dirt hidden beneath his well-trimmed nails.

Zac pulled his shirt from his pants and flung it to join his vest. "You don't even know the meaning of those words."

Prudence was startled by his accusation. "How dare you—"

"How dare I suggest your ignorance of life, or how dare I undress in front of you?"

"Both," she snapped. Her eyes helplessly focused on the thick muscles that spread across the wide expanse of his naked chest.

He grabbed her by the arms, pinning them to her sides. "I'm your husband, and if I wish to undress in front of you, I will. If you loosened that attitude and corset some, you might discover a part of life you've been missing."

Prudence grew flustered at the mention of a tightly strung corset she didn't wear and an attitude she most certainly didn't possess. "You, Mr. Stewart, are no better than the Indians the Army has locked away on the reservations."

Zac roughly shoved her away from him. Her backside hit the bed and she steadied herself.

"I would befriend and trust an Indian before a Bostonian any day. At least an Indian accepts a man for himself alone. He judges by character and strength, not by background and money. He doesn't concern himself with what a friend wears but with what a friend needs."

Zac advanced on her. "And he adapts to his surroundings, living with the land not clinging to stupid white gloves that have no place out west."

He reached for her hands, tugging at the gloves

115

with every intention of removing them permanently. She screamed and scrambled across the bed, her skirt tangling around her legs and impeding her progress. Finally, she slipped off the other side of the bed and braced herself against the wall.

"Take them off," he ordered, moving toward her. "Since the first day I met you, you haven't been without those damn gloves."

"I need my gloves," she cried, nearly in tears.

"For what?" he yelled. "To protect you?"

"Yes," she said, answering honestly. "I need their protection."

Zac didn't understand that she referred to the emotional protection. He thought her vain and uncaring. "Take them off," he repeated harshly. "I want to see my wife's lily-white hands."

"No! No!" she cried, pushing herself flat up against the wall.

"Damn it, Prudence! I said off!" Zac lunged for her, his arms out straight and his hands spread wide. She attempted to outmaneuver him, dashing to the side. He was too quick, too sure of his ability. His hands found her instantly and they wrestled to the bed together.

"Stop, Zac! Stop! You don't understand," she pleaded, fighting to keep her gloves from his reach.

Zac couldn't stop himself. To him the gloves represented her high-and-mighty attitude. He wanted to change that, to make her see herself and him for what they were—a man and a woman, not a gunslinger and a society lady.

They rolled around on the bed, fighting. Her skirt tangled around his legs, while her hands flew in all directions. She tried desperately to keep her gloved hands from his grasp. She shoved them above her head, to her sides, and even attempted to hide them

116

beneath her bottom.

Zac had had enough of her stubbornness. Those gloves were coming off . . . now. He grabbed her by the waist and twisted her beneath him. Without a second's hesitation, he flung his leg over her, straddling her just below her belly.

Prudence was stunned into stillness. He rested flat and hard against her. Even through her layers of clothes, she could feel the perfect fit of him, every inch of him. There was no doubt he felt it, too. She had learned to read his eyes, to judge his emotions, but this time it was his body that spoke clearly.

He pressed into her, leaning forward, inching his way closer and closer. His chest hardened considerably from the effort of his slow descent. His midriff held not a trace of fat, only taut, hard flesh. His navel and a smattering of dark hair peeked from beneath his waistband and below that. . . .

Prudence gulped and shut her eyes as he applied even more pressure. A pressure that forced the sudden moistness between her legs to intensify.

"You've got something I want."

His tone was neither harsh nor tender. It rested in that dangerous spot somewhere in between, which left one feeling uncertain and wary.

Prudence's eyes opened wide. She didn't know whether her heart thudded so from fright or from anticipation.

He was inching his way down over her like a victorious bird of prey claiming its foe. Was he going to kiss her? Or was he going to claim his husbandly rights?

His face rested only a hairsbreadth away from hers.

She held her breath, afraid to breathe in the nearness of him.

Suddenly his hands shot out, grabbing her wrists and yanking her up. She was locked between his legs, unable to move her own limbs. He didn't wait for her to gather her wits, as he swiftly plucked her gloves off.

Prudence didn't even have time to protest. She steeled herself against the inevitable and felt a sadness descend upon her as her fingers came into view.

Zac winced when he saw the two end fingers of her left hand. They hugged each other and were slightly bent. The deformity wasn't hard to look upon. It didn't bother Zac in the least. What did bother him was the thought of the pain and hurt Prudence must have suffered over the years while growing up. He understood now why she had kept them hidden, but here, out west, it wasn't necessary.

"If you put my gloves back on, you won't be forced to view my affliction."

Zac's look wasn't angry, nor was it one of pity. It was warm and caring, and it tugged at Prudence's heart.

"Why didn't you tell me about this?" he asked, holding her fingers up.

Prudence forced herself not to look away. It wasn't that she was ashamed of her deformity. It was the memories it brought back and the pain of being different. "What was I supposed to say? 'Zac, it seems that I have these two useless fingers I thought you should know about'?"

Zac saw the tears pool in her eyes and the effort it took to control them. She hurt deeply and he felt it as though her pain were his own.

"Tell me about it," he said, suddenly needing to share the weight of her burden.

"Why?" she asked, bewildered by his interest.

"Because I want to know."

"Everything?"

"Yes, Pru. Everything." He moved off her then but didn't release her. He sat next to her, holding her hand, ready to listen.

Prudence wasn't sure where to begin or even if she should. Why should she trust him? Why should he care? She looked at him a moment, all her doubts and insecurities evident in her sorrowful expression.

Zac released her hand quickly, lifted her chin, and kissed her. His lips were tender and persuasive. They slipped over her with an infinite skill that caused her stomach to flutter.

"Tell me," he whispered and kissed her again, this time so lightly that she tingled from the strange sensation.

She didn't understand Zac Stewart. A notorious gunslinger. A man handsome in features. A man women melted over. A man who appeared to care about her. It was unlikely. Impossible. But she wanted to believe it. Oh, how she wanted to believe he actually cared.

Her voice trembled as she spoke. "I was born this way. It was no accident. The doctor told my father these things happen. It could have been worse. You can cover them up, hide them away, he assured my father. He insisted I was lucky."

Zac listened quietly, having once again taken her hand in his. He held on to her, offering his strength and support, feeling her tremble and squeezing her hand gently to still her nervous tremors.

"It didn't trouble me until I was old enough to understand. Until I made friends . . . at least I had thought them friends. They made fun. Called me *deformed*. And of course my looks didn't help any. Being plain and larger than the other girls only added to my problems."

Zac stared at her, his eyes intent. She assumed he regarded her affliction as most people did and turned her head away in embarrassment. He grabbed her face with his fingers and turned her head sharply to look at him.

"Finish," he ordered, and none too gently.

"My mother's death didn't help. When I needed her the most, she was gone. My grandmother helped me. My father was too lost in his sorrow. My grandmother had several pairs of gloves made and instructed me to wear them as often as possible. When etiquette dictated otherwise, I learned to hide my hand well, always wearing my skirts a little extra full so I could conceal my hand in the folds of the added material."

"Your mother—"

Prudence didn't allow him to finish. "—isn't dead. Which makes all the more sense when you stop to think about it. She gave birth to a daughter who had an affliction, wasn't pretty, wasn't petite. Surely a disappointment to a woman who possessed such beauty. So she left, leaving her little girl behind to face the cruel world on her own."

The knock at the door came just in time for Prudence. Zac released her hand, and she had time to turn away and wipe the tears that had hovered so dangerously close to her lashes.

Zac didn't even bother to slip his shirt back on. He opened the door, hurried the man inside with the tray of food, then hurried him out again.

He was annoyed and angry. How could a mother leave a daughter who needed her so desperately? And why did he find himself believing Pru's story about her mother? Perhaps it was the raw hurt so evident in her offered words.

"Eat," he said with more sternness than he in-

120

tended. He was surprised when she obeyed without question.

He watched her as she prepared the table with the plates of food and the silverware, making certain all were in their correct places. Always the lady, no matter what the circumstances.

He was furious at the treatment she had suffered as a child. Still suffered. She had been told so often she was plain and large that she actually believed it. No one had bothered to comment on her natural beauty. She had the kindest green eyes, a narrow nose, and full cheeks that held a smattering of freckles. And her lips were sleek and sensuously inviting. The kind a man ached to kiss.

Then there was her body. *Ample* was the word that came to mind. And ample was the type he liked. He wanted to feel a woman full in flesh when he touched her, no matter where he touched her.

And her hair. He looked at her pinning it neatly back up into place. He liked it free and wild. The way it was when they had struggled on the bed. Its redness seemed to flame with her temper and he smiled. Prudence had many attributes and a few flaws, but he liked them as well. There was much he liked about Prudence Agatha *Stewart.* Too damn much.

The meal was eaten in silence. After having washed up, Zac joined her at the table. Both were at a loss for words and remained so into the evening.

Prudence was grateful that the room contained a privacy screen. She could wash and freshen up without worry of Zac watching her. Not that it mattered. It appeared he wasn't the least bit interested in her. He was her husband now and could rightfully demand she perform her wifely duties, yet he made no mention of it. She could only assume that he wouldn't have married her if over a dozen rifles hadn't intervened, and of course, there was the substantial fee from her father for her safe return.

She slipped into a clean white blouse and sighed. She could continue to dream. No one could take her dreams away from her. In her dreams a handsome man, similar in features to Zac, would follow her to the ends of the earth, declaring his love and insisting she marry him. Then he would carry her away and make love to her.

"Melodramatic," she whispered to herself and smiled. The idea that a man would go to such lengths to claim her filled her with tingles and chills.

"Stupid childish dreams," she admonished softly, and her smile faded. "No one will love you that much, not even Zac Stewart."

"Did you call me, Pru?" Zac asked from where he lay on the bed.

"No, and my name is Prudence," she corrected, annoyed with herself and her silly dreams.

"I like Pru. It's short and to the point. And don't bother to correct me again. I'll call you what I like."

Prudence couldn't help but smile. He was so dictatorial at times and so tender at other times. A gunfighter and a gentle man. What a combination. She giggled quietly. She liked the gentle side of him, but the gunslinger side added that air of danger and mystery that fascinated her.

"What? No arguing? No insisting I do as you say?" Zac asked teasingly.

Prudence stepped around the screen.

Zac grinned wickedly and shook his head. "Honey, that's not what I would expect my wife to wear on our wedding night."

Prudence blushed, hating the swift heat that rose to paint her cheeks a deep red. She stiffened her posture and reprimanded him with a "Mr. —"

"Be careful, honey. Remember my warning. And this time if I kiss you, I won't stop. I'll take it further and discover if that sweet blush starts at your toes and works its way up your entire body."

Her first thought was that he was no gentleman. But then was it a gentleman she wanted in her bed? Or the notorious, sometimes savage gunslinger?

"Next time wear a nightgown," he ordered roughly. "I'm not in the habit of ravishing Bostonian virgins."

Prudence gasped, her hands flying to her chest at the audacity of his remark.

"You mean you're not a virgin?" Again he produced that wicked smile that captivated women and held them spellbound.

"I most certainly am," she said indignantly, feeling her racing heart would burst from her chest any moment.

He held out his hand to her, and his face took on a more serious and thoughtful expression. "Come to bed, Pru. We'll discuss your virginity another night."

There was an underlying meaning to his words. Prudence was sure of it, but she wasn't certain just what it was. She walked to the bed, tired and weary from the long day and all that had happened.

"Come on," he coaxed gently. "You're exhausted and need rest."

He sounded so sincere and she wanted so badly to trust him. She reached out to him.

His fingertips grazed hers, slipping across her hand until he had captured hers softly in his. He pulled her down upon the bed beside him and covered her with the quilt, tucking it around her waist. He leaned over her, his dark eyes reflective. "I'll do whatever I can to help you find your mother."

His words stunned her. She had thought him about

to kiss her, but somehow his offer of help was so much more potent.

"Go to sleep. We have a busy day tomorrow," he said softly, and tainted her lips lightly with his own. Then he moved away from her and turned down the oil lamp on the nightstand beside him.

The room was engulfed in darkness. A quiet calm had settled over the street outside, except for the occasional howl of a dog or the distant burst of laughter from the saloon at the far end.

Zac stretched his long legs out and raised his arms above his head, bracing his hands against the wooden spindle headboard. He felt wired, strung taut. And there was no way to release his pent-up emotions. In teasing Pru, he had succeeded in teasing himself and to a dangerous degree. Right now he ached to strip her of that damn white blouse and gray skirt. And all the garments beneath it, until he reached her naked flesh.

Hot. Her skin would be hot. He had no doubt. She was a virgin, inexperienced. Damn, she probably grew moist from the slightest suggestion of sex.

The muscles in his arms flexed as he exerted more pressure on the headboard. It was a good thing she slept in her clothes. If she had a nightgown on right now, his hand would most certainly be finding its way beneath it. And he'd play. Oh, how he'd play with her.

"Stop it!" he whispered harshly to himself.

Prudence moaned and turned in her sleep, snuggling into the cradle of his arm. Her face found his bare chest and rested comfortably against it, while her hand slipped low upon his belly, dangerously low.

She was getting too deep beneath his skin. Much too deep. He had no business entertaining such ideas. Hell, he had no business marrying her. But he

124

had, and now there were consequences to face.

He lowered his arm, running his hand down along hers until his fingers locked around her wrist. Would she try to escape him again? No, she was his wife. She wouldn't do anything so foolish now. Or would she?

Zac closed his eyes and tightened the grip he held on her wrist. He wouldn't let her escape. No, he damned well wouldn't. Not again.

Zac bolted up from the bed at the sound of the screeching train whistle. He didn't get far before he felt a tug at his wrist. He stared up at his arm. His wrist was neatly tied to one of the wooden spindles of the headboard.

"That's it!" he yelled, and tore at the knots.

His anger escalated to a dangerous degree when he realized just what she had used to secure him to the bed. She had taken his leather holster thongs and tied them together. His temper ignited further when he found the knots too intricate to open.

He heard the train whistle, announcing its departure. He soundly cursed her and urgently worked on the knots.

Chapter Nine

Prudence stood on the train station platform, close to the building, out of view of the crowd waiting for the train to Plattsmouth.

She had arrived in Hastings an hour ago. The train's slow progress across the flat land had worried her. She assumed that Zac was an excellent horseman. If he could find the right horse, there was the possibility he would arrive in Hastings just before or right after her, depending on when he woke and how fast he could untie himself.

Her decision to escape him hadn't been hasty. She had risen early and watched him sleep in the faint light of morning. He was so handsome, his body so powerfully built. Then there was his caring side. The side of himself he hid quite skillfully but that Prudence glimpsed on occasion.

She recalled his touch, his kiss. Then she had sobered up. A man like him could never love her. Unfortunately, she fancied herself in love with him. She reasoned it was his pursuit of her that had brought on this ridiculous notion. She fantasized that his quest for her was pursued out of love, not due to her father's generous fee. It was a foolish young girl's dream. One that had become much too strong a craving. A craving she fully understood would never be quenched by the likes of Zac Stewart. She couldn't — wouldn't — leave herself open to another hurt and disappointment.

With a tear in her eye and regrets for what could never be, she tied him to the post and took her leave quietly. Now she waited, most anxiously, to see if he would catch up with her. She had no doubts he would follow. He had wired her father, promising her safety, and he would certainly keep his word.

She glanced once again around the platform. Zac was nowhere in sight. No one paid any particular attention to her, except for the large man standing in the middle of the platform. He had turned his head, glancing in her direction quite often. He didn't look familiar. He was burly built and dressed in a dark suit that seemed a bit too tight. His moustache was fat and wide, his eyes set close. His open crown hat was too small for his wide head and looked as though it would topple off at any moment. He seemed out of place and his presence suddenly worried her.

The train whistle screeched the signal for all to board. In minutes she'd be on her way. She sighed in relief.

"Excuse me, ma'am."

The voice, so near, startled her and she jumped, turning to see the large man standing beside her.

"You are Prudence Agatha Winthrop, aren't you?" he asked.

"Who are you?" she demanded, anxious as to who would be familiar with her identity out here.

"Sorry, ma am," he apologized, respectfully removing his hat. "I'm Barney Osgood. Mr. Granger Madison hired me to locate you and escort you back to Boston."

127

"Granger hired you?" she asked, bewildered. "Why?"

"He told me how much in love you two are, and about the little spat you had with him, and how you got it into your mind to go west."

Prudence wondered if love had anything to do with Granger's hiring Mr. Osgood, or if it was the fact that he saw his dream of a banking empire crumble. "How long have you been following me?"

Barney Osgood scratched his chin. "Actually, I've been following Mr. Stewart. But I lost him. I went on a bit, hoping to run across him again. It's just plain luck I saw you here. Now we can head back to Boston together."

"I have no intention of returning to Boston with you, Mr. Osgood."

"Gee, ma'am, I was afraid you were going to say that."

Prudence took a step away from him. She didn't care for the determined glint in his eyes. That, together with his size, made him appear formidable. "I have a train to board," she said, dismissing him and attempting to move around him.

His hand reached out in a flash, grabbing her arm. "Afraid I can't let you go, ma'am."

Prudence was incensed. Everyone thought themselves in control of her, and she was fed up with it. "Get your hand off me," she said distinctly.

"Can't do that, ma'am," he said, placing his hat back on his head.

"You have no right to do this," she demanded loudly, purposely trying to draw attention.

To Prudence's relief, people began to stare at them. She hoped someone — anyone — would offer help.

"Afraid I do. I'm carrying papers written by Mr.

128

Madison explaining the situation and how it would be best for your own safety to return with me."

"That is ridiculous."

"Perhaps, but why don't you just come along nice and quiet like with me. Then when you get back to Boston, you can settle all this with Mr. Madison."

Prudence struggled futilely in an attempt to free herself. "Let go," she cried, swinging her other hand and hitting him smack in the middle of his chest.

It did little good. Her hand hurt, while his chest suffered no ill effect.

"Now come along nice and quiet," he repeated once again, pulling her alongside him.

"I'm not going with you and that's final!" she yelled, kicking him square in the shin. She hurt her foot and caused him a small, annoyed grimace.

"That's enough," Barney Osgood warned.

"My sentiments exactly. Now take your hands off my *wife!*"

Prudence had no choice but to turn with Barney, since he swung her around with him at the sound of Zac's demand.

"Your wife?" Barney repeated.

Zac walked up to him. They were both of equal height, but Barney weighed considerably more. "My wife!"

"I can't let her go until I check with Mr. Madison," Barney said, still holding on to Prudence.

Zac shook his head slowly. "We have a real problem."

A crowd had gathered around them. They whispered and mumbled among themselves about the notorious gunslinger Zac Stewart being here in Hastings.

"I don't carry a gun," Barney informed Zac.

Prudence detected a quiver of fear in the man's voice. She didn't want to see him hurt. And she didn't want to see Zac forced into drawing his guns to defend her. "I refuse to go with either of you," she cried out dramatically. "Now let me go!"

She yanked viciously to free herself while swinging her other hand, hitting Barney about the head and chest with her wild blows.

Barney quickly lost all control of the situation.

Zac stepped forward, shaking his head and raising his voice. "I swear, it's easier to face another gunslinger than to deal with a wife like you."

Just then Barney ducked to avoid another blow from Prudence. It missed him completely but connected solidly with Zac's jaw, sending him stumbling back.

Barney released Prudence instantly. She stood in shock, her eyes widespread, staring at her fist and then at Zac. She couldn't believe what she had done.

"I've had it," Zac growled, marching straight for her.

Barney stepped in front of him, in a manly effort to protect Prudence. But Zac was past reasoning. When he saw Barney raise his hands, Zac raised a fist and connected squarely with his jaw. The large man stumbled back, cleared his head with a shake, rubbed his jaw, and threw a punch back.

The crowd roared as the two men went at each other.

Prudence quickly stepped out of the way and watched along with the crowd. Cheers filled the air as blow after blow was thrown. Neither man reacted noticeably to the stinging punches. It was as though they were both made of solid rock.

It was the first sign of blood that concerned Prudence. It ran from Zac's nose after his head had been sent back with a sharp snap by a hard blow from Barney. He ignored the damage, though, and it seemed to fire up his blood. His punches took on an angry intensity, and Barney soon began to stumble backward as Zac converged on him with repeated blows to the face.

Barney went down, rattling the planks of the train platform as his large body landed with a bounce.

Zac stood over him. The set of his firm jaw, the menacing look in his eyes, his fists clenched at his sides and smeared with blood, warned Barney to remain where he was or suffer further pain.

Barney closed his eyes and grimaced from the pain. "I'll wire Mr. Madison that Prudence is safe in your care, Mr. Stewart."

"A wise decision," he said, then quickly searched the area for Prudence. She stood only a short distance away, near the edge of the platform. Her posture retained its usual stiffness, and her chin was tilted in that autocratic manner that so often annoyed him. He wondered if she had been at all tempted to return with Barney to Granger. He noticed her eyes then. They were different. They were wide with alarm and aimed intently on him.

There was no doubt he looked battered. The blood on his knuckles and under his nose and mouth probably made his condition appear worse than it actually was.

Was the alarm so evidently registered in her eyes intended for him? Did his condition concern her? The thought baffled him, since she constantly reminded him they were not *fit* for each other. Though he had the feeling they would *fit* perfectly. The misplaced thought fueled his imagination. And · he couldn't help but smile over the fact that their fit would be as perfect as that of the finely stitched white gloves she always wore.

He took his white handkerchief from his pocket and wiped his face clear of the blood. He did the same to his hands, though he noticed two knuckles on his right hand had already begun to bruise. He then retrieved his hat from the platform and walked over to her.

"I'm not going with you," she blurted out before he could speak.

He dumped his hat on his head and pushed the brim back. "You most certainly are."

"You don't fit into my plans."

He stepped closer to her, his body planted almost on top of hers. "Oh, I *fit* all right, Pru. And you're going to learn that right quick."

"I refuse, absolutely refuse, to go," she said adamantly, crossing her arms solidly upon her chest.

"Suit yourself, wife," he said, pausing one moment, then leaning over, scooping her up, and flinging her over his shoulder.

"Put me down!" she cried, her hands fumbling to keep her bonnet in place. Her cheeks colored with humiliation as her eyes focused on the strength of his long legs and her skirt-covered derriere brushed his face.

He ignored her shouts and, grabbing her bags, marched through the crowd that laughed and rooted for him.

"Teach her who's boss," yelled a man.

"Don't take no nonsense," added another.

Prudence's face flamed even more in embarrassment. How could he be so inconceivably thoughtless? He had no right to treat her this way. He was a brute. A savage. Absolutely no gentleman.

He carefully boarded the train with his distraught baggage and deposited her in a seat next to a window. He sat beside her, turning halfway in his seat to look at her.

Her hat sat askew. Loose strands of her reddish brown hair hung down her back and a few dangled in her face, and her cheeks flushed with the hottest, most tempting shade of red.

Prudence removed her hat and fumbled to right her hair. "You are—"

"Take them off," Zac ordered, his tone dead serious.

Prudence's hands came to a stop on top her head. She saw where his eyes were fixed: on her gloves. The warning in his voice was evident and so was the message. If she didn't remove them, he would.

She glanced around the passenger car. The few people about were busy settling in their seats and paid them no heed. There was no danger of someone being upset by the sight of her affliction. Off the gloves came, with only the slightest bit of hesitation.

"Happy?" she asked, placing her hands over the folded gloves on her lap.

He reached over and covered her hands with his right one. "There's no need to hide them away. The only problem with your hand is the way you've been made to feel about it."

She was about to argue the point, when she looked down and saw the tender black and blue bruises running across his two knuckles. She slipped her one hand from beneath his and ever so gently touched the swollen area. "It must pain you terribly."

She was right. He was in pain, deep pain, but not from his hand. It was her touch that shot the spark through his body and caught his attention. An extremely painful attention.

Her fingers skimmed across the bruises, making his skin tingle and sending the hot sensation up his arm. *Damn, but her simple, light touch was erotic.*

"Does it hurt?" she asked innocently.

"Yes," he said, almost choking on his words.

Her look and tone were sincere. "I wish I could ease your hurt."

"You can." He was playing with fire, but at the moment he didn't care.

"What can I do?" Her voice trembled in a whisper, its softness stirring him all the more.

He leaned closer to her. "Kiss it and make it all better." He expected a harsh protest, followed by a lesson in gentlemanly behavior. Instead, she stared at him a moment, her eyes glassy and her lips moist.

Her hand moved beneath his and carefully cradled it in her own. She brought his hand up slowly to her mouth, so slowly that Zac thought time stood still around them.

Her head bowed slightly as his hand reached her lips, then she kissed the bruised area so delicately, so thoughtfully, so potently, that Zac thought he would burst right there in his seat.

She lifted her head, her eyes misty with a steamy passion. "Have I made it all better, Zac?"

"Worse," he choked.

She kissed his bruises once again and this time he could have sworn he felt her tongue graze his skin. It sent a jolt of pure sexual adrenaline running through him. He pulled his hand away from her and sat back in the seat.

"It's better," he said in a ragged breath.

A tense smile played across Prudence's face as she

sat back in her seat and turned her head to look out the window.

The train whistle blew and in minutes they were on their way. Their speed was slow as the steel wheels meandered along the track to Plattsmouth.

The scenery that passed before her wasn't compelling, but her thoughts were. His injury had disturbed her. She had sought to comfort and aid him. When he had asked for the kiss with such candor, she had believed him in pain and meant only to quell it, along with her guilt.

Instead, she had brought suffering upon herself. His flesh had been warm, near to hot when she pressed her lips against it. And his taste . . . It still stung her tongue where she had dared to sample him. It was a vibrant, manly flavor. One she wouldn't soon forget nor mind savoring again.

Prudence closed her eyes against such shameful thoughts. She had no business thinking this way. But a daring voice interfered, asking her, *Why not?* He was her husband. She had the perfect right to harbor such notions. There was a good chance that this would be her only marriage. That this would be her only opportunity to experience the *intimate* side of marriage. Should she take advantage of the situation to satisfy her carnal curiosity? Or was this just an excuse to sample the likes of Zac Stewart, himself? Hadn't all the women in Boston hinted about, but never spoken openly of, his base needs and how he satisfied them?

Her cheeks reddened with the sinful thoughts. Whatever was the matter with her? She was a lady, born and bred. Such thoughts were unacceptable.

"Pru."

His voice was smooth, thick, and addictive, like

rich syrup. She could almost taste the heavy sweetness of it on her tongue. The shameful idea jolted her senses, and when she turned to view him, her chin was once again angled high in her proper manner.

Zac watched her defenses materialize step by step. She used her formidable breeding as a shield to ward off emotional attachments. He could understand her reluctance to open up. She had been hurt in more ways than one. The sad thought prickled his manly defenses, and he suddenly experienced an overwhelming desire to protect her while breaking down that blasted shield at the same time. Not that she'd let him. She was proud and stubborn, and he had to admit he admired her for that. Yet he selfishly needed to protect her. It was as embedded in him as her proper upbringing had been embedded in her. Damn, but this relationship was at odds. The crazy thought excited him.

She regarded him with impatience, or perhaps it was her own impatience he read in her features. The thought intrigued him.

"You wanted something?" she asked.

He couldn't prevent his smile, wicked that it was, from betraying his thoughts. "Yes."

His short, curt answer stung like an angry bee in her bonnet. He was being the devil himself again and she'd have none of it. "Well?" she said, attempting to ignore his devastating smile and the way her stomach fluttered in response.

"Tell me of this skill you possess with knots," he ordered mildly, and was rewarded with a pleasant and, if he was not mistaken, proud grin.

Her grin spread and Zac was caught by the beauty of it. Her plain features suddenly sparkled, highlight-

136

ing the softest green eyes he had ever seen. Then there were her cheekbones, high and replete with a warm blush that titillated his already-peaked senses even further. And a mouth so luscious and inviting that he ached to taste it.

"I owe it all to my uncle, rascal that he was," she said.

He liked the lilting tune of her voice. "Your uncle taught you such skill?"

"Yes. Whenever his ship was in port, he would visit."

"A sailor?"

"No." She shook her head.

"Forgive me," he said and amended, "He was a sea captain."

"Correct, and a fine one."

"Of course. A Winthrop could be nothing less."

"Naturally," she said, doubting he understood the importance of her family background. "He was a wonderful man and so patient."

"A virtue not many people possess."

"You have such insight into other people's short-comings."

"A talent of mine," he praised himself.

Prudence couldn't help but turn her head away in laughter.

"You don't agree?" he asked, enjoying her relaxed mood.

She looked at him. "I'm sure you have many talents, possibly even insight, but knots . . ." She shook her head forlornly.

"Then you must teach me," he insisted good-naturedly.

Prudence was surprised. She had thought he would protest, yet he had conceded her more knowledgeable

137

in that area and had even requested instruction. She nodded her agreement and added, "You will teach me, in return, about the West?"

Zac was heartened by her willingness to learn of her new surroundings. "I'd be delighted."

Prudence felt as though a truce had been reached. How long it would last was doubtful. But for now she would enjoy the peace. She sat back in her seat and watched the passing land slip by. It further soothed her already-contented state and caused her eyelids to droop in fatigue.

Her head lolled from side to side, and she ached for a soft pillow. As though her thoughts could be heard and answered, she felt her head rest upon a solid form. A pillow it wasn't, since it was hard. She didn't protest. It felt good, as did the arm that held her firm. Her mind might wonder who cushioned her, but her heart had no trouble deciding. The notorious gunslinger, Zac Stewart, allowed his wife to use him as a pillow. Prudence smiled in sleepy contentment and cuddled against him.

Chapter Ten

Plattsmouth was a busy town. The train station and steamboat depot saw to that. Travelers could arrange transportation to all areas. And these travelers were good for the economy of Plattsmouth, stocking up on supplies whether traveling by train, steamboat, or wagon. There was always a necessary item to buy before departure.

Zac had that exact intention in mind, but first he needed to learn when the next steamboat was headed up the Missouri River.

Prudence had followed close beside him since leaving the train. It was obvious he was in a hurry. Their baggage had been hastily deposited with the stationmaster, whom they left grinning as he counted the numerous bills Zac paid him in return for his watchful eye. She worried over their destination. She needed time. Time he refused to give her.

"Just a few inquiries," Prudence found herself pleading after her previous requests were repeatedly rebuked. "What can it hurt?"

Zac continued walking as he spoke, though he slowed his pace. "Ordinarily, I would say it could hurt nothing, but in your case . . ." He allowed his words to

139

trail off purposely, an obvious hint of his distrust of her.

Prudence chose tact instead of anger. "This is important, Zac."

An explanation wasn't necessary. He understood the importance of her finding her mother. After all, he had firsthand knowledge of the damage her desertion had inflicted on Prudence. He would love to find the woman himself so he could voice his own sentiments toward her. Yet another part of him worried and wondered if Pru's confrontation with her mother would help heal or would only worsen old wounds.

Zac stopped abruptly, having reached a decision. He took her arm, directing her out of the path of passing couples. "After I purchase tickets for the next steamboat up the Missouri and reserve us a room for the night, I'll see what I can find out for you."

A slim thread was all that was left of Prudence's patience, yet she fought to keep the slender emotions intact. "That will take time. I could begin the inquiries now and meet you at the hotel."

"Are you suggesting I should trust you not to run away?"

"Be reasonable . . ."

"I'm trying, but you've made it difficult."

Prudence could accept his reluctance to trust her. After all, she had escaped him more than once. "Where would I go? There are no more trains today. It is already late in the day. And the information I seek is here. Why would I want to leave?"

She was correct on all accounts, but he still didn't trust her. He envisioned her hightailing it out of Plattsmouth, information in hand.

"I promise I will meet you at the hotel at the specified time," Prudence insisted. "I won't get into any trouble and—"

A burst of laughter from Zac interrupted her. "You're sure you won't get into trouble, are you?"

Prudence wore a serious expression. "I most certainly won't. I will ask appropriate questions, in appropriate places, and determine what I can."

"Appropriate places?" he questioned, leaning indolently against the building and crossing his arms over his chest. "Then tell me how you happened into Sadie's place?"

"I was perhaps a bit overzealous," she said pensively, but the slight turn of her lips betrayed her pride.

He straightened with a hastiness that made Prudence take a step back. Damn, but that wicked little half smile could unman him. It teased and poked and promised all in one. And the worst thing about it was she didn't even realize she was capable of seduction.

"Where did you think of starting your inquiries?" he asked, judging a bit of separation from her might prove beneficial.

"The hotel," Prudence was quick to answer. She was hopeful that he would permit her this. If not, she'd have no choice but to free herself of him once again.

"And?" He wanted her intentions spelled out. He wanted—actually needed, for his own sanity—to know her whereabouts until they were reunited at the hotel.

Prudence was prepared. "The mercantile, bank, seamstress, and if leads take me elsewhere—"

"The saloon?" he interjected, waiting with a look that could only be termed murderous.

Prudence bravely placed her hand flat against his chest. The hard muscles beneath his shirt tantalized her fingers and her senses. But she felt contact, physical contact, was important at this moment. He had to understand her desperation. He must. "If my search takes me in that direction, I will wait until we meet and allow you to proceed from there."

141

He covered her hand with his, pressing it more firmly to his chest. "Promise?"

Hard. The one word bounced into her thoughts, and her cheeks were suddenly speared by red heat. She dropped her readable wild gaze to the ground. "I promise."

"A docile, obedient wife, now isn't that a most welcome change," he whispered. His hit was direct and intentional. He liked when she got all fired up and uppity. She was a force to be reckoned with, and he damned well wanted to reckon with her.

Prudence slowly raised her face, the red heat, now a fury, highlighting her cheeks. "If docile and obedient are what you are searching for in a wife, I assure you, you will be sadly disappointed with me."

Zac ran his finger slowly down her hot cheek to the corner of her lips. "I doubt I'll be disappointed, Pru. I doubt it very much."

His looks were hungry and her emotions ravenous. Not a good combination at the moment. She took a step back.

He gained control, with much difficulty, over his fervor. "One hour is all the time I'll grant you. In one hour, meet me at the Hotel Lillian."

Prudence nodded and made to turn, when his hand caught her arm. It was a commanding grasp and she looked up at him.

"Be careful." His words were strongly issued, but he couldn't hide his concern.

Prudence smiled and reached up to plant a light kiss on his cheek. "I'll be fine . . . and thank you."

Zac stared at her retreating back as she weaved through the crowd. She was an enigma to him. One minute proper, the next brawling with Barney Osgood, a man three times her size, then hitting him and sending him stumbling to boot. And now kissing him sweetly. He smiled. What was the opposite of that sweet kiss? Blistering passion? He'd find out. Yes sir, he sure in hell was going to find out.

Prudence found her task more difficult than she had expected. Many of the local residents were new to the area and could offer no help. A few suggested she try Granny Hayes. Everyone agreed the old woman had been around before the town even got its name and if anyone could help her, she could. Of course, there was only one place to find Granny this time of the day . . . the saloon.

Prudence cringed when she heard that and cringed again when she recalled her promise to Zac. Why had she allowed herself to be trapped in a promise? She could have phrased it differently, allowing herself her familiar freedom and appeasing him in the process.

Honor-bound as she was, Prudence hurried to the Hotel Lillian, hoping Zac had completed his business and would be there waiting for her.

She weaved through the crowd of people, stepping around a potted plant, its large green leaves hiding her view of a section of the large lobby. Zac was nowhere in sight. She had been advised that he had secured them a room but had informed the desk clerk he would return later. That had been over an hour ago and still he hadn't returned.

Prudence needed to talk to Granny Hayes, and she didn't want to wait. Mr. Lewis at the mercantile had told her Granny would be at the saloon for only so long. The old woman, he had said with a laugh, didn't like it when the rowdy young'uns came in.

This was important. It couldn't wait. Zac would just have to understand her position. After all, it wasn't as though he were her real husband, who would have certain rights. She walked out of the hotel convinced Zac would see things her way.

Piano music flowed loudly from the Golden Cage saloon, as did laughter and singing. A joyous bunch occupied the bar inside, there was no doubt about that. Prudence stood to the side of the wooden swinging doors. She now understood clearly the necessity for saloon doors to swing. Most occupants of the saloon were too drunk upon leaving to locate a handle. And when a fight broke out, swinging doors made it easier for the barkeep to throw the rowdy ones out.

She waited, considering the consequences of entering the saloon. She recalled Sadie and the misunderstanding there, and Prudence firmly assured herself she wouldn't allow such a dreadful thing to happen again. She would just march right in there with her head up and with a most stern, maidenly expression, and quickly search the room for Granny Hayes. She would talk with the woman and then be directly on her way. Zac would never know.

Prudence tied the white silk ribbon of her bonnet more tightly beneath her chin, giving her face a squashed expression. She threw her shoulders back, which thrust her chest out, making her appear one determined lady.

She gave the swinging door a hard shove and walked in, forgetting the door would swing back. It did, hitting her solidly in the back and sending her sprawling face first on the floor.

Prudence landed on her hands and knees, a most undignified position. Too shocked to move and too embarrassed to raise her face, she remained there for a moment, until realizing the music had come to a dead stop. She assumed everyone had focused their attention on her, and why not? She had made a perfect fool out of herself.

She managed to lift herself onto her knees with some dignity before her bonnet fell down in her face, covering her eyes. She had tied it too tightly, and the silk ribbons still hugged the sides of her face while the bonnet tilted forward. She couldn't see and as she tried to fix it, she lost her balance and fell to the side, bumping into a chair and landing on her backside. This time she felt her whole body flame in embarrassment. Then the laughter started. Low at first, until it grew into a roar.

"Here, dearie, let me help you," a woman's voice said. Her hands untied the silk ribbon and pulled Prudence's bonnet off.

Prudence looked up into the oldest and most wrinkled face she had ever seen.

"Granny Hayes, child. You must be the city gal I heard's been looking for me," she said, holding her prune-skinned hand out to Prudence.

Prudence gratefully accepted it, surprised by the strength of the old woman's firm handshake. Granny Hayes helped her up without a grunt, groan, or protest.

"Sit yourself," she ordered, directing Prudence to a table and chairs in the corner near the doors.

Prudence obeyed, still unnerved by the laughter that continued to rumble and the chuckles and comments that circulated loud enough for her to hear. She didn't at all care for the insulting phrases.

"Wonder if she's that clumsy in bed?"

"That's one position I like women in."

"She's got a nice-shaped rump."

Prudence tucked herself in the chair closest to the corner and out of everyone's view.

Granny signaled the barkeep. "Another whiskey, Harry, and—" She looked at Prudence.

"Cider, please."

145

Granny shook her head. "Waste of money," she mumbled, smiling, then yelling, "Cider, the good stuff."

Prudence found her attention glued on Granny. She had thought she had met her share of unusual characters, but Granny outshined them all. Her age was difficult to read, due to the thousands of wrinkles, but it had to be somewhere between eighty and ninety. Her pure white hair was tucked up and under a floppy gray felt hat. She was reed-thin and wore a bright multicolored skirt similar to the ones Prudence had seen on a few Indians. A blue man-styled shirt was covered by a blue denim jacket, and a long necklace made from string and rattlesnake tails hung around her neck.

"So what is it you want from me?" Granny asked directly, leaning back in her chair.

"Information," Prudence answered immediately, wanting to avoid any misunderstanding.

"Well, the first bit of info I can give you is to get rid of that stupid-looking, useless hat."

Prudence glanced at the hat in question, sitting on the table. It was dirty and dusty and looked battered beyond wear.

"You need something to keep the sun off that pale skin of yours. Don't you ever go out and breathe the good clean air God gave us?"

Prudence attempted to answer, but Granny didn't wait for a reply. "You're not from around here, though you look the type that could survive out here. You're strong and big-boned. Won't have any trouble giving birth and can do your fare share of the chores. That's a good sign in a woman. Too many women aren't strong. They need a man to rely on. Men are good for nothin'." She smiled and amended her last statement. "Well, they're good for one thing."

146

Prudence couldn't help but laugh. She liked Granny. "Thank you for the compliments."

"Ain't compliments, just sayin' like it is."

Prudence intended to do the same. "I need to know if you know of a woman I'm looking for."

Granny held up her hand, signaling silence. The barkeep came up behind her and walked around to place the glasses on the table.

When he had returned to the bar, Granny spoke. "You don't trust anybody in a saloon. Gossip travels like fever in here."

"You mean everyone in town will have known I've been in here."

"Darn right."

Prudence sighed and reached for her cider. She swallowed several gulps, licking the delicious, odd taste from her lips.

"So tell me about this woman," Granny said after swallowing a good portion of her whiskey.

"She would have been here around eight, maybe nine years ago, in her thirties, shorter than myself, with long dark hair. A soft voice, gentle eyes, an excellent cook—"

"Does she cook a hell of a rum cake?" Granny interrupted.

"Yes," Prudence said anxiously, then drank more of the cider.

"Sounds like a woman I might have known. What's she to you?"

Prudence hesitated a moment.

"Don't bother lying, dearie. I want the truth or you don't get any answers."

Prudence's response was sharp. "She's my mother."

Granny Hayes looked at her intently, reached for her glass, and downed the remaining whiskey. She signaled the barkeep once again. "Two more of the same, Harry."

Prudence waited, wondering over the old woman's strange stare.

"I knew a woman that fits your description. Whether she was your mother or not, I can't say."

Prudence got the distinct feeling that Granny Hayes was trying to protect the woman she spoke about. "Do you know where I could find her now?"

Granny shook her head. "Can't say. She just took off one day."

"What was her name?"

"Called herself Lee."

Prudence lifted her glass but found it empty.

"Harry, two more," Granny yelled again with a wave of her hand. "She walk out on you and your pa?"

The familiar ache reached her chest, and Prudence found herself choking on her words. "Yes, she left us."

Granny leaned forward. "Some women have good reasons for leaving their families."

Prudence was about to disagree, when she saw Harry approach. She waited until he had deposited the glasses and left. "There is no acceptable reason for a mother to desert her child." She lifted the glass and, closing her eyes, swallowed half the contents.

"Age brings wisdom, child. Don't judge her too harshly."

"Is there something you can tell me about her that would help change my opinion?" Prudence asked, still sensing Granny's attempt to protect Lenore Winthrop.

"Ain't my place. It's you who needs to make peace with your ma."

"If I can find her," Prudence said, her words sounding funny to her ears. Her head felt light and her mouth dry. She reached for her glass once again.

"Don't rightly know where to tell you to look,"

Granny said. "She could have gone anyplace from here."

Prudence ran her hand over her face. "It's rather warm in here."

"You just ain't used to Harry's special cider."

Prudence stared at Granny, rocking back and forth in her seat. Until she realized it wasn't Granny who was rocking. "What do you mean *special* cider?"

"It's spiked with the finest whiskey made in Plattsmouth."

"Oh no," Prudence moaned, attempting to stand. She didn't make it. Dizziness engulfed her and she immediately plopped back down in the chair.

"Don't fret so, child. It ain't gonna kill you," Granny said.

"No, it isn't, but I just might," an angry voice boomed.

Prudence moaned and hid her face in her hands. She was in no condition to deal with her husband at this moment.

Granny turned in her seat and smiled. "Heard you were in town. Good to see you again, Zac. You know this woman?

"It's good to see you again, Granny, and believe it or not Prudence is my wife."

"Wife? Prudence? Neither fit you," Granny said with a firm shake of her head.

"Maybe not, but I'm stuck with her," Zac said, and sat in the chair between the two women.

Prudence didn't want to be *stuck* with any man. She wanted a man to love her unconditionally and irrationally. It wasn't fair. Nobody loved her. Nobody except her father, but then he was her father and would love his daughter no matter what her flaws.

"You promised to stay out of the saloon," Zac said, interrupting Pru's musing.

She peeked through the split in her fingers where they covered her eyes. His features were so handsome that it actually hurt to look upon him. She closed her eyes to make his face vanish.

"Pru?" His voice was low and soft.

If she refused to acknowledge him, perhaps he would go away. Perhaps this was all a dream. Perhaps she cared for Zac Stewart more than she cared to admit.

"Three glasses? Damn, Granny, that was three too many."

She heard the incredibility in his voice. What did he think? That she was incapable of holding her liquor? "I quite enjoyed them," she heard herself respond, then add, "And kindly watch your mouth, *Mr. Stewart.*"

"Them kind of manners ain't gonna suit her out here, Zac," Granny said, giving him a wink.

"She'll learn," he assured her.

"You gonna teach her?" Granny asked, her grin growing wide.

Prudence couldn't hear his response. It was as though he spoke from far away. But she did hear Granny laugh, and she didn't need to look at Zac to know he wore that sinful smile.

His hand suddenly covered hers where they were clutched to her face. His touch was gentle, not at all demanding. He carefully pried her fingers away and looked into her bleary eyes.

"Come with me, Pru."

His voice was so deeply intoxicating that she would have followed him anywhere, but her deep-rooted Bostonian upbringing cautioned her to ask, "Where?"

Zac leaned close to her. The rough texture of a near day's growth of whiskers whispered dangerously close to her cheek as he murmured, "To bed."

Chapter Eleven

"Bed?" Prudence said, her eyes resembling two bright red suns about to burst.

"The best place for you. Unless, of course, you would prefer food?" he asked, much too sarcastically.

Her stomach protested even at the mere suggestion, rumbling in a most unladylike way. "I'm not hungry."

Zac played the gentleman, not adding to her misery by smiling, though the devilish side of him couldn't help but tease. "I didn't think you would be. Then my invitation to bed suits you?"

It did not suit her at all, at least not the way he phrased it. His implications were obvious and so was the joy he derived from her discomfort. "Bed sounds appealing, especially since I find myself rather *sleepy*."

"You two are a hoot," Granny said, her wide smile highlighting her numerous wrinkles. She lifted her half-filled glass of whiskey in a salute. "To a long and happy marriage. And plenty of young'uns." She downed it in one gulp, waved, and was out the swinging doors before either Prudence or Zac could respond.

Prudence was surprised and envious of the old woman's agility. There was no way she, herself, could move that fast, at least not in her present condition.

Zac stood. He looked even taller to Prudence than usual. His chest seemed wider, his smile nastier, his stance more commanding. But then everything seemed out of proportion, even sounds.

The glasses clinking together, the liquor being poured, the men talking, the piano keys tinkling, they all blended into a sea of discordant sounds.

Alarm registered on Prudence's face, and the distraught look wasn't lost to Zac. He held out his hand to her.

She thought of refusing but deemed that unwise. She reached for her bonnet first, taking a moment to still her dizziness before attempting to stand.

Zac no longer found the situation amusing. He could tell from her clumsy movements that the *special* cider had taken its toll. "Let me help you," he offered, moving to stand behind her.

"I assure you, Zac, I am quite capable of standing on my own," she said, and moving slowly to guarantee her steadiness, Prudence stood. One moment she thought all was fine, and then she began to teeter as though on a precarious edge. The foreign sensation that gripped her so strongly brought with it a deep feeling of apprehension.

She closed her eyes and her cry was urgent. "Zac!"

His arms swiftly circled her waist and he brought her gently back to rest against him. "Easy, honey, I've got you."

A flush of relief washed over her. He was holding her, protecting her; she had nothing to fear. She placed her hand over his forearm, and the strong muscle she felt beneath his waistcoat brought her a sense of peace. "I don't feel well, Zac."

"I know," he commiserated. "It's best we get you to the hotel so you can rest."

"Zac," she said calmly, though she felt far from it, "I don't think I can walk."

Zac couldn't help but grin, glad she was unable to see it. Even in her inebriated state, her speech was polite. "I'll manage to get you there."

"I —" She stopped a moment, giving her words second thought. "I've embarrassed myself enough for one day. "I don't wish to add to my disgrace."

"Always proper. Always the lady," he teased.

"Well, as you have pointed out yourself, I'm not exactly a lightweight. I'm sure you would find it difficult, shall we say, supporting me."

Zac's dander jumped. When the hell had he ever implied that she was heavy? Never, because he had never even held such a ridiculous notion. "Are you insinuating that I'm incapable of carrying you?"

"I have no desire to be toted like a common piece of baggage," she said indignantly.

"By all means we must consider propriety."

"If you would but support me with your arm about my waist, I think, perhaps, I might make it."

"You're quite certain that is how you wish my help?"

"Of course. Just do as I've instructed and all will be fine," she said, her speech slurred. After all, it wouldn't be proper for him to discover she wanted nothing more than for him to lift her in his arms and carry her off. The idea was so romantic but quite improper.

"You instruct, I follow. Is that the way of it, Pru?" he asked softly near her ear. Dangerously soft, and if Prudence's head hadn't been so muddled, she would have recognized the threat behind his words.

"A good husband tries to please his wife."

"And does a good wife please her husband?"

"Naturally," she answered, amazed it was necessary to instruct him in such rudimentary behavior. But, then, he was a gunslinger.

She heard the menacing laugh. Low and strong, it rippled like a wave, growing in strength. And just when she thought it would burst, it ended, and she was snatched up into the air to land abruptly in Zac's arms. Her head spun and she had difficulty focusing on his face. "What do you think you're doing?"

"I don't think," Zac said, walking out the swinging doors to a round of approving applause.

"That's obvious," she said, refusing to place her arms around his neck and give him the satisfaction of her accepting his brutish assistance.

"I know *exactly* what I'm doing," he said, walking casually down the street and nodding politely to the startled and not-so-startled people they passed.

Prudence was mortified by the snickers and smiles she received. Lord, but this was outrageous. She was being carried down the street like common baggage, and she didn't even have her bonnet on her head. "What precisely are you doing, *Mr. Stewart?*"

He laughed and hugged her closer to him. "I'm about to have my wife please me."

Two bright red spots colored her cheeks. "You . . . I . . . you . . ."

"You've got that right, honey. It's you and I and the long night that lies ahead."

Prudence was beside herself. He wouldn't take advantage of her in her besotted condition, or would he? He did whatever pleased him. He had no manners. He was barbaric. He was her husband. And, if she would admit it, she was truly attracted to him. She couldn't help it. He was the type of man women dreamed of and fantasized about. Perhaps she could live out one fantasy, just one.

Impossible. The word shot through her like a jolt of thunder. Don't be a fool, Prudence Agatha Win— Stewart. He's only teasing you. He doesn't desire you.

154

Don't be an utter moron. You have disgraced yourself enough for one day.

Without thinking, she laid her head on Zac's shoulder. If nothing else, she would take this moment and remember it as the day Zac Stewart carried her down the street of Plattsmouth to the Hotel Lillian. She would leave the rest, for others who heard of it, open to speculation.

Prudence refused to open her eyes and look about when they entered the hotel lobby. It wasn't necessary, since the gasps and busy chatter were enough to tell her people were stunned and probably offended.

Well, she didn't give a hoot. He was her husband and it felt good being in his arms. His chest was the most comfortable pillow she had ever laid her head upon. And best of all, his heartbeat was strong and steady. He hadn't exerted himself at all by carrying her.

He even deposited her gently, not roughly, on the bed. She closed her eyes, attempting to control the dizziness, but it escalated as his all-male scent drifted around her. She allowed herself the luxury of a dream, pretending their marriage was real, born of love and desire. No one could rob her of her reverie. She would savor this moment in her memory forever and . . .

"Take off your clothes."

Prudence bolted up to a sitting position, immediately regretting her rash action. Her head spun and her stomach revolted. But she refused to be sick, absolutely refused. It just wasn't dignified. "Pardon me?" she said in her most affronted manner.

"Off with your clothes," Zac said slowly and sternly.

"I most—"

"—certainly will obey your husband," he finished for her, removing his waistcoat, vest, and shirt much too quickly for Prudence's way of thinking.

She folded her glove-covered hands primly in her lap and stiffened her spine. She pinched her legs tightly together beneath her skirt and crossed her feet as though bolting a lock. Then she prepared to speak, though her head throbbed unmercifully. She had every intention of delivering a scathing sermon to her husband on proper bedroom decorum.

"Forget it, Pru," he snapped. "You would only be wasting your breath. You will remove your clothes and that's all there is to it."

"I will not," she insisted. "And a proper husband wouldn't expect me to or demand that I do."

Zac hung his gun belt on the bedpost. Prudence stared at the muscles running across his chest and the hard thickness of his arms. They actually bulged as though he had swung an ax day after day. His gorgeous body seemed capable of tremendous power and promise.

Zac watched her eyes as they scanned his naked torso, much too suggestively and much, much too desperately.

He spoke cautiously, not trusting that his own words wouldn't add fuel to an already-volatile situation. "I'm far from a proper husband, Pru. A proper husband would respect his wife's privacy, allowing her ample time to change into her nightgown before he entered her bedroom. He would extinguish the light, allowing her the courtesy of the dark when they made love. He would arrange her nightclothes so as not to subject her to all of his naked body. He would be the perfect gentleman, and sex with him would be totally proper and totally boring."

Prudence was about to take him to task for his brash remarks and for causing her embarrassment. But Zac wouldn't allow it. He bent down over her, forcing her flat upon the bed. He pinned her down by her shoulders and spoke directly into her face. "I'm not finished. I wouldn't allow my wife the privacy to change before I entered *our* bedroom. I'd help her remove every piece of clothing she had on and I'd take my time about it, or if I was in a hurry, I'd rip them off her. I wouldn't extinguish any light. I'd want to see her naked and I'd want her to see me naked. I'd want her to watch our bodies join together, feel me move against her, inside her. There would be no room for well-bred manners in our bedroom. Though there would be breeding, hot and heavy, and it wouldn't be long before she was swollen with my child. And you know what, Pru?" he asked, his voice anxious.

She shook her head, her breathing too labored to speak.

"Even with her swollen belly, I'd still make love to her, and do you know why?"

Prudence didn't respond this time. She just stared into his passion-filled eyes.

"Because I'd want to. I'd want to feel the life we made together, watch her belly stretch, love her as she should be loved."

Prudence fought to trap the tears, to keep them locked behind her closed lids. Each word had cut deeply. Each word had made her see that Zac Stewart was exactly the kind of man she could love, would want to love, perhaps did love, but who would never love her. The familiar pain was there, stabbing at her chest, reminding her he was out of her reach now and always.

She had to protect herself against the pain, push it deep down inside as she had when she thought her mother dead and as she'd done again when she found out otherwise. She had to forget these foolish dreams and thoughts. He had been sent to do a job and that was precisely what he was doing. Once he delivered her safely to her father, it would be over. He would be rid of her and she of him. He would be free to find the woman whom he could love and with whom he could share his life.

She felt the pain in her heart again, but instead concentrated on the pain in her head. She focused on its relentless throbbing, willing all other thoughts away.

"Take off your clothes."

His words were but a whisper, his breath tickling her face so near was he. Did he want his way with her just because she was there? Convenient?

"Come on, honey, you're tired. Let's get you out of these clothes." He sounded sincere, concerned about her tipsy state. This was an example of the tenderness he would show his wife. He would look after her, care for her. The tears threatened once again and her defenses automatically rose to shield her.

Her tongue was quick and sharp. "You would ravish an inebriated woman?"

His laugh sounded tinged with annoyance. "Ravish? Not likely. I just want to make certain you stay put tonight. Your nightgown would prevent any hasty flights."

Prudence felt the quiver begin in the tip of her chin. It was slight at first, and she fought against it turning into a tremble but wasn't successful. Her whole chin shook and the sob trapped in her throat escaped, as did the deep flood of tears. She cried like a newborn babe, wailing most unmannerly.

She raised her hands to her face, trying to hide her embarrassing display of emotions. He didn't want her body. He just wanted to make certain she wouldn't escape. She cried on in humiliation. Her tears soon soaked her gloves. Her head continued to throb unmercifully, and she felt positively awful. She was making a complete and utter fool of herself.

Zac reasoned her outburst was due more to the special cider than to anything else. She wasn't exactly accustomed to hard liquor, and the stuff they brewed around here wasn't very gentle.

"Pru. Pru," he said softly, too softly, since he couldn't be heard above her crying. He pried her hands away from her face. "Pru."

"Leave me be in my misery," she sobbed.

"You're going to make yourself sick," he said and, with a playful twinkle to his eyes, added, "And then I'll have to play nursemaid to you."

Her eyes popped open at the ludicrous thought. "You — *hiccup* — will do — *hiccup* — no such — *hiccup* — thing — *hiccup*."

Zac's grin spread and he could see his amused expression didn't please her. "Then let me help you get out of these clothes."

"No," she snapped sharply. "I'm quite capable of undressing myself."

"You're positive about this?"

His grin had grown and it irritated Prudence. She would certainly save him this duty. "I'm more than positive."

"Suit yourself," he said, and moved off her.

Prudence felt a sudden empty chill when he moved away. She sat up slowly and was relieved to discover that her head didn't spin as badly as before. She would actually be able to tend to herself. She wouldn't need his assistance. Of that she was glad. Or was she?

Of course she was, she scolded silently, and moved cautiously to the end of the bed. She sat there a moment, taking several deep breaths, then slowly pushed herself up to stand.

A mistake. A big mistake. The room spun about like an out-of-control merry-go-round. She reached out, searching for something to grab on to, and felt the floor suddenly rush up to meet her. She screamed. "Zac!"

He grabbed her before she could hit the floor.

This time her tears were soft and few. "I'm so sorry for being such a fool."

Zac laid her gently on the bed. "You're no fool, Pru, and don't ever say you are again," his voice scolded lightly, yet with a sternness to it that warned her he meant it. "Now let me help you out of these clothes."

"It really isn't proper," she said between deep, heavy sighs. "Though I do find myself incapacitated."

"And I am your husband," he offered easily, slipping the gloves off her hands without any protest from her.

"But I couldn't very well run away in my condition," she argued, while he opened the buttons of her basque and lifted her to remove it.

"You'll be much more comfortable in your *condition* in a nightgown," he suggested, silently cursing the tiny pearl buttons on her white blouse. One by one, he opened them as Prudence drifted closer to slumber.

"Lift up," he instructed gently, attempting to remove her blouse. She did as told, sticking her chest out in the process. The blouse came off, and Zac's eyes met with two full, firm breasts. They hid beneath the thin cotton chemise, but the buds of her dark nipples were visible through the fine white material.

"Damn," he mumbled.

"Mr. Stewart," she reprimanded sleepily.

Zac looked at her closed eyes and smiled. She was chiding him for his language, not for his nasty thoughts. And nasty they were. He ran the pad of his thumb lightly over the material that covered her nipples and watched them change instantly from soft to hard. He brushed over them again, and this time Prudence moved uneasily in the deep sleep her intoxication had forced upon her.

He was playing with fire and he didn't care. He had an awful urge to get scorched. He knelt over her and removed her petticoat and stockings. Her limbs were neither slender nor heavy; they were just right, oh, so right.

His fingers went to the top of her bloomers, and he was about to pull them down when she moaned. The throaty sound interrupted him. "Damn," he muttered. He didn't want her asleep when he stripped her. He wanted her awake, responding, writhing, aching for him.

"Take a peek," his devilish side whispered. Just a glimpse of what awaited his pleasure and hers.

"No!" The voice sounded entirely too respectable to his own ears. And what was worse, it sounded like his own.

"You're my wife," he murmured, trying to justify his actions. He splayed his hand over her stomach, drifting down until his fingers whispered over her mound. "We have a date, Mrs. Stewart. One I intend to make certain you never forget and one that will seal our future forever."

He moved off the bed and, taking the folded quilt from the bottom, covered Prudence up to her chin. "That will protect you for now," he said, then kissed her lightly on the forehead.

Prudence woke the next morning with surprisingly nothing more than a slight headache. She stretched her arms above her head while stretching her toes at the same time. It took a few seconds for her to realize she wore only her chemise and bloomers. She yanked the quilt up to her chin, mortified by her state of near undress. She turned quickly to find the other side of the bed empty, though her relief was short-lived when a strong voice answered her silent questions.

"I figured what I left on you was sufficient to serve as a nightgown."

Prudence looked over at Zac. He was running his straight-edge razor down the side of his lathered face, finishing his morning shave. "Thank you," she said, pleased, yet in some small way disappointed he had acted the gentleman.

"Don't bother," he said, rinsing the remainder of the lather from his face and drying it with the towel next to the washbowl. "I'm not in the habit of *ravishing* besotted virgins."

"I thought, perhaps, you had learned some gentlemanly manners. I can see now I was wrong," she said, sitting up and clutching the quilt to her chest as she looked about the room for her traveling case.

Zac reached for a white shirt from his satchel. He snapped the clean, crisp shirt open and slipped it on. "I told you once and you'd do well to remember it: I'm no gentleman."

Prudence stood, the quilt slipping from her grasp. Her full breasts were dangerously close to tumbling from her chemise. Her bloomers were pushed up high on her legs and showed more of her firmly shaped limbs than was proper. Even her reddish brown hair was far from dignified. It fell in wild disarray. She had the distinct appearance of a woman who had just spent the night sharing passionate love and had thoroughly enjoyed the sexual episode.

Zac found her state of near undress quite appealing, and he smiled. "If you remember correctly, *Mrs. Stewart*, I told you that my wife would view me naked, as I would her, and no lights would be turned off, no garments left on."

Prudence scooped up the quilt and hugged it to her

162

chest. She stood firm at his approach.

He tore the quilt from her grasp and threw it aside, then took her chin in his hand and raised her face up. "Make no mistakes about it, *Mrs. Stewart*. My wife's time will come."

He released her and turned away.

Prudence wasn't certain she interpreted his meaning correctly. Was he telling her he would wait to make love to the wife he chose of his own free will? Or was he informing her that eventually he would make love to her? And if so, for what reason? He certainly didn't love her.

"Get dressed. The steamboat leaves in two hours, and there are a few things I need to purchase before we depart."

She didn't bother to argue. Her mind was too muddled—from the cider or from his words, she wasn't sure.

"I'll be in the dining salon," he said, securing his gun belt around his waist, then putting on his waistcoat. "Can I trust you to meet me there in twenty minutes, or do you have plans of running away again?"

"There's no point in my running away now. I will stay and confront my father and this marriage situation. Afterwards, when all is taken care of, I will continue my search for my mother. I will meet you downstairs in ten minutes. You have my word, Prudence said, and lifted her traveling case to the bed.

Her decision was sensible, she told herself. There was no point in running off on her own when she had no leads to her mother's whereabouts. Once her father arrived, she would discuss the matter with him and request his help. Hopefully, he would agree, and if not, she would continue the search on her own.

"Ten minutes, then," he repeated, and walked out the door. He stood outside their room a minute and shook his head. "Damn," he said.

"Mr. Stewart!" the staunch voice reprimanded him from behind the closed door.

Zac laughed all the way down the hall and into the dining salon.

Chapter Twelve

Prudence looked casually around Mr. Lewis's mercantile. His store was large and held an array of items. There were ropes, shovels, picks, and buckets hanging from pegs, while glass jars filled with striped candies lined the counter. Materials from muslin to various prints or plain cotton were displayed in bolts, while needles, threads, and even patterns were stacked nearby. Then there were the ready-to-wear garments. Those were the ones that interested Prudence.

She had taken careful note of the way the local women dressed. Her clothes might be proper back in the East, but she was beginning to realize they were far from practical in the West.

The dark brown grosgrain skirt and matching basque she wore were much too heavy and unsuitable for this rugged life and late spring climate. In contrast, the women here outfitted themselves in cotton or muslin skirts and sturdy blouses minus the frills and bows.

If she wanted to fit in, to blend, to be part of the West, the best place to start was with her clothes. She saw that Zac was busy speaking with Mr. Lewis, and satisfied she had enough time, Prudence set about choosing her purchases.

Mrs. Lewis, a robust and cheerful woman, helped her gather the appropriate items, suggesting articles that would be "necessary."

"Now for a hat," Mrs. Lewis said, looking over her inventory of bonnets prominently displayed on shelves behind the counter.

Prudence surveyed them herself and found not one she felt suitable for her journey. They were either overly decorated with fanciful *stuff* or plain as the day they were made. And of course, she couldn't go around bareheaded.

Mrs. Lewis tapped her puckered lips with her finger while sizing up the situation. "You need something special, yet practical."

Prudence tended to agree with her.

"I've got it," Mrs. Lewis cried, hastily disappearing behind the gray curtain that separated the back rooms from the store. She emerged in minutes, a huge smile on her face and the perfect bonnet in her hand.

Prudence beamed when Mrs. Lewis handed it to her.

"It's you, dear," Mrs. Lewis insisted. "Different and ever so beautiful."

Beautiful? Yes, that was what she had said. Prudence had heard it clearly. Mrs. Lewis had suggested that Prudence was beautiful.

"I told Mr. Lewis that only a special woman could wear that hat. Mind you, it's nothing fancy, but the strawberry-blond color of the straw and the pale pink of the silk scarf running around it and down through the sides to tie under your chin . . . well, it just takes perfect coloring to wear it. And you have that coloring. The red in your hair will just burst out and the creamy complexion of your face will radiate a pinkish glow. Yes, it's perfect, absolutely perfect for you."

Prudence was speechless, an odd occurrence for her.

"Why don't you just slip back into my private quarters and switch to that darling light gray skirt and white blouse you bought. The hat would look wonderful with it, and I even think I have a short cape in gray that would match the skirt."

Prudence felt like a young girl buying her first party dress. She took a quick peek to see what Zac was about and found him still busy with Mr. Lewis.

"Would the outfit be appropriate for travel on the steamboat?" Prudence asked, not wishing to embarrass Zac by wearing ill-suited clothing.

Mrs. Lewis shook her head and smiled. "My dear, there isn't much that is and isn't appropriate out here. We make do with what we must. As long as one is clean and respectful, one has nothing to fear. Now come with me. I think your hair needs some changing. You wear it pulled back much too severely for one so young and pretty."

Pretty. The woman had called her pretty. Prudence followed Mrs. Lewis willingly, feeling each step she took transformed her from a plain moth into a beautiful butterfly.

Zac finished with his order. Mr. Lewis promised he'd have it delivered to the steamboat with time to spare. It had taken longer than he had expected, but every time he had glanced around the store, keeping Prudence in sight, he had seen she was busy with women's things. He was glad she had kept herself occupied. But now that he was ready to leave, he couldn't find her. Zac didn't think she would have left the store without telling him. He didn't know why, couldn't explain it even to himself, but he felt her more attached to him. Not dependent. Prudence would never be totally dependent on anyone. No, it was as if she was accepting him as a husband; strange as the idea was, she appeared somewhat satisfied with the notion.

167

He found himself liking the notion of her accepting him. She was a lady and often reminded him that he was no gentleman, a status she placed much importance on. But was she finding that importance misplaced? Was the unruly West opening her mind? Was it making her see reality and not just the confines of the cultured society to which she was accustomed?

He hoped so, since beneath that refined facade lurked a woman he intended to get to know on more intimate terms. Terms he had every right to insist upon, since she was his wife. But he had a gut feeling she was going to be quite put out by the decision he had reached concerning their marriage.

Zac smiled. Hell, he needed a wife. He owned a big spread, and he wanted a large brood of children to fill the house he had built. Wasn't that why he had built it? And he'd never be able to teach kids the proper manners Prudence could. With her obstinate nature and his strength . . . damn, they'd grow into little commanding giants.

He laughed at the idea, though he doubted Prudence would. Actually, it didn't matter what she thought. He held the key that would secure their marriage, and when the time was right, he'd use it. For now, though, he needed time alone with her. Here in the West. Not in Boston.

"Looking for the missus?" Mr. Lewis asked, bringing Zac's attention back to the important fact that Prudence wasn't anywhere to be seen.

"Actually," he confessed, "she's kind of difficult to keep track of. Will of her own, if you get my drift."

"Sara's the same way," Mr. Lewis whispered, "though I find it to my liking. Can't abide those pampered women with no mind of their own."

"I'm in total agreement, Mr. Lewis."

"Your wife's probably in the back with Sara. She's

always taking the new arrivals under her wing. I'll go see."

Zac waited with a minimum of patience. He was anxious to be on his way. He suddenly felt tired of the confines of the cities and towns he had been through. He longed for the peace and solitude of his ranch.

"Zac."

He turned, ready to tell her it was about time, but his words caught in his throat. She looked beautiful. The gray skirt she wore fit more than perfectly. It accented her ample hips to the point of being sensual. The short matching cape wasn't completely closed, and from beneath it he could peek at the simple white blouse that curved invitingly over her full breasts. But it was her hair and bonnet that brought the mumbled "Damn" to his lips.

If Prudence had heard it she ignored it, so intent were his eyes upon her. He didn't even smile, just stared, but oh, what a stare!

He loved the way the wide-brimmed straw hat rested back on her head, leaving her coppery-colored hair to frame her face. And frame it it did, with small springy curls teasing her forehead and temples, while the pink silk ribbon that dangled in a knot beneath her chin added a soft rose color to her complexion. Nature had bestowed upon her a natural beauty, and the West was just beginning to bring out her full potential.

Zac walked over to her. "You look beautiful."

His words were neither forced nor expressed with any hesitation, a surprise to Prudence. Could he actually mean it? "Thank you," she said, hearing the uncertainty in her own voice.

"Have you gotten everything you need?" he asked, feeling a bit awkward. He seldom told a woman she was beautiful, especially since he hadn't met many he felt deserved that high a compliment. Whenever he did, it was always in private and usually when they were naked. Suddenly, he felt rather exposed, vulnerable, and uncomfortable.

Prudence sensed his uneasiness and wrongly attributed it to his statement. He hadn't meant a word he had said to her. She had never been beautiful, so how could she suddenly become so? She was being a fool again. Too often she had allowed herself the fantasy of hearing such compliments, so that now when she actually did, she believed them. Her defenses rose once again. "I have purchased everything I need. I don't need any help from you."

Zac took a step back, stunned by her caustic response. She marched right past him with that superior tilt of her head.

"Damn, what did I do now?" he mumbled, sending a quick nod and a pleasant smile to Mr. and Mrs. Lewis before he stormed after Prudence.

"That girl's a real beauty and a spitfire," Mr. Lewis said and, with a sly grin, added, "Just like you, Sara."

Sara winked at him and sashayed behind the gray curtain, with Mr. Lewis quick on her heels.

Zac looked up and down the busy street outside the mercantile. Prudence was only a short distance away. He headed for her with the thought of a good tongue-lashing in mind.

"Zac Stewart!"

The voice boomed like a cannon, halting most people where they stood, especially Zac and Prudence. Zac was all too aware of that voice. It didn't actually belong to anyone in particular. It was the tone. The tone a man used when he thought himself ready to test his skills on the best. And Zac Stewart was the best. No man was faster with a gun.

Zac was cautious when he turned, taking in all of the scene around him. His eyes darted with precision

170

to the buildings, the rooftops in particular, seeing if any "friends" lurked about. Just as quickly, he canvassed the area around the young man who stood no taller than a few inches over five feet.

Zac surveyed the man so swiftly that his opponent didn't even notice. His instincts told him there was no real threat. The man's fingers were too close and itchy on his gun, which meant he was unsure of himself. And an unsure gunslinger was an inexperienced one. And a dead one, though he had no desire to see the young man with a bullet through him.

"You are Zac Stewart?" the man asked, his voice shaky and his finger inching closer to the butt of his gun.

Zac walked toward the man with a slow and steady gait. There was no hesitation to his steps, his confidence all too apparent. "I'm Zac Stewart." His voice was strong, his tone threatening.

The man attempted to speak, but his voice croaked some and he had to clear his throat. "I'm Jeb. Jeb Smith."

Zac wanted to laugh in the young man's stupid face, then give him a good thrashing and send him home to his mamma, where he belonged. "Well, Jeb Smith, what can I do for you?"

"I hear you're the best," he challenged, and people began to spread away from them.

"Heard the same thing myself," Zac said, a haunting smile fixed upon his face. He pushed his waistcoat back behind his holster, an action meant to frighten the boy, since he had no real intention of drawing on him.

The young man swallowed hard upon seeing Zac's shiny silver six-shooters. "Well, I've come to find out for myself."

"You will do no such thing!" Prudence yelled, stepping around Zac and walking straight up to the startled young man. She raised her hand and pointed her finger right in his face, like a schoolteacher about to chastise an unruly student. "Your manners and actions are appalling. You should be ashamed of yourself."

The boy was stunned and took a step back.

She took a step forward. "Go home to your mother and have her teach you proper behavior and—"

She was grabbed roughly by the waist, lifted a few inches off the ground, and deposited near the door of the mercantile.

"Don't say a word, Prudence," Zac warned with a murderous glint in his eyes, which intermittently focused on her and on the boy.

"I—"

"So help me, I'll gag you."

She snapped her mouth firmly closed. *Let him get killed. See if she cared.*

Zac advanced on the boy, sending him stumbling back in fear. He spoke low but with brutal authority. "You're right, son. I'm the best. I've killed more men than you've probably known and never blinked an eye. I've been told I'm so fast that my opponent can't even see my gun leave my holster. Many a man stood in shock and watched his own blood spill from his chest and wondered how it happened, since they never saw my gun move. I haven't killed in a while. Haven't had the taste for blood, but you've whet my appetite. What'd ya say? Shall we see if you can see my gun leave my holster?"

The boy turned pure white and so did Prudence. She began to shake, while the boy's response was much more embarrassing.

Jeb Smith took off without a word to Zac. He ran down the street, mounted his horse, and rode out of town as fast as the animal's legs could carry him.

172

The crowd laughed and cheered and began to disperse as Zac made his way to Prudence. She stood pressed flat against the building. He loomed over her. His look was menacing as he braced his hands beside her face, trapping her.

"Don't ever interfere again," he said. "You were lucky this time. He was young and inexperienced. An experienced gunfighter would have knocked you out, if he felt kind, and if not, he would have shot you."

Prudence tried to speak but found only a spurt of breath leaving her mouth.

Zac felt her fear and was glad for it. She had to understand what a stupid thing she had done. She had been lucky, very lucky. It was important for her to learn a lesson, since people rarely got a second chance out here. One mistake was all it took, and that mistake usually proved fatal.

"I've told you many times, there are few if any gentleman out here."

Prudence blinked her eyes and took a deep breath in an attempt to rid herself of the fear. She had known Zac was a famous gunslinger, but until this moment she had never fully understood the consequences of such a profession. He actually killed men.

Her heart beat like a wild drum and her voice was shaky. "You're not a gentleman."

It wasn't a question. It was as though she finally understood, but he answered, anyway. "No, Pru, I'm no gentleman."

He grabbed her arm roughly and marched her down the street to the steamboat.

The chaotic activities that the loading of cargo and passengers entailed brought a welcome relief to Prudence. She focused on the bustling commotion, chasing away her fears and doubts if only for a short time.

Zac guided her around trunks and crates waiting for

loading. He held her arm firmly as he assisted her up the gangplank. Prudence was amazed at the variety of people here. Her eyes were widespread with excitement. She was eager to take in all she could.

They arrived all too soon at the cabin door, and with regret, she craned her neck and cast a glance about for one last look.

"It isn't necessary for you to remain in the cabin," Zac said, noting her enthusiasm over their venture. "I just wanted to make certain you knew where our lodgings were located. You may walk about the boat, but I request that you stay on board. With all this jumble of activities, I don't wish to take the chance of *misplacing* you."

Prudence smiled over the emphasis he placed on the word. He was being tactful. Actually, quite tactful, since he hadn't demanded she remain on board but rather requested she do so. "I won't venture off the boat, but I will gladly take the opportunity to explore the vessel."

"Be careful, and when our departure is announced, please make certain you return here to meet me."

Prudence walked over to the wooden railing bright with its new coat of white paint. She patted the top. "I'll meet you right here so we can watch Plattsmouth fade away."

"Is that an invitation?" Zac asked teasingly, though in truth he found the prospect of such a simple shared act appealing.

Prudence felt lighthearted and dreamy, emotions she rarely experienced. She allowed her defenses to drop and her heart to open, leaving herself vulnerable to the notorious gunslinger. "It's an invitation. Will you accept?"

Zac heard her doubt, felt her uneasiness, and knew this exposure of emotions was difficult for her. "I'd be delighted," he accepted, without hesitation and with a heartbreaking smile.

Prudence reached out and gently touched his arm. "I'll be waiting."

Zac nodded and hurried off. His "Damn" was inaudible to anyone but himself, it was so low and harsh. Her touch had been soft, but it wasn't really the touch that disturbed him so. It was the fact that she had reached out to him at all. It hadn't taken long for him to realize she feared giving her love and trust and accepting it from another. She was cautious with those emotions and guarded them strongly, much too strongly. He assumed her mother's desertion of her at an early age had much to do with it. And he wondered just how difficult it would be for her to accept a man's love.

Prudence watched Zac disappear down the gangplank, anxious to inspect the room she would share with him. She turned and entered the cabin.

She left the door open to allow sufficient light to enter. There was no window, so the room was otherwise bathed in darkness. The quarters were small, and smelled of strong lye soap. There was a small chest of drawers, with an oval mirror above it on the wall. To the side of that sat the washstand, with the porcelain basin snug in its brass holder and the matching pitcher beneath snug in its holder. The bed, built into the wall, was narrow, more adequate for a single person than for two people.

Pleased with the accommodations yet a bit apprehensive about the size of the bed, she left the room.

She walked along the upper deck, pressing flat against the wall several times to allow the crew members to pass with armloads of baggage. She easily took the steep steps to the lower level and strolled along there, watching the activity on the dock.

Lively piano music caught her attention, and she entered the open doors to her right and behind her. It was the dining salon. The large room was light and airy, since its doors and shutters were spread open wide. Round tables were decked out in pristine white linens, and a bowl of fresh daisies sat in the middle of each one. A long table covered in the same white linen cloth sat against the far wall, but where the others were empty, this one was not. Coffee, cider — which Prudence made a point of avoiding — muffins, breads, cakes, eggs, sausages, ham, and crystal jars filled with honey and jams lined the table.

Prudence served herself after watching the other passengers do the same. An elderly woman, Mrs. Hampton, joined her at one of the tables and they talked. Actually, Mrs. Hampton talked almost nonstop about her son and his family, whom she was going to visit.

Finishing the delicious food, she thought of Zac and wondered if he had eaten. Prudence politely excused herself and walked out onto the deck once again. She stood against the wooden railing, looking about for her husband. She saw him on shore and anxiously raised her hand to wave and draw his attention, when she suddenly realized he wasn't alone. She immediately dropped her hand.

The woman with him was attractive. She was blond and petite and, from the looks of it, ever so charming. Their conversation appeared lively. And Zac was smiling.

Jealous. The ugly thought reared its head, but she wondered if she was jealous of the woman and her appearance, or the fact that Zac seemed taken by her. She wished she had had more experience with men and relationships. So often she thought herself foolish, but perhaps her feelings were commonplace and shared by many women. If only her mother had been there to guide her.

She noticed then that Zac had seen her; he was waving, quite strenuously. Her first thought was to turn her head and ignore him. But Prudence thought better of such a rash and improper action, waving and smiling instead.

The whistle blew and the call for departure was issued. Zac pointed to the upper deck, reminding her where she was to meet him. She pointed to the dining salon behind her and motioned with her hand to her mouth, then pointed to him. He nodded his willingness to meet her there and patted his stomach to demonstrate his hunger.

Prudence's laughter was light as were, once again, her emotions. She often thought this was the way a marriage should be, trust and caring being the most important aspects of the relationship. And at the moment, she felt she shared those notable traits with Zac. But was the feeling really mutual?

She hurried into the salon that was now filling with passengers. She fixed a plate for Zac, and one of the crew members, who helped serve, carried it to a table near the door while she poured two cups of coffee. Prudence was seated at the table when he entered.

People, she noticed, were instantly struck by his appearance. How could they not be? He was so tall and formidable and, lest she forget, handsome. He was minus his hat and the blonde, for which Prudence was grateful.

"I thought you wanted to watch the boat pull away?" he asked, standing as though he'd forgo his meal so she could view their departure.

His consideration warmed her. "We'll go out on deck when you finish."

To Prudence's disappointment, other people joined

them. She had wanted to be alone with Zac so they could talk. She suddenly had an overwhelming urge to learn more about him, and since she wasn't certain how much time they had left together, each moment seemed precious to her.

She was glad when he finished and excused them both to walk out on the deck. He directed her silently with a light touch of his hand to the lower part of her back. They were soon on the upper deck past their cabin at the front of the boat, watching the beauty of the Missouri River pass before them.

"Too many people on the lower deck," he said in explanation.

"You don't like crowds?" she asked, anxious to share this time with him.

"Sometimes they're a necessity and I admit I enjoy them. Though most of the time I prefer the company of my few good friends and the solitude of my ranch."

She liked the way his hair ruffled in the warm breeze that drifted off the river. She noticed his hair wasn't as dark a brown as she'd first thought, and she admired the color that sat somewhere between dark and light. "How large is your ranch?"

"Over a thousand acres and growing," he beamed proudly.

"You've thought of expansion already?"

"I intend to have the biggest cattle ranch in the territory," he stated, his firm tone suggesting he would settle for nothing less.

"How did you get into ranching?"

"Don't you mean what made me give up being a gunslinger?"

She caught the defensive glint in his eye and met it with one of her own. "No, I didn't, but since you mentioned it, whatever made you become a gunslinger?"

Zac liked her fearless nature. "Necessity."

Prudence remained silent and attentive.

Realizing she intended to hear him out without comment, he continued. "I was young and not much good at anything. My father drifted from town to town and job to job, and I tagged along with him. If I didn't, he would have just left me behind without a thought. My mother died when I was five. Don't recall much about her except she always smelled good, like fresh flowers."

In contrast, Prudence thought, her life had been perfect, even considering that her mother had left her and her father. At least she had a father who loved and cared for her.

"I started fooling around with a gun when I was about eight. It fascinated me, and I learned right fast that men who knew how to use one were quickly respected. I started teaching myself. Day after day I'd practice my aim. Then I practiced my draw. Then I combined both until they were perfect and I didn't miss one moving or nonmoving target."

Prudence was caught by the faraway look in his eyes. It was as though he were reliving his troubled youth.

"The first time I killed a man I got sick. Didn't plan it, didn't intend for it to happen. My father got into trouble in the local saloon in a town whose name I've long since forgotten. One of the men was a gunslinger and called my father out. Said he'd been cheating at cards, though I don't know how he could have been, since he was too drunk even to see straight. I was fifteen and scared."

He stopped and looked straight at Prudence. "Just like that kid who challenged me in Plattsmouth. Only I didn't want to challenge this man. I just wanted to prevent my father from being killed. God knows why."

Prudence knew why. He was the only one Zac had. If his father died, he'd be alone.

"My legs shook, but my hands, they were steady. I had one six-shooter in a single holster and that gun was sparkling clean. I stood in that smoky, dirty saloon, looked at my father passed out in a drunken stupor on the table and then at the gunslinger who stood smiling at me at the other end of the bar. His hand moved, I thought, way too slow. My gun was out before his slipped from his holster. I fired once and he went down . . . never got up."

Prudence listened, feeling close to tears.

"Word got around fast about my speed with a gun. It didn't take long for more to challenge me. I had to leave town. Sheriff asked me nice and polite."

"Did your father go with you?" she asked.

He shook his head sadly. "He died the very same night I killed that gunslinger to protect him. Doctor said it was too much liquor . . . rotted his gut."

Prudence placed her hand on his back, offering comfort.

"My reputation grew after that. There wasn't a man I couldn't outdraw. Then one morning I woke up and realized that one day a young man just like myself would challenge me and that would be the end. That's when I started hiring out for money. Mostly to the towns that needed cleaning up. I put away almost every cent I earned until I had enough to buy the first hundred acres of my ranch. Then about four years ago the ranch started showing a profit, and it's been booming ever since."

"Why do you still wear your guns?" Prudence asked, worried that someone more talented might challenge him.

Zac turned and leaned against the post. "Honey, I'd be a fool — actually a dead fool — to go anywhere out here without them."

"But if you didn't wear them, no one would bother

180

you," she said, needing to find a way to protect him.

Zac raised his hand and ran his finger along her cheek. "It wouldn't matter. I'd be given time to get one . . . probably have a gun handed to me."

"You could refuse," she insisted.

"No, Pru, I couldn't," he said softly. "It's a matter of honor."

She opened her mouth to protest.

He placed his finger over her lips. "I must do what is proper," he teased, sending her a sinful wink.

Prudence wanted him to kiss her. Right there and then, no matter who was about. She needed to feel his lips, hot and alive, so frightened was she that he would die. But how? She couldn't just tell him she wanted a kiss, needed it, ached for it. She thought a moment. No smile came to her lips, though she felt it when she sternly announced, *"Mr. Stewart."*

"Ahh, Pru," he whispered, realizing full well why she had addressed him so. And he lowered his mouth to hers, to savor, to taste, and to enjoy.

Chapter Thirteen

The cabin was hot.

Prudence sat on the edge of the bed, tugging at the neckline of her blouse.

"Shall I open the louvers on the door more?" Zac asked, amused by her uncomfortable state and reaching to adjust the wooden slots meant for ventilation.

She shook her head. "No, I'm fine."

Zac, in a playful mood, added to her discomfort with the statement, "I thought it rather cool myself, especially with the late spring breeze blowing off the river."

"It must have been all that coffee I drank at supper," Prudence offered, watching Zac remove his gray vest and add it to the gray waistcoat hanging on the peg near the chest. He had looked so handsome this evening when they had gone to supper in the dining salon. He had changed from his usual black outfit to a gray one. The dusky gray color set off his striking features, sending the females in the salon into apoplexy. He, himself, took no note of it, but Prudence did, finding their stares, giggles, and blatant overtures unmannerly.

"Perhaps if you changed into your nightgown, you would feel more comfortable," he suggested, removing his shirt.

Prudence had never undressed in front of anyone, not even Tess, her personal servant. Buttons, stays, and hooks were seen to after she had clothed herself enough to avoid embarrassment. She had never really thought her full figure pleasant to look upon and had even refrained from viewing herself naked.

"I could help, if necessary," Zac said, startling her as he stepped toward her.

Her eyes settled on his chest, broad and solid and oh, so lovely to look upon. "Not necessary," she cried in a high-pitched squeak.

He stifled the chuckle that rushed to escape. "But you're so hot and bothered, removal of those garments is the perfect solution," he argued. "And besides, you would never be able to reach the back buttons."

He had her there. She wouldn't be able to reach behind her.

"Come on, stand up and turn around," he offered, holding out his hand to her.

It was obvious to him that she was reluctant and doubtful. She didn't assault him with her usual fervor, which meant she was nervous and uncomfortable with the situation. He had sensed she had wanted this all evening. He had read it clearly in her eyes, in the way she constantly watched him, in her movements that were edgy and awkward. Yes, he was certain she wanted him to touch her intimately. "I am your husband, so it is proper."

That was true, and that was what disturbed her. He was her husband, and she wanted more from him. So much more that it frightened her.

She reached her hand out slowly to him, and before she could change her mind, he grabbed for it, lifting her off the bed and turning her around.

He worked silently, unbuttoning her blouse. She could hear his breathing, soft and steady. His breath was warm, tingling the back of her neck, causing gooseflesh to rise across her back and down her arms.

He slipped it off her shoulders, pushing the soft material slowly down along her arms before tossing it to the bed. Treading lightly, he ran his hands back up her arms, then over her shoulders and down again, wrapping his arms around her waist to ease her back against him.

"Feel better?" he asked, his cheek resting beside her temple.

"Much," she said, thinking his touch heaven and longing for more unearthly sensations.

His hands worked at her skirt. She felt the tug but made no move to protest. She wanted this, wanted him.

By the time he finished, she stood in her chemise, bloomers, and stockings.

He turned her around then and tilted her chin up to look at him. "Better?" he repeated.

She nodded, her mouth too dry to speak.

He moved his hand to her waist and ran it beneath her chemise, around her back to dip dangerously below her bloomer band. "If you still feel hot, perhaps I should remove more?" he asked solicitously but with a spark of passion in his eyes.

Prudence suddenly felt apprehensive. He was leaving the decision totally up to her. He had no intention of forcing himself on her. If she was willing, then so was he. Should she satisfy herself and learn the secret knowledge of womanhood?

When no answer was immediately forthcoming, Zac took matters into his own hands. He had to; he couldn't wait. His need for her had heightened with each touch until it had grown into a frenzy, and his only thought was to touch, taste, and make love to her.

He moved her gently to lie upon the bed, lying beside her. Strands of her coppery red hair teased her shoulders, and Zac brushed them out of the way as he hooked his finger beneath the thin strap of her chemise and

184

pulled it ever so slowly down.

Her full breast tantalized him as inch by inch it came into view. The abrasion of the material and—he hoped—his nearness had puckered her large nipple into a welcoming bud.

He looked at her as he moved his mouth toward it. Her eyes were wide like those of a frightened doe, and although he wished to ease her trepidation, he couldn't wait. He offered words that were meant to comfort but caused her passion to flare. "I'm going to taste you, Pru."

His tongue lightly licked her hard nipple. She pitched backward slightly and shivered. He stayed her with his hand to her midriff, soothing her by gently caressing her warm flesh.

His tongue continued to lick, circling the bud and bringing a hardness so torturous to his loins that he thought he'd burst from the thrill of it.

He suckled her then, slipping his hand up from her waist to cup her breast. She was so ripe, so full, that it excited him even more. He savored the taste of her and enjoyed the way she squirmed against him. She was so inexperienced that she didn't understand her own feelings, didn't know what pleasure to expect.

He would go slowly and fill them both with pleasure and satisfaction. He lifted his head and brought his face to hers. She looked at him almost pleadingly, and he smiled before he lowered his mouth to hers and captured it in a kiss.

She responded with equal eagerness, tasting him as he did her. He pulled his mouth away to allow them a breath, and while she inhaled slowly, he teased her lips with his tongue, brushing them, tracing them, nipping them until she moaned in deprivation.

He continued to tease as his hand moved beneath her bloomers, running across her belly and dipping down between her legs. While his tongue sought her mouth, penetrating her sharply, so sought his finger.

He felt her heat and moistness at hand. His blood raced, his heart pounded, his shaft throbbed unmercifully. He tore his mouth from hers, moved his finger slowly, and whispered, "I want to feel you, taste you, and see every inch of you."

Prudence's passion was high, soaring beyond description. She had never thought pain and pleasure could be synonymous, but they were. She wanted him to feel her and taste her . . . but see her naked? The thought of such extreme exposure, of such vulnerability, caused a sudden fear to rear up in her. She tensed once again, raising her defenses. "No," she stammered.

He stilled all movement. His fingers rested against her moistness. His lips touched hers. He drew his head away from her to look into her eyes, afraid of what he would see.

They were icy green, full of coldness and reproach. Had she just realized who was touching her? Did the fact that he was a gunslinger and not of her breed make him acceptable for dallying with but not for anything further?

Her chin went up defensively.

"I have no intention of forcing you, Pru," he said, and quickly moved off her to stand.

She reached for her blouse, pulling it over her, covering her exposure, shielding herself.

He reached for his shirt, roughly tugging it on, and then grabbed his waistcoat. He opened his mouth to speak and then, thinking better of it, shut it and walked out the door, slamming it behind him.

Prudence sat up, still holding the blouse firmly against her chest. What was the matter with her? All evening she had wanted Zac to touch her intimately. That was all her mind could think about. All through supper she had watched his fingers as they skillfully and gracefully moved, and she had fantasized how they would feel caressing her. She had worked herself up into such a heated state that the cabin had become a furnace to her.

He had offered, really quite gentlemanly, to ease her discomfort. After all, he was her husband. And she had given much thought to experiencing such things with him, realizing it might be her only chance. And his touch had been more than she had imagined. It had awakened in her feelings she had never even *dreamed* possible. Yet her self-doubt had risen once again to torment her. So what if he saw her naked and wasn't pleased? Surely, he wouldn't be so rude as to embarrass her. He'd just complete the task and she would be none the wiser. Perhaps somewhat wiser, for then she would learn the womanly secrets that she had only touched upon this evening. Secrets her body still ached to experience.

"But how will you ever get him to touch you again after this evening's disgraceful display?" she asked herself. Perhaps if she undressed and waited in her nightgown and was pleasant to him . . . It might work. It was worth a try.

She hurried to change, hoping her pink cotton nightgown with its high-neck collar and long sleeves would appeal a little and not turn him off entirely.

After brushing her hair loose and not braiding it as usual, she hurried to the bed to wait. Time ticked by slowly and the breeze outside turned into an angry wind, churning the river and the boat.

Prudence felt the change. It wasn't much, but after all the upset this evening it was enough to rattle her stomach. She released a woeful moan and prayed the remainder of the evening would not turn disastrous.

Zac walked along the upper deck to the cabin. He had spent the last two hours drinking and playing cards. The booze had left a sour taste in his mouth and the card game had left him with an empty pocket. He berated himself for being a fool. A fool for drinking and playing cards when his mood was foul, and a fool for not calling Prudence to task for her objection to his making love to her. He should have put his foot down, asked questions, demanded answers. But his temper and pride had been riled, so instead he had stormed out of the cabin afraid of saying or doing something he would regret.

After losing the last hand in cards, he realized he wouldn't be satisfied until he confronted her. Now standing in front of the cabin door, Zac wondered if his idea had been an intelligent one, or if it was his pride — or perhaps his body — that needed stroking. With that lustful thought and an added smile, he opened the door and walked in.

The room was dark, the oil lamp having been extinguished. He fumbled his way to the bed, calling out to Prudence.

He thought her still angry and that she was purposely ignoring him. He called out to her again, more sternly. "Pru."

Still no answer. His concern deepened with the furrow of his brow. She had to have heard him. "Damn it, Pru, answer me."

When no answer came this time, he turned in the direction of the lamp and lit it. Prudence was gone.

Panic immediately set in. Then he recalled they were on a steamboat sailing up the river, limiting her ability to escape. But where could she have gone and why?

He was suddenly furious. He had had enough of her flights for freedom. Especially now since she was his wife. If she didn't mind him, then he'd tie her down. The thought held promise, and he stormed out of the cabin in search of her.

The wind had picked up and the threat of rain appeared close at hand. Zac's fury quickly gave way to worry. He had searched the upper deck and hadn't found her. He was now almost finished searching the lower deck, and still no Prudence.

He made his way to the front of the boat near the stacks of cargo. He walked around them, wondering why he was wasting his time. Prudence would never come here. He was about to turn and walk away.

Then he saw her, huddled against a large crate. The wind blew her hair across her face. Her nightgown flapped at her feet and her hands gripped her shawl around her.

He was at her side instantly, kneeling before her to block the raging wind. "What the hell are you doing here?"

Prudence looked up at him, ever so grateful he had found her. "I don't feel well, Zac."

Her voice was weak, her face pale in the moonlight. He removed his coat, wrapped it around her, and lifted her up into his strong arms. He said nothing. He wanted to get her back to the safety and comfort of their cabin.

She clung to him, her hands fastening around his neck and holding on tightly, her face buried in the crook of his neck. She had no intention of ever letting go.

Zac kicked the door shut with his foot and placed her gently on the bed. She was shivering and she wouldn't take her hands from around his neck.

"Pru, let go," he said gently.

She made no move.

"Pru, let go," he repeated. "We need to get you warm."

When again she refused to release him, he grabbed her hands and pried them loose.

"Don't leave me," she cried out to him.

"I won't," he assured her, and reached for the wool blanket to wrap around her. He threw his waistcoat on the chest and hurried into bed with her, drawing her

189

cocoon-wrapped body into the safety of his arms.

She snuggled against him, anxious to get as close as possible.

He held her firm as she tucked her head beneath his chin. "Why did you leave the cabin?"

"I felt so sick and the closed quarters made it worse." She didn't add how frightened the approaching storm made her. She had never liked storms, having feared them since childhood. The wind and then the thunder, loud and bold, and finally the torrential rain . . . She shivered.

He pulled the blanket away from her. "Let me take that from around you. It's better if you lie next to me. My body heat will keep you warm."

She didn't argue. Actually, she preferred being as near to him as possible. She melted comfortably against him as he arranged the blanket over them.

A crack of thunder signaled the approaching storm. Prudence jumped in fright.

He held her firm, running his hand soothingly up and down her arm. "Have you always had a fear of storms?"

"As long as I can remember. My mother would come to my room when there was a storm and sleep with me. She'd sing to me and tell me stories to help me through the night."

"Well, I'm not much of a singer, but I sure can entertain you with stories."

His sincere concern pleased her. "Fairy tales?" she teased.

"Sometimes I wonder," he said with a laugh.

The thunder rumbled loudly again and a spattering of rain turned quickly into a downpour.

"I'm all ears," Prudence said, anxious to hear anything but the storm.

"Remember," he joked, "you asked for it."

The storm and Zac's stories continued throughout the

190

night. Some brought laughter and some brought tears to Prudence. She learned much about him, and as the storm rumbled angrily off into the distance, she realized the meaning of true love. She had no doubt the ache in her chest, the comfort, the churning emotions she was experiencing, were all part of love. The love she felt for Zac Stewart.

The morning brought sunshine, along with mixed feelings, to Prudence. She was confused. All her life, she had thought of matters as either black and white, proper or improper. Yet the emotion that absorbed her now was beyond anything as simple. There was no easy explanation for it, no sound reasoning. She supposed that was why her friends had scoffed at her and laughed when she had asked for a description of the feelings they were experiencing. All had agreed it was indescribable.

Prudence sighed, releasing some of her frustration as her hands gathered her long hair to pin it up. About to fasten it in place, she recalled Zac's request just before he left the cabin. "Leave your hair loose. I like it that way."

She allowed the coppery, thick waves to fall down her back. With a smile she took a pink ribbon, which she had bought at the mercantile, and slipped it under her hair to tie at the top.

She was tugging on her gloves when Zac entered. He was so handsome in his dusky gray suit that she felt her heart race and her legs tremble.

"Breakfast is hot and ready, and the salon—" he stopped, spying her gloves.

"I don't want you wearing them," he said sternly. He walked over to her and took her hand, pulling at the tips of the glove.

Prudence yanked her hand back and away, but his

191

hand closed firmly around her wrist and held her still. "These are no longer necessary."

"To me they are," she snapped. "You have no right."

"I have every right. I'm your husband."

Dictatorship was not to Prudence's liking, and her response was quick and sharp. "In name only."

His head jerked up sharply to look at her as he plucked the glove off her hand, discarding it on the bed. "That can easily be rectified."

Prudence felt her feet go cold, so to speak. After all, last night she had decided she wanted him to make love to her, had even counted on his doing so when he returned to the cabin, but then she had gotten ill and frightened by the storm. Now that he suggested precisely what she had intended, she panicked.

"It's morning," she said without thinking, assuming it would be explanation enough.

His hand touched her breast, squeezing it gently. "All the better to view you."

Panic gripped her like a steel band and she stiffened. "I — I — I'm hungry."

His hand didn't move, though his fingers covered her nipple and teased it into hardness. "So am I."

She was intelligent enough to realize his hunger was of a different nature, and the idea of exposing herself to him in full daylight horrified her. She searched quickly for an avenue of escape, one that would not make him think she was completely uninterested.

Prudence forced a smile, hoping he didn't notice her trembling. "My stomach is still a bit queasy from last night. I could really use a cup of tea to help settle it."

He responded instantly and with such sincere concern that her deception troubled her. "I had forgotten. Forgive me. Let's get you to the dining salon immediately."

He snatched her cape from the chest but left her bonnet where it lay. He threw the cape around her shoulders and fastened the ties. "Not many passengers are up and about yet, so we shall have the salon almost to ourselves."

She turned to reach back for her bonnet, but he tucked her arm down and around his. "All set," he announced as he firmly directed her to the door.

Prudence thought of demanding her bonnet and gloves, thought of giving him a lecture on the proper deportment of a young lady when she went out, but she left those thoughts unspoken. Today she would enjoy. Today she would pretend her marriage was real and her husband loved her.

The day turned magical for Prudence. Zac treated her just as she thought a husband should. Other passengers even commented on what a considerate husband Prudence had. It warmed her heart and made her proud.

Late in the day Zac reluctantly left her in the company of Mrs. Hampton, having received a request from the captain to speak to him. He had been thoroughly enjoying his wife's company and didn't wish to leave. He had given her a quick kiss and promised he'd return soon.

Prudence enjoyed her conversation with Mrs. Hampton. The older woman was a storehouse of information concerning the West. Prudence listened intently while sharing a late afternoon snack of coffee and honey cakes in the dining salon.

"Have to watch out for them injuns . . . can't trust them," Mrs. Hampton said, licking the honey from her fingers. "Savages they are, never know when they might scalp you. Best to keep your distance."

Prudence wiped the sticky crumbs from her fingers with her linen napkin. "The few I have seen appear harmless. And I heard that many are on reservations."

193

Mrs. Hampton waved her chubby hand in dismissal. "Not all of them. You just mind what I say and don't trust them. Same goes for gunslingers."

Prudence placed her coffee cup back on the saucer, not taking the drink she intended. "Really? Why is that?" Her tone was curt, though the older woman didn't notice or else chose to ignore it.

Mrs. Hampton reached for her fourth honey bun. "The gunslinger has an air of danger and mystery about him most women find attractive. What these young ladies don't realize is that these men live and die by their guns. That's the only thing that matters to them. Their real love, their passion, if you understand what I mean, is when they face an opponent."

"There must be some who change and—"

Mrs. Hampton shook her head. "No, my dear, once a gunslinger, always a gunslinger. And let me tell you, those gunslingers aren't faithful to any woman. They love them and leave them, so to speak. But you needn't worry about them. You're a well-bred young woman, that's obvious, and you have a wonderful husband who loves you. You're one of the lucky ones."

Prudence watched as the woman reached for her fifth honey cake. Crazy thoughts muddled her brain as her eyes focused on Mrs. Hampton's full cheeks chewing the sticky cake. Could she be right? Or was Zac different from the others? He hadn't chosen to become a gunfighter. Or had he? Was the story he told her of his youth the truth or a tale?

Zac returned to the dining salon and found his wife's carefree mood gone.

By evening's end she had reverted back to the proper, well-bred, stuffy Prudence Agatha Winthrop. Even her attire had changed. She dressed sedately in a plain brown skirt and basque for supper. She had drawn her hair, so coppery bright when loose, tightly back to sit in a large knot at the nape of her head. She looked god-awful.

The only item she failed to wear was her gloves, having heeded Zac's sharp warning look. She'd left them sitting on her traveling case.

All evening he tried to understand what had gone wrong. He had already surmised that she had an aversion to being seen in the rough. He attributed this to two factors, one being her genteel upbringing and the other her obvious low opinion of herself. Two obstacles he saw no problem in overcoming. But this sudden turnabout of emotions bewildered him, giving rise to speculation that was not to his liking.

Did she once again view him as an infamous gunslinger? Was he once more an unacceptable character in her eyes? Had his stories been too vivid? Did they portray the raw side of his life too profoundly to be to her liking?

Zac stood over the bed where Prudence slept. She had requested, quite primly, that he give her a few moments to see to her nightly toilette. He obliged her with a curt nod, leaving her to undress. He understood, somewhat, her need for privacy, though he had plans that would bring it to an abrupt end.

When he returned she was in bed, with the covers tucked snug beneath her chin and her eyes squeezed shut. A signal that required no explanation to Zac. It read loud and clear. *Don't touch.*

He shook his head and ran his hand through his rumpled hair. He still held the key and the solution to their problem. Yet the time wasn't right to use it. It was time he needed, and time he had, and time he would put to good use.

He reached down and brushed a silky strand of hair off her cheek. "You're my wife," he whispered, the simple statement explaining everything.

Chapter Fourteen

"That's Fort Sully," Zac said, walking up to Prudence as she strained her neck out over the railing to see the large log structure one hundred yards or so ahead on the right bank.

"We'll be stopping there?" she asked unable to keep her enthusiasm from showing.

He was glad she at least still found their journey exciting. He only wished he could say she felt the same sense of elation about him. "For a day or two, then we're off by wagon to my ranch."

"How long will that take?"

Zac shrugged. "Four or five days, depending on the weather conditions."

Prudence looked questioningly down at her willow-green day dress and then up at Zac. "Not suitable?"

"Hardly," he said, touching the thick velvet material and wondering how she wasn't suffocating in the heavy garment. The late spring air was warm, exceptionally so. But it didn't fool him. He knew a cold front could blow down from the north in the next hour and bring with it a good snowstorm. He doubted it would, though, since he had a feel for such things. No, he expected the summer-like weather to continue.

"I'm afraid I'm quite unprepared for the trip to your ranch. Most of my clothes are similar to these, with the exception of the outfit I purchased at the mercantile," she explained, concerned about her lack of functional clothing.

"There's a trading post at the fort. We should be able to find you suitable garments for the trip." As an afterthought, he added, "I like that outfit you bought. It suits you much better than your Boston clothes."

Her manners being what they were, Prudence immediately thanked him for the surprising compliment, then quickly resumed looking at the fort that they were fast approaching.

Zac stepped behind her, pressing into her back as his hands stretched past either side of her to rest on the polished rail. She felt trapped.

"If I'm not mistaken, either tonight or tomorrow night is the fort's spring dance. Would you like to go to the dance, Prudence?"

There was no pretense in his request. Zac sounded as though he actually favored escorting her to the event. The exciting thought sent shivers up her spine and she shuddered.

"Mmmm, do that again; it felt good," Zac said, leaning farther into her.

"Mr. Stewart!" she said, so shaken by his words that she failed to remember the consequences of addressing him as such.

He chuckled as he spun her around to face him. Prudence caught the mischievous glint in his eyes and the teasing, yet tempting smile on his lips. She found it impossible not to respond when he lowered his head and kissed her.

He was unhurried and gentle, almost as though it were their first kiss. Tentative and questioning. Should he seek more? Should he refrain? Does she like it? Does he like it?

197

Will she allow me to kiss her again? Does he want to kiss her again?

Prudence found the crazy thoughts stirring.

His lips regrettably released hers, taking a moment to taint her mouth with a last brush and whispered words. "I love the taste of you, so sharp and vibrant. It stings my senses."

Prudence felt as if all the air had been expelled from her. Her legs wobbled. Her heart beat madly. And she tingled between her legs.

Zac supported her limp weight against him. "I like the effect I have on you, *Mrs. Stewart.*"

Prudence's returned breath brought with it her dander. She opened her mouth to speak.

"Don't bother to deny it, Pru. The condition of your body is proof enough. Can't even stand on your own two feet."

She glared at him, eyes ablaze and ready to battle. Then suddenly, as though doused with a bucket of cold water, she smiled. "Oh, hoot, you're right," she said, and rested her head upon his chest. She just couldn't argue with the truth. It didn't make any sense. And besides, she had decided after a most disturbed night's sleep that she might as well enjoy being Mrs. Stewart while it lasted.

Zac wrapped his arms around her and hugged her to him. "Hoot, is it? You do adapt fast, Pru."

"I'm very adaptable, I'll have you know," she said proudly, slipping her arms around his waist.

"At first I had my doubts, but after watching you handle yourself out here, I must say I'm impressed."

She pulled back enough to look up at him. "Really? You think me capable of surviving out here?"

"Of course I do. You're quite a woman, Prudence Agatha Stewart."

She grinned, and although she didn't realize it, it was a

wicked grin. "And you're quite a man, Mr. . . ." She purposely didn't finish.

Zac shook his head and captured her chin with his fingers. "Don't you know, dear wife, that thoughts can be even more dangerous than words?" He leaned down and once again kissed her. This time it wasn't gentle. It was the kiss of a hungry man, starving for his wife.

Fort Sully was bustling with activity. The passengers who disembarked were immediately embraced by family or friends, and soon hugs and kisses were flying freely while crates of supplies were unloaded.

Prudence was wrapped in a huge hug by Mrs. Hampton's son Benjamin, a bear of a man. She was proud and not a bit surprised when Benjamin shook Zac's hand and her husband didn't even wince. Zac pumped the large man's hand back with just as much, if not more, vigor.

"You must come to the spring dance tomorrow night," Mrs. Hampton insisted. "It's so much fun. Families come from miles around to attend, and there's so much dancing and singing that it's simply grand."

"We'll be there," Zac assured her, and Prudence smiled, eagerly anticipating the event. It would be the first dance she attended as a married woman. And she didn't care that it was in a fort miles from civilization. She planned on enjoying herself.

"I've made arrangements for us to stay in one of the small one-room cabins in the fort for the next two days," Zac explained, walking with her through the open wooden log gates of the fort. He had thought Prudence might find Fort Sully primitive and not at all up to her standards. But from the looks of her unpretentious excitement, she appeared to be having the time of her life.

Prudence was surprised by the many people who called to Zac, announcing they were glad to see him back. He apparently wasn't considered a gunslinger around here and that pleased her. At least she wouldn't have to worry about someone trying to challenge him.

There was a camaraderie at the fort that astonished Prudence. Everyone seemed willing to help each other. She actually felt a bit out of place. Her dress was too stylish. The woman wore simple clothes suited to their surroundings and climate. Prudence was sorry she hadn't worn the outfit she had brought from Mrs. Lewis.

She hurried along after her husband toward the several cabins that occupied the east section of the fort. Zac explained they were made available to folks who were passing through and needed lodgings for a night or two.

Their cabin was neat, clean, and sparse. One bed, none too big, a bureau, scarred from use, a table and two chairs, and a rocker by the hearth were the only furnishings. One window allowed sufficient light to enter and oil lamps sat ready for use.

Zac placed her bags and his on the floor by the bed. "I need to tend to a few things. As soon as I'm finished, I'll take you to the trading post."

Prudence was a bit disappointed. She wanted to explore the fort and the trading post while excitement still stirred her. Zac didn't suggest that she go off on her own, so she assumed it was best she was accompanied by him and didn't question his judgment.

She took off her hat, removed her gloves, and turned to speak to Zac. Her words lodged in her throat. Prudence paled considerably before heat rushed up her entire body to singe her cheeks.

He stood, his back to her, completely naked. She felt as though she had turned to stone. She was unable to move, to breathe, to think. His body was simply gorgeous.

Wide shoulders gave way to a trim waist that connected with a nice, firm, round bottom that attached to legs thick with muscles. She spied the scar that she had noticed on another occasion and saw that it traveled down to the middle of his firm cheek. She wondered with sympathy and simultaneous arousal just how he happened to come by it.

"Shall I turn around so you can inspect the rest of me, Pru?"

Prudence blushed to the roots of her hair and swung around. "I — I — I'm sorry. I — I — didn't mean to — to —"

"Admire me?" he asked teasingly.

Prudence closed her eyes. Even though Zac was behind her and no longer in her view, she felt it necessary to do so. "If you had told me you were changing clothes, I would have —"

"I don't mind you seeing me naked," he interrupted. "Actually, I like the idea. You can look at my body any-time, honey. And you are definitely welcome to touch it if you'd like."

Prudence groaned.

"Now, that hungry sound is best saved for another time."

Prudence didn't think she could blush any more than she already had, but she did. The red heat scorched her cheeks and she could have sworn her temperature hit well over one hundred degrees.

"You can turn around now. I'm decent," he announced candidly.

Prudence hesitated and turned slightly to peek from the corner of her eye. He was dressed, and much differently than she had ever seen him.

"Buckskins," he said and held out his hands, turning around for her inspection. "Not as great as me naked, but . . ."

He was wrong about that, Prudence thought. The buckskins were tight in all the right places, leaving very little to the imagination.

"So what do you think?" he asked.

"You look" — she paused a moment, searching for the proper word — "very nice."

That wasn't what she really thought and they both knew it. Zac was about to call her to task for it, when a knock on the door interrupted him.

"Mrs. Hampton," he said in greeting as the short, round woman walked right past him into the cabin.

"Hello, Mr. Stewart," she said, her smile generous. "Prudence, I'm on my way to the trading post . . . most of the women are. Thought you'd like to join me and meet a few of the ladies."

She was about to accept, when she recalled Zac's offer to take her there later. "Would you mind if I went with Mrs. Hampton?" she asked him.

He was surprised that she sought permission. Since he'd met her, she had done exactly as she pleased, regardless of his opinion. It was nice to see that she'd begun to consider his feelings. "Not at all."

"Good, good," Mrs. Hampton chimed. "Fetch your bonnet, but don't bother with that jacket. It's a warm one today."

Prudence followed her direction, leaving her discarded jacket on the chair but reaching for her gloves.

Zac caught her intention and was about to object as unobtrusively as possible, when he noticed her hesitation and then the slight shake of her head. He was overjoyed to see that she, herself, had decided against wearing them.

Mrs. Hampton bid Zac good day. Prudence followed with a quick smile to her husband and an "I'll see you later" tossed over her shoulder.

Before she could take another step, his strong arm snaked around her waist and pulled her back hard against him.

She gripped his fingers, tugging at them for release, but they were firm and she could not budge them. "Zac," she pleaded softly.

"She forgot to give me a good-bye kiss," he called to Mrs. Hampton, who had turned to see where Prudence had gone.

The older woman smiled, nodded, and walked ahead, respecting the young couple's privacy.

"A kiss isn't the only thing you forgot, Pru," he said, giving her a light peck on the cheek.

She was flustered. "What did I forget besides the kiss?"

"You forgot to tell me what you really thought of my buckskins."

"But I did," she insisted. "You look nice, very nice."

His face still rested next to hers and she felt him shake his head. "No, Pru. I want to know what your first thought was. The one that made you catch your breath and stop speaking."

"I don't know —"

"Oh, yes you do," he contended strongly. "And I'll hear it, or here you'll stay in my arms until I do."

Mrs. Hampton had stopped and glanced back.

"She's waiting," Prudence said, squirming against him.

"That she is. Now tell me."

There was no dissuading him. He'd have his answer or else embarrass the daylights out of her. "Appetizing," she mumbled, and wiggled more strenuously to free herself.

"What?" Zac asked, hearing what she had said but wanting her to repeat it.

"Appetizing," she said with strength but not with pitch.

Zac grabbed her hand and spun her around. "You can taste me any time, honey."

Prudence blushed. Zac kissed her. And she was sent off to join Mrs. Hampton with a gentle pat to her backside.

Zac Stewart was not the ordinary, proper husband she had envisioned she would marry. The thought brought a mighty wide grin to her face as she walked toward the trading post with the talkative Mrs. Hampton.

* * *

Prudence found Old Bill, the man who ran the trading post, chock-full of information. He knew everything, from the best recipes for rattlesnake meat to the surefire cure for a sore tooth.

"Pull that sucker right out the mouth," Old Bill told her. "Never bother you again. 'Course, you gotta pour the rotgut on it and that burns like hell, but you can't let the pus set in. Pus sets in and you know you'll be kissin' heaven's gate in no time." Prudence was fascinated by his fountain of facts. She stood listening intently. Mrs. Hampton had warned her that once you got the old geezer going, there was no shutting him up. But Prudence had already seen to her purchases and had conversed with the other woman about fashions and such. Now she wanted more information on the West, and Old Bill certainly was a professor when it came to that.

"Now take the injuns," Bill said, pausing a moment to spit a wad of tobacco directly into the brass spittoon not far from his foot. "They're an altogether different breed of folk."

"Yeah, savages," commented a man on the way out the door.

Bill ignored him and continued as though uninterrupted. "They know things we don't, 'else they wouldn't have survived out here in this wilderness so long on their own. They're a special people. Much can be learned from them, but as usual, the government sticks its two cents in and messes everything up.

"Got a good recipe for rabbit stew," Old Bill said, changing the subject, which he did often.

Prudence took it all in, making a point of remembering that it was the wild onions that give the stew its special flavor.

"Granny Hayes once told me—"

"You know Granny Hayes?" Prudence asked, startling those around her, since usually no one could or would interrupt Old Bill when he was talking.

"Sure do. Do you?" he asked, not a bit put out by her interruption and not bothering to wait for her answer. "Me and Granny go way back. We used to hunt beaver together, even tried mining for gold once or twice. She's a mighty good woman."

Prudence found it hard to contain her excitement. If he knew Granny, then perhaps he knew of her mother. Since he had paused, she jumped in with her question. "Did you know of a woman called Lee? Long, dark hair, not as tall as me, big eyes—"

"Sure enough," Bill said, a wide toothless grin brightening his aging face. "One nice woman. Good cook. Taught me a thing or two. She was—"

"Here?" Prudence asked anxiously. "Is she still here? Where can I find her?"

Old Bill shook his head and scratched his short gray beard. "Wish I could help you there. Was sad myself when she just up and disappeared one day. She'd listen to my stories for hours and never complained. Never shared any of her own. Thought she might, but she kept her business to herself. Some people like that, and there ain't no sense pestering them. They talk in their own good time. Yes sir, sure do miss her. Baked the best rum cake around."

Old Bill went on talking, but Prudence only half listened. She remembered her mother's special rum cake. She'd bake it at Christmas and for special occasions. Prudence was only allowed a small piece, since it was soaked in rum. Her father, however, would fill himself with it, as would holiday and party guests.

Why? Why did she leave her husband and child? It couldn't have been the lure of the West that had enticed her mother, although Prudence could understand its strange attraction. There was a sense of freedom out here for a woman that was hard to find back east. So what was

205

Lenore Winthrop's motive? Everyone Prudence had spoken to had commented on what a wonderful woman she was. Why would a woman whom so many thought so highly of walk out on her family?

By the time Prudence returned to the cabin she was depressed. She deposited her packages on the bureau and sunk down into the rocking chair before the empty hearth. Lenore Winthrop never stayed long enough in one place. Was she afraid of being discovered? Was she frightened that someone was following her? Or did she want to make certain her family never found her?

It was just plain luck she had spoken to Old Bill and discovered her mother had been here. She had no idea where to go now. Lenore just kept disappearing. Each time Prudence felt her in her grasp, she'd slip away again.

Perhaps this journey was unwise. Perhaps it would have been better if she had gone on thinking her mother dead. At least then she would still believe her mother loved her, cared for her, and was taken away through no will of her own.

Dreaming again. She'd been doing a lot of that lately. And it usually only brought her more hurt, more pain, and more regret.

Better to live in the real world, to face its problems and complexities, instead of dreaming of what could be, what might be.

A tear fell from her eye while shadows darkened the room. Dusk had settled over the area, bringing with it the calm and quiet of early evening. A time for families to gather and share the evening meal, as well as the news of the day's events.

She was alone. Far from home and the one person who loved her, her father. The only sure love in her life.

The tears continued to roll down her cheeks and splatter onto her beige blouse, staining the delicate silk. She had never been given to tears lightly. She was always in control of herself and her feelings. That was why it was so hard for her to contain this unwarranted show of emotion.

The shadows further bathed the cabin in darkness and Prudence continued to sit alone, crying and rocking.

Zac approached the cabin and worried that Prudence hadn't returned yet, since no light flickered from the lone window. It had taken a bit longer than he had intended to make the necessary arrangements for them to leave day after tomorrow. Then he had remembered they had no food and had stopped at the fort's cookhouse to see if Curly had something to spare. The large, jovial man gave him more than he needed, but he accepted it graciously upon Curly's insistence.

He pushed the door open with his elbow, since his hands were full, and walked in. He was surprised to see Prudence rocking in the dark and more surprised to hear her sobs.

He placed the packages on the table and approached her with trepidation.

"Pru?" he summoned her softly. She didn't respond but continued to rock.

He walked up alongside her and tried again. "Pru," he said more strongly. Still no answer.

He stepped in front of her and bent down before her. "Pru, honey," he said gently, and placed his hand on her thigh. He was taken aback by her flood of tears and by the condition of her tear-stained blouse. It appeared she had been crying steadily for some time. Her eyes were proof enough. They were red and puffy, and her lashes resembled thick, wet spikes. His heart nearly broke considering the pain she suffered, and a gut-wrenching anger tore at him and toward the person who had been the cause of her hurt.

"Honey," he said, moving his hand to cup the side of her face. "What happened?"

Prudence looked at him and the distress that registered in her eyes filled him with grief. "M — my mother di — didn't love me."

Zac wanted to strangle Lenore Winthrop with his own bare hands. He half hoped Pru was wrong and she was dead; then at least Pru would know her mother had loved her. The other half of him wanted her alive so he could tell her exactly what he thought of her.

He pushed his own anger aside to comfort her. "You don't know that," he said, wiping her tears with his finger only to have others follow.

She nodded and sighed heavily. "Yes, I do. She hated me. She was ashamed of me. She —"

"You don't know any of that. You're just assuming it all. When we find her then you'll find the truth just like your grandmother told you."

"I'll never find her. Every time I think I'm close, she disappears. Old Bill knew her, he even ate her rum cake. The rum cake she always made at Christmas. The one she would let me help her bake."

Zac heard the hurt and disappointment of a small child, could even understand it. He often thought of his mother, remembering only the fresh scent of flowers that had surrounded her. But there must have been more she had shared with him. Something good and kind for him to be able to care and love, since his father had displayed no emotions toward him. And he also understood that his mother hadn't wanted to leave him, that she loved him, always had and always would. Not so for Pru. Her mother had deserted her. A sure signal to a small child that she wasn't loved.

Zac wiped her eyes, but it wasn't the tears he wanted to remove. It was her pain. "Will you make the rum cake for me?" Perhaps if she shared it with someone else, her hurt would ease. She could build new memories.

She smiled, almost shyly. "I don't think I'd make it as well as my mother did."

He grinned and thumped his chest with his other hand. "You can practice on me. I eat anything."

Her face brightened some and he didn't have to wipe any more tears away. "Old Bill told me about his rabbit stew. It sounds quite delicious. Perhaps I could cook that, too."

"Sounds good to me. When we get to the ranch, I'll hunt you a rabbit. Then you can make the stew for us. Which brings us to food and my empty, protesting stomach. How about you?"

She nodded readily. "Yes, I am rather hungry."

"Good," he said, standing. "I brought us a feast. But I think we best light some lamps if we want to see what we're eating."

Prudence smiled and stood herself. "Let me help."

They worked in friendly companionship. Prudence recounted some of Old Bill's stories and Zac added some of his own.

"Where did you get all this food? It's delicious," she said between munching on a tasty chicken leg.

"Curly, the fort's cook. We're long-time friends. I did him a favor once, and he always makes certain I have plenty to eat when I'm around."

Prudence focused on Zac's face while he spoke. She hadn't expected such tenderness and understanding from him. He was turning out to be a good husband, far better than she had first thought and one she wouldn't mind having for the duration.

She reached for another flaky biscuit. "It must have been *some* favor."

Zac shook his head, his eyes lighting in amusement. "It was. I saved his life."

For the next thirty minutes Prudence sat intrigued by

the story. Each tale she heard taught her more and more about the West. And it taught her the importance of true friendship and trust.

After clearing off the table, Prudence took her night-gown from her traveling case. She held it over her arm as she searched the room for some tiny nook of privacy where she could change. She found none and worried over the dilemma she now faced.

Zac watched her. She had been through enough for one day; he wouldn't put her through anything else. "I'm going to step outside a few minutes."

Prudence smiled at her stroke of luck, then realized it had nothing to do with luck. "Thank you," she said. He winked as he closed the door behind him.

She was in bed when he returned, snug up against the wall, leaving distance between them.

Zac doused the lights, slipping out of his clothes and into the bed. He didn't need to see her distance; he felt it. But then he had suspected she would pull away, avoid contact.

He wouldn't pursue the issue now. He had time. Then he heard the sobs, soft and pitiful. She was trying so hard to hold them back.

"Damn," he mumbled and reached out, pulling her against him. "It's all right, honey. It's all right. I'm here."

Prudence clung to him. His hard, warm flesh felt good. She was safe in his arms, protected. He was there for her.

She cried even harder as she listened to his whispered words of comfort. And her thoughts cried out the words her lips kept locked away. *You'll leave me, too*.

Chapter Fifteen

The dance was like none she had ever attended. And she loved every minute of it.

The building used as a mess-house for the soldiers had been scrubbed clean. Tables had been arranged off to the sides for people to eat at, while leaving sufficient room for dancing in the center. In the back, out of the way of the dance floor, sat the food table.

There were no fancy sandwiches or artful cakes dripping in sweet icing upon silver trays and pure white linens. The fare was plain, hardy, and delicious, served in sturdy crockery on wooden tables covered with bright red and white check tablecloths.

Curly had outdone himself as had the women, who brought platters and bowls laden with mouth-watering food to add to the already-abundant selections.

Prudence had dressed in the gray skirt and white blouse she had purchased at the mercantile. She was scrubbed and shining from her recent bath. She allowed her coppery hair to remain free, except for the two ivory combs that swept the sides up and back. She told herself it was a more practical style for the evening's event.

Zac had teased her, insisting she had recalled his preference for her hair loose and sought to please him. She had remained staunchly silent, not wanting to argue against the truth.

Prudence tapped her foot in time to the music. It was a lively tune, and the dance floor was crowded with couples swirling around.

Several pairs of female eyes were busy assessing her husband. She learned quickly that the women had no qualms about asking the men to dance. And Zac looked mighty tempting in his black trousers and white shirt. His hair was a bit rumpled, but on him it didn't look unkempt. It looked "damn" sexy.

Spying a young, attractive female making her way through the crowd toward Zac, Prudence grabbed his hand. "Let's dance."

Zac smiled as he took her in his arms on the dance floor and swirled her about. He liked her possessiveness. It felt good. He didn't want to ruin it by telling her that the woman, Sally Fry, was a friend of his. A very married friend.

The pleasurable evening wore on and turned into a night filled with unforgettable memories for Prudence. She was swamped with invitations to dance. Never in all the years she had attended socials had so many men asked her to dance. She felt like the most popular young girl at her first social. It was all simply wonderful.

Zac didn't agree. At first when he couldn't get another dance with his wife, he shrugged it off. He wanted her to have a good time, hoped sincerely that she would. But he had never expected the men to monopolize her. He had to admit she looked damn pretty. Her face was flushed a soft pink color from the exertion of the dances and probably from her laughter. Her full breasts and generous hips were quite nicely displayed beneath her skirt and blouse. And her hair shone coppery bright, highlighting the scattering of freckles across her nose. Yes sir, she looked mighty appealing. Actually too damn appealing.

Zac marched onto the dance floor, where Prudence was occupied in a dance with a young man. He knocked the man on the shoulder, causing half his body to sag as he turned.

"Mind?" Zac asked, so malevolently that the man rapidly shook his head and scurried off.

"You scared him," Prudence scolded softly, but she was happy to be held in her husband's arms once again.

"I don't care," he snapped wolfishly. "You're my wife and should behave properly."

Prudence was struck by the vehemence of his statement. He meant it. And she couldn't help but smile at the irony of it. "You're calling me to task on acting properly?"

"Yes," he said, his firm hold increasing around her waist so his fingers bit into her flesh.

"My decorum is impeccable. There is no justification in your accusation."

His eyes narrowed and his lips were set firmly in determination. "A married woman doesn't dance with every man around."

Prudence was affronted. "I have not danced with every man here. And besides, you have no right to dictate what I can and cannot do."

Zac yanked her closer to him. Her body hit his, and with much difficulty, she managed to pull away to the proper distance.

"I have every right," Zac said, loudly enough for her ears alone. "You're my wife."

"In name only," she retaliated.

Zac yanked her back again and this time kept her smack up against him, to the surprise of those around them. "That can be rectified quite easily."

Prudence babbled, distracted by the fact that her body found his hard one much to her liking. "You — you — you —"

"Your husband," he finished. "And you had

213

best behave like my wife."

The warning was sharply issued and left no room for retort. Prudence remained tight-lipped and finished the dance.

A high-stepping tune started almost immediately, and Old Bill swept her into his arms as Zac was escorting her firmly by the arm off the dance floor.

"Come on, gal. Ain't danced with a young pretty one like you in a long time."

Prudence didn't hesitate. She went with him. If she stayed with Zac, she would probably scratch his eyes out, so angry she was. The impudent thought pleased her, since it was far from proper. And that was the distance she sought from anything "proper" — very far.

Old Bill was a terrific dancer. His steps were spry and quick for his seventy plus years, and Prudence found herself having difficulty keeping up with him. She was certain, had no doubt, that the West raised a different breed of people. Strong and resilient.

Bill kept her busy with a second dance, and when that finished she was grabbed by Ned Fry and swung onto the dance floor again. It continued like that for the next thirty minutes. Prudence thought she'd collapse from the exertion, but she was having so much fun that her body adjusted and she kept on dancing.

She caught sight of Zac stalking the sidelines of the dance floor like a predatory animal. He looked coiled and ready to attack. Her sensible side warned her to join him and soothe the beast within him. But her womanly side, the one that enjoyed seeing a man seethe with jealousy, especially since she had never experienced this sensation before, cajoled her to push further. And she did.

She entertained three more partners, smiling, swirling, and having the time of her life. By the time she walked over to where Zac stood, she was flushed and breathless.

"Oh my," she said, smiling up at him and taking several deep breaths. "I didn't know dancing could be so much fun."

He stood with his hands behind his back and a stern expression on his face. "Enjoying yourself, are you?"

"Very much," she answered honestly. "And I'm very thirsty." She thought he might act the gentleman and get her a glass of cider, but he remained still, not moving an inch.

Prudence looked around, ignoring his obviously bad mood, and spied the cider bowl. She licked her parched lips in anticipation, pressed her hand to his chest, and gazed up into his dark eyes. "I'm going to get myself a drink."

He grabbed her wrist, keeping her hand solid against his chest. "No you're not. I'll get it."

Her stubbornness asserted itself. He was acting quite the heavy-handed husband. And she would have no part of it. "I'll get the cider myself." She tugged at her hand to free it as she stepped to walk away. She was brought to an abrupt halt when her hand was not released but met with even further resistance.

"I'll get it," he said, sounding as though he were issuing a threat instead of offering his assistance.

Not wanting to cause a scene, she nodded.

"You wait here," he ordered. "And don't dare let me see you on that dance floor again." He dropped her hand and marched off.

Prudence could only stare at his retreating back. He was behaving quite oddly. Why should he care whom she danced with? Or how often she danced? He acted like a jealous husband. And their marriage status really did not warrant it. Perhaps it was for the benefit of those around him, or possibly for the sake of his image. It wouldn't look good for him, an infamous gunslinger, to have a wife who openly disobeyed him.

Prudence shrugged, tired of trying to understand his odd mood, and turned to watch the dancing. She was grabbed instantly by Old Bill.

"Come on, gal. We're gonna kick up our heels in a reel," he said, tugging her along beside him. She had only a moment to look back and see Zac, glass in hand, looking furiously at her.

Prudence had never laughed so hard or had so much fun in her life. She wasn't familiar with the steps, but Old Bill directed her with such skill that it didn't matter and in minutes she was swinging along with him.

Old Bill deposited her at Zac's side when the dance was over. "Got yourself some gal there. Not only pretty, but a good dancer. You're a lucky man." He slapped Zac on the back and walked off.

Before Prudence could say a word to him, another man came up to her and asked her to dance.

"No!" Zac said menacingly. "She's tired."

"That wasn't pol—"

"Don't bother," he snapped. "I'm not in a polite mood."

Prudence was annoyed by his grumpy attitude. "Then perhaps we should leave, since you seem so displeased with the evening."

He grabbed her hand. "My precise intentions."

Prudence was being hurried past people who called out "Goodnight" and "Glad to have met you" and "Hope to see you again." She answered as best she could, feeling herself blush when she heard the word *newlywed* followed by giggles.

Zac didn't bother to slow down once outside. He kept up the brisk pace, pulling her right along.

There was a bit of a chill in the air tonight and Prudence felt it through the light cotton of her blouse. It tingled her warm skin, flushed from so many dances.

Zac paid no heed to the briskness of the weather. He just marched straight for the cabin. Once inside, though, he immediately saw to building a small fire in the stone hearth. That task accomplished, he turned in full fury on Prudence, who was shaking the wrinkles from her nightgown.

"I thought your *refined* upbringing taught you better than to act as you did tonight."

Prudence stood wide-eyed with her mouth agape. She couldn't believe what she had heard. And Zac intended for her to hear more, much more.

"You're a married woman and should act accordingly. Dancing with every man who asks you is disgraceful," he admonished while pacing back and forth before the hearth.

"Accordingly? Disgraceful?" she spat, throwing her nightgown on the bed.

"Exactly," he yelled, stopping his pacing long enough to shake an offending finger at her.

That really upped Prudence's temper. "I'll have you know I've always acted accordingly and never—I repeat, never—have I acted disgracefully."

"Well tonight certainly proved that it wasn't for lack of trying. You know exactly how to do it."

Prudence marched up in front of him, forcing him once again to stop pacing. She raised her hand and, as she spoke, emphasized each word with a poke to his hard chest. "You have no room to talk. You behaved like a raging, jealous husband tonight, an uncalled-for exhibition of your insecurity. You just didn't want the mighty Zac Stewart's, infamous gunslinger's image to be marred. After all, how would it look for his wife to do as she pleased? Not to jump when he ordered. Not to sit when he commanded. You're a self-centered bore."

Zac was looking down at her rather chillingly. "Are you finished?"

"No," she said, her tone lacking the confidence it had

had when she started her tirade. "You, *Mr. Stewart,* are no gentleman."

A muscle in Zac's cheek twitched, warning her he was fighting for control. She took a step back, but his hand was too fast. It reached out in a flash and gripped her wrist, dragging her back to him.

"I told you once before I'm no gentleman, and I told you *not* to call me Mr. Stewart."

Prudence eased her head back away from him, but his other hand grasped a handful of her hair along her nape.

"It's time you learned your lesson, Mrs. Stewart."

While his hand forced her head toward him, his lips came down to meet hers. She had expected urgency, perhaps even brutality, but his kiss was light, merely a whisper. It fanned her lips while his tongue bid entrance to her mouth. It wasn't a demand. It was a request, a sensual request. One she found hard to deny.

His warm lips changed from a whispered touch to a caress, while his tongue slipped in and skimmed the tip of her tongue. As she withdrew hers, so did he. Then his was back again.

This sensuous, teasing game of his was spine-tingling. Her body began to heat, to respond, to want more of what he offered. The movement of his lips now turned from a caress to a pleasurable pressure, and his tongue again sought hers.

Tentatively, it touched hers and withdrew again, but this time Prudence followed. She wanted more, so much more. She caught him as he left her mouth, and with only a bit of hesitancy did she reach out and stop him.

The tip of her tongue teased his with a flicker and slowly she drew him in. They played with each other, mindless of everything but their sensually playful tongues.

His hands slipped around her waist and brought her

closer, while her arms went around his neck without pause.

Zac dragged himself away from her mouth. Neither was willing to relinquish the other, but it was necessary for them to breathe. He then kissed her closed eyes, one after the other.

"Your taste is intoxicating," he whispered and kissed the tip of her nose. "I can't get enough of you."

He kissed each cheek, hot and red from their encounter. He kissed along her jaw, beneath her chin, down her neck and up again.

Prudence moaned with regret when he stopped, only to find herself turned around, her body brought solid up against his. His arms wrapped around her so his hands could cup her breasts while he feasted on her ear and neck.

He nibbled at her earlobe and along her neck, raising gooseflesh over her arms and bringing a pitiful moan from deep within her throat.

"You like that, don't you, Pru?"

She only had the strength to give a slight nod and his response was a soft chuckle. "There's lots more to like," he whispered, and his thumb and forefinger pinched softly at her nipple through the cotton material.

"Mmmm," she moaned in pleasure.

"Tell me you want more, Pru. Tell me to go further." He moved his one hand down low over her belly and pushed her back against him.

There was no mistaking that he wanted her, and the thought excited her even more. He actually desired her; she could feel it.

He moved into her, pressing against her skirt while his fingers continued to torment her hardened nipples. "Tell me, Pru. Tell me you want me. Tell me to strip you naked. Tell me to touch you, taste you, take you."

His words burned like fire in her ears and her body.

Her legs trembled and she went wet between her legs. She hugged them closed, frightened by how much she needed him.

"Don't!" he said harshly, moving his hand down along the front of her skirt to urge her legs apart. "Don't lock me out. Your body wants me. You want me. Don't deny us this, Pru."

Finding a small amount of courage, she spoke. "I'm frightened, Zac."

He pressed his face alongside hers. "I know, honey, but don't be. I won't hurt you, and you won't be sorry. I promise. Trust me. Let me love you."

Love you. Yes, she wanted him to love her. Oh, how she wanted him to love her.

"Don't think, Pru," he urged. "Don't think." With that, his hand began to release the band of her skirt.

Chapter Sixteen

The flickering light of the fire cast strange shadows around the room. The odd forms dipped and swayed gracefully. Their peculiar shapes reminded Prudence of dignified couples with their heads and bodies bowed in conversation. It was odd, for she imagined their whispers concerned her. She could even hear their faint hisses and sneers of disapproval.

Shocking.

Outrageous.

Disgraceful.

She shivered though she stood before the warmth of the fire's glow. All that remained of her clothes were her undergarments and grateful she was for their meager protection.

"Zac," she whispered, grasping his hand before he could remove her cotton chemise.

Zac heard the uncertainty, ragged and breathless, upon her lips and felt the reluctance in her shiver. "Don't think about the doubts, honey. Lock them out. Push them away. Tonight there's just you and me."

She was frightened, not of the intimate act they would share but of how he would view her. She would be naked, yet worse, vulnerable. Could she trust him to understand? This man who was her husband but not by his choice. This man who didn't love her.

His hand shifted its way beneath the thin chemise to cushion her heavy breast. "Do you know how good you feel to me? Do you know what touching you does to me?"

Her back was still to him, and his face nested in the crook of her neck, close to her ear. A sensitive spot that tingled each time his breath fanned it. She turned her head to shake the no that would not come to her trembling lips. The slight awkward movement could be read otherwise.

The invitation, even if it weren't meant as such, was too much for Zac to resist. "Pru." His warm breath rippled along her sensitive flesh, sending goosebumps down her arms. He ran the wet tip of his tongue along the column of her neck as his lips traced in feathery lightness.

This time the tingle shot to her toes.

His hand, cushioning her breast so gently, began to massage it in alternate strong and soft squeezes. "I want to taste your nipples, Pru. Will you let me taste them?"

Her mind was muddled with emotions she didn't understand. Didn't want to understand. At the moment all that mattered was that Zac not stop touching her. She nodded, her voice failing her once again.

His hand left her and she protested with a desperate sigh.

"Easy, honey, easy," he urged, taking only minutes to slip out of his clothes.

His touch returned to her, but this time to unfasten the remaining garments and strip them from her body before she could change her mind.

Prudence almost faltered, fear suddenly attacking her senses, fighting its way through the fog of sensual pleasure Zac had created.

He had expected this moment of resistance. That was why he was now bent in front of her, removing her last garment. After tossing it aside, he came upward slowly, carefully inspecting each inch of her with a soft, tentative touch until he reached her flat belly.

He kissed her then, right below her navel, and he felt her sharp intake of breath. He circled her navel with the tip of his tongue, before slipping up along her midriff to between her breasts. He didn't pause or give thought to his actions. He had planned every move.

His tongue flickered across her nipple like a fluttering butterfly wing, and Prudence's legs gave way. Zac grabbed her, turning her back to him and turning them both to face the fire's light.

Prudence's breathing was rapid. Her heart beat madly. And she could swear her legs were no longer attached to her.

The fire's light bathed her in a shimmering reddish glow, making her pale flesh appear simmering hot and appetizing.

"You're beautiful," he whispered, stationing one arm firmly around and beneath her breasts while his other hand ran over any part of her flesh he could reach. "Your skin is like plush velvet. It excites me. Your hips are full and strong enough to take the strength of me. And your legs are not thin slivers, but taut and strong. Lord, but I can't wait to have them locked around me."

The sensual fog still muddled her brain, but a small voice cried out like a beacon, "Does he mean it?" She wanted to believe they were so strongly connected that he could read her thoughts and that this caused him to answer her concern.

"The truth, Pru. What I tell you is the truth. I would never lie to you. Never hurt you. You're my wife and the most 'damn' beautiful woman I've ever seen naked."

She wanted to cry and scream all at once. But most of all, she wanted to tell him how very much she loved him. She settled on the closest thing to it. "Make love to me, Zac."

"All night, honey. All night," he whispered, and swung her up into his arms and carried her to the bed.

He laid her upon the bed and rested alongside her. Propped on one elbow, he looked down over her, running his hand soothingly across her breasts, her stomach, her thighs.

Prudence felt as if she were being stroked with a velvet glove, so soft was his caress.

"I can't touch you enough." His hand slipped between her legs, and his mouth moved over hers and captured it with such tenderness that Prudence thought she would cry.

Odd that his touch in such an intimate place should feel so comforting, so right. She didn't flinch when his fingers slipped inside her. They felt too good.

"Like that, do you?" he teased, nibbling along her bottom lip.

"Yes," she whispered, since she found herself quite breathless.

"Good, because I intend to do more, much more." His fingers came alive with the skill of a master lover. And his mouth feasted on her breasts, tormenting the hard nubs with light nips that puckered her nipples even further.

Prudence ached all over with a painful pleasure. Never, never in her wild imaginings had she thought it would feel like this. And never had she thought she would want so desperately to touch a man. But she didn't have the courage and she wasn't certain if it was the proper thing to do.

He raised his head and moved his fingers down her thighs to knead the inside of each one, spreading them farther apart.

"I've never tasted a virgin." He smiled just before the tip of his tongue touched between her breasts and traveled down the length of her body in deliberate slowness.

"Zac," she cried in a high-pitched squeal, understanding full well his intentions but not understanding how he could even think to do such a . . .

Her thoughts evaporated the instant Zac's tongue licked her bud of pleasure. She moaned so deeply, so agonizingly, that Zac couldn't help but laugh before doing more of the same.

There wasn't an inch of her intimate zone that his mouth or tongue didn't taste.

"Damn, Pru, I want you so bad, I hurt," he mumbled, swinging himself over her like a majestic beast about to ravish her.

"I don't want you to hurt." Her words were sincere, as she failed to realize what he meant.

He smiled as he placed his hands on each side of her head, holding himself stiff above her. "Yes you do, dear wife. You want me hurting badly, very badly."

That was when Prudence felt him. He shifted his body just enough for his stiff manhood to rest between her legs. He was hot, thick, and pulsating with life. It frightened the hell out of her and she snapped her legs closed.

"Don't!" he ordered more harshly than he had intended, and immediately softened his tone. "If you don't resist me, it won't hurt. Please, Pru, trust me."

Her answer came in the tentative reach of her hands to his arms, locking onto them as if for dear life.

"Another night when you've grown accustomed to

me, I'll give you a rough ride. Tonight I will be gentle," he coaxed, attempting to ease her quietude with a brush of his lips across her breasts. "Now relax and let me become part of you."

Prudence needed no instructions; his words alone told her all. She parted her legs to accommodate him. He probed gently with his shaft, easing her sheath to welcome him.

Zac threw his head back and fought the overpowering urge to rush into her. He had promised her he wouldn't hurt her, and he had no desire to cause her pain. Perhaps a pleasurable pain, but certainly no physical discomfort. He was well aware of the trust she had placed in him, and he would not harm that fragile gift for anything.

But staying under control was so difficult. The throbbing organ between his legs was issuing orders that his mind was fighting desperately to ignore. *Rush,* it insisted, urged. Get into that wet, hot sweetness as fast and furious as possible.

He shook the damaging demands away and looked down into her face. Her eyelashes, so long and coppery, fluttered faintly and her mouth sat open just enough to make *him* tingle. Her chest heaved with each breath. Her soft whimpers and sighs reminded him of a helpless kitten, reaching out to him for stroking and satisfaction, adding to his explosive state.

"Damn," he whispered.

"Mr. Stewart," Prudence smiled artfully, then released his arms. She slipped her hands up around his back and pulled him down to her.

His returned smile was gratifying, and he came down over her slowly, entering her deeper as he went. Inch by inch she took him inside her. When she tensed he eased back, but a shake of her head warned him it

226

wasn't necessary. And with a control he had doubted he possessed, he slid farther in until he saw her bite at her lower lip.

"Pru?" he questioned gently.

"Please, Zac. Please, I want you so much." Her voice ached with that want, and without hesitation she pulled him roughly toward her.

He rushed into her then, unable to stop himself. She cried out and he stilled for a moment.

"Don't, please," she begged.

He needed no further encouragement. He moved gladly within her, and as his rhythm increased, so did her eager response. He had been right about her. She was no shriveling prude. She was a hot-blooded woman and all his.

Their tempo escalated to a wild cadence. He pulsated. She throbbed. They matched each other thrust for thrust, their frenzied pace urging, pushing, and finally erupting.

Zac captured her strangled cry with his mouth, wanting to savor the moment of her fulfillment. It tasted like nothing he had ever experienced, unearthly and magical.

He found himself unable to move off her, out of her. He wanted, actually needed, to remain locked within her. He felt one with her, so deeply cushioned in her female womb, like a newborn unwilling to give up the comfort and love surrounding him.

His concern for her overrode his nesting instincts, and he raised himself only slightly to look at her. Her sweet, yet fretful smile warned him she still felt vulnerable, uncertain, and her doubt caused him pain.

His words now were important, very important, and he chose them wisely and truthfully. "I feel as though I've just lost my virginity."

Her eyes widened and the corners of her mouth rose.

He kissed her. "I've never — ever — felt the way you've just made me feel."

"Zac." She touched her finger to his mouth, sending a shiver racing down his back. "You are telling me the truth?"

He laughed and wiggled his butt. "A man can't lie, honey. Can't you feel what your touch does to me?"

She giggled in relief.

"Don't laugh, you hussy. I've never gotten aroused so fast after just making love to a woman. I always needed time to recoup."

Prudence felt his pulsating swell, stimulating to say the least. She teasingly rotated her hips beneath him.

He groaned. "Are you trying to kill me or tempt me?"

"A little of both," she whispered.

"You learn quick, Mrs. Stewart."

"I adapt, Mr. Stewart."

He smiled and lowered his mouth to hers.

Prudence stood at the lone window watching the blackness of the night give way to the dawn of a new day. And a new day it was for her. She tugged the white wool shawl up over her bare shoulder. The fringe tickled her bottom and she sighed.

Whoever thought she'd stand naked before a window with only a knitted shawl as a cover? And that her husband would be sound asleep only a few feet away?

"Improper behavior, Prudence," she scolded with a giggle.

Her giggle faded and her expression grew serious. She had always thought she would marry a man equal to her in social status and that they would share a life like those around them, practical and boring. She would perform her wifely duties accordingly, give birth when expected, and retire to her own room, only to share her husband's bed when he extended an invitation.

But now, now she had tasted of a far different lifestyle. A far different husband. The type of husband that had haunted her dreams and wouldn't let go. He was everything she had ever wanted and more. Strong, yet tender. Handsome, but not self-centered. Domineering at times, yet caring and thoughtful. And best of all, he liked looking at her nakedness, actually admired her form. He even told her she was beautiful.

An emotional cloud descended over Prudence just as the sun's rising glow lit the horizon. There was no doubt in her mind now. There couldn't be after last night. She knew herself too well. She could never give herself to a man as she had given herself last night to Zac unless . . . she loved him.

Tears threatened her eyes and she fought them back. How could this happen? How could she fall so deeply in love with Zac Stewart?

"You're going to be hurt again, Prudence," her inner voice warned.

"I don't care," she answered. For once she intended to follow her heart. She would enjoy her husband while she could. When she left, she would take her memories with her to keep her warm in her old age.

"You look awfully cold, honey," Zac called from the bed.

Her head snapped up, surprised to hear her husband's voice. He looked rumpled and sexy, as though he'd spent the whole night making love. She smiled. He had done just that and with her.

"I'm awfully warm," he said, kicking the covers down

229

off him and turning on his side to rest his head on his elbow. "Actually, I'm damn hot."

"I can see that." She gave him an approving glance that came to rest on the swelling length of him.

"Why don't you come over here and cool me off, and I'll warm you up?"

Her smile spread. God, she loved the way he spoke to her. There was nothing proper and mannerly about him where making love was concerned, and that excited her. She walked toward him.

"Take it off," he said roughly. "I want to watch you walk naked to me."

Prudence deliberately let the shawl slip slowly from her as she took each step. When she reached the bed, he grabbed for her, pulling her beneath him.

"Now it's my turn to tease." He eagerly lowered his mouth to her nipple.

Chapter Seventeen

"Good God! I told you hiring Zac Stewart was a mistake. Now look at the mess Prudence is in," Granger shouted, waving his hand in dismissive disapproval.

James Winthrop tried to ignore the man's wild ranting, but he was beginning to weigh on his nerves. "I've explained to you numerous times that Zac had no choice in the matter. Prudence is now safely in his care and *I* feel relieved, as should you."

"Relieved? Relieved to know the woman I intend to marry is now married to another man, and a gunslinger at that?" Granger shot back.

James had had enough. Granger had not once expressed concern for Prudence. "And what about Prudence? Don't you care what she must be feeling now?"

The changed expression on Granger's face betrayed his concern, not for Prudence, but for how James Winthrop viewed him.

"Of course, of course," he faltered, searching for the correct words to soothe the man. "I've been concerned about Prudence since the very first day she undertook this venture. Women are fragile creatures and need protection. They cannot survive without a man to lead them and keep them in line."

James shook his head in exasperation and dropped

into his leather chair behind his desk. His daughter had been right all along. Granger wasn't interested in her. His only interest was to merge two banks and build a banking empire.

"You feel you know Prudence well?" James asked, anticipating the answer but wanting to see if Granger would dig his own grave deeper.

"Yes, I most certainly do." His words possessed an air of testiness. "I don't even see how you could question me on that matter. Prudence is a well-bred lady. She seeks what all women with such impeccable status seek. A fine home and children and, of course, charity work to fill her time. We would make the perfect couple. She would fulfill my needs and I would fulfill hers."

Granger's stupid words exasperated the already painful throbbing in James's temples. He massaged them, applying pressure to the pounding veins on the sides of his head.

"This marriage must be annulled immediately," Granger demanded, slamming his fist down on James's desk for emphasis.

James slowly removed his fingers from his temples and looked up at Granger. "That decision will be up to Prudence."

Granger took a step back, hand to his chest, aghast at what he heard. "Prudence doesn't know her own mind. She proved that by running off on this ridiculous trip. When she becomes my wife, she will follow my orders and behave appropriately."

"That remains to be seen," James argued, thinking that his daughter was better off with a man like Zac Stewart for a husband than with this milksop standing before him.

"What—what do you mean 'remains to be seen'? An annulment is the wisest course of action in this matter. Do you want her ostracized by her friends?"

James stood, his large form intimidating enough to cause Granger to take another step back. "At the moment, I don't care what her friends think. Prudence is my first and only concern."

"Naturally, naturally. I am just as concerned, but we must also take into consideration the results of such a disastrous situation and make provisions for the outcome. The easier we can make it for Prudence, the better it would be for her."

James hated to admit it, but Granger did have a point.

"You wouldn't want her to return to Boston after such a traumatic ordeal and be shunned by her friends. We must make the transition as smooth as possible."

"A point well taken," James said, trying not to let the words choke him. "How do you propose we do that?"

"Simple," Granger answered, as though James were foolish for not thinking of it himself. "Have the annulment papers drawn up before you leave and seek special dispensation for Prudence and I to marry immediately. The talk of her first, unfortunate marriage will fade in the wake of the preparations for her forthcoming marriage. She will be too busy with wedding plans to think of anything else."

James nodded. It might be wise to have an alternate plan. He didn't wish to see his daughter hurt or depressed by past events. "I suppose there's some sense to what you suggest."

The smile Granger wore was broad and satisfied. It resembled that of a cat who had just swallowed a rather large bird. "Yes, yes, there is. We should see to this matter without delay."

James reached in his vest for his pocket watch. "I suppose we have time to see to this today. I leave in two day's time, though I could postpone it some until the necessary papers are secured. Zac did say all was fine and not to worry or hurry."

Granger didn't care for the "not hurry" phrase. "Yes, let's arrange for the annulment papers, and then I'll secure a ticket on the same train as you."

James looked at him oddly. "It really isn't necessary for you to join me."

"I understand that, but I would appreciate your permission to go along. I do find myself overwrought by Prudence's absence and wish to ascertain with my own eyes her safety."

James decided to give Granger the benefit of the doubt. After all, it was Prudence's decision whom she would marry, not his. "If you feel that strongly, by all means join me."

Granger reached out, grabbing James's hand and shaking it. "Thank you. You won't be sorry. You'll see how relieved Prudence will be to see me and know you've made a wise choice."

James nodded, not worrying about his choice but concerned with his daughter's. He hoped she would choose wisely.

"All set," Zac said, trying to hold back the grin but failing miserably.

"You don't like it," Prudence said, looking down at her long denim skirt, light blue cotton shirt, denim jacket, and pair of sturdy brown boots.

"On the contrary. I love it," he answered, meaning every word. She was ten times more attractive in wilderness clothes than in her Boston attire. "I also love your long hair braided like that and that straw bonnet. It brightens your features."

234

She opened her mouth but Zac cut her off.

"Don't ask me if I mean it. You know damn well I do." He reached for her, grabbing her around her waist. "And don't bother to reprimand me with a Mr. Stewart, unless you want to find yourself dragged back to the cabin and flat on your back, on the bed, under me."

The idea had merit and she smiled wickedly.

"You sinful hussy," he teased, planting a kiss on her lips before hoisting her up onto the seat of the wagon. He climbed up next to her and leaned close. "I'll take care of you tonight."

He never issued idle threats and Prudence was glad of that. She had thought after last night and this morning that he had had enough of her. But it didn't appear that way, and as long as he still sought her favors, she had no intention of denying him.

He grabbed the reins, then released the brake. The horses meandered off. Many in the fort waved and called their good-byes to them as the wagon rolled out the open gates.

Mrs. Hampton had stopped by earlier in the morning just after Prudence and Zac had finished making love. Prudence was flushed from their heated encounter, but if the older woman suspected something, she gracefully kept it to herself.

She shared a cup of tea with Prudence while Zac went off to see to the preparations for their journey. Prudence was surprised when Mrs. Hampton presented her with a gift. "For the bride," she had insisted.

Prudence was stunned and grateful for the exquisite hand-embroidered white linen napkins, twelve in all. Mrs. Hampton had remarked on how much she knew Prudence would appreciate their beauty. They hugged and parted with promises of visiting each other. Prudence only hoped the promises could be kept.

"We'll travel most of the day, only making necessary stops. I had Curly pack us some food. . . ." Zac stopped as though in thought and then continued. "I know you can bake a rum cake, but by any chance can you cook anything else?"

Prudence stuck her chest out proudly. "I'll have you know I spent a good portion of my days pestering Bessie — she was our cook — to teach me."

"Glad to hear that." Zac couldn't help but wonder what a lonely little girl she must have been to seek out the cook's attention. "And what scrumptious delights did she teach you?"

"All the basics and then some, though . . ." It was her turn to pause in thought. "I'm afraid some of the ingredients will be difficult, if not impossible, to find out here. But I can adapt many of the recipes."

Zac admired her for that. She did adapt well except where her mother was concerned, but then he couldn't blame her for that, either.

"I would like to try Old Bill's rabbit stew recipe. He told me to make certain the wild onions were picked fresh the day I intended to use them. Will you show me where I can find wild onions?"

Zac switched the reins to his left hand and patted her knee with his right. "I plan on showing you a lot, honey."

She slipped her arm through his and leaned close. "Promise, Zac?" she asked in such a breathless whisper that it made him shiver.

He cursed his instant reaction. "Promise and then some."

They rode for a ways in silence, Zac lost to his thoughts and Prudence caught by the beauty of the land around her. The farther they traveled from the fort, the more dense the trees became in their majestic

236

beauty. Prudence was awed by the startling blue of the sky and the puffs of huge white clouds that floated across it. The air even smelled different. It was fresh and clean and heavy with the scent of pine.

She realized that she had fallen in love twice. The first time was with Zac Stewart. The second was with this land. She wished she never had to return to Boston and its stuffy confines. She wanted to stay here and carve out a life with her husband, raise children, watch his ranch grow, and watch their love grow.

But love hadn't entered the picture, and so her dreams were for nothing. She had to live for today and enjoy. Enjoy as much as possible before it all came to a rapid end.

Zac stopped to let her stretch and fetch some food for them to eat on the way, while he tended to the horses. They munched on fried chicken, the best Prudence had ever tasted, as they continued on.

"Would it upset you overly much if we spoke about your mother?" he asked through bites.

Prudence had to swallow before answering, but her head was already shaking in response. "No, I'd like to speak of her."

"You mentioned Old Bill knew your mother."

"That's right. It was her talent as a cook that Sadie, Granny Hayes, and Old Bill recalled about her. That was her one quality that stood out and made her memorable."

"I don't know about your cooking, but you've got memorable eyes."

"I have memorable eyes?" Prudence asked, about to bite into her buttermilk biscuit but stopping.

Zac nodded, snatching the biscuit from her hand. "At first I didn't notice them. I think it was all that foggy air in Boston."

Prudence playfully slapped his arm. "The only foggy air in Boston is near the harbor. An area I don't happen to frequent."

"Then it must have been your corset being strung too tight."

"I don't wear a corset," she said smugly.

"Then that explains it." He laughed and bit into the biscuit.

"Zac, swallow that and tell me what you mean," she ordered.

Zac obliged with a swallow. "Your stiff posture dulled your eyes."

"I am not stiff," she said defensively.

"No, and I thank God you're not and I thank God I am." He laughed again.

It took Prudence a moment to decipher his reference. Upon doing so, she brazenly slipped her hand over his crotch. "Not stiff enough," she declared.

He laughed even harder. "Honey, keep that up and you'll find yourself touching solid rock."

She looked at him then and he caught the mercurial passion in her eyes. He took her hand and moved it off him, replacing it in her lap with a pat. "I think we better finish the discussion about your mother." It was a safer subject, especially since his desire was raw and ready, and if he took her now, it would be fast and furious in the bushes. He was certain she was too tender at the moment for such rough play.

Prudence calmed her racing heart with several deep breaths, but the uneasiness between her legs remained uncontrollable. She would simply have to suffer through it. "I really would like to find her, but she seems always to have managed to leave a place without anyone's noticing. It was as though she thought someone was following her, or she wanted to prevent someone from finding her."

"That would make sense, although one thing doesn't."

Prudence was anxious to hear anything she might have overlooked. "What's that?"

"Her ability to survive out here. It's almost as though she were familiar with the area. Where did she come from originally?"

"I think my father met her on a business trip to Philadelphia, but I don't recall if that is her place of birth. I don't remember her ever speaking of her birthplace or Father mentioning it."

"Well, perhaps she's as adaptable as you?"

"Perhaps," she said, puzzled. "But when she left Fort Sully, where could she have gone?"

"Wilderness surrounds the place." He shrugged. "Unless she took the steamboat. Then her destination could have been anywhere."

"Do you think my quest hopeless?"

"No. I think it is important you find her. When you do, I think you'll have your answers."

Her answers. Would they hurt or would they help? Prudence remained silent for a while, lost in her thoughts until she realized she was building new memories. And she wanted many to take back to Boston with her.

She turned to Zac and smiled. "Will we be stopping soon?"

He nodded and mumbled beneath his breath, "Not soon enough."

The wagon came to rest a few hours later. Zac fixed a fire so Prudence could heat some of the food Curly had sent along, then he again tended to the horses.

Hunger pangs assaulted his senses so badly that he found himself arguing with the horses, not that they answered him. His was not the kind of hunger that required food to quench it. No, he required a bit more sustenance. And with that satisfying thought, he hurried to finish his task.

Prudence couldn't prevent the yawns from attacking her. No matter how hard she tried to hold them back, they would break free and another would escape. She supposed it was being up most of last night, rising early this morning, and riding in the wagon most of the day that had done it.

Her body was beginning to protest and that's all there was to it. She raised her hand, covering her mouth as yet another yawn presented itself. She shook her head, attempting to shake away the fatigue that was fast overcoming her.

She stood and stretched her arms up, reaching out for the unreachable sky, trying to rid herself of the lassitude and aches. She took a deep breath, inhaling the fresh, cool air of dusk, only to find another yawn sneaking up on her.

"Tired?" Zac asked. Concern made him realize what Prudence had been through in the last twenty-four hours.

"Just a little." She didn't want to appear too tired for them to make love. She had thought about his touch all day, especially since they had sat so close on the wagon. His leg, so thick with muscles, had rubbed against hers most of the time. Intentionally or not, it didn't matter. The friction it had generated was enough to spark her passion.

"You look tired. We'll eat and then get some rest." He noticed the slight droop of her eyelids and the weighted sag of her shoulders. He should have taken her sleepless night into consideration and not pushed so hard today. They could have stopped an hour or so ago. It would have given her more time to relax. But he was anxious to put distance between them and the fort. He was selfish. He wanted her all to himself.

Prudence didn't like his bossy tone. If she said she wasn't tired, then she wasn't tired. "I'm fine, really. You needn't concern yourself with me."

Zac held back his retort. Fatigue always brought out the crankiness in a person. "I'm starving."

Prudence's head shot up and she stared at him. She was just thinking how hungry she was and it wasn't for food. She had the overpowering urge to taste her husband. She regained her senses and, with only a bit of stammering, spoke. "I—I found the beef Curly packed and heated it, plus the biscuits. And there's hot coffee."

"Sounds great to me." He rubbed his hands together in anticipation and joined her by the fire.

Their meal was sprinkled with only a smattering of conversation, but highlighted with several uncontrollable yawns from Prudence. When supper was finished he offered to help clean up. She didn't refuse.

Prudence was putting the last of the tin plates away when a lone wolf cry sounded in the distance. Her weariness had made her so glad they had stopped for the night that she had all but forgot to wonder where they would sleep. Apparently here, out in the open, virtually unprotected. She looked to Zac.

He took the bedrolls from the wagon and spread them next to each other by the warmth of the fire. He patted the one next to his. The one closer to the flames and heat. "Come on over here and tell me what's wrong?"

Prudence hurried over and sat down on the bedroll, releasing an anxious sigh. "Did you hear that howl?"

"Sure did. It was a mournful one."

Prudence glanced out at the darkness that surrounded them. "Do you think the animal is close?"

Zac realized that she was nervous over their accommodations. Even though she prided herself in adapting easily, sleeping out under the night sky for the first time was an experience, especially for a proper lady from Boston. He reached out and cupped her chin. "There's nothing to worry about. The fire will keep the animals away, and this part of the territory is pretty much safe."

She smiled, accepting his explanation and hoping the animal wouldn't howl again tonight.

He released her chin. "Get some sleep. We have a long day ahead of us tomorrow."

She nodded and turned to stretch out, when she felt the kink of tension in her neck and shoulders. She moved her head from side to side, then slowly rolled it around.

"Problem?" he asked, stretched out on his side next to her.

She rubbed at the nape of her neck. "Sore muscles," she complained, and then the thought struck like lightning. "Would you rub it for me?"

Her voice, dripping with sweetness, enlightened Zac to her obvious intentions. He supposed if she felt she wasn't too tired for them to play, then why should he? "Take off your jacket," he ordered.

His strong command sent a shiver of anticipation racing through her and she quickly shed the garment.

Zac knelt behind her, taking her long coppery braid and placing it to rest over her breast. While his hands were there, they carefully unbuttoned her shirt and slid it down her shoulders. "Cold?" he asked, his warm hands racing up to rub her bare shoulders.

She was far from cold; she was boiling. "No, not at all."

"Good. It's too difficult to massage someone through

242

layers of clothing." He started then, his thumbs pressing into the base of her neck, working on the taut muscles. He soothed them, cajoled them into relaxing.

Prudence thought his touch rough at first, but the more he massaged, the more languid her body became. She felt like a limp rag doll, all her strength gone. She was pliable to his touch and she closed her eyes, giving herself completely over to him.

He bent her head forward and concentrated on her neck, kneading the last tension spots away. He brought her head up before his hands moved down her back. He eased her shoulders back slowly, forcing her chest out. He took a moment to run his hands lightly over her breasts before returning to her back. He focused on the knots of tension running down her shoulder blades and with each stroke, with each pressure, her body surrendered to his masterful touch.

"Feels good?" he asked, his hands working their way farther down her back.

"Mmm," was her only reply.

He smiled, pleased with her response, and continued. A few more strokes, a few more whispers, and she'd be ready. He was. He was so damn hard, he thought he'd burst. But he worried that she might be sore from their previous night's adventures, and he wanted her relaxed enough to take him.

He eased her slightly slumped body back to rest against his. Her head nestled on his shoulder while his hand cupped her breast. He heard the steady rhythm of her breathing and sensed her lack of response as he gently squeezed her nipple. "Damn," he muttered, looking down into her closed eyes.

"Damn," he muttered again. This wasn't fair. He had expressed his concern for her fatigue, but she had insisted, most emphatically, that she wasn't tired. Now

243

here she was sleeping soundly while he suffered the tortures of hell.

She moaned softly in her slumber, turning into his chest for comfort and protection.

Shaking his head, he eased her shirt back over her shoulders and buttoned it. Then he stretched Prudence out on her bedroll, covering her with the wool blanket. He debated whether he should even bother to attempt to sleep. He was too wound up. Too tense. Too damn hard.

He threw himself back on his bedroll and focused on the thousand twinkling stars . . . and began to count.

Chapter Eighteen

The grunts were what did it. They proved to Prudence beyond a doubt that Zac was upset. He had grunted his every answer to her questions since sunrise, when he had roughly shaken her awake and ordered her to make breakfast so they could be on their way. Not that he ate any food. He drank three cups of coffee and ignored the biscuits and smoked bacon she had prepared.

They had been traveling for hours in silence. Every effort at conversation was met with a grunt. She was even beginning to distinguish the difference between the various ones. A short one meant "fine." A long one meant "leave me alone." And the one in between meant "I don't care."

She tried to understand what had brought on this miserable mood. A few days ago it wouldn't have disturbed her if he had remained silent. She probably would have cherished it. Now things were different. She found she actually took comfort in their conversations. He always managed to offer some words of praise or a compliment, and her spirits were lightened considerably by his thoughtfulness. But this strange mood was incomprehensible.

Most women back in Boston wouldn't even consider

their husbands' lack of communication a problem, but this wasn't Boston and Zac wasn't any husband. He was hers.

Prudence lifted her chin and stiffened her back. If he thought she was going to put up with such nonsense, he was crazy. "You didn't like breakfast?"

A short grunt produced her answer, and she assumed that if she measured his grunts correctly, his behavior wasn't related to the morning meal.

"The weather seems pleasant enough," she tried, wondering if he was concerned with the possibility of an unexpected storm.

Another short grunt was released.

So the weather didn't disturb him. What other possibilities could there be? Perhaps he was concerned with her? "I had a wonderful night's sleep."

His grunt was the longest she had ever heard. A growling grunt, she thought, and wondered over its translation. Her practical side finally emerged and took over. She turned in the seat and looked directly at him. "Whatever is your problem this morning? You're acting abominably."

He turned, too, lifting his head only a fraction so his dark eyes appeared even darker in the shadow of the brim of his hat. His lips wore no smile. No frown marred his handsome features. He displayed no emotion at all. She felt chilled by his empty stare and wondered if this was the mask he wore when he faced another gunslinger.

"Why do you presume I have a problem?" His tone was low and controlled, each syllable being enunciated with just the right amount of cool force.

His frostiness didn't in the least disturb her. "You've done nothing but grunt all morning. Those are the first civil words you've spoken to me."

"Perhaps I'm not in the mood to talk."

"No, perhaps you're not, but you are in the mood to be ill-mannered."

"And perhaps I have reason for such ill manners."

Prudence raised her brow. "There is no logical reason for ill manners."

"None?" he asked sharply.

"Children," Prudence answered, "are prone to ill manners, being they don't know any better and must be taught appropriately. Adults, on the other hand, should know better and confront a problem with intelligence."

Damn! Did she always have to make sense? He'd been stewing in his own pot since last night. His problem was one of his own making, not hers, though he'd like to believe it was.

"You've got a point," he admitted reluctantly.

"At least that's a start." Content that she had broken through his chorus of grunts, she said, "Now let's discuss it."

Zac pushed his hat back to see her better and turned on his outrageous smile. "Honey, I don't think you want to do that."

"Of course I do," she said seriously. "A matter cannot be dealt with and settled unless discussed honestly. Too many misunderstandings occur when both parties assume things. I don't wish that to happen to us."

"What if the matter is delicate?" he asked.

Prudence nipped at her lower lip and thought for a moment. "I think a husband and wife should be able to discuss anything. So many of my married friends find various subjects off limits with their husbands. I don't wish that type of relationship between us." She didn't bother to add "for the limited time we have to share."

Zac liked her directness and the thought that they could discuss anything. He'd never considered holding

247

a conversation about sex with a woman, but he'd try anything. Anyway, he couldn't wait to see Pru's expression when he explained his *mood*. "If you feel comfortable with open discussions, I have no problem with it."

"Good." A sharp nod of her head confirmed her satisfaction. "Now what's wrong with you?"

"Sex!"

Prudence almost lost control, almost but not quite. The years of enduring the cruelty of other children when they noticed her useless fingers had taught her to hide her emotions well. So although she was shocked, she didn't show it. She calmly answered, "Sex is a subject I have little knowledge of, but my limited experience has been a pleasurable one."

Zac laughed. He had to hand it to her. She handled the situation like no other woman could. And damned if he didn't enjoy talking to her like this. "I'm glad I brought you pleasure, Pru. I thought perhaps you might find the act not to your liking."

"No, no." she was quick to defend. "I found it so much more satisfying than I was led to believe."

"Your married friends told you tales?"

"Many times."

"During tea?" He couldn't help but ask, thinking of all the proper ladies sitting about, teacups in hand, munching on sweet cakes and discussing the conditions of their husbands' crotches.

"Usually," she answered, and couldn't help but smile herself.

"Were any pleased with their husband's performance?"

"No, I'm afraid many just tolerated their husbands' fumblings."

"Fumblings?"

"Yes, most referred to it, for polite reasons, as fum-

248

blings. Others called it disgusting, beastly, degrading, barbaric—"

"I get the point," he said. "Not even one enjoyed it?"

She shook her head. "Not one."

"You would have been the exception."

She smiled broadly. "Oh my, yes, although I would have never discussed you with them."

"Why?"

"Silence many times speaks louder than words. Their own vivid imaginations would be enough to drive them crazy, and besides, what you and I share is private. Something personal and special, not something discussed over tea and cakes."

Zac had to admit the lady had class. It might irritate him at times, but at other times it made him damned proud she was his wife.

"I still don't understand the problem, Zac?"

Now what was he going to do? Tell her she's got a horny husband?

She reached out, resting her hand on his forearm.

The soft, languid look in her gentle green eyes did him in. He didn't know how to handle this situation. He had been in many gunfights, stared down many a man, but never had he been as nervous as he was at this moment. He had always been better with actions than with words. He hoped she would understand.

He kept a steady hand on the reins while his other hand reached over, took hers, and slowly brought it to rest between his legs. His hand remained covering hers and he squeezed it gently.

Prudence thought to pull away at first, so startled was she. But his hand was firm and his manhood warm and hard. She clearly understood his problem.

"You're so damn desirable. I can't stop thinking about you."

"You desire me?" she asked, surprised by the strength of his passion.

"*Desire* isn't a sufficient enough word for what I feel."

She didn't move her hand and neither did he. "Tell me how you feel, Zac?"

"Like a wild man, Pru," His answer held no hesitancy. "You would be frightened if I told you the things I wanted to do to you."

"I don't fear you, Zac."

"You should. At this moment, you should." He squeezed her hand more tightly over him, and she felt the strength of him, so hot and alive to her touch.

"I can't," she whispered and stopped herself from adding *I love you*. Instead, she asked, "When do we stop for the noon meal?"

He looked at her long and hard. She didn't turn away from his stare, she matched it. She was brazenly offering herself to him, without any qualms or doubts. "About fifteen minutes or so, up a piece, there's a stream the horses can drink from."

"Good," she said, turning her head to watch the path, leaving her hand to rest against him.

It was the longest twenty minutes of Zac's life. He saw to the horses, while Prudence gathered some food and wandered toward the shade and solitude of a large weeping willow tree not far from the stream.

As he approached, she patted the spot on the wool blanket she had spread out for them to share. "I have cider, bread, and cheese, if you're hungry."

He laughed at the way she hastily added the last statement. "I'm not hungry for food, Pru."

"I didn't think you'd be."

His hand reached out, cupping the side of her face, and she turned into it, kissing his warm palm. He took a deep breath, releasing it slowly. "You've changed, Prudence Agatha Winthrop."

"Stewart," she corrected. "I told you I'm —"

"Adaptable," he finished, laughing, drawing her to him and beneath him all in one swift motion. He focused on her eyes as he unbuttoned her shirt and slid her chemise straps down and out of his way. The light breeze combined with his intention was enough to bring her sensitive nipples to immediate arousal.

He grinned and lowered his mouth to the hard pebble nub beckoning him, while his hand ran down over her belly.

Her unchecked passion had grown to match his. Both found their sensuality at a high peak and impossible to control.

"I can't wait, Pru." He moved his mouth to feast on her lips.

She welcomed his quenching kiss. "Neither can I," she murmured between their frenzied tastes of each other.

His hand slipped to her skirt, pushing the mounds of material out of his way. He cursed the damn undergarments he'd have to battle. He was pleasantly surprised and relieved to find she wore nothing beneath. His brow rose in question.

She grinned and shrugged her shoulders. "I thought you might be in a hurry."

He laughed and bent down and kissed her while he released himself from his pants. He didn't wait. He entered her swiftly, and she cried out from the strength and pleasure of him.

He leaned over her, bracing his weight on his hands, and moved at a slow and steady tempo, giving her time to adjust. Then his tempo increased and each thrust grew more forceful, more exhilarating. He was riding her with a fury that knew no bounds, and the powerful

251

sensation was like none she had ever dreamed possible. It was beyond reality, beyond conception. It was *wicked*.

She heard the groan deep in his chest. It bubbled forth as did her own, climbing, reaching, struggling to grasp. . . . They exploded together in an eruption so utterly powerful that they both cried out in unison.

Zac collapsed on Prudence, and she cradled him against her, feeling the ebb of the once-heavy throb fade blissfully in the distance. She squeezed him tightly inside herself and shivered as the very last tingling sensation rippled away.

"Mrs. Stewart," he breathed heavily, "if you continue to eliminate your undergarments, we'll never make it to my ranch."

She giggled and rubbed his back possessively. "I must say I find it much less confining, as I did when I decided to shed my corset permanently."

Zac pushed himself up. "Does this mean there'll be nothing but your beautiful naked bottom beneath your skirts from now on?"

She winked boldly at him. "Perhaps, but perhaps not."

"You wicked woman." He kissed her soundly. "I'd like to spend the rest of the day here lost in your arms . . ."

"But," she finished, "you really want to get on to your ranch."

His smile was warm and thoughtful. "I'm anxious for you to see it. And I'm anxious, for various reasons, to get home." He moved off her, sliding her skirt down before he stood and adjusted his own clothing. He needed to get her home. He needed time alone with her. Time for her to grow accustomed to life on his ranch. Time for her to grow to love him.

Prudence sat up, buttoning her shirt and slipping

252

into her denim jacket. "Tell me about it . . . the ranch, I mean."

He held his hand out to her. She took it and he pulled her up to him, kissing her gently. "I will, if you don't mind listening and eating while we're traveling."

"No objection," she said, gathering everything up.

They were on their way in no time. The cider jug sat between them, and the cheese and bread were cushioned in Prudence's lap on a bright red and white checkered towel.

"Is the house made of sod or log?" she asked, breaking off a hunk of bread to hand him.

He took it, finding his appetite ravenous since he had neglected breakfast. "Couldn't call the first house on my land a house. It was a one-room log cabin, not fit for man or beast."

"But you loved it, didn't you?"

"Every inch of the place, and do you know why?"

She shook her head, although she had an idea.

"It was mine. That one-room cabin with a fireplace, bed, table and two chairs, and no window was all mine. It was the first time in my life I had owned anything with permanence to it. I finally had a place to come home to."

"You must have some wonderful memories."

"Wonderful and harsh, but both were to be expected. I was prepared . . . still am."

"And now?"

"That cabin remains on my land. I couldn't bring myself to tear it down when I had the house built. And besides, the house is miles from where the cabin stands. Now I have a twelve-room house. The house I'd always dreamed of building."

"Twelve rooms? Do you plan on having a large family?" she asked without thinking.

253

"I certainly do," he said proudly. "There's a large master suite upstairs and four bedrooms for the children when they come along. Two in each room makes eight in all. A good size family, don't you think?"

"A very good size." she agreed, recalling how she had always envisioned a large brood of her own.

"Downstairs are the receiving parlor, the family parlor, the dining room, my study, a sewing room, and the cooking area, complete with a water pump next to the sink and a brand-new cast-iron stove."

"And the sewing room is complete?" she asked.

"A new Singer sewing machine just waiting patiently. I bought some thread and stuff but wasn't certain what was really needed, so I thought I had better wait. You can order whatever you need from the catalogs or see if the dry goods store carries it."

Prudence was startled that he should offer her the use of the sewing machine. She thought he would want it saved for his permanent wife. She was tempted to refuse his generous offer but resisted. A few stitches on the new machine wouldn't hurt, and some needles and threads, pincushions, and thimbles would probably be appreciated by his next wife.

"The place could use some curtains. Are you handy with a needle?"

"Yes, I like to sew and surprisingly am quite good at it."

"Most women are. Why would anyone be surprised at that?"

She shrugged. "My useless fingers give everyone the impression that I'm incapable of doing anything with my hands."

"Ignorance. Ignore them."

She smiled at how easily he defended her. It was nice

to have a champion. "There's a town nearby your home?"

He shook his head and laughed. "If you can call Stewart a town."

"Stewart?"

"Yes, it's named after me. The land once belonged to me, and I donated it to some settlers who were interested in forming a town since several ranches sit about. It's in its infancy stages but growing nicely. There's the dry goods store run by two women. They also handle the mail. There's a small jailhouse that's never been used. It's more of a deterrent for people passing through. Sort of announces that our town is law-abiding. And Charlie Biddle just opened up a smithy. We hope to have a church built before the end of the year, and who knows what else."

"Sounds like a wonderful place." Prudence was anxious to see it for herself.

"It is, but it's a far cry from Boston," he warned.

Prudence totally ignored him. Her thoughts were elsewhere. "After the church is built, you could build a large hall beside it. It could double as a schoolhouse until an appropriate one could be built. Then Stewart could have a spring dance just like the fort's. Wouldn't that be wonderful?"

He agreed with an eager nod, surprised at her enthusiasm. But then she had told him often enough that she was "adaptable." He was beginning to doubt that and to believe that Prudence belonged in the West. It was in her blood. She had taken to the lifestyle too fast and too easily. For some inexplicable reason, she belonged here. She had come home.

Chapter Nineteen

"This is wonderful!" Prudence said as Zac reached up to help her down from the wagon.

He placed her gently on the ground beside him and glanced around, wondering if they were looking at the same town, Stewart. There was the blacksmith building as they rode in, the small jailhouse next to that, and then down at the opposite end of the wide dirt street to the right was the general store where they now stood.

"Wonderful?" he repeated, wanting to make certain he had heard her correctly.

Prudence grabbed his hand and squeezed it in excitement. "Yes, just imagine the possibilities. A church, right over there," she pointed to the right. "Nestled amongst those giant trees. And look to the side of it. A perfect clearing for a church hall to hold socials and dances. And before you know it, the street will be lined with stores. Wonderful, absolutely wonderful." She marched up the two steps, tugging a bewildered Zac along beside her to enter the dry goods store.

Prudence removed her bonnet and adjusted the short cape of her gray outfit. She wanted to make a good impression on these two women who had braved the wilderness to establish their business.

The wide open room reminded her of the mercantile. It was stocked to the brim with an extensive variety of merchandise.

"Anybody minding this store?" Zac called out humorously.

"Gosh almighty, you're back!" a woman's high-pitched voice squealed from somewhere in the back room.

In a flash, a short, round barrel of a woman came rushing through the swinging doors that separated the back room from the front. She headed straight for Zac.

Zac opened his arms in greeting and took the impact of her solid form without flinching. "So you missed me, Bertha?" He hugged the woman, who only reached his chest, tightly to him.

Bertha giggled like a young schoolgirl and stepped back, her cheeks flushed and her fingers nervously patting her brown curly hair that refused to stay confined by two ivory combs. "I most certainly did."

"I missed everyone here myself," he admitted. "And brought a surprise back with me." Zac slipped his arm around Prudence's waist, bringing her to stand before him. "Bertha, I'd like you to meet my wife, Prudence Agatha Stewart."

"Gosh almighty, your wife!" she cried and grabbed Prudence's hand, shaking the life out of it. "It's a pleasure to meet you, Prudence. Actually, a shock, since no one here in Stewart ever expected Zac to marry. We figured he'd have to search pretty far and probably have to pay a woman to marry the likes of him."

Bertha stopped shaking Prudence's hand and stared

wide-eyed in embarrassment at her. "Gosh, he didn't have to pay you, did he?"

Prudence laughed and shook her head. "No, but the decision wasn't really left up to him."

It was Bertha's turn to laugh. "A decision concerning Zac not left up to him? Not likely."

Prudence turned quickly and looked up into her husband's face. He winked at her and she wondered over Bertha's reply. Had Zac been forced to marry her? Or hadn't he?

"Where's Silver Fox?" Zac asked. "I want Pru to meet her."

"She should be here soon. She went to deliver some items to Charlie Biddle that arrived late yesterday," Bertha explained.

"So Charlie still keeping you dangling?" Zac teased.

Bertha dismissed his words with a wave of her hand and a coy smile. "No sir. I told him that if he expects my home cooking so frequently, then he better put a ring on my finger or he could eat his own horrible cooking permanently."

Zac craned his neck to get a better look at Bertha's hand. "Don't see a ring."

Bertha blushed, her cheeks matching the color of her pink gingham dress. "Charlie's traveling to Plattsmouth in a few weeks on business. He's getting it then."

"Congratulations. It's about time," Zac said.

Prudence was about to offer her own congratulations when another woman's voice, soft and sweet, interrupted.

"You've finally come home, Zac Stewart."

Bertha turned quickly, anxious to be the first to spread the news of Zac's marriage. "He's married, Sil-

258

ver Fox. Do you believe Zac actually got married? The poor, dear girl doesn't know what she's in for." Bertha giggled.

Prudence was surprised, though she kept it from showing. She hadn't expected one of the women to be an Indian, and beautiful at that. She took her for about forty, with a figure that was still trim and fit. She wore her long, dark hair parted in the middle and braided. There was a streak of silver rushing through the front and running down on either side of the part. Her dress was a plain brown skirt and white blouse. Her eyes were kind, as was her smile, and Prudence took an instant liking to her and to Bertha.

"So you bring a wife to us," Silver Fox said, extending her hand in friendship to Prudence. "Welcome."

Prudence accepted it gratefully. "Thank you."

"Let's have tea," Bertha suggested. "Prudence can tell us all about the wedding."

Zac tugged at his wife's waist, stepping back with her in tow. "Another day, ladies."

"That's not fair, Zac," Bertha complained. "We want to hear all the details."

"So you can make certain you spread the news first," Zac added with a laugh.

Bertha nodded in total agreement. "Of course. Everyone will be expecting me to fill them in."

To Prudence's surprise, Zac kissed her on the cheek before he spoke. "It will have to wait. I want to show my bride her new home."

Prudence was anxious to see his home, and the way he spoke of it as *her* new home gave her chills. It might only be a fairy-tale marriage, but she was enjoying it and wanted it to go on as long as possible. "Perhaps you and Silver Fox could join me for tea tomorrow at a time convenient for both of you?"

"That sounds great," Bertha called as Zac began pulling Prudence toward the door. "Three would be good. We could close down for a couple of hours."

"Three is fine," Prudence cried, waving good-bye as Zac yanked her through the door.

Prudence wasn't prepared for the beauty of Zac's home. It was a two-story log structure. It looked sturdy enough to withstand the wild elements, yet welcomed visitors with its wide end-to-end front porch.

The inside was even more surprising. His furnishings were a combination of classic and wilderness style, and they blended perfectly. The old wooden rocking chair before the stone hearth in the family parlor looked as at home and in place as did the apricot medallion love seat near the window next to the tabouret table. Each room was one surprise after another. Prudence was about to go up the stairs to the second floor, when Zac's hand on her arm stopped her. "I have to go check on things with my ranch foreman. You can acquaint yourself with the house. Feel free to roam about; there's nothing off-limits. It's your home."

Temporarily, Prudence thought, and immediately chased the depressing thought away. For now she would enjoy.

Zac stepped close to her, raised her chin to look up at him, and brushed her lips with his. "One thing," he whispered. "Are you wearing anything beneath that skirt?"

Prudence felt a warm tingle rush up from her toes and was about to answer, when he spoke.

"Don't tell me. I'll never make it out that door if

you tell me nothing stands in my way of making love to you but that skirt."

Prudence couldn't prevent the little moan that slipped from her lips.

Zac ran his finger across her mouth and Prudence reached for it with her tongue. "Damn, Pru, you're making this hard on me."

"No," she murmured, nipping at his finger with her teeth. "I want to make *you* hard."

Zac brought his head to rest on her forehead and kept running his finger across her lips for her to enjoy. "You're one hot-blooded woman, dear wife."

"You made me that way." Her breath was heavy with desire.

He could argue that point but chose not to, since he heard the approach of a rider and assumed his foreman, Josh, had arrived. "I have to go, Pru."

She moaned and her teeth tugged lightly at his finger.

He pulled his finger away and replaced it with his lips, tasting deeply of her, leaving her breathless and begging. "Promise me one thing, Pru."

"What?" she asked, her chest heaving.

"Say you promise," he urged, kissing her breathless again.

She nodded her promise, unable to speak.

"I want you naked on my bed when I return."

Her already laborious breath caught in her throat at his lustful suggestion.

"A promise is a promise. I'll be back by dusk." He kissed her on the cheek and quickly slipped out the front door.

It took Prudence a good ten minutes to calm herself

261

enough to realize her word had been given and was expected to be kept.

She walked up the curving steps to the second floor, opening the first door on the right as she began inspecting the rooms and tried to rid herself of her nervous state. Prudence stood there, shocked. The room was stunning, the massive bed seductive. The rosewood headboard stood high and was carved with cherubs and vines, mingling and entwining like lovers. She shivered at the thought of herself lying naked upon it, waiting to mingle and entwine with Zac.

She turned her back on the envisioned scene and focused on the remainder of the room. The colors were a gentle blend of muted greens and beige, with just a small amount of apricot thrown in for a subtle effect.

Two matching rosewood wardrobes stood side by side against one wall. Prudence opened the first, which turned out to be empty. The other held Zac's clothes. A dressing table sat between the only two windows in the room, with a silver brush set the only item on it. Like the wardrobe, it was waiting for the permanent mistress of the house to arrive to add her personal touch.

A large stone fireplace with a heavy wood mantel occupied the wall opposite the wardrobes. A beautiful painting of the wilderness hung above it and a clock sat in the middle of the mantel.

Prudence turned around and around slowly. A smile formed on her lips as she thought of the touches she would add to make this more of a home. Plain beige lace curtains on the bare windows to start, her personal items on the dressing table, a chair with a footrest for Zac's relaxation, and a carpet in hues of deep green would do much for the room.

She explored the small room off the bedroom and found it to be two, one a bathing room and the other a dressing room, privacy screen and all.

She hadn't expected such luxuries in the West, but now knowing and understanding Zac, Prudence could see how hard he had worked to provide himself and his future family with such amenities. And she realized that while keeping the best of the rough young West, he had also added things that would help it age gently.

Prudence had a couple of hours before dusk and was suddenly filled with energy. She would unpack her clothes, build a small fire in the bedroom hearth, run a bath, bring up a tray of food, and leave a trail to seduction. She turned quickly on her heels and left the room.

Zac ran his hand through his hair again. It was still damp. He had taken a dip in the stream, though it chilled him to the bone. It made him feel clean, as did the fresh clothes he had switched into.

His thoughts had troubled him since he left Prudence on the steps. All he could think about was her naked on the bed, waiting for him. He wondered if she'd find the confidence to do as she had promised. He hoped so, for then he would know she trusted him deeply. And that was important to him. Very important.

The house was quiet when he entered. An instant fear gripped him as he wondered if she might have run away. But he pushed it aside. There was no place for her to go, and he sensed she didn't wish to leave him just yet.

He climbed the steps slowly. There was no need to rush their union. He enjoyed the anticipation of what was to come. The kisses, caresses, the intimate touches and purposeful teases. Yes, he was going to enjoy her tonight, perhaps even introduce her to something new, something shocking.

He was smiling most devilishly when he opened the door quietly and peered in. The bedsheets were drawn back but the bed was empty.

He stepped into the room, his anger on the rise, and walked around the bed to where the small fire flickered and crackled.

He stopped dead in his tracks.

Prudence lay on a quilt on the floor, sleeping. A silver tray sat nearby with meats, bread, cheese, whiskey, and cider. She had planned everything. Had waited for him. Had wanted him. There was no doubt in his mind about it. She was stretched out on the quilt, arms resting above her head, stark naked.

The smile he wore fast faded to a frown. She was exhausted. The long, uncomfortable ride in the wagon had finally taken its toll. She hadn't once complained. Although it was obvious at times that she experienced discomfort, she had kept it to herself. An admirable trait in a woman and one he admired.

Of course, he hadn't helped the situation any. He hadn't been able to keep his hands off her. He couldn't get enough of her, night after night, under the star-studded sky, next to the warmth of the fire, her flesh alive and hot to his touch.

"Damn," he mumbled, shaking his head. He had told her often enough he was no gentleman. And since he had proven it on several occasions, he should have no qualms about joining her now on the quilt and making love to her. So what was stopping him?

His concern for her well-being. There would be other nights and days to share with her. Now she needed rest.

He shook his head in total disbelief at his actions. "I can't believe I'm doing this." He bent down and carefully slipped his arms beneath her, picking her up to cradle her against his chest as he stood.

Her body was brushed with the warmth of the fire and the heat penetrated his shirt, whispering against his chest. He didn't waste any time but hurried to the bed and laid her down, pulling the quilt up from the foot of the bed, where it was folded, and tucking it securely around her.

He forced himself to turn away, not trusting his ungentlemanly side. He spied the decanter of whiskey on the tray. He walked over, picked it up, and began unbuttoning his shirt as he moved toward the door.

A stiff drink would do him good and so would that cool stream he had left only a short time ago. Then maybe, just maybe, he could enter their bed to sleep.

"Fat chance," he mumbled, then closed the door behind him.

Chapter Twenty

"I can't believe Zac is married," Bertha said, reaching for one of the sweet buns on the pink flowered china plate.

Prudence had taken extra pains in preparing for Bertha and Silver Fox's visit. She had set the serving table in the receiving parlor with the pink flowered china she had found in the dining room cupboard. Its tiny buds with traces of pale yellow and soft green leaves were beautiful. And she did so want to make a good impression.

"It was bound to happen," Silver Fox said, accepting the teacup Prudence had just filled for her.

"But you know Zac." Bertha giggled. "He's so fussy when it comes to women."

"Fussy?" Prudence asked, curious to learn more about her husband.

"Not fussy," Silver Fox corrected softly. "He was looking for someone special. Someone who would eagerly and happily share his dream of building this ranch and a large family."

Bertha nodded. "That's true enough. Zac loves kids, always has. He'll make a wonderful father."

"I'm sure he will," Prudence agreed a bit sadly.

Silver Fox smiled at her as though in understanding. And her eyes held Prudence's for several moments. "I'm sure you and Zac will have many children and share a wonderful life together."

Prudence attempted to return the woman's smile, but she was made momentarily uneasy by the intensity of Silver Fox's gaze.

"They certainly will," Bertha said, "and that's why Stewart needs a church built now. Where would their baby be christened? I tell you, we need a church. A church will bring more people. It will show we're serious about establishing this place. That it's a God-fearin' place where families are welcome and safe."

"A church is a good idea," Prudence said, adding her opinion. "And I was thinking the perfect spot would be near your store under those large trees with that clearing next to it. Then a church hall could be built and we could hold socials and dances and—Oh, Bertha!"

Bertha and Silver Fox waited for Prudence to explain her startled expression.

Prudence reached out and hugged Bertha's hand. "We could hold your wedding there. Just think of it—the food, the dancing, the music, the celebrating."

Bertha grew just as enthusiastic. "Then all the families can come from miles around. We could even fashion beds for them to sleep over in the hall, since the wedding celebration would probably continue into the night."

"The building must start soon if it is to finish before the first snow," Silver Fox said. "I don't want to sound discouraging, but I don't think there is sufficient money in the church fund to start the building."

Prudence smiled and thought about the money she

had upstairs, tucked away. "Oh, I think something can be arranged."

After much planning and decision making, Bertha left to reopen the store. Silver Fox insisted on remaining to help Prudence clean up, although she had argued it wasn't necessary. Prudence had to admit, though, that she enjoyed the womanly companionship and conversation as they tended to the clean up.

"You like the West," Silver Fox said, her tone without question.

"Yes, very much," Prudence agreed. "At first it took some growing accustomed to, although I can't say it was difficult. I found the lifestyle to my liking, so much better than where I come from."

"And where is that?"

"Boston."

The teacup Silver Fox was drying almost slipped from her hand and she steadied it. "Tell me of your life there? It must have been very different."

Prudence laughed at the memories, something she had never thought herself capable of doing. "*Different* doesn't come close. It is a whole other world. Not bad, mind you. It has its good points, but I find myself so much more relaxed here. People seem to accept things more readily."

"It wasn't always so. There was a time—and in some places this still exists—when the West was much like the East. I was not accepted in many places due to my half-breed heritage."

"Half-breed?" Prudence asked, having heard the word many times but not paid much heed to it.

"My father was white and of Irish descent, and my mother was Cheyenne, not an acceptable mixture in most parts."

268

"I must admit my ignorance of such matters, although I suppose it is similar to back home, where one's importance was determined by one's social status."

"That was why I was so relieved to find Stewart. It is sort of a haven to me, for which I am grateful."

Prudence placed the last dish away in the cupboard. "All finished."

Silver Fox smiled and reached for Prudence's hand, taking it gently in hers. She touched the two immovable fingers. "It is good to see that you do not hide your hurt, but display it bravely and without shame."

Prudence slipped her hand away. "It wasn't always so. I have Zac to thank for that."

A shadow of sorrow passed over Silver Fox's face as Prudence spoke.

"Back home it was difficult, especially when I was young. Often the other children would make fun of me, and I hid my pain behind pretty gloves and a false smile."

"There was no one to help you through this time?" Silver Fox asked with sadness in her tone.

"My grandmother was very good to me, but I wished for the comfort of a mother."

Silver Fox nodded slowly as though in understanding. Prudence almost thought she saw her eyes grow moist in sympathy. "We will talk again."

"I'd like that," Prudence said, feeling she had made a valuable friend. A friend who lent her shoulder for Prudence to lean on and who shared her heart.

She walked Silver Fox to the door and was surprised to find Zac heading toward the house. She had seen him only briefly this morning upon waking, when he was already dressed and on his way out. She had assumed he wasn't angry with her over last night, since he had to have been the one to place her in bed. It was one time she wished he didn't act the gentleman.

He took a moment to speak with Silver Fox and then he was bounding up the steps.

"Get enough sleep?" he asked, grabbing her around the waist and pulling her alongside him into the house.

"Plenty," she assured him. He looked so handsome in tight denims and a white shirt with his sleeves rolled up, displaying the strength of his thick muscled arms. His hair was rumpled in that devil-may-care way that always managed to excite her. His smile was lusty and sensual all in one, and she ached to taste the heady combination.

"Expecting any more guests?" he asked, his eyes straying to the stairway.

"No." Her answer was short and to the point. She had no plans except to get her husband upstairs and into bed.

He turned her in his arms to face him. "All this time until supper and nothing to do."

Prudence teasingly placed a finger to her lips in thought, then pointed it at him. "I have an idea."

"What's that, Mrs. Stewart?"

"We could talk."

"About what?"

"Sex!" she said without stopping to think, for if she did, she would certainly have lost her courage.

"A most interesting topic, but . . ."

Prudence's heart dropped. Perhaps he wasn't interested in making love to her.

"The bedroom is the only *proper* place for such deep discussions."

"And we must be proper." She nodded seriously.

He snatched her up into his arms, to Prudence's surprise and pleasure. "Proper only goes so far, Pru. And one place it has no room is in our bed, so to speak. What I intend to do to you now is far from proper."

Her smile never faltered. She had only so much time to enjoy him, to pretend this would go on forever, and she would steal whatever moments she could with him. She was building a treasure chest of memories and she wanted to fill it to the brim.

He walked to the steps. "No objections?"

"None," she answered without modesty.

"But it's daylight."

"Wonderful!" She playfully snuggled her face into the crook of his neck. "Then I'll be able to see you better."

"I can arrange for you to see every inch of me."

She pulled her head back and looked him square in the eye. "I'd like that."

Two parts of Zac's anatomy reacted in extreme opposite. One softened and the other hardened, and the only thing he could say was, "Damn."

"Mr. Stewart," Prudence scolded softly. "You're going to pay for that."

Zac brought his lips to hers and whispered across them, "Promise."

"Promise," she repeated, reaching out and tracing his lips with the tip of her tongue, while sending shivers through the both of them.

"We're wasting time." He turned, taking the steps steady and quick.

A hard pounding on the front door stopped him near the top. He turned as the door flew open and Josh, his ranch foreman, hurried in.

"Sorry, Zac, but Lucky's showing signs of an early delivery and it don't look good."

Zac lowered Prudence to the step, gave her a quick kiss, mumbled an even quicker apology, then raced down the steps and out the door.

Prudence stood bewildered and distraught. She stamped her foot like a spoiled child and mumbled her disappointment. But after several minutes of exasperation, she recalled Silver Fox's words about Zac's dream of building the ranch and how he wanted his wife to share in it. And here she was complaining instead of offering her help.

She picked up her skirt and ran upstairs to change into her denim skirt. She couldn't help but glance regretfully at the large, empty bed.

"Tonight," she reassured herself. "Definitely tonight."

She hurried out the door and down the path that lead to the corral and barns. The late spring air was cool and fresh, and all around her signs pointed to the approach of summer. The trees were majestic in their height and their leaves were brilliant greens. Wildflowers grew in profusion, their pinks, yellows, and reds adding cheer to the deep green of Mother Nature's carpet.

The ranch hands respectfully tipped their hats in greeting as she passed by, and one stepped aside so she could enter the barn. Zac had been wrong, she thought. There were many gentlemen in the West.

Prudence spotted Josh. They had been introduced briefly shortly after her arrival at the ranch. He stood by a stall, looking down. He was a tall, lanky man with the thickest moustache Prudence had ever seen and kind blue eyes that didn't fit his rough cowboy exterior. Inside, Josh had a tender heart.

She approached slowly and when Josh saw her, he held his hand up for her to remain silent but motioned her forward.

Prudence joined him, looking down into the stall. Zac was kneeling beside Lucky, talking softly and soothingly to her while stroking her neck.

"It's going to be a long night," Josh whispered to Prudence. "Lucky's our top mare and this colt is the beginning of good horse stock for the ranch."

"Will she be all right?" Prudence asked.

"Can't say. Just have to wait it out and do what we can."

The night passed slowly. Prudence was kept busy making coffee and sandwiches for the ranch hands who were helping with the difficult birth.

It was close to midnight when Lucky finally delivered and easier than they had all expected. A roar was heard throughout the barn when Lucky produced the most beautiful male foal Prudence had ever seen. Of course, it was the *first* foal she had ever seen, but that didn't matter; the newborn was still beautiful to her. And the way Zac tended to the mother and son was heartwarming. She thought with envy of the care and tenderness he would provide for his wife and newborn babe. It was hard to believe that hands that were so fast and lethal with a gun could extend such comfort and care.

Prudence looked at him, so tired and worn from the night's strenuous event. She could see his weariness in the way he rubbed his neck and twisted it back and forth as he stood.

"I can handle it from here, Zac," Josh insisted.

Zac nodded, still rubbing his neck. "I'll be out early tomorrow to check on them both."

"Okay, boss," Josh said, then added, "That's some missus you brought home. She's one fine woman."

"That she is," Zac agreed, and he reached out his hand to Prudence.

She took it and smiled her thanks to Josh for the sincere compliment, before walking from the barn. She held firm to Zac's warm grasp. He pulled her into the crook of his arm as they walked toward the house.

"Lord, but I'm tired." He rested his face against her hair, enjoying its sweet, fresh scent.

"You need to rest," she said in fierce protection of him. She was overwhelmed by the need to care for him. She was certain it was part of being in love, this over-protectiveness, this need to shelter.

Prudence directed him straight upstairs, and once in the bedroom she fussed over him. She immediately built a small fire to chase the night chill from the room. She then motioned in her most staunch manner for him to sit and proceeded to help him remove his boots. His shirt was next, and she couldn't help but admire the strength of him, so thick and broad.

"I need to wash up," he said, getting up from the bed.

"But you're tired."

"And dirty," he added, disappearing into the bathing room.

Prudence turned down the bed and quickly undressed. She changed into her pink nightgown, tying the thin pink silk ties at her throat and chest.

Zac entered the room with only a towel draped around him. He didn't waste any time but headed straight for the bed, discarding the towel just before he crawled in.

Prudence got a quick peek at his bare backside and muscled thighs. She sighed with regret, pushing away her disappointment.

She climbed into bed, slipping beneath the covers, trying not to disturb him. He laid on his stomach quietly. She assumed he had already fallen asleep, which was why she jumped, startled, when he spoke to her.

"My neck is killing me, Pru. Could you rub it some for me?"

"Of course," she said, getting up to kneel beside him.

Her hands worked at the muscles in his neck, which were thick with tension. She kneaded them roughly, forcing him to relax. His skin was warm to her touch though damp from the strands of wet hair that brushed his neck.

"That feels great." His voice was muffled from his face being half buried in his pillow. "Rub my shoulders?"

She didn't hesitate. Her hands moved to help ease the tension there. She worked on his back down to his waist, where the blanket lay across it. She liked touching him, feeling his potency beneath her fingers as they dug into his flesh. He was so powerfully built that it excited her, and she was tempted to slip the cover away and touch him even further. He was hard and virile, and she wanted badly to stretch herself over him, to connect closely, to join with him and feel the pleasure of him.

Instead, she continued to work on his back while her imagination worked elsewhere.

"My thighs, Pru. Do my thighs," he begged. "They ache like hell."

She swallowed the lump in her throat and her inhibitions all at once as she drew back the covers, exposing the rest of him to her view.

With great difficulty she stifled a moan, which was pleading to escape her lips. She bit hard to hold it back as her fingers dug into the heavy muscle of his thigh. Her eyes roamed as her fingers worked most diligently. The firm swell of his nicely curved backside connected perfectly to his thighs, as though a master sculptor had fashioned him. And her memory taunted her with vivid recall of what lay snug in the darkness between his slightly parted legs.

"That feels so good," he groaned in relief.

She was glad he was so pleased, because she was suffering mightily. Perspiration tickled her brow, and the small fire made her feel as though she were roasting. She wiped at her face and sighed.

"Hot, Pru?" he asked softly.

"A bit. Must be the fire."

"Must be," he agreed. "Take off your nightgown."

Her hands stopped and rested on his thigh a moment before continuing again, this time with added fervor. "That's not necessary."

"I think it is. You're hot and bothered. You'll feel better with it off."

"No, I won't," she insisted a bit more sternly than she had planned.

"Don't argue with your tired husband," he ordered just as sternly.

"It's really not—"

He turned swiftly on his back and her hand now rested on the top of his thigh, dangerously close to his groin. Her eyes caught there immediately, and she squeezed them shut upon seeing the full size of him, potent and ready.

"Take your nightgown off and come here to me," he demanded in the harsh sensual tone of a man hungry for his woman.

Her fingers trembled as she reached to untie the pink ribbons at her throat. The trembling increased when she pulled the ribbons free at her chest.

"Take it off," he ordered once more and with impatience.

She eased the gown up and over her head, tossing it to the side. She was still kneeling, her back rigid, her chest out, and her eyes finally open.

"Come here." He held his hand out to her.

She took it and he pulled her to him, adjusting her to straddle him. Her bottom rested on his belly and his one hand stayed locked with hers.

He tugged her forward slightly so his other hand could reach up and capture her breast. She stretched up, arching her back, offering herself to him.

"I love how your nipples harden so quickly to my touch and how you shiver and moan when I play with you." He raced his fingers down her stomach to the junction of her thighs, then over the small bud that sprang to life as soon as he caressed it.

The results were instantaneous. She shivered and moaned.

"I'm not going to play fair tonight, honey," he warned, grasping her backside firmly in his hands.

She looked at him in alarm and anticipation.

He just smiled and yanked her forward. His tongue was electrifying, and she cried out as spasms of rapture assaulted her. This was pain and pleasure in its purest form, and she never wanted it to end.

He teased and tormented her until she thought she would go mad, rushing her to the brink of release, then easing her back again to start his torture all over.

She begged and pleaded for him to stop and not to stop. Prudence was lost in a mindless void where nothing mattered but his touch and the magic it brought her.

She wasn't aware of him slipping her off him and tucking her beneath him, or of how gently his hands eased her legs apart, or of when he entered her. Her only thoughts were of his powerful thrusts. Deep and forceful, they were delivered time and time again, and she clung to him, aching to feel each one.

"Come with me, Pru," his voice urged from somewhere in the distance. "Come with me."

She raced up to meet him, throwing her hips against his, matching his power, filling herself with him as he filled her. Together they exploded, clinging, yearning to feel every bit of that infinite moment.

Zac cradled Prudence in his arms afterwards, wanting her close to him.

"Tired?" he asked, concerned about her stillness.

"Satiated."

He laughed and hugged her to him even tighter. "So I filled you up, did I?"

"More than I ever imagined possible," she said, squeezing his leg between hers.

"You like what I do to you?"

She shook her head against his chest. "No, I *love* what you do to me."

"Well, there's lots more to learn," he teased.

She stiffened slightly in his arms. He could feel the

change in her, as though she were alarmed. "Something wrong, Pru?"

She cuddled closer to him. "No, nothing."

But he knew her better and he knew what disturbed her, knew her fears. Soon he would use the key that would ease her worries and still her pain. Soon he would unlock his heart and tell her how very much he loved her. How he had since the first time he kissed her. Very soon, but not just yet. He didn't want to give her an ultimatum. To force her to make a choice between ranch life and Boston. He wanted her decision to be based on one factor: her love for him. Given a little more time, that would be possible. He was certain of it, as certain as he was of his love for her.

Zac slept easily that night, convinced he had Prudence in hand, convinced there were no obstacles to overcome, convinced he had everything under control.

Chapter Twenty-one

"I can't believe she's been here only two weeks and has accomplished so much," Bertha said, setting out fresh baked breads and homemade jams on the long table already stocked with a variety of foods.

Silver Fox moved some of the warm fruit pies around to make more room. "At the rate folks are turning up for this church raising, we'll need two more tables to accommodate everyone."

"Zac's already ordered the men to fix up two more tables," Bertha informed her, smiling as she accepted a crock of baked beans from Mrs. Gooden.

"Looks like the church will be ready in plenty of time for your wedding, Bertha," Mrs. Gooden remarked with a smile. "Everyone around these parts is looking forward to the big event."

"It's thanks to Prudence I'll have my wedding in a church," Bertha commented appreciatively.

"That young lady is a whirlwind of activity," Mrs. Gooden said with glee. "She's added a whole lot of life to this town. Why, Sam can't stop talking about that dance she held out at her place last week, and Norma Bennet can't wait for next Wednesday and the Ladies Social Club meeting. And this church . . . My, oh my, she's something else."

"Yes, she is very special," Silver Fox added warmly.

"Well, I'm off to help the other ladies with the quilt we're working on for you-know-who as a belated wedding gift." Mrs. Gooden nodded toward Prudence, who was walking toward them.

"I'll be over to help later," Bertha whispered.

Mrs. Gooden waved her slim hand and was off with a short stop by Prudence, telling her how wonderful everything was going and how proud all the citizens were of the new church.

Prudence joined Bertha and Silver Fox at the table, checking on the supply of food and laughing at the abundance of it. "And I was worried there wouldn't be enough."

"Do you ladies mind if I take a minute to bring some cider to Charlie? He looks mighty thirsty," Bertha said, glancing appreciatively at Charlie's solid bulk as he helped raise one of the church walls.

"Go ahead," Prudence said, having just returned from a similar errand of mercy.

"You have made a good home here," Silver Fox said after Bertha had left.

A shade of sadness descended over Prudence's face. "Yes, I have."

"Is something wrong?"

"No, nothing," she answered, and forced a cheerful smile to her face. She wanted to scream and yell, *Yes,* . . . she didn't want to lose her husband or her home or the friends she had made here. But time was running out and soon she would say good-bye to it all. She had even found herself fantasizing that Zac loved her and perhaps would beg her to stay, insist that she stay. But again it was only her fanciful dreams.

"Something troubles you."

Prudence nodded her head. "Much troubles me."

And suddenly she found she wanted to speak of the one thing that she hadn't discussed with anyone since her arrival. "I came west to find my mother. She left my father and me many years ago. I was lucky and picked up her trail, but each time I got close I'd lose her track again. It saddens me to know that I didn't succeed in my original reason for venturing out here."

"Sometimes things are better left in the past," Silver Fox offered in comfort.

"I suppose they are, but memories die hard, especially in a little girl who loved her mother more than anything and had thought her mother felt the same way."

"Perhaps she did. People don't always leave because they don't love. Many times it is because they do and wish to protect."

Prudence regarded Silver Fox strangely. "I never thought of that. I can't imagine what she would have been protecting me from. But perhaps if I looked differently at her reason for leaving, it would help me to understand her better and hopefully find her."

"Keep your heart open and you will find success in your quest."

"Thank you," Prudence said, grateful for the sincere advice. She turned to take yet another dish from a new arrival.

The day couldn't have gone better. Everyone was in high spirits. By dusk the outside of the church was almost complete. There was still much to be done and many volunteers to do it. In a few weeks the church would be complete, and by early autumn it would be dressed in its finery for Bertha's wedding.

Prudence kept her eyes on her husband as he prepared their wagon to leave. An overpowering urge to rush into his arms and beg him to take her home this very minute and make love to her shot a nervous shiver through her. She was gripped by a dreadful premonition that she would not have many more such opportunities.

She waved her good-byes to Bertha, Charlie, and Silver Fox, then hurried to join her husband. Her hand touched his shoulder and a feeling of comfort swept over her.

He turned, grabbing her around the waist in his familiar way and drawing her to him. He kissed her soundly. "Ready to go home, honey?"

"Yes, more than ready," she said, her breath catching in little gasps, betraying her excitement.

Zac brushed a strand of loose hair from her face. "Your words tell me we'll be lucky if we make it home."

She didn't smile, her expression becoming seriously sensual. "We need to make it home, Mr. Stewart, since I intend to make love with you all night, perhaps even into the day." She had the most awful feeling that this was her last chance to hold him, to love him, to share with him.

Zac felt her nervous tremble and he crushed her tightly to him. "I think we'll make it back to the ranch in record time tonight."

She released a tremulous laugh, remaining locked protectively in the strength of his arms. "Let's get started."

Zac was about to agree wholeheartedly, when a shout announced an approaching wagon.

Bertha, Charlie, and Silver Fox stood on the steps of the dry goods store, staring down the street at the slow meandering approach of the wagon.

Prudence tugged at Zac's shirt. "Let's go, Zac. Now. Please."

The urgency in her voice concerned him, as did the fright in her eyes. If it was who she assumed, he was glad, actually relieved, they were here. Finally, matters would be settled, and it was about time. "We'll see who it is first, Pru. Perhaps someone needs help."

He took her hand and almost had to pull her along, around their wagon, to face the new arrivals.

"Prudence!"

She cringed at the sound of Granger's squealing voice, then cringed again when the wagon halted and Granger climbed clumsily off, almost toppling to the ground in his haste and ineptitude. Her father followed, but his footing was sound and sure.

She felt the reluctance in Zac's hand to release hers as she stepped forward to welcome her father. She walked straight past a startled and perturbed Granger. "Father," she said, her voice choked with emotion as she kissed him on the cheek.

"Prudence, my love," James Winthrop said in relief, hugging his daughter to him. He filled himself with the knowledge that only holding her could bring — that she was safe and sound — then held her at arm's length to inspect the change he had been surprised to see when first he laid eyes on her. "You look positively radiant."

"Nonsense," Granger interrupted sharply. "She looks disheveled. Whatever are you doing in that common cotton dress? And why isn't your hair pinned properly in place?"

"Granger, please," James said, his nerves nearly shot. "I'll handle this."

"Then handle it," Granger yelled. "Just look at what he's done to her. It will take weeks to return her to her well-groomed self. What will people say when she re-

284

turns to Boston looking so sunburnt and so—so common!"

The voice that spoke next was threatening. "Prudence isn't going back to Boston."

She turned to see Zac walking toward her. His steps were purposeful and sturdy, his stance probably a bit frightening to those who did not know him. He was a commanding figure even without his six-shooters, especially when he wore that cold, expressionless mask. The one that registered, *shoot to kill*.

Granger automatically stepped out of his path of fire, his face having paled considerably.

Zac possessively hooked his arm around her waist and stood like a stalwart guard beside her. Prudence showed no signs of protest. She was too shocked to respond.

Granger finally managed to gather some courage, though he kept his distance. "And why isn't Prudence returning to Boston?"

Zac stared at the man so intimidatingly that Granger took another step back. "Simple," Zac answered. "She's my wife."

Another step back appeared to add a notch to Granger's courage. "You mean 'rich' wife," he said. His remark was highlighted with an ugly laugh.

Zac's expression didn't waver. It was as though Granger's barb had hit steel and bounced off. But his response was chosen well. "Wife, Granger, in every sense of the word."

Granger burned a bright, furious red. He sputtered and mumbled, attempting to contain himself and his mounting wrath. But his tongue would not hold, and he directed it at the one person he felt certain of intimidating. "Prudence, how could you lower yourself? Circumstances *forced* him to marry you. Circumstances did not *force* you to share his bed. Your conduct is appalling."

"Enough, Granger!" James interrupted angrily. "This is a private matter and should be discussed as such."

"There's nothing to discuss. Prudence is staying with me," Zac calmly informed them all.

Prudence felt on the brink of tears. In her emotional state, she was close to breaking down. Granger wanted her for her family's money. Zac's reason, she supposed, was obligation. He had lain with her, taken her virginity, and felt obligated. No one, absolutely no one, loved her.

"I think it best we return to the house and settle this matter," Prudence suggested with a normalcy to her tone she didn't think possible.

"A wise idea," her father agreed, his glance straying to the three people standing in front of the store.

"They're friends, Father," Prudence said, reassuring him. "They will understand this outburst."

James nodded his head but couldn't help but glance again at the three, especially the woman standing behind the gentleman. The one with the long, dark hair.

Prudence saw his hesitation and weariness. "Would you like to meet them?"

James wasn't certain if he wanted to, but he nodded his head in favor of his daughter's suggestion, anyway.

Prudence held Zac's hand as she, along with her father, walked toward the trio.

The introductions were made. Bertha was her usual boisterous self, while Silver Fox stayed back somewhat in the shadows of the storefront porch.

Prudence noticed her father's preoccupation with Silver Fox. His glance darted often to her, and he seemed confused and unsure. His response to questions put to him was hesitant and distracted. She assumed the long trip had taken its toll and decided it was best she take him to the ranch so he could rest.

Good-byes were casually issued, as well as handshakes. James was about to take his leave, when he turned one more time and stared most strangely at Silver Fox.

Prudence suddenly became alarmed as her father turned pure white.

"Oh, my God!" James cried and took a step forward, toward Silver Fox. She had retreated farther into the shadows, like a frightened animal.

"Papa?" Prudence questioned, fearful of her father's strange actions.

James stepped swiftly forward and halted a few inches from Silver Fox. He reached his hand out, but she backed away. His voice was low, yet rich in pain. "Lenore!"

Prudence, on her way toward her father, stopped dead still. Zac wasted no time in coming up behind her.

"It is you, isn't it, Lenore?" James asked for reassurance, though it wasn't necessary. His wife might have gotten older, but she was just as beautiful as the first day he had met her.

"Yes, James, it's me."

If it weren't for Zac's strong arms around her, Prudence would have collapsed to the ground.

"I don't understand," James said sadly. "All these years I tried, but I couldn't understand why you left me."

Tears filled Silver Fox's eyes and spilled onto her cheeks. "It is difficult to explain."

"You didn't love me?" James asked the question that had haunted him for so long.

"Oh no, James, I love you more than anything in the world," she argued, her hurt evident in her labored tone.

"Then why?" he demanded, suddenly angry for the wasted years.

"*Because* I loved you so much. That is why I left."

James shook his head. "That doesn't make sense."

"Nothing makes sense," Granger cut in caustically as he walked up beside James. "Particularly the fact that your wife is alive and is a half-breed. Which makes your daughter part savage. That should make for some startling gossip in Boston."

Prudence felt the sting of his words and the fact that what he said was true. She was part Indian, or as he put it, part *savage*. Tumultuous feelings overwhelmed her. Silver Fox was her mother. Silver Fox was part Indian. Silver Fox had known all along that Prudence was her daughter and had allowed her to go on hurting.

"Zac!" Prudence cried, welcoming the darkness that swallowed her up as much as the strong hands that caught her and held her tightly.

Chapter Twenty-two

"Three days, Pru. Three days you have refused to speak with your father or mother," Zac said, pacing in front of the bed where his wife sat.

"I don't wish to speak with anyone," she reiterated for the third time.

Zac was close to erupting. He had had enough of all the nonsense going on, but most of all he was concerned with his wife's health and well-being. She looked pale and she hadn't been eating properly. Her eyes were constantly red from her constant crying. It had to stop.

He stopped in front of her. "Prudence." His voice was stern and held authority.

Her head snapped up, and she tilted it in that defiant manner he always found challenging. She was all but informing him she'd do as she pleased, like it or not.

"I am going to town to pick up your father, and I am returning with him and your mother. You are going to sit and talk to them, just as they have been talking to each other and, might I say, making remarkable strides in mending their relationship."

"I—"

"Don't bother to tell me you won't talk to them," he warned. "If I must, I'll carry you downstairs myself and tie you to a chair and force you to listen to them."

Prudence shut her mouth and crossed her arms firmly across her chest.

"Being pigheaded isn't going to do you any good."

She refused to rise to his bait.

He knelt down in front of the bed where she sat, placing his hands on her knees. "Have a heart, honey. Your mother and father are concerned about your reaction to all this. They need time to talk things over with you. And besides, Granger needs someone to cut him down from the corral post that he's been tied to for the last two days."

"Zac, you didn't?" Prudence cried, and couldn't help but smile at the crazy picture it brought to mind.

He patted her knee in reassurance. "No, I'm only teasing. I wanted to see you smile again. But I warn you, I'll do more than just tie him to a post. I'm liable to shoot the stupid idiot."

"Zac, really," Prudence admonished.

"Honey, he's a danger to himself. If he's not insisting one of the ranch hands take him into Stewart, he's upstairs sulking in his room. When I refused his request and offered him a horse, he didn't bother to tell me he didn't know how to ride and mounted the animal backwards. It took five men to calm the horse down and get him off, since he was facedown on the animal's rump, holding onto his tail for dear life."

Prudence couldn't help but burst into laughter at the comical scene Zac's words had painted. "You're teasing me?"

"No, I'm not. And he's carrying on horribly because he has to eat in the mess house with the cowhands. It's the one issue on which he feels I should exert husbandly authority. He thinks I should put my foot down and force you to come downstairs and cook the meals."

"Oh, he said so, did he? And what did you tell him?" Prudence's tone was brisk and annoyed.

"I told him I had you right where I wanted you." Zac stretched up and over her, forcing her back onto the bed. He held her captive with his body, emphasizing his superior position by pressing against her with a decisive sensual wiggle.

"I don't feel like making love," Prudence lied. Her arms were still locked across her breasts, hiding the twin stiff peaks, proof that she certainly was interested in his playful teasing.

"I can change that," he offered, and kissed her breathless.

"Stop that," she yelled when she was finally able to pull her mouth away.

"Didn't like it?"

She cast him an evil glare.

"I like that look. It's sinister and wicked. And I love when you're wicked." He kissed the tip of her nose.

"Zac!" she cried.

"In that much of a hurry, are you? Well, let's hoist up your skirt and get to it." He reached down to open his pants.

"Zac, so help me!"

Zac looked seriously into her soft green eyes. "That's exactly what I'm trying to do, help you. You can't continue like this, Pru. It isn't you. Yell. Scream. Tell your parents how rotten you feel, but don't lock your feelings away."

"I don't know if I can," she said wearily.

"You have no choice," he insisted. "You must confront them. It's the only way to settle things."

Her hand came up to rub his thick jaw. "You're strong enough to take punches and come back fighting. I don't know if can."

He took her hand and brought it to his lips, kissing her palm. "I'll be right there beside you. It isn't necessary to face this alone."

She was close to tears. He was being so kind to her and she couldn't understand why. Nothing, absolutely nothing, made any sense anymore. "I'll speak to my parents."

"Good," he said, then kissed her soundly. He pushed himself off her and held out his hand to help her up. "I'll go fetch them right away before you change your mind."

She nodded her agreement.

He slipped two fingers beneath the coppery curl that fell on her forehead and fondled its silky texture. "Will you be all right while I'm gone?"

"Yes, Zac. Don't worry. I'll be fine."

"I won't be long." He hurried to the door, anxious to be on his way and anxious to return. He stopped suddenly, his hand on the handle, and turned around. "After this matter is settled with your parents, there is much we must discuss."

"Yes, there is," she agreed, dreading the moment they would face each other to say good-bye.

"Be back soon." He waved and walked out the door.

Prudence washed her face and repaired her messy hair. She changed into a plain blue skirt and white cotton blouse, then went downstairs to await her parents return.

Her spirits bounded from high to low, and her only consistent feeling was one of confusion. There was so much to think about. Yet her one major worry, the one that invaded her thoughts night and day, involved the overpowering love she had for Zac Stewart and the reality of their marriage coming to an end.

She walked into the family parlor and stopped as though she had run up against a brick wall. Granger was standing by the fireplace.

"So you have finally decided to join us, have you?" he said arrogantly. "I must say, Prudence, your manners have been abominable. But under the circumstances, I can now understand why."

Prudence's brow rose. "And why is that, Granger?"

He tugged at his brown vest, making certain it properly covered his trouser band, and adjusted the starched white collar that cut into his throat.

Prudence was familiar with his delay tactics. They were meant to intimidate her. "Do you know why, Granger?" she asked impatiently.

"Yes, of course," he snapped. "I had thought to spare your feelings, but since you appear so adamant . . . It is because you are part *savage*. Everyone knows savages cannot be completely taught to live as decent white people."

Prudence took a step back, as though he had struck her in the face. This was one time she found it difficult, if not impossible, to hide her stunned reaction.

"Of course," Granger continued without caring how his ignorant remark affected her, "it isn't your fault you carry heathen blood in you. And I am willing— although it will take much understanding on my part,—to overlook your character flaw and marry you anyway. Our friends in Boston, naturally, must not hear of this, or our social standing would be ruined. At first, of course, you'd be a rarity, but the novelty of your situation would wane and eventually we would be cast out completely."

"Marry you?" Prudence repeated, wondering how

he could think she would even entertain such a ridiculous notion.

"Yes. Your father had annulment papers drawn up before we left. Once they are signed and validated, we'll be free to marry almost immediately."

"Why?" she asked, completely confused by his nonsensical idea.

"What do you mean why? We planned on marrying before you took it into that empty head of yours to go frolicking off to the West. And now, who else would marry you? Ex-wife of an infamous gunslinger. Part heathen. Why, I bet those crooked, ugly fingers were caused by the impure blood inside you."

Prudence shut her eyes against the vicious remark. She took a deep breath and opened them slowly. They were burning bright green with anger. "I have no intention of marrying you. I never had any intention of marrying you. I wouldn't marry you if my life depended on it. Do I make myself clear, Granger? I want nothing to do with you." She turned and stormed out of the room, her head held high.

Granger rushed after her, grabbing her arm and swinging her around. "You think the handsome gunslinger wants you? You think he took you to his bed because he wanted to? Think again. Your father *paid* him to protect you. He doesn't enjoy touching you. You're too plain. Too big. Money buys anything, my dear Prudence. And your father's money not only bought you a husband, but it bought you his kisses and all the pretty lies he tells you when he's forced to perform his conjugal rights."

Prudence's response was instantaneous. She swung with all her might and slapped Granger square in the jaw, sending him stumbling back. He landed with a solid thump to his backside on the floor.

"Heathen!" he spat, cupping his sore jaw.

Prudence stopped halfway up the staircase and placed her hand on the bannister, holding her body erect with grace and pride. "I may be a heathen, Granger, but I'm a *rich* heathen. And as you said, money can buy anything."

Granger paled, his eyes bulged out from his head, and his mouth hung open so wide that it reminded Prudence of a perfect fly trap.

"Prudence, please. I was upset . . . not thinking properly," he begged, realizing too late his mistake. "Please, please forgive me."

"Forgive you?" She shook her head sadly. "I pity you." She walked up the stairs, ignoring his pleas, his vows of love and concern for her, and his promise never to speak so inconsiderately again.

She closed her door, locking it and leaning her forehead against the thick wood. She had forgotten her father had paid Zac to look after her, to protect her, to return her to him safely. She had been a fool. A stupid fool. And the memories she had collected were worthless. They meant nothing. His words meant nothing. They were all lies. All lies.

She wiped at her tears and hurriedly packed a small traveling bag. She grabbed her wool shawl, threw it around her shoulders, and ran out of the room.

Prudence made her escape down and out the back way so Granger wouldn't see her. She searched for Josh, finding him by the corral watching the mare and her new foal.

"Josh," she called, "I need your help."

"What's the matter? That easterner bothering you?" he asked and, with a menacing look, took a step toward the house.

"No," she said, reaching out to grab his arm and

stop him. "I just need to get away from everyone for a few days. I need time alone. To think. To straighten things out. Is there someplace you could take me?"

"Alone?" he asked. "Are you sure you want to be alone in these parts? You're still pretty new to things around here."

"I'm adaptable." She almost laughed.

"Yeah, Zac says that all the time." He shook his head and smiled.

"Please, Josh, just three days. You can come check on me. Please."

"Never could turn down a pleading woman," he mumbled. "I'll get the wagon. You go tell Tom, the mess house cook, to throw some food stuff together for you. Then meet me the other side of the barn."

Prudence was so ecstatic that she threw her arms around Josh and kissed him on the cheek. "Thank you," she cried, and rushed off to do as he had directed.

Josh shook his head and rubbed his moustache. "Zac ain't gonna like this one bit."

"She's gone!" Granger shouted as Zac, James, and Silver Fox walked through the door. "I've searched the entire house. She's no place to be found."

"She's probably down by the corrals. She's taken with the new colt and enjoys watching him," Zac said, not the least bit worried.

Granger shook his head and tugged at James's coat sleeve. "I tell you, she's gone. I heard a wagon pull out of here a short time ago, and being she was upset I'm sure—"

"Upset over what?" Zac asked, his tone curt. "When I left her she was fine."

Granger shrugged, while a nervous twitch started in the corner of his right eye. "We had a discussion. She became upset upon realizing all the problems she faced."

James rubbed his forehead and shook his head in regret. "I should have never brought you along, Granger."

Granger was insulted. "And why not? Who else would have been honest with poor Prudence and told her the truth? You would have kept her in a fairy-tale world. You would have had her believe that this marriage could actually work and, worse yet, that Stewart actually cared about her."

Zac wasn't pleased with the way Granger pointed an accusing finger at him, nor did he relish the thought of the exchange that must have taken place between him and Prudence. He had a dreadful feeling that Granger had damaged, if not completely destroyed, all the trust and confidence he had steadily built within Prudence.

"What exactly did you say to her?" Zac asked.

"I told her the truth," Granger defended.

"And what is the truth?" James snapped. "What vile opinion did you attempt to force on her?"

"James, really," Granger said. "You're acting more and more like your daughter. Don't let this uncivilized land turn you into a savage, too."

"Savage?" Zac repeated. "You called her a savage?"

Granger cleared his throat in an attempt to explain. "I merely pointed out the obvious and what others would comment on once we returned to Boston. And, of course, I reminded her why you so conveniently married her."

"Why did I marry her, Granger?" Zac asked in such a menacing tone that Granger paled considerably.

"Her—her money, naturally," he stammered. "Or what James paid you already. Why else would you marry someone so plain and with a deformity?"

Zac shut his eyes against the pain he was certain Granger's thoughtless words had caused Prudence. He had an overpowering urge to shoot the senseless bastard, but unfortunately—or fortunately for Granger—he wasn't wearing his six-shooters.

He opened his eyes and relived his wife's pain when he glanced at Silver Fox and saw the tears rolling silently down her face.

Zac took a step toward Granger.

He backed up swiftly and threw his hands up to protect his face. "You're not going to hit me, too, are you?"

Zac stopped in front of the cowering man. "Who hit you?"

Granger turned a bright scarlet. "Prudence, in her anger, slapped me."

Zac laughed and shook his head. He had to hand it to her. She was one spirited lady.

"Do you have any idea where she could have gone?" James asked Zac, concerned for his daughter's safety.

"There's a few possibilities. I'll check them out," Zac said. "You and Silver Fox make yourselves at home. And, Granger?"

Granger stepped forward. "Yes, what can I do to help?"

"You've given me all the help I can handle." He smiled, then leaned back and threw such a forceful punch to the man's face that it sent him onto his backside, sliding across the floor, to land against the wall.

Zac walked over to him, grabbed him by his collar, and pulled Granger's head up, shaking him awake. When he was certain he had his attention, he spoke.

298

"Don't ever call my wife a savage again, or the next time I'll kill you." Zac released him, and his head hit the bottom step with a loud thud.

"I suppose my daughter's safety is in your hands once again," James said.

"That it is," Zac agreed as he reached for his hat on the hall table. "Only this time it isn't your daughter I'm going after. It's my wife, and she's going to be damned sorry she challenged me on this one."

James opened his mouth in defense of his daughter.

"Don't bother saying a word. This is one time she's not going to get away with it."

Silver Fox stilled any further comment from her husband with a gentle hand to his arm.

"Zac."

All three faces turned to see Josh standing in the open doorway.

"I need to talk with you," Josh said, motioning for him to follow outside.

"I think we have our answer," Zac said, then followed Josh out onto the porch.

Chapter Twenty-three

Prudence listened to the woeful tune of the wind as it whipped around the outside of the cabin. It reminded her of a wailing woman, crying out her grief and sorrow over the loss of a loved one. It was punctuated every now and then with the lonely howl of a wolf or the deep hoot of an owl. The once uncommon sounds were now a soothing melody to her, and she sat at the wooden table listening with pleasure to the strange symphony.

Josh had built a fire in the stone hearth before he had reluctantly left her on her own. He had predicted rain, insisting that a slight chill would accompany it. She was grateful for his expertise and for the wool shawl now draped around her shoulders over her blue nightgown.

The rain, she had no doubt, would start soon. She didn't worry overly much since the cabin was snug and warm, locked away from the outside world. She studied the small interior, amazed at how Zac could have spent so many years in this one room.

A wide bed occupied one wall, a chest another, the fireplace took up the third, and the door almost covered the fourth. Four square solid walls, no window, and no light, except when the door was open. A table and two chairs stood before the fire, and Prudence thought of the many nights Zac had probably sat as she did, watching the flames and dreaming of the future.

She shook her head, forcing the thoughts from her mind. She hadn't come here to make matters worse. She had come to decide what course of action to take. She didn't care for the idea of returning to Boston. She liked it here and she liked the people. But could she stay if she was no longer Zac's wife?

An odd noise interrupted the symphony outside, and Prudence listened to the changed melody. She thought she had heard a horse but wasn't certain.

She listened more closely, jumping clear out of her chair when a pounding sent the door rattling.

"Prudence, let me in!"

Prudence sighed in relief upon hearing Zac's demanding voice. She rushed to the door, lifting the board that held it locked against intruders. Zac was admitted with a gush of wind and a splatter of rain.

Prudence stepped back as he forced the door closed. He slipped off his long coat and hat, hanging them on the pegs near the door, then turned.

She protectively tightened the shawl around her shoulders, clinging to the ends in front of her chest. He looked so handsome and so angry. The simple mixture and soft glow of the flames highlighted his good looks and brought an audible sigh of regret to her lips.

Zac remained where he was, watching her assess him. This wasn't going to be easy. He wanted her. Hell, he ached for her. Her coppery hair fell wild and loose over her shoulders, and he'd bet anything her bottom was bare beneath her nightgown. But it

301

wouldn't do to rush things. She needed to trust him, to believe in him once again.

"Have any coffee?" he asked. "It's chilly out there."

She nodded her head and placed a tin mug in front of the chair opposite where she had been sitting. She took a thick pot rag and picked up the coffeepot from near the hearth, where she had kept it hot, and poured Zac a cup.

"Thanks." He sat and cupped his hands around the hot mug.

"Hungry?" she asked, unwrapping a cloth napkin to offer him a honey biscuit.

He took it though he wasn't hungry. He wanted to keep her talking, relax her so that when he reached out to touch her she wouldn't jump like a frightened kitten.

"Josh told you I was here," she said, taking her seat.

"He was concerned about your safety."

"He never intended to let me stay here alone, did he?"

Zac shook his head. "Wouldn't be the wise thing to do, Pru."

"But I need some time alone," she insisted.

"Do you? Or do you need a place to hide?"

The implication of his words stung. "I wasn't running away."

"Weren't you?" he argued. "You were running from your father, mother . . . and me."

"I'm not ready to talk to anyone yet."

"You mean you're not ready to confront anyone yet?" he corrected.

"I can face my problems. It's people I prefer not to deal with at the moment."

"People or issues?"

302

Prudence stood and slammed her fist on the table. "Stop talking in circles and spit out what you have to say to me, then be on your way. I don't want you here."

Zac stood, too, and planted his hands flat on the table, leaning toward her. "You won't confront your mother about why she left you. You wouldn't confront your father about why he didn't tell you the truth. You won't confront the fact that you're part Indian. And you won't confront me with the reason I married you."

"I know why you married me." She held her pride and head high.

"Really? And why did I marry you?" he asked, standing straight and tall.

"You were staring down the barrel of several rifles. You had no choice in the matter. Besides, my father paid you handsomely to see to my safety."

Zac shook his head sadly, running his hand through his dark hair in frustration. "You don't know me at all, Pru, if you think a bunch of men with rifles could force me to marry someone I didn't want to."

"What choice did you have?" she asked incredulously.

"Pru, I've cleaned up towns filled with tougher men than the ones that were toting those rifles. Nobody forces me to do anything."

"You actually expect me to believe you married me because you wanted to?"

"Is that difficult to believe?"

"No, just preposterous."

"Damn, woman, you don't make things easy."

"What is it you want easy?"

"Your acceptance of my love."

303

Prudence opened her mouth, ready to argue, then shut it immediately. "You can't love me," she said softly after gathering her wits.

"Why?" He walked around the table slowly toward her.

"You were paid to take care of me, which included marrying me if necessary, making love to me, and telling me I'm pretty."

"What was I paid, Pru?" He stood near her but back, not wanting to frighten her away.

"Money, and plenty of it. My father is filthy rich and so am I. You did it for his money and probably mine."

"I did, did I?" His voice was so gentle and patient, it caused Prudence to tremble.

"Yes," she snapped defiantly, and stuck her chin out and up. "How much? How much did he pay you to tell me all those lies?"

"The price was steep," he said, advancing on her and forcing her to back up.

"And naturally my father agreed. Why wouldn't he? He loves me!" The back of her legs brushed the bed and brought her to a dead halt.

"It isn't your father who owes me," Zac said, stopping in front of her. He looked down into her challenging green eyes, bright and shining in defense of herself. "You owe me, honey."

"I most certainly do not. What could I ever owe you?"

"You owe me the very thing that I offer you freely and that you've been hiding, tucked away, too frightened to give it to me." He seized her arms and brought her up against him. "Your payment is due now. I want it. I demand it. I deserve it."

"You don't deserve anything," she protested, twisting in his arms to free herself.

He tightened his grip and stilled her movements. "Not even your love, Pru?"

Startled, her eyes widened and she drew in a sharp breath.

"I love you, Prudence Agatha. I have since that night in the garden when I kissed you. I'm not being gallant. I didn't realize then that I loved you. But I felt something strange and exciting, and damned if I didn't want to feel more. When your father informed me of your unexpected journey and asked for my help, I couldn't say no. I didn't want to."

"But—but he paid you," she stammered, shaking her head disbelievingly.

"My fee was that he see to the investment of some stock, which he would have done anyway since I had an appointment with him the following day to ask him to do just that."

"You came after me because you wanted to?"

"Correct."

"You love me?" she asked tentatively, almost fearfully.

"Yes, Prudence, I love you."

"Honest?"

He laughed and roughly pulled her up more firmly against him, forcing her head back so she could look into his eyes. "Honest, I love you. All of you, from the tip of your naked toes, up those sexy legs and doubly sexy bottom, to those gorgeous breasts and to the prettiest face I've ever laid eyes on. You're mine, honey, and I'm never going to let you go. Do you honestly think I'd make love to you and allow you to walk out of my life?"

305

"Could it be obligation you feel toward me? I mean, since I was a virgin and inexperienced, perhaps—"

"Obligation has nothing to do with our relationship. Love is the only factor here. Before anything had occurred between us, when I wired your father about our marriage, I told him it was a permanent situation. There would be no annulment."

"But he brought annulment papers. I assumed you—"

"You assumed wrong," he finished. "He explained to me that he wanted to give you a choice. I told him you had no choice. You were my wife and would remain so for the rest of our lives."

"You really love me?" she asked again, fearing that this was all a dream and she would soon wake and find herself alone.

"Yes, I *really* love you. And if I must tell you over and over for the rest of our lives to convince you, then so be it. I *really* love you."

"Oh, Zac, I don't know what to think. I'm so confused, so tired of being hurt," she cried and laid her head against his chest, seeking the comfort he had often given her.

He wrapped his arms around her. "I understand, Pru. We'll take this one day at a time. But I honestly love you. Cross my heart," he whispered.

She buried her face against his chest. She wanted to believe him. Oh, how she wanted to believe him. But her hurt was so raw that she was afraid to open herself up to him and tell him that she loved him. If she did, she'd be vulnerable, and she wasn't certain if she could handle that delicate feeling right now.

His hand rubbed her back in a steady and sure motion. It was a simple, reassuring touch, but one that stirred her need for him. Perhaps if it was too difficult to speak her love, she could at least demonstrate it. She pulled away from his chest, holding on to his arms, and looked into his eyes. They burned with the same hot desire.

"Make love to me, Zac." Her whisper was a soft ache.

He nodded slowly, understanding what she was trying to tell him. "I love you, too, Pru." He took her in his arms, drawing her back onto the bed.

His touch was like magic. It brought her body alive. She had never felt so sensitive, so attuned to his every caress. His lips found and worshiped every responsive spot, raising gooseflesh across her warm skin.

Her breasts ached and her stomach fluttered, each stroke of his hand and tongue making her more wet with anticipation.

It wasn't long before she begged him to fill her and quench her raging thirst. And when he did, she cried out his name repeatedly, until she exploded and his name echoed from her lips. His words that joined hers, more softly but with equal strength, were simply, "I love you."

They lay wrapped in each other's arms, content to listen to the howling of the wind and rain outside. It had turned into a worse storm than was expected.

"You're not afraid?" he asked.

"Afraid?" she asked, cuddling against his warm naked body.

"The storm. On the steamboat, you were afraid of the storm."

Prudence listened for a minute and noticed that the intensity of the rain had picked up considerably.

There was even a distant rumble of thunder. "No," she said, surprising herself. "I'm not afraid. I feel safe and secure."

"And here I thought I'd have a good excuse to entertain you with more of my stories."

She poked him playfully in the ribs. "You can still tell me your stories. I enjoy hearing them."

"Good." He wrapped his leg over hers and began a tale that made Prudence laugh so hard, it brought a flood of tears to her eyes.

"You tell some tall tales, Mr. Stewart," she said, wiping her tears away.

He kissed her slightly swollen lips, a remaining effect of his insatiable hunger for her. "I tell nothing but the truth, Mrs. Stewart, I swear." He covered his heart with his hand in demonstration of his good faith.

"I suppose I have no other choice but to believe you."

"No choice, honey," he said seriously. "I always tell the truth."

She swallowed the lump in her throat. He was once again telling her his love for her was real and true. But she still couldn't bring herself to admit her own love for him.

Chapter Twenty-four

The rain continued into the next day, not that it mattered to the couple nesting inside. They were impervious to their surroundings. They were the only two who existed.

Prudence sat at the table eating the biscuits and eggs Zac had prepared for them. She wore only his white cotton shirt, which was secured by just two buttons, leaving her breasts barely covered. Her coppery hair was in total disarray and gave her an air of wildness that Zac found appealing. Her lips were swollen from too many ardent kisses and her cheeks flushed from too much lovemaking. Her odor was one of pure lust, lingering around her like an enticing perfume.

"I make good eggs, don't I?" he asked, deciding food was a safe enough area to discuss.

"Great eggs," she agreed, eagerly popping the rest of her biscuit, dripping with yolk, into her mouth. She licked her lips with a small laugh, wiping the last drop of yolk away with the tip of her tongue.

"Your father and mother are worried about you."

"You said they have been speaking with each other?"

"Quite successfully. And they hope to talk with you."

"My father has accepted my mother's reason for

deserting us?" she asked, slamming her knife down on her tin plate.

Zac calmly continued. "That is something you will have to ask him. I know they have spoken. I know tears have been shed by all. And I know it is time to lay this thing to rest."

"Does Silver Fox still love my father?" It was an important question. If she did, then there was hope her mother still loved her.

"I don't think she ever stopped loving him."

"Then why did she leave us? And why didn't she tell me who she was when I first met her? I was so young when she left. My only memories of her were in fashionable clothes and a lovely swept-up hairstyle, becoming her natural beauty." Prudence's questions were asked with bitterness and sorrow that came from failing to recognize her own mother.

"I don't know, but did you ever stop to think it might have something to do with her Indian heritage?"

"No one knew." She shook her head sadly and amended her spoken thoughts. "My grandmother must have known. That's why she sent me to find her. She told me I'd find the truth."

"Does the truth disturb you?" Zac asked, worried she might be ashamed of her Cheyenne heritage.

"I don't know. I was raised in a world vastly different from this." She waved her hand around the sparse cabin. "I was lead to believe that there was only one way to live, one way that was acceptable to society."

"And what do you believe now?"

She shrugged her shoulders. "I don't know what to believe. When Granger called me a savage, I experienced, firsthand, the meaning of prejudice.

310

And it hurt."

"So you hit him," Zac couldn't help add with a laugh.

Prudence grinned and held up her fist. "I should have punched him with this."

"Your slap was sufficient. It left its mark."

"It did?" she asked, sitting up straight and feeling proud.

"It did. A nice red tender welt. A perfect match for the black eye I gave him."

"You didn't?" She covered her mouth in feigned shock.

He winked. "You knew damn well I would."

Her humor faded and she looked seriously at him. "Do you think my father and mother will mend their relationship?"

"Without a doubt, I'd say it's close to mended already. You're the last thread that needs stitching, so to speak."

"My father is worried about me?"

"Your father and mother are worried. Your mother in particular."

"How would you know that for sure unless—" She paused a moment, realizing. "You've spoken to Silver Fox about me."

"She needed to talk, to make someone understand that she never meant to hurt you. She's desperately worried that you will be ashamed of what she is. What she passed on to you. You need to speak with her. I think then you'll understand."

Prudence shook her head slowly. "I don't know if I'm ready."

"You may never be ready, honey. It's just something you must do."

"I suppose you're right," she agreed reluctantly. "But can we wait another day? I want some time to think this through."

"We're not going anywhere in that rain."

Prudence listened to it thrashing against the cabin. She relaxed back in silence in her chair, sipping at her coffee and growing lost in her thoughts.

Zac watched her with interest. This time was difficult for her. The mending process hurt; accepting all she had learned would be hard. It would do her good to talk with her mother, open old wounds, and help them heal properly.

"Zac," she interrupted his musings. "That night you—" Prudence stopped abruptly, obviously fearful of pursuing her question, then thinking better of it, she tried again. "The first time you made—" She halted once again and shrugged her shoulders in a defeated gesture.

"Are we about to discuss sex?" he teased with a smile that was anything but playful.

She leaned forward in an effort to confront him but hesitated, then sat back in her chair in a disappointing slouch.

"We spoke about being open and honest with each other," he said, attempting to lure her out of her fears and doubts. "You can ask me anything, Pru. I'm your husband and wish to share all your misgivings and joys equally."

She decided to give it one more try, forcing her words to race from her mouth before she gave them consideration. "That night you made love to me and told me I was pretty and such, did you mean it?"

"Every word," he answered without hesitation.

"You don't think I'm plain or too . . . big?"

312

"Big?" he repeated with a laugh. "Who the hell ever told you you were big?"

"Granger," she admitted.

Zac shook his head angrily, stood, and carried his chair to set it before the fire. He sat down and held his hand out to her. "Come here."

She went to him, holding out her hand in tentative trust. Zac took it and pulled her to him, his knees spreading her legs apart for her to straddle him. She fit perfectly over him and he cursed the interference of his denims.

"You're not big," he corrected, unbuttoning the two protective buttons that hid her from his view. He opened the shirt, pushing it gently aside.

Prudence sat still, her hands on his shoulders. She watched his eyes scrutinize her. They held no disgust, only pure lusty passion.

"Your breasts are full and perfect to nibble on," he teased, leaning into her as he drew her forward to taste her rigid nipple.

She wiggled against him from the sweet pleasure that he stirred in her.

"Mmmm," he murmured, basking in the feel of her familiar movement. "That brings us to those luscious hips. Big, no," he shook his head. "Full. Sexy. Sinful. Definitely yes." His hands cupped the cool cheeks of her backside, lifting them to fit more firmly over him.

She nested comfortably on him, wishing he were free of his denims so she could feel him against her. A rash and wicked thought hit her and she wondered if she should dare. Instead of giving it consideration, she moved into action. Her hands reached for his button.

He looked with surprise and suspicion at her.

313

"You know what will happen if you release me."

She nodded, her fingers working slowly.

He sucked in a deep breath when he felt her hand slip inside his trousers. Her fingers felt like ice stroking his hot shaft. He found speech slow and difficult. "I won't take you to the bed."

"I didn't ask you to," she said, enjoying the feel of him so smooth and powerful to her touch.

"You'll ride me here," he warned her, closing his eyes as she pushed his pants aside and continued to stroke him, until he was crazed with the want of her.

"You'll show me how?" she asked. Her innocence fueled his desire.

Zac pushed her shirt down and off her, needing to see every inch of her naked flesh. "I'll show you." He reached up and squeezed her breasts, so ripe and full and ready for his touch.

Her hand still enjoyed him and they pleasured each other before the fire's glow, until both were hotter than the flickering flames.

Zac positioned her over him, bringing her down on him with infinite slowness, driving them both crazy. Then he held her bottom firmly and taught her the rhythm and moves. She caught on quickly, and soon she was riding him without his help, skillfully, confidently, maddeningly.

Zac leaned back and savored every motion. He held firm to the edge of the chair and allowed her the lead. Allowed her to love him.

It was pure torture and pleasure all rolled into one. And when he knew she was near, when he felt his own passion mount, he reached out to her, forcing her to ride harder and explode with him in a tremulous conclusion.

She collapsed against him and his arms encircled her. Their breathing was heavy, their bodies weak.

"I never imagined I would enjoy riding so much," she whispered near his ear.

He shuddered from the tickle of her warm breath and it sent a quiver through her, since they were still solidly joined. "You can ride me anytime," he said.

"Be careful what you offer, Mr. Stewart. I may just do that," she said, half teasingly and half meaningfully.

"I repeat, Mrs. Stewart, *anytime.*" He bit playfully into the soft flesh of her neck.

She moaned and tilted her head, offering more of herself to him. "I wish we could stay like this forever."

"We can." He continued to taint her flesh with his warm lips.

"Promise me," she said fiercely.

"I promise, Pru," he answered with just as much fierceness.

They stayed wrapped around each other, kissing, tasting, touching, until Zac lifted her off him and carried her to the bed. She held her arms out invitingly to him and he covered her with himself.

The storm continued outside, but the lovers inside were lost in their own passion.

Prudence sat astride the saddle, waiting for Zac to finish closing up the cabin. She didn't want to leave. Didn't want to return to the outside world. She just wanted to stay locked away with Zac forever.

Here in this tiny cabin she could believe all he told her. Believe his unending words of love. Believe he really thought her beautiful. Believe their marriage was

315

forever. But in the outside world reality interfered, letting in doubts and fears.

"All set." Zac hoisted himself up behind Prudence. He reached around her to take the reins. "We'll come back here often, just you and me."

"Promise?" she heard herself ask again.

"Promise," he said, then laughed.

"What's so funny?"

"I just knew there was a reason why I didn't want to tear this cabin down."

"Don't ever tear it down," she cried.

"Never," he assured her with a hug.

He turned the horse around and the mare plodded slowly along, like Prudence, in no hurry to return to the ranch.

James sat on the apricot-colored medallion love seat next to Lenore. She would always be Lenore to him. Even though others referred to her as Silver Fox, to him she was his Lenore.

They had talked on and off for days, reasoning about and attempting to vanquish the past. It had been difficult at first, even to look upon her had caused him pain. The years had treated her well. The only traces of age were a few lines and wrinkles barely noticeable except to those who had known her in her younger years. Her dark hair was still long and lustrous, the only difference being the silver streak that ran down the middle, which didn't detract, but rather added to her uncommon beauty. Even her trim figure had remained the same, and James found himself falling in love all over again.

"I can't believe you didn't tell me of this when it

happened." Having heard her explanation yet again, he was hurting with her pain as well as with his own.

"I was frightened of his threats. I thought he would hurt you and Prudence," Lenore said, recalling the ugly threats Ralph Madison, Granger's father, had issued.

James reached over to her cupped hands resting in her lap and took one in his, gripping it firmly. "And did you doubt my acceptance of your heritage?"

She nodded, dropping her head sadly. "I wasn't sure of your reaction. How you would feel about my Cheyenne blood. If you would be shocked and disgusted. I couldn't face the thought of you turning away from me in disgust."

James felt both anger and sadness. "I love you, Lenore. I wouldn't care if you were full-blooded Indian. You should have trusted my love to see us through such an ordeal."

"But Ralph said it would ruin you. That when it was discovered I was a half-breed, people would shun you and Prudence. That you would be brought to financial ruin. I couldn't take that risk."

"So you left?"

"Either that, or become Ralph Madison's whore."

James released an exasperated sigh. "I wish Ralph hadn't died last year so I could kill him myself."

"I had experienced much prejudice growing up. After my mother's death when I was ten, my father, being a trapper, didn't feel it was fitting for a young girl to travel with him. He saw that the Indian way of life would soon perish, and not wanting that fate for me, he took me to his sister in Philadelphia."

James squeezed her hand. "It must have been difficult for you."

317

"More difficult than you know. My Aunt Laura was kind and generous and did all she could to train me in the ways of the white world. But I always longed for the freedom of the West and my home. Until I met you and fell hopelessly in love."

"You should have confided in me, trusted me," James urged.

"Fear is a powerful emotion. And my fear for you and Prudence far outweighed any other thoughts."

"Perhaps if I hadn't been so blind, so wrapped up in thinking our life perfect, I would have been able to see your distress," James offered, attempting to take the blame for all that had happened.

Lenore shook her head anxiously. "No, it was my foolishness that has kept us apart and me away from the daughter I love dearly. I should have been strong and had more faith in our love, perhaps even in myself, but I was young and frightened."

James hugged her hand to his chest. "I'm angry for all the wasted years, for all the love lost. I want us to be together again."

"You can forgive me for what I've done?" She looked through a pool of unshed tears at his face, which had remained as handsome as when she had first met him.

"Forgive?" he repeated. "*I* should forgive *you* for sacrificing all you held dear to protect your daughter and me? It is I who should ask for forgiveness for not being the husband I should have been."

Lenore reached up and touched his face, as though making certain he was really there beside her. "No, James. You were a wonderful husband and father. When I saw you the other day, my heart almost broke in two. I realized how very much I love you and how

318

much I've missed you. And when you looked at me with such pain and regret, I thought I would die."

He kissed her hand and held it tightly. "I was angry and confused when I recognized you. Then I experienced an overwhelming relief, which was instantly replaced by a raging anger at what you had done. After talking these last few days, I've come to understand so much. You could have left when you discovered who Prudence was—"

She stilled his words with her fingers to his lips. "I was so happy to meet her. I couldn't bring myself to leave her again. I wanted so much to get to know her. I had run enough. It was time for me to face things."

"Prudence can be stubborn," he offered in way of explanation for his daughter's refusal to speak with Lenore.

"She has a right to feel as she does. I hurt her terribly."

"She survived. She's strong and resilient. A true Winthrop," he said with pride.

"I have spoken with her, James. She has many emotional scars from my desertion. It will take time, much time. And our relationship may never mend."

"She is confused, as I was. Talk with her and she will understand," he urged, anxious for his wife and daughter to be reunited so they could once again be a family.

"I will try my best."

He squeezed her hand reassuringly. "We have much to discuss and decide. You're not getting away from me again, even if I must grow my hair long and wear moccasins to keep you. We will spend the rest of our days together."

A teardrop fell from Lenore's eye and James

reached up to brush it away. "I love you," he said, and leaned over to kiss her. His kiss was tentative at first; he was fearful that she would reject him. But when she didn't back away, when she welcomed him as though they had never been separated, he kissed her as he had many years ago.

"I love you," she whispered as he slipped his arm beneath her legs and lifted her to rest on his lap. He held her close, touching her and kissing her in a way that was old, yet new.

"We're still married," he teased with a passionate glint in his eyes.

"And my desire for you is still as fierce as it always was," she said, her smile inviting.

He stood with her in his arms.

"James," she said, concerned, "you can't carry me upstairs."

"I most certainly can. I'm not *that* old. And I'll prove just how virile I've remained."

"Is it anything like when you were younger?" She placed her arms around his neck as he walked to the door.

"Worse. I doubt you'll make it out of the bedroom before nightfall," he warned most seriously, not having the least bit of trouble carrying her up the steps.

"I love you so very much, James," she said, reaching for his lips with her own.

James walked down the hall, through the guest bedroom door, his lips firmly locked with hers. He kicked the door closed.

It was almost nightfall when Prudence and Zac walked through the front door. The house was silent,

320

reminding Prudence of the solemnness of the situation. She was relieved they had left the cabin later in the day. Glad she had spent the morning hours making love with her husband. Glad the occupants of the house were asleep in their beds and it wouldn't be necessary to face them until tomorrow.

"Tired?" Zac asked from behind her while his arms circled around her waist to hug her to him in comfort and support.

"Weary," she sighed, squeezing his hand.

"I think bed is the perfect place for us." He kissed her cheek.

"I agree," she said and turned in his arms, hugging his waist and burying her face against his chest. Tomorrow was soon enough to talk with her parents. To face her past and lay the sorrows that had plagued her to rest.

"Pru," he said softly, tightening his arms around her, "I don't want you to worry or be afraid. I'll be there with you. I will always be there with you."

She nodded, not trusting her voice. She was too close to tears, too close to losing the emotional balance she had tried so hard to maintain.

"Let's get you to bed." Without waiting for her response, he lifted her up into his arms.

Zac pressed his cheek against the silkiness of her coppery hair. The soft strands smelled of fresh air and spicy pine. He had sensed her need to hide away when she had tucked her head in the crook of his neck. She didn't wish to confront the situation or accept what she had learned. She was fighting it every step of the way.

He supposed he could understand her reluctance. She feared being hurt once again. That was why she found it so difficult to admit her love for him. And he had no doubt she loved him. She demonstrated it in her actions and looks, and especially when they made love.

It was almost as though that were the only way she could reveal her love to him. And although it pleased him, he still wanted, needed to hear the words race from her lips. Perhaps when she healed things with her mother, she would have the strength to admit her love for him openly and with pride.

He entered the room and lowered her to stand near the bed. He lit the lamp and when he turned, she was quickly shedding her clothes. Her actions were desperate and her eyes close to tears.

Zac didn't hesitate as he began removing his own clothes. He understood her actions. She needed proof that what had transpired between them at the cabin was real and not a dream. That he would love her no matter their surroundings.

Zac went to her, and his large, gentle hands worked fast to rid her of the remaining garments. He lifted her, naked in his arms, and walked to the bed. He lay down on the mattress with her, covering her, pressing into her.

"I love you, Pru," he whispered.

She looked at him, her eyes pooled with tears. She opened her mouth and fought for the words that seemed locked tightly away. Frustrated, she tossed her head from side to side, allowing the tears to spill, then reached up, capturing his face with her hands and drawing him to her. Her lips caught his and she kissed him hungrily.

Chapter Twenty-five

"It's been two days since you've returned and she's still managed to avoid her mother," James complained to Zac as they shared their morning coffee on the front porch.

Zac poured himself another cup from the pot Silver Fox had left on the table for them. He still couldn't get used to the idea of calling her Lenore. The name just didn't fit her. "You have to understand—"

"I'm tired of being an understanding father," James snapped. "Prudence is being unreasonable and I intend to put my foot down."

Zac leaned back in his chair, cup in hand. "I don't think so, James." His voice was stern and his tone strong. "Prudence is my wife and no longer comes under your rule. I won't have her dictated to by anyone."

James looked at him in surprise. "You really love my daughter, don't you?"

"Yes. Had you doubted I did?"

"Well, I must admit I had some doubt. Didn't think she was your type, although," James added hastily, "when I arrived here and saw you two together, saw

323

the change in Prudence, I began to think it was possible that you did actually love her."

"I *do* love her," Zac corrected. "She's stubborn, quick-witted, proper beyond belief, and an excellent knot maker."

"Knot maker?" James repeated.

"Don't ask, you don't want to know, and I'd be too embarrassed to explain. Needless to say, I love everything about her."

James held his hand out. Zac put his cup down and took it. It was a warm, hearty shake and James smiled broadly. "Welcome to the family, son. For a while there, I was worried that Granger just might become my son-in-law."

Zac laughed. "I doubt it. Prudence has too much common sense and intelligence to make such a drastic mistake."

"Your belief in her is heartwarming."

"Prudence needed someone to believe in her. Though she appeared strong, she still harbored the misgivings of the little girl who had been hurt so badly by her mother's desertion."

"I've explained to Prudence why Lenore left," James said sadly. "I thought it would be enough to make her understand that her mother did it out of a desire to protect her."

"I think she does realize that, but her little girl doubts still haunt her."

"Then all the more reason she speak with Lenore," James insisted. "They need to talk. I just don't understand Prudence's obstinacy in this matter."

"I don't think Prudence understands it herself." He leaned forward in his chair, closer to James. "I have an idea that might bring mother and daughter together, at least to talk. But I'll need your help."

"Anything. You name it. I'll do anything that will help," James assured him.

"Good. The first thing is that Granger must be made to leave the house for the rest of the afternoon. I want no interference from him."

James nodded his agreement. "I'll take care of that."

"How? I want to make certain he remains away."

"I'll tell him I'm thinking of opening a bank in Stewart, and that I want him to assist me in looking over some locations and meeting some of the local people to see if it's worth the investment. Naturally, he'll join me, since he'll try to talk me out of it."

"Stewart could sure use a bank." Zac's smile was persuasive.

"My sentiments exactly. A growing town needs financial support to help bring in business and families, and to help existing ranches prosper."

"Sounds to me as though you've already made up your mind."

"I've been tossing the idea around," James admitted.

"Does it have anything to do with Silver Fox?"

"Yes. She's content here. She's finally come home. I don't wish to rob her of that, and besides, I don't think she would want to live far from her daughter."

"Then we best get the two together," Zac said, relieved that Prudence would have time to build a solid relationship with her mother and heal the old wounds gradually.

"What else do I do?" James asked.

"You tell Silver Fox that you've missed her rum cake and ask her if she would bake one for you."

"Rum cake?" James asked. "That's your plan? To have her bake a rum cake?"

325

"Didn't Prudence as a child love to help her mother bake a rum cake?"

James nodded slowly at first, and then understanding dawned. "And you're going to ask Prudence to bake you one, throwing them together in a task they shared as mother and daughter."

"Right."

"It just might work," James agreed, standing. "Let's not waste any more time. Give me some time to talk with Lenore and to get Granger out of here."

"Thirty minutes enough?"

"Make it twenty," James amended. "I'm anxious to see this plan work."

James set off for the kitchen and Lenore, with the tray of cups and coffeepot. Zac started toward the sewing room, where Prudence had cloistered herself since early morning.

"Curtains all finished?" Zac entered the room, closing the door behind him.

"The ones for our bedroom are almost complete," Prudence answered, and stiffened her posture in preparation for another lecture from her husband. She had put off talking with her mother, but not for the reasons everyone thought. When the confrontation with her was over, Prudence would have to confront her feelings toward Zac and make a decision. And that she wasn't ready to do.

Zac fingered the fine beige lace and marveled at his wife's skilled workmanship.

"You didn't come here to talk to me about curtains, Zac."

"No, I came to ask you a favor." He leaned down beside her, running his finger along her cheek in a teasing manner, dipping it down her neck and over

326

her breast, stopping to trace circles around her nipple. It hardened instantly, and he squeezed at it playfully.

"Zac, we can't. There are people in the house," she said, although her reasoning sounded false even to her ears.

Zac smiled and teased the other nipple equally. "I don't care how many people are here. If I want to make love to my wife in the sewing room, I will."

Prudence brought her head forward, resting her forehead against his. "You are wicked, Mr. Stewart."

"And you love it," he affirmed and kissed her, taking her lips roughly.

Prudence jumped at the knock on the door, pulling away from Zac just as her father opened it and stuck his head in.

"I'm off to town with Granger. Be back for supper," he announced, then left with a wave.

Zac was still bent down beside her. "Before I get carried away, I better request my favor."

"I thought you had," she said disappointingly.

"No, that was a preliminary of what I have planned for tonight." He ran his hand beneath her skirt and stopped suddenly. "Damn, Pru, you don't have anything on underneath."

Her smile was a carefree taunt. "I thought it would give you something to think on."

He shut his eyes and forced his hand to stay put. If he moved it, even just a little, he'd be lost. He fought for control of his warring emotions, since part of him insisted he hoist her skirt up and satisfy them both, while the other half argued that it was important she talk with her mother now.

"I have a taste—"

"Mmmm," she said softly, slowly licking her lips. "I have a taste, too."

"Good." He forced himself to respond and quickly removed his hand as though it lay on hot coals, which was exactly how her naked flesh felt to him, hot and ready. "Then you'll bake us a rum cake."

"Rum cake?" she asked, bewildered.

He stood, taking her hand and pulling her up with him. "Yes, rum cake. I have this urge to try it, and you promised to make it for me."

Prudence was out the door of the sewing room and propelled down the hall before she could object. "Zac, I don't understand," she said. Before she could say more, she was deposited in the kitchen.

Her eyes met her mother's, both of them registering shock upon seeing each other. Her mother wore a clean white apron over her blue calico dress. Bowls, flour, eggs, and the like were spread out on the table before her. Prudence now understood everything. She backed up, only to hit the solid wall of her husband's firm body.

"Well, isn't this a coincidence," Zac said, holding Prudence firmly by the shoulders and pushing her stiff body farther into the kitchen.

"I was just going to bake a rum cake for your father," Silver Fox began nervously. "Perhaps you would like to help, like you did when you were little?"

Zac felt his wife's shoulders sag and was glad he held her firmly. He was certain Silver Fox's words disturbed her, and he hoped she would put her doubts aside and accept her mother's invitation to do more than just help.

Prudence's response was slow and shaky. "I'd like that."

Zac kissed her cheek. "I'll leave you two to your baking," he said, but whispered for her ears only, "I'll be right out back if you need me." He released her, giving her hand a quick squeeze of support before walking out the kitchen door.

"He loves you very much," Silver Fox said seriously.

Prudence walked to the table and pulled out one of the chairs, sitting down to join her mother. "You really think so?"

"I know so. It is written clearly on his face. He cannot hide his feelings for you. They are too strong. And you love him."

Prudence was surprised she stated the fact and did not question it. "Yes, I do, but I can't seem to bring myself to tell him."

"The right time will present itself and you will," Silver Fox assured her. "You must learn to trust."

Her words opened up the way for Prudence to speak, and she didn't doubt that Silver Fox had stated them just for that reason. "I trusted once, but I was hurt badly. Now it is hard for me to trust those that profess to love me."

Silver Fox handed her the eggs to crack, just as she had done when Prudence was a child. "Sometimes we love so much that we make rash decisions, thinking them the best at that moment, only to find them foolish later."

"But how can you leave someone you love?" Prudence demanded, cracking the eggs more forcefully then necessary.

"It isn't easy." Silver Fox mixed the batter, her eyes steady on the bowl.

Prudence felt the ache deep in her heart and the tears close to her lashes. "Father told me why you left us, and I suppose I understand your concern for us at the time. But I loved you so very much, and it hurt so very badly when I was told you had died. It hurt worse to discover you had not . . . that instead you had chosen to leave us."

Silver Fox allowed her tears to fall. Her ache was just as painful as her daughter's, if not more so. "I loved you then and I love you now, Prudence. It broke my heart to leave my little girl, but I thought I was doing the right thing. It was so very foolish of me," she admitted, shaking her head ruefully.

Prudence sniffed back her tears, determined to keep them at bay and finally determined to face her mother with her fears. "When I learned you weren't dead, I thought that you left me because I wasn't as pretty as you and because I was deformed."

Silver Fox's eyes widened in disbelief and shined bright from her tears. "I thought you were the most beautiful child in the world, and whatever do you mean *deformed?*"

It was Prudence's turn to be stunned. She held her hand up, displaying the two fingers she no longer hid away in shame, thanks to Zac.

Silver Fox smiled proudly and nodded. "That isn't a deformity."

Prudence looked at her hand as though her fingers had miraculously healed and she had missed the transformation. "They are crooked and useless."

"They are a symbol amongst my family that only a chosen few women bear. It is believed that those who are born such possess strong spirits, and they are regarded with great esteem. I was extremely disappointed when my mother explained this to me, since I did not possess it. She bore the same symbol as you,

330

and when you were born that way I was proud, for I knew you were endowed with great strength."

Prudence stared at her fingers. "And all these years I hid them, thinking them ugly."

Silver Fox bent her head, staring down into the bowl. "It is my fault you felt that way. I should have been there to help you."

For the first time since learning of Silver Fox's identity, Prudence regarded her as her mother and understood the pain she must have suffered herself all these lonely years. "I think we should stop blaming and start forgiving . . . Mama."

Silver Fox raised her head. Her eyes were damp and her lips trembled. "I often dreamed of hearing you call me that once again."

"Then why didn't you tell me who you were when we met?" Prudence asked, confused. "You knew how badly I wanted to find you."

Silver Fox fought her tears unsuccessfully. "I couldn't bear losing you again."

Prudence's tears joined hers. "You wouldn't have lost me."

She shook her head. "But I am part Cheyenne, and I distinctly recall the world you were raised in. I didn't think you would find me acceptable as a mother."

Prudence couldn't help but laugh as she wiped her tears away. "Being acceptable, even proper, at one time might have mattered to me, but then I came west . . . I came home. Will you teach me of your heritage? This part of me I know nothing about?"

Silver Fox nodded. "I will teach you. I love you, my daughter." She held out her arms to Prudence and the lonely years faded away as her daughter ran to her once again, a small child of eight aching for her mother's love.

The next hour was spent in a mixture of tears and laughter. They renewed their relationship, building on it, strengthening it, giving it a solid base to grow on.

"So how's the rum cake coming?" Zac asked, entering the kitchen.

Both women burst into laughter as they looked down at the table, the partially mixed rum cake completely forgotten.

"Well, I'll get that rum cake one of these days." He smiled and left mother and daughter alone, content that they were mending the past. Now he could begin to build on the future with Prudence.

Chapter Twenty-six

"You can't mean this," Granger said in astonishment.

James glanced around the empty field with a twinkle in his eye. He hadn't felt this young and vigorous in years. It was almost like beginning life anew.

"James, did you hear me? I said you can't mean this," Granger repeated, shocked by the mere suggestion of such a ridiculous notion.

"But I do, my boy, I do." James stepped to the middle of the field, stretching his arms out and turning slowly. "This is perfect, just perfect. Couldn't ask for a better place to build a bank."

"Oh come on, James. You really can't be serious," Granger insisted. "This is a joke, right?"

James found it comical the way Granger stared like a wide-eyed little boy at him. "Granger, use your imagination. We could build a good size bank, keeping the growth of the town in mind."

"Of course," Granger agreed with a shrug of his shoulders, convinced James had finally managed to lose his mind.

"I'd make certain to add a private office in the back for me to handle business and where Lenore and I can share lunch in private," he added with a broad, happy smile.

Granger threw his hands up in the air in defeat.

"Comfortable chairs, potted greens, curtains. Why, I bet Prudence would sew the curtains for me if I asked her. She's a whiz with a needle and thread."

Granger shook his head. "James, I think you're dreaming. Prudence couldn't possible sew with those useless fingers."

James's look contained a mix of pity and contempt. "You don't know much about my daughter, do you?"

Granger was intelligent enough to realize he had already trodden on enough dangerous territory. "I assumed it was necessary to have the use of all fingers to be able to sew."

"Did you ever bother to ask Prudence if she had any skill with a needle?" James asked candidly.

Granger proceeded with caution. "I never did, but if she takes pleasure in the craft, I'll gladly see to having a special room prepared for her in my home for her use when we marry."

James dismissed his remark with a hasty wave of his hand. "Prudence is married to Zac and intends to remain so. Stop fooling yourself and accept the fact."

Granger stood erect and raised his hand, shaking his fist toward James. "I object to this marriage most strenuously."

"You have no right to object to it."

"I most certainly do," Granger insisted. "I had approached you and spoken my intentions. You led me to believe Prudence would be open to my interest. I had plans. I would be able to give her a good life. A fine home. Social acceptability. What can that gunslinger give her? A home in the wilderness? No social

334

contacts except maybe a dance at the local church hall on occasion?"

"What about love?" James added, folding his arms across his chest.

"You can't honestly believe that man loves her?"

"I most certainly do. He's a fine, honest, hardworking man, and I'm proud to have him as a son-in-law."

"This is too much," Granger cried. "He's a gunslinger. *Gunslinger.* He's killed men, and might I add for money. This is the type of man you want your daughter to spend the rest of her life with?"

"He did what he had to do. I wonder if you could do the same?" James said in defense of Zac. "Or," he added with anger in his voice, "would you have chosen to behave as your father—underhanded and cruel?"

Granger was affronted by his outrageous insult. "I beg your pardon, James?"

"I had promised myself I would not bring it up to you, that you weren't responsible for your father's past actions. You were only a young boy. How could you know what he had done?" James shook his head.

Granger began to sweat. He had the most dreadful feeling.

"You know nothing, do you?"

"No, James. I know not of what you speak, although I would like a clarification on the matter."

"That I shall gladly provide for you." He looked the young man straight in the eyes. "Your father was the reason my wife left all those years ago."

"What? That's ridiculous." Granger shook his head in disbelief.

"No, it isn't. Your father discovered Lenore was part Cheyenne. How, I don't know, though I wish I did. Someone had to supply him with the information, and I wish I knew who it was. He threatened her with exposure. Threatened the safety of her husband and daughter. Threatened to use the information to cause the financial ruin of the Winthrop Bank . . . unless she agreed to become his mistress."

Granger was shocked and disgusted. His old man never could keep his pants on. Now, even in death, he came back to haunt him, to destroy his chance of building a banking empire far superior and more powerful than anyone had ever imagined. There was much work for him to do if he was still to see his dream become a reality.

"No comment, Granger?" James asked, disturbed by the other man's silence.

Granger rubbed his hands and sadly shook his head. "What can I say, James? Sorry doesn't seem sufficient for the hurt my father's deviousness has caused you and your family. If there were a way I could repay you, I would. I regret most sincerely that my father caused your family such pain."

James was touched by Granger's sincerity. He had expected rejection and disbelief of what Ralph Madison had done. He also felt a sense of guilt for laying the blame at Granger's feet. It wasn't his fault. "You did nothing wrong, Granger. I should never have mentioned it to you."

"No," Granger insisted. "You had every right, and now I can at least extend my apologies to Prudence. I owe her that much."

"As you wish, Granger," James said, sorry he had even brought the matter up.

Granger took advantage of his moment of weakness. "James, if you intend to open a branch of the Winthrop Bank here, who will run the bank in Boston?"

James thought on his question. "I'll have to give it much consideration. It is a huge responsibility."

Granger pumped his chest out and stood tall. "Yes, a major responsibility. You will need a person who is trustworthy, dependable, and knowledgeable in the field of finance."

"I will give it thought," James said. "Now about this field. I'm thinking of purchasing it. It sits in a good central location."

"A wise decision, James. Very wise," Granger agreed, with a smile that would have made the devil himself cringe.

Prudence knocked on the door of Zac's study, then opened it slowly and peeked in. "Busy?" she asked, her cheeks flushed and a smudge of flour clinging to her chin.

"Never too busy for my wife," Zac winked, before holding out his hand to her.

She smiled like a small child about to spill a tale to her parent. She hurried to him, taking his hand in hers and squeezing it. "Oh, Zac, I can't thank you enough for forcing me to speak to my mother."

Zac pulled her into the protective circle of his arms and kissed the tip of her nose. "I didn't force you, honey."

Her smile turned generous. "Sure you didn't. I walked into the kitchen on my own. Your hand on my back, pushing me, had nothing to do with it."

"Prudence Agatha," he said authoritatively, "if you didn't really want to talk with your mother, God himself couldn't have kept you in that kitchen."

Her expression changed to one of wonderment. "You're right. I stayed because I wanted to and for no other reason, and I'm so glad I did. I've learned so much."

"Things patched up?" He gave her waist a friendly squeeze.

"Partially," she admitted. "We still have a ways to go and much talking to do and . . . oh, wait until you hear about my fingers." She wiggled them eagerly in his face.

"Don't tell me," he teased. "They're not really yours."

She looked at him in surprise and then at her fingers. "How did you know?"

"Now wait a minute," he said with a serious shake of his head. "The last time I looked, they were yours."

She laughed with a lightheartedness that brightened Zac's own spirits.

"Well, they are and they aren't, in a way," she began, and excitedly told him of her discussion with her mother.

Zac listened carefully and attentively. He studied her easy smile and the brightness in her green eyes and the way she waved her hand to emphasize a point. And then there was her ample body leaning up against his in so relaxed a manner. She was content, and that pleased him. Perhaps their confrontation, when it came, wouldn't be as difficult as he had anticipated.

"So what do you think?" she finished, looking at him expectantly.

He brought his hand up, unable to keep his thumb from wiping the smudge of flour from her chin. "I think that you and your mother have started off on a

338

good path."

Prudence smiled, pleased by his response.

They stood for a moment in silence, watching each other. Their stares grew more expressive. The mood surrounding them had changed considerably.

"Tell me," Zac said in a sensual whisper, "do you still have nothing on beneath your skirt?"

Prudence felt a rush of flutters in her stomach, and her voice sounded slightly breathless. "Yes."

Zac dropped his hands away from her waist and stepped around her to the door. He secured the lock, then turned to face her. He held out his hand once again to her, only this time his command wasn't silent. "Come here, honey."

Prudence felt the tremble start in her legs and grow, until she was fearful her jellylike limbs wouldn't support her another minute. It was the way he called her "honey" that did it to her. His voice didn't drip with sweetness. It was thick with sexual innuendo, as though to tease and titillate her. Which it did, significantly.

"Come on," he cajoled in a dangerously soft voice, which weakened her unsupportive legs even farther. And he added to her distress by unbuckling his belt.

Prudence sighed and felt a warmth spread down her belly to between her legs, while somewhere in the back of her mind orders were issued to her limbs and she walked toward him.

He grasped the hand she held out to him and pulled her roughly against him. "Damn, I want you so bad it hurts."

She smiled playfully, recalling his words of weeks before. "And I do want you hurting, don't I?"

His other hand grabbed the hair at the nape of her

339

neck and forced her head back, while his hand that held hers twisted her arm back behind her to assure her captivity. "Not this bad, honey."

He brought his mouth down over hers, completing her capture. His kisses were untamed and turbulent. Prudence could express her answering excitement only with her mouth, and even that was difficult since he had taken absolute control of her.

She managed to free her mouth for a few seconds. "Zac, someone may hear us."

"Then no screaming allowed," he warned, taking charge of her mouth once again.

She enjoyed his rough, commanding play. She felt protected by his strength, and his sharp, manly power heightened her passion.

His mouth left hers and dropped to her breast. He took her nipple, covered by her cotton blouse, in his mouth and nibbled at the tip through the cloth. It hardened instantly, sending shivers along her warm flesh.

Zac lifted her then and hurried to the settee near the cold hearth. He placed her back against the arm, pushed her legs up and spread them, and flung her skirt up.

He held her eyes with his as he placed one knee between her legs and reached down to release himself.

A knock to the door startled them both and Prudence made to sit up. Zac stopped her with a hand to her chest and a firm shake of his head that warned she damned well better stay put.

"Zac, are you in there?" James called.

"Yes, I'm here," Zac answered, his voice sounding calm and normal, to Prudence's surprise. "And I'm busy."

"Don't want to disturb you. I just was wondering where my daughter was. . . . Thought I'd talk to her."

Prudence felt her face grow scarlet. She embarrassingly fussed with her skirt in an attempt to cover herself. Zac would have none of it and pushed the skirt right back up. Then grabbing her beneath her backside, he pulled her farther down on the settee. Her blush deepened, since she was now more exposed to him then before.

"Prudence is resting." His smile was evil.

"Is she all right? Perhaps I should check on her," James said anxiously.

"She's fine. No need to worry."

Prudence buried her face in her hands. She was shameless. Even though her father stood right outside the door, her desire for Zac had not diminished in the least. She wanted him, now more than ever. She was a wicked hussy, absolutely wicked.

"Well, if you say so, but you never know. She could be upset or not be feeling well or—What's that, Lenore?" James said, interrupting his own rambling. "What? What's that you're saying? I can't hear you. Huh? Oh! Oh! Yes, a cup of tea would be nice. Sorry to disturb you, Zac."

Prudence buried her face in her hands and shook her head. Her father knew. He knew she was in here and he knew what they were up to.

"Fathers can be a troublesome lot at times," Zac teased.

"He knows," Prudence cried out, removing her hands from her face.

"Knows what?" Zac asked with all the feigned innocence of a young boy.

"What we're doing," she said, reverting to a whisper.

"What are we doing?" he whispered back.

Prudence clamped her mouth shut and crossed her arms over her chest. "Nothing. We're doing absolutely nothing."

"Wrong, Prudence Agatha," he said firmly and lifted her bottom, providing easier excess as he entered her.

She cried out from the pleasure and shock of his entrance. He didn't come down over her as she had expected. He stayed positioned upright between her legs, giving him the power of deep penetration.

Prudence closed her eyes against all else and surrendered to him.

Zac watched her eyes flutter and close as his controlled thrusts cast her into a web of relaxed sensuality. He was in no hurry. He savored the feel of her, so snug, wet, and hot. She fit him perfectly.

He reached out and touched her, adding to her pleasure and his. He brought a moan to her lips and a cry from deep inside her. Her rapture heated his own and his movements took on a new dimension, taking them one step beyond.

His name slipped pleadingly from Prudence's lips and she reached out to him. He gripped her hands, their fingers locking firmly as he drove them farther and farther beyond reality.

She pulled at him, urging him to come to her, but he refused. He meant to use his strength to bring them to an earthshaking climax. And he did, forcing Prudence to cry out his name repeatedly.

He covered her with himself then, capturing her face with his hands and kissing her sweetly. "I love you, Pru," he whispered through his kisses. "I love you."

Prudence closed her eyes and was glad when Zac bit playfully at her lower lip, preventing it from trembling. Her love was locked deep within her heart and she still feared releasing it. Why? Why couldn't she declare her love for him as easily as he did for her?

Chapter Twenty-seven

Summer was right around the corner. The weather was surprisingly warm and the trees were alive with bright green leaves. Flowers bloomed as though the season had already arrived, their vibrant yellow, pink, and red colors adding a sparkle of contrast to the surrounding area.

"It looks picture perfect," Zac said, sitting in relaxed comfort on the front porch with Prudence, James, and Lenore.

"But it isn't always so," Lenore added, standing to refill the empty glasses on the round table that separated her and James from Zac and Prudence. She lifted the large pitcher and poured a generous amount of cider into each glass, handed one to James, and returned to her rocking chair beside him.

"Sil—Lenore," Zac corrected, attempting to help the woman reestablish her identity as James's wife and Prudence's mother. "Lenore is right. The winters can get pretty brutal around here."

"There's much snow?" Prudence asked eagerly, reaching for Zac's and her glasses. She handed his to him.

He took it and, with his free hand, patted her thigh. "Like the snow, do you?"

344

"She loves it," Lenore answered, her smile wide. Then realizing she had trodden on the past, she dropped her nervous gaze to her lap.

Zac looked to Prudence and she understood his message. It was distinct. It informed her that Lenore needed a daughter as much as Prudence needed a mother.

"Mother's right," she said. "She should know, since I drove her crazy when I was little. Every time I saw a snowflake fall, I would beg to go outside to play."

James cast his daughter a grateful look, though it wasn't necessary. Prudence was glad that she could finally look back on her past with some fondness.

Lenore leaned forward in the rocker and smiled broadly, her whole face lighting with pleasure. "I would bundle her up until she looked like a round ball. Then we would go out and play in the yard. I taught her how to make pictures in the snow."

"And I cried when we had to go in," Prudence added.

"Then you will enjoy the winters here." Zac sent a sly wink to Prudence and added, "We can play in the snow together."

She grinned at his suggestiveness and hid her doubts. Would she be here this winter, or would she find herself returning to Boston?

Talk went on around her while she remained lost in her thoughts. Zac had declared his love for her often and with much insistence. She could almost believe he meant it. Yet there was that little nagging doubt that tormented her. Why? Why couldn't she just shove it aside and accept his word? Why couldn't she speak openly to him of her love?

"When do you think you'll be leaving?" Zac asked, snapping Prudence out of her musings.

"Two, three weeks," James answered. "I want to set

345

things up here before I go. This way, the bank will be almost ready to open when I return."

"Which will be?" Zac questioned.

James shrugged his shoulders. "Probably not until the fall."

Lenore placed her hand on James's arm. "You must not wait too long to return. Once the snow starts, the journey will be difficult."

He patted her hand in reassurance. "We'll be back before then. I know how much you want to be here for Bertha's wedding."

"But I'm not going with you," Lenore said, surprised.

"Of course you are," James corrected. "We've wasted enough years. I refuse to waste any more."

"James," Lenore said patiently, "my skin has darkened some from my many outside activities. My looks betray my heritage now. I don't wish to bring shame to your family name. And besides, many believe me dead."

James took her hand in his. It was important she return with him. It would erase all doubts that his love for her was anything but complete and without qualification. "You bring me no shame. I love you and want the world to know it. You *will* return to Boston with me. Let people believe they're seeing a ghost." He squeezed her hand and cast her a wide smile. "It will be our second honeymoon."

Lenore leaned over and placed a delicate kiss on his cheek. "I look forward to it as much as I did our first."

Prudence was happy to see her parents' relationship on the mend. "I'm glad you've decided to establish a Winthrop Bank here, Father. It will help bring more families to Stewart."

"I was thinking the same thing myself," he said proudly.

346

"Let me know exactly when it is you'll be leaving so I can be ready," Prudence said, thinking it was best to go away at least for a while.

Three pairs of eyes turned on her.

"You're not going anywhere," Zac said, his statement sounding nonnegotiable.

"I think it best if I —"

"Run away," he finished.

"I'm not running away," she insisted. "I thought, perhaps, time alone would help us to —"

"What? Feel frustrated and lonely?" he demanded. "I repeat: You're not going anywhere."

Prudence didn't like his dictatorial attitude. "I'll go where I want."

"The hell you will!"

"Zac, your language —"

"Will get worse if you don't stop this damn nonsense."

Prudence stood. "You can't tell me what to do."

Zac stood up, almost tumbling the rocker off its gliders. "The hell I can't. I'm your husband."

Prudence jammed her hands on her hips. "What difference does that make?" she asked sarcastically.

James cleared his throat to remind the warring couple of his and Lenore's presence. "Lenore and I will see you later," he said, and they both stood to leave.

"No!" Zac yelled. "Stay and enjoy the pleasure of the late afternoon sun. This confrontation has been a long time coming and it's about time it was settled." He grabbed Prudence by the hand.

"I'm not going any —"

Zac placed his finger over her lips, shutting off her objection. "Fight me on this, and I'll haul you over my shoulder like I've done before and cart you off."

"You wouldn't —"

"You know damn well I will," he warned, his tone dangerously low.

Prudence stiffened and held her head high. "Mother, Father, please excuse us," she said in her proper Bostonian accent.

Zac shook his head and mumbled beneath his breath, before yanking her by the hand and practically dragging her into the house.

James leaned over to his wife. "Did I hear him correctly?"

"What is it you think you heard?"

He shook his head again as though it didn't make sense. "Little, stubborn, commanding giants."

Lenore agreed with a nod. "Yes, I heard that, too, though it doesn't make sense."

They both shook their heads and decided to take a walk to the corral to see the foal and his mother. The raised voices inside the house made it impossible to enjoy the afternoon sun on the porch.

Zac slammed the study door, rattling the books and prints on the shelves and walls. "I've had enough, Prudence."

"So have I ," she said, and yanked her hand free to walk a safe distance away from him.

"You," he laughed wryly. "You've had enough? You haven't been shackled with a stubborn, pigheaded—"

"Shackled! Pigheaded!" she yelled, storming toward him and stopping only inches from him. "My father has papers that will easily release you from your shackles."

He grabbed her wrist and twisted it as he brought her up flat against him. "Don't tempt me!"

She gasped. "I'm not tempting you. I'm giving you your way out."

"I had my way out back in Alexandria."

"Oh yes," she said derisively. "I keep forgetting. It really wasn't necessary for you to marry me, even though all those *rifles* were pointed at you. Zac Stewart, the infamous gunslinger, could have shot his way out."

His grip tightened, burning Prudence's flesh. "My guns weren't necessary. My intelligence would have sufficed."

"And what words of wisdom would you have expressed that would have freed us?"

"Simple," he answered. "I would have announced that you were already my wife. That you had run away and I had been searching for you."

Prudence stared at him in disbelief. "They would never have believed that story."

"You underestimate my charm. The hotel clerks along the way never doubted we were man and wife."

"It wouldn't have been that simple," she insisted.

"Yes, it would, and if it didn't work, there was always an alternative."

"Which was?"

"Pull my gun on one of the men and warn them to back off or I'd shoot."

Prudence was stunned. "You wouldn't have?"

"If I didn't want to marry you, I wouldn't have thought twice."

"I don't believe you," she said more calmly.

"That's our problem, Pru. You don't believe in me . . . or yourself."

He couldn't have said it more clearly. She didn't believe in his love or her own.

"What is necessary to make you understand how much I love you? And for you to admit your love for me? Unlike you, I harbor no doubts of your love. Even though I don't hear the words, I know you love me."

Prudence pulled at her wrist and winced. "You're hurting me."

"I want to beat some sense into you." His voice was an angry growl and he released her wrist with a shove.

She grabbed it and rubbed at the tender flesh, shutting her eyes against the soreness and against the truth.

"Let me see it," he demanded, forcing her to open her eyes.

She was tempted to refuse, but the stern look in his dark eyes warned her against such foolish actions. She offered him her arm.

Zac took it, touching the redness with infinite care. "You make me so angry," he said in way of an explanation and apology.

"I didn't mean to." Her words were whispered as though she were afraid to speak.

He brought her wrist to his mouth and kissed it, sending a tingle up her arm. "I don't want you leaving here, honey. This doubt you have must be laid to rest. You can't do that in Boston. You need to be here . . . with me."

"I don't understand, Zac," she cried. "I'm confused."

He brought her into the protective shield of his arms. "That's only natural with what you've been through. So much has happened and changed for you in such a short time. You're just beginning to learn to trust someone's love again. But don't run away like your mother did. Face the problem and solve it."

Tears clouded her vision. "I want so much to work things out, to feel secure and safe in our love."

"Then give it a chance," he said harshly. "Give us a chance to learn from each other and strengthen our relationship. I'm not asking you to declare your love for me right this very moment. Take your time, feel your way, but don't run away. Not this time."

She rested her head on his chest. "You are not what you seem to be."

350

"I'm not," he said, hugging her to him.

"No. When I first heard you speak in Boston, I thought you an arrogant, egotistical man who couldn't possibly care for anyone or anything, except his guns."

"And now?" he asked.

"You're still arrogant at times," she teased, then added seriously, "but you care. Care so much more deeply than I ever thought possible."

"I'm glad you saw through my facade to the real me."

She ran her hands around his waist to hug him as he hugged her. "I find it difficult to believe you actually killed men."

"I never enjoyed it, never wanted it. Like you, life forced situations on me. I dealt with them."

"Much better than me," Prudence added.

"A compliment I'll gladly accept, though not entirely agree with."

"You're a gentleman, Zac Stewart." Her smile was hidden against his chest.

"What?" he cried in feigned shock. "Did you say *gentleman?*"

"Accept it as another compliment," she ordered, "for I doubt you'll hear me say it again."

He laughed warmheartedly. "I graciously accept it, dear wife, and thank you for it. I shall cherish it forever."

Zac felt the sudden stiffness of her posture and gently rubbed her back to help ease whatever doubts had snapped at her.

"Will you cherish me forever, Zac?" she asked, needing to hear a promise that he would never stop loving her.

He reached down and drew her face up to look at him. He kissed her softly. "I'll cherish you through this lifetime and beyond."

Prudence began to cry and Zac held her tightly, allowing her tears free rein.

Prudence sat alone in the family parlor. Zac had been called down to the stables, and her father and mother had retired early. She had promised Zac she would wait for him to return. The tender kiss and intimate touch he had left her with suggested she wouldn't be disappointed if she did.

"Prudence."

The lace curtain she was hemming almost fell from her lap, so unexpected was Granger's voice.

"I'm sorry if I startled you," he apologized, entering the room farther and coming to stand in front of her.

"Nonsense," she assured him with a slight shake of her head. "I was lost in my thoughts, that's all. Please join me." Her proper manners were the reason for her polite response, even though she would have preferred to ignore Granger and the last rude encounter she had had with him.

Granger took the chair to her right. "I was hoping to have some time alone to speak with you."

Prudence was prepared for another attempt on his part to see to the dissolvement of her marriage. He was certainly tenacious; she'd give him that much. "Well, here I am, Granger. Speak your mind."

It was obvious her brashness irritated him. He preferred when she held her tongue and spoke when a lady should.

"It is difficult for me to approach this subject, for I have only recently come to understand how much you've been hurt by past actions and don't wish to see the past repeated."

Prudence looked at him strangely.

352

"I wish to apologize for my father's horrible actions. What he did is unforgivable and I have no right to ask your forgiveness. I can only hope you will not hold his past transgressions against me. I wish for us to remain friends."

Prudence was stunned by his sincere expression of sorrow. "I would never hold you to blame for your father's actions. What is done is done. We can't change the past. We can only build on the future."

Granger nodded sadly. "This is true, and I wish you much happiness in your marriage. I had hoped for such happiness for us, but now I see it will never be and I wish the best for you and Zac."

Prudence leaned over and patted his hand. "You will find a woman more suited to your needs, Granger, and have a most wonderful marriage. I wasn't right for you."

A slight stiffening of his posture was the only sign of visible irritation, and it wasn't lost to Prudence's acute attention.

"I suppose you're right. You do seem much more content out here, but then I imagine it has something to do with your heritage."

"Which is another part of me you would find difficult, if not impossible, to accept," she offered without any malice.

"I do find it difficult thinking of you as part Indian," hc admittcd. "Though I fecl in time I would be able to deal with it. You must admit, it isn't easy to accept, even you must have reservations about it."

"Of course I do," she agreed. "One doesn't accept something like this lightly. It will take time. And I look forward to learning about that newly discovered part of me."

"I hope your discoveries are pleasant ones."

"Thank you, Granger," she said, still surprised at and dubious about his sudden change of heart.

"I will be returning to Boston with James and Lenore. I will do my utmost to see that your mother's reemergence into Boston society is smooth and without incident."

"That would be much appreciated."

Granger stood. "Again, Prudence, I apologize most profusely for my father's past transgressions and wish you much happiness in your marriage."

"Thank you, Granger. My wife and I appreciate your sincere good wishes."

Granger and Prudence turned together at the sound of Zac's voice. He stood leaning casually against the door frame, as though he had been there for some time.

Granger was unnerved by his presence. Zac commanded authority and respect with such ease that it galled Granger. It took some men years to achieve such consideration, while others always hungered for it yet never tasted it. Granger was one of the hungry, and he eyed Zac with envy.

"I thank you for your hospitality, Mr. Stewart, and hope I can return it whenever you visit Boston," Granger said. He gave a slight nod to Prudence, then left through the other doorway.

"He certainly has had a change of heart," Zac said, walking over to his wife. "Though I wonder how sincere it actually is."

Prudence folded up her sewing and placed it in the basket beside the chair. "Perhaps he is feeling repentant."

Zac laughed and bent down in front of her. "Perhaps we should get good Preacher Jacob to speak to him. He could cleanse Granger's soul in evening prayer."

Prudence laughed and shook her head. "I don't think

Preacher Jacob would care to cleanse a man's soul during evening prayer. His taste ran more for the female flock."

Zac raised an inquisitive brow. "Exactly how so?"

"He wanted to hear all the wicked things, in detail, that had been done to me and even appeared to want a demonstration, with him in your role."

"What did you do?" Zac asked, his tone a bit sharp.

Prudence recalled her hasty and successful escape with pride. "I got out of his reach just before his hands connected with my bottom."

Zac sprang up like a shooting bullet. "Why the hell was your bottom in reach of his hands?"

Prudence looked at him in surprise. "I had been on my knees in prayer for several hours and my limbs were numb. I fell over when I attempted to stand and get out of his way."

Zac ran his hand through his already-tousled hair, thereby making himself look all the more appealing. "Do you realize the danger you put yourself in?"

"Nothing happened," she defended.

"But it could have," he insisted. "You were foolish to take such chances."

"They were necessary at the time."

"You will never do anything so foolish again," he ordered. "And if I ever get my hands on that preacher, I'll wring his neck."

Prudence couldn't hide the smile that tugged at her lips.

"You find this funny?" he yelled, his agitation growing.

"Heartwarming," she corrected.

He looked at her as though she had just lost her mind. "Heartwarming?"

"Yes," she nodded and stood, walking over to him.

She placed her hand on his blue shirt, running it up and down his chest slowly. "It is heartwarming to know you care so much for me."

"I love you," he said, waiting for her response.

She kissed him tenderly and smiled, then her fingers began unbuttoning his shirt.

Chapter Twenty-eight

"Prudence, I'm giving you fair warning." Zac held her shoulders firmly. "You'd better be here when I return. I'll be gone three . . . four days at the most. And I'll only be at the far west end of the ranch. If there's an emergency, send one of the ranch hands with a message."

Prudence rolled her eyes heavenward. "You make it sound as though I'm just waiting for you to leave so I can rush off."

"Which you've done to me on several occasions, feeling justified each time."

"I was," she corrected him.

His grip on her tightened, and he brought her up closer to him. The rim of his black hat shaded both their faces from the morning sun. "This time you would definitely be wrong."

She attempted to correct him once again, but he silenced her with a bullying stare. "We need to talk more and you need to settle these fears of yours. We can't do that separated. You will stay put or else . . ."

Prudence didn't care for the "or else," though she was aware it was issued out of love and not demand. "Where would I go? There is much work to do here. The garden is ready for planting. I promised to help Bertha stitch her wedding dress. There are the curtains to be made for the receiving parlor. The list is endless."

"Good." He brushed a kiss across her lips.

Prudence frowned like a disappointed child. "Four days you'll be gone, and I receive a schoolboy kiss as a farewell?"

Zac's laughter was a playful rumble. "I thought after last night your lust for me would be satisfied."

She slipped her arms around his neck and drew herself up against him. In a whisper that was more sensual than low she said, "I think you've become a steady part of my diet, one that I find I'm unable to survive without."

He took her lips and fed off them as she did with his. They parted breathless and wanting.

"Or else." He repeated his warning once again before turning and mounting his horse.

Prudence went to him, placing her hand on his leg and looking up. The sun glared bright behind him and she could barely make out his features. "There's no danger to you, is there?"

"No." His answer was quick. "A small problem with some of the cattle. Nothing serious."

She smiled, pleased and relieved by his explanation.

"See you in a few days." He waved as he rode off with Josh.

Prudence felt a sense of deep loss as she watched him fade off into the distance. She couldn't shake it. It was an uneasy feeling, one that troubled her.

"He'll be back," her father assured her, walking out the front door and meeting her as she climbed the porch steps.

"I know." She smiled, although it was a forced one.

Her father drew his arm around her in the comforting embrace he had often offered her as a child. "Your

358

mother and I must leave in two days. I don't like leaving you here alone and despondent."

Prudence relished his fatherly concern. "I'm fine, really. And I'm not alone. Bertha and I will be busy sewing her wedding dress, and there's the Ladies Social Club meeting . . ."

Her father shook his head as her words trailed off, and he reached for his handkerchief in his back pocket. He wiped at the tears that fell slowly from her eyes onto her cheek. "Come and sit down a minute."

"I don't know what's the matter with me," she said, sitting in the rocker on the porch.

James sat in the other rocker beside her, pressing his handkerchief into her hands. "You're in love."

Prudence agreed with a nod. She reached her hand out to her father and he took it in a gentle squeeze. "Why can't I express my love for him? Why do I find the words so difficult to say to him?"

James felt the guilt weigh heavy on his shoulders. This was all his fault. In protecting his child, he had shielded her from fears and hurts and never allowed her to learn to deal with the normal pains of life. "You fear the hurt of losing that love and don't wish to open yourself to that pain again."

Her tears flowed more freely down her cheeks and she didn't stop them. "Why didn't you tell me the truth about Mother?"

James had been waiting for this moment, had expected it. He squeezed her hand once again, asking for forgiveness or acceptance, he wasn't certain. "I couldn't bear to see you hurt, to see the pain I knew her leaving would have brought you. I wanted to protect you."

"As Mother wanted to protect us?"

James shook his head sadly. "Sometimes we make decisions we think are right." He stopped a moment and shook his head even more strenuously. "But later we regret them and realize how very wrong we were. And then it's too late and they can no longer be mended."

It was Prudence's turn to squeeze her father's hand in comfort. "I'm glad I found Mother for us."

James smiled in pleasure. "You always were tenacious and stubborn."

"Determined," Lenore corrected from the doorway.

"Yes. I like that description of me much better," Prudence agreed. "I do have a determined nature."

"I have some sweet buns left from breakfast," Lenore offered. "Shall we all steal a late morning snack?"

James sprang out of his seat, realizing Lenore was offering more than buns. She was offering, by the simple shared act, that they become a family once again. "Don't have to ask me twice."

Prudence patted at her damp eyes before she stood. "I'm with you, Papa."

James took Prudence's hand and reached out for Lenore's. She extended her hand to him without hesitation. "How lucky can a man get to have the two most beautiful women in the world by his side."

Lenore laughed.

Prudence stared wide-eyed at him. Her father had never called her beautiful the whole time she was growing up. The sincere words touched her heart. She entered the house with her parents, filled with a sense of peace and appreciation.

The late afternoon sun shone through the dining room windows, filling the room with warmth and brightness. Prudence noted, with pride, the way the sun spotlighted the highly polished table.

She sighed with satisfaction and draped the ivory

lace cloth over the middle, then added a tan pitcher filled with wild yellow and white daisies.

"All ready," Prudence said, and was surprised when a voice answered her, since she had assumed she was still alone, her mother and father having gone off on a walk.

"For what, may I ask?" Granger inquired.

"The Stewart Ladies Social Club meeting on Thursday," she answered, having grown more relaxed around Granger since he had ceased his attempts to convince her to marry him.

"I wouldn't have thought there would be enough women in these parts to form such a group."

"There are more people around than you think. It's just that the ranches are spread out, and neighbors don't always get to see each other as often as they like. That was why I formed the club."

"And organized the building of the church?"

"Someone's been talking to you," Prudence said, motioning for him to follow her to the kitchen.

Granger sat at the plain wooden table, though he was obviously uneasy in such common surroundings. "Everyone I meet sings your praises. They tell me how much you have done for this town and how they are certain Stewart will prosper because of your help."

Prudence poured them each a glass of cooled mint tea. "They just needed someone to organize things."

"You always were good at that," Granger offered in way of a compliment.

Prudence accepted it with a gracious smile, since it was the only one he had ever paid her.

"Zac won't be back to see your parents off?"

"No, he had business to tend to at the far west end of the ranch."

"That's a shame. I did want to thank him for his hospitality," Granger said, sipping at his tea.

"Does business often take him away for days?"

Prudence shrugged her shoulders. "I really can't say. I haven't been here long enough to know the complete workings of the ranch."

"I was under the impression that the owner of a ranch didn't actually involve himself in the work . . . that he hired the appropriate men to do that."

"Zac has many ranch hands and there's Josh, the ranch foreman. But Zac keeps his hands in the thick of things to make certain all goes well."

"Then this must have been something terribly important to have taken him away and to leave you on your own to say farewell to your parents."

Prudence was about to agree, when she realized she didn't really know just how important the matter was.

"I know it won't be easy for you to bid them goodbye, even if only for a few months. After all, you haven't seen your mother in years and she's leaving again."

Prudence didn't respond. She sipped at her tea.

"But you're strong and resilient. I guess it's sort of like taking a punch and bouncing back, so to speak. You're made of strong stock, Prudence. A quality trait and one I vastly admire."

Prudence nodded and remained silent.

Granger didn't, continuing on. "I suppose the men out here, in the West, are different. They tend to leave their womenfolk on their own much of the time, feeling them capable of handling all matters. Boston men have a tendency to protect their women, sort of shield them from everyday problems."

"I don't need shielding," Prudence offered more sternly than necessary.

"Of course not. Just look at what you've accomplished on your own, with no help from Zac. He was

362

lucky to have found you. I bet any other woman he had brought here would have perished from the isolation. But you were accustomed to being alone, finding pleasure in your own company."

"What are you getting at, Granger?" Prudence snapped, not caring for the direction of this conversation.

Granger appeared startled by her vehement response. "Nothing, my dear. I'm just saying how safe you are tucked away here in the wilderness. There's no need for you to concern yourself with your common looks any longer or hide your fingers. Out here it doesn't matter. There aren't that many people who will take notice or care."

Prudence understood his intent perfectly. He assumed that Zac had married her for his own benefit, as well as for the town's. That Zac didn't actually love her or think her attractive. And that Zac was proving just how much he didn't care by not being there to help her through her parent's departure.

"I think this life will suit you well." Granger stood. "And Zac, I'm certain, will make the perfect husband. I will inform all your friends in Boston how happy and content you are."

Prudence leaned casually back in her chair. "Yes, by all means do tell everyone of my happiness. And what a wonderful husband Zac has made. I just know the women will be green with envy, since so many of them found him attractive."

Granger stiffened his posture. "I will tell them. They will probably find the subject fascinating."

Prudence stifled a laugh. "Yes, I should make for at least a month's worth of juicy gossip."

Granger could hide his true distaste for her brash responses no longer. "Doesn't your husband find your outspoken remarks distasteful?"

Prudence allowed her smile to spread wide. "Actually, he finds me quite *tasteful.*"

Granger turned several shades of red, mumbled and spat something unintelligible, then hastily left the kitchen.

"That wasn't at all proper, Prudence," she scolded herself. "But who gives a hoot. He deserved it."

Granger was purposely trying to place doubt in her mind about Zac's love for her. He couldn't accept the fact that she was happy with what he assumed was much less than he was willing to offer her. He measured attachments by money and possessions. Granger would never love a woman for herself. He would love—if you could call it that—only what she could offer him.

Zac was different. He honestly loved her. There wasn't anything he wouldn't do for her. He'd follow her to the ends of the earth, his love for her was that strong.

But would he follow her to Boston?

The strange thought nagged at her. She was aware that Granger had planted the seed of doubt and that it had taken root. Should she test the Fates and see how strong his love really was? Would that force her to open up to him and declare her love?

Or else! His warning echoed loudly in her ears.

She really wasn't one for taking orders.

She stood. "Now where did I put my traveling cases?"

"Prudence, you can't mean to go through with this," her father said for the third time.

"I most certainly do," she answered firmly, pulling her gloves on with a vicious tug.

James Winthrop shook his head and looked to his wife for help. Lenore shrugged her shoulders.

"Some time apart will do us good, and *if* Zac wishes to *join* me, then he can follow and catch up."

James shook his head. His daughter was being anything but intelligent at the moment. She was acting more like those all-too-senseless women who insist a man must prove himself worthy of her love. James knew that Zac was not going to like this one bit.

"Prudence has a point, James," Granger joined in. "Many of her friends back in Boston will be thrilled to hear the news of her marriage and will wish to host various social functions for the couple. I'm sure Zac will catch up and they will enjoy the trip together."

James wanted to shake some sense into the two. Lenore placed her hand on his arm, and with a gentle smile, shook her head.

"If Prudence wishes to join us, James, it is her decision," Lenore said calmly.

James opened his mouth to disagree, thought better of it, and shut it.

"Good, then let's be off," Granger said, reaching for Prudence's case.

She stopped him with a hand to his arm. "I can manage myself."

Prudence was the last to leave the house. She looked about one final time, checking to make sure her note to Zac was on the hall table. A shudder ran through her as she remembered similar past actions, and she hastily closed the door behind her.

"She's making a serious mistake. Why don't you say something to her?" James asked, standing next to his wife on the steamboat and watching it pull away from the dock.

"It isn't my place," Lenore answered.

"You're her mother, and you know as well as I do she expected Zac to catch up with her before we made it this far and demand she return with him."

"She must learn from her own mistakes."

James ran his fingers through his hair in frustration. "Look how long and how much we suffered because of our mistakes. You wish the same for your daughter?"

"No, James," Lenore said softly. "But Prudence wouldn't go back now no matter what either one of us said. Her pride is hurt, and unless Zac comes for her, this marriage, to her, will be over."

"But he loves her," James growled through gritted teeth.

"Then he will come."

James sighed and ran his fingers through his hair once again. "Women!"

Lenore smiled and hugged her husband's arm.

"Boston should be beautiful now. The flowers surrounding your home should be in full bloom and Glenda should be in a state of near panic with her plans for her summer social," Granger said. He strolled casually along the upper deck of the steamboat with Prudence, her arm draped around his.

Prudence stopped and turned to Granger. "I'm afraid I'm not feeling well. Would you be so kind as to get me a cool drink?"

"Of course I will. Shall I help you to your cabin first?"

"No, that isn't necessary. I prefer the fresh air, but require something cool to quench the dryness in my throat and soothe my upset stomach."

Granger patted her arm. "I'll only be a moment."

Prudence sighed with relief when he left. She

couldn't stand him another minute. All he talked about was Boston and their old life there. He seemed to have no doubts about them returning to the way things were before she had left. She hadn't thought that possible a few days ago, but now . . .

"Are you all right, Prudence?" Lenore asked, coming up behind her.

Prudence turned with a smile, which disappeared at the sight of her mother. She burst into tears.

Lenore placed her arms around her daughter and directed her toward the front of the boat, where there were less people about.

"I was so stupid," she cried against her mother's shoulder.

Lenore patted her back as if she were a small child needing comfort. "You thought the decision wise at the time. We all make mistakes."

"I should have stayed. He kept expressing his love for me, and here I go off and leave him, and for what reason? . . . To make certain he loves me. It wasn't his love I was trying to prove. It was mine."

"Then go back."

"I can't. I would feel like a fool," she cried, having trapped herself in her own good intentions.

"Do not be foolish and allow your pride to stop you," Lenore warned. "I speak from experience."

Prudence looked up at her. "You thought of coming back to us?"

"Many times, but I feared the reception I would receive and could not face the doubts."

"But we would have welcomed you with open arms."

"I did not know this."

Prudence's shoulders sagged. "You think I should go back to Zac before it's too late."

Lenore cupped her daughter's face in her hands and

shook her own head slowly. "I cannot tell you what you must do. Only you can decide. But I beg you to choose wisely and from your heart."

"Mama," she cried, throwing herself into Lenore's arms.

Chapter Twenty-nine

Prudence glanced over her shoulder for the tenth time in twenty minutes. Nothing had changed in the chaotic scene of people hurrying about, preparing to board the train at Plattsmouth.

It was different from the last time she was here. Then she was heading in the opposite direction, and she had prayed that Zac wouldn't show up. Now she prayed he would appear and demand she return home with him.

"There's still plenty of time to change your mind," her father urged, coming up behind her. "I could change your ticket and you could get the early train back tomorrow morning."

"There's an early train tomorrow morning?"

He nodded in excitement, hoping that Prudence would realize her foolishness and return to Zac. He had to at least try to convince her to return, or the guilt would haunt him for the rest of his life. "I spoke with the station-master and he informed me there would be no problem exchanging tickets."

Prudence fought against the urge to run inside the ticket office and scream for her ticket to be exchanged. If Zac hadn't made the effort to come after her, perhaps he didn't love her after all.

"Zac could have been held up by that problem at the ranch," her father offered, almost reading her thoughts. "Or perhaps he's been hurt."

The awful prospect registered clearly on Prudence's face.

Her father played on her fear further, hoping it would force her to return. "You really should consider the possibility. He might need you at this very moment. He could be seriously injured. You should go back immediately."

"I'm sure Zac's ranch foreman would have sent a wire somewhere along the way, informing Prudence if such a mishap occurred," Granger said, joining father and daughter.

Prudence's sigh was audible. "He's right, Father. Josh would have wired me."

James wanted to strangle Granger with his very own hands. "I still feel it wise for you to return."

"Nonsense, James. Why, Zac is probably taking his time and intends to join Prudence in Boston," Granger suggested, and reached for Prudence's hand. "Allow me to assist you in boarding the train." He took her hand and they walked off.

James stepped forward to protest, when he was stopped by Lenore's hand to his arm. Prudence and Granger walked ahead.

"Let it be," she said softly.

"But she's making a mistake. A dreadful mistake. I can't just stand by and watch her throw her life away," James insisted. His frustration mounted with each step his daughter took with Granger toward the train.

"You cannot force her to return. It would do her no good. She must walk this passage of her life herself. Her strength and courage will guide her."

James looked doubtful. "Her life experiences have been limited. She isn't mature enough to understand the implication of her foolish actions."

370

Lenore addressed him with a gentle and patient smile. "She has experienced much more than you think. Allow her this *folly* and watch over her with a hopeful heart."

"This certainly is a folly. My heart is breaking in two, knowing what a dreadful mistake she's making and not doing anything to stop it."

Lenore guided him toward the train upon hearing the blast of the boarding whistle. "Watch and see, James. It will all work out."

James muttered beneath his breath while boarding, thinking women were not, nor would they ever be, practical creatures.

The train chugged forward with a start, rocking the passengers in their seats. It pulled away slowly, picking up speed as it drew more power from the mighty engine.

Prudence felt her heart break with each chug of the train. She had envisioned Zac coming after her. The scene had been so vivid in her mind's eye. He'd wear his black waistcoat and trousers. His silver six-shooters would be strapped on and his hat would ride low in that familiar fashion that shaded his eyes from view, yet allowed him the privilege of scrutinizing those around him.

He would declare his love for her and demand that she return with him. He might even throw her over his shoulder and storm off to the nearest hotel.

Her cheeks flushed to a pale pink from the heat her mental wandering had brought upon her. Prudence had to admit she missed the intimacy they shared. She no longer felt shy around him. She was familiar and comfortable with him, and she liked the easy feeling.

She sighed and rested her head against the pane of the train window. She would miss this land and the people. But most of all she would miss Zac. It had taken her departure to make her realize her love for him was just as strong as his love for her. She shouldn't have questioned or tested it. He had offered it to her freely. Had spoken of it openly. He loved her, *from the tips of her toes to the top of her head,* and that's all there was to it.

"You're doing the right thing, Prudence," Granger said, patting her hand that rested on her lap.

Prudence turned to him. "Why do you say that, Granger?"

"If the man truly loves you, he would have followed you immediately. As soon as I heard about you and Zac, I insisted on joining your father. I wanted to ascertain for myself your reason for marrying Zac and if you wished to remain married to him."

"Then you feel Zac doesn't really care for me?"

"No, no, dear. I'm sure Mr. Stewart cares about you, but I doubt he's capable of proper love."

"Proper love?"

"Yes." Granger nodded, his expression somber. "Proper love. Love that is given and experienced with respect and concern for a woman's delicate nature."

"Delicate nature?"

Granger cast a hesitant glance about him, then spoke in a whisper. "Most women object to the marriage bed and must be handled delicately so as not to cause distress."

Prudence lowered her voice to a whisper. "You mean like not upsetting your wife by undressing in front of her and performing conjugal rights with the lights off. And by retiring to your own bedroom during your wife's *delicate condition.*"

Granger appeared startled. "Zac treats you so . . . like a gentleman?"

Prudence wanted to laugh in his face. Zac made love to her like a man in love should, without restraints or doubts. She shook her head sadly, sighing dramatically for effect. "No, he doesn't allow me privacy. I must undress in front of him. And the lights, they're on all the time. And he says that when I bear his child, he will remain in my bed and touch me often."

Granger gasped, bringing his hand to cover his heart in shock. "How awful it must have been for you, my dear."

Prudence raised her hand to cover her mouth and the giggle that threatened to escape. "Yes, awful. Simply awful."

"Do not worry, Prudence. I will be there for you to help you recover from this dreadful ordeal. I will treat you as a lady should be treated, and soon you will forget these horrible memories."

Prudence didn't respond. Her mind was busy sifting through her treasure chest of memories. They would keep her warm in the lonely ensuing years. And she would have no one to blame but herself.

"Don't fret, my dear," Granger comforted, assuming she was upset. "I'll be beside you."

Prudence raised her head at her father's choked cough. He had overheard their exchange and was voicing his objection most strenuously, since his cough continued and grew louder until it was silenced abruptly. Prudence bit her lip to hide her grin.

The blast of the shrieking train whistle startled everyone. Then the slowing down of the mighty metal vehicle caused fear and panic to set in.

"Holdup! Holdup!" someone screamed.

Several women began to cry and small children added their fearful wails.

Granger began to sweat, the watery beads popping out along his forehead and running down his face.

Prudence shook her head in disgust and turned her attention out the window. There was no band of outlaws or Indians in sight on either side of the train. Yet the train continued to slow down until it finally came to a dead stop.

Passengers began to jump from their seats, some hugging their children to them, others grasping their traveling cases tightly to their chests as though in protection.

Loud squeals and cries of fright from the passengers in the car in front of them caused even more chaos.

"Stay calm and stay put," James called back to Prudence and Granger.

Prudence was proud of the way her father sat steadfast and unnerved in the seat before her. Even if he were fearful, he didn't display the emotion. Granger, on the other hand, trembled uncontrollably, shaking the whole seat and Prudence in the process.

High-pitched screams and the connecting car doors squeaking open caused a rush of nervous tension to run through Prudence. She squared her shoulders and angled her chin defiantly, prepared to meet the unknown foe.

Shock and relief mixed with excitement and anticipation when her eyes met those of her husband. His look was cold and furious. She was in trouble. Definitely in trouble.

"Please, ladies and gentlemen," Zac said calmly, turning on his most disarming smile, "you have nothing to fear. I'm not a train robber. I'm actually here to *collect* a notorious thief!"

A unified gasp echoed throughout the car.

He began walking slowly toward the back where Prudence sat. His steps were measured, his pace slow and sure. He was obviously attempting to intimidate, and he was doing an excellent job.

He even looked formidable, just like the day he had entered the Devil's Den saloon. He was in black, only this time he wore a white shirt opened casually at the neck, improper but suggestively appealing. His dark waistcoat was drawn back behind his six-shooters, which firmly hugged his thick thighs. He was minus his black hat, though Prudence wished he had worn it. His hair was too rumpled, which gave him an even more dangerous air of appeal.

"Is this thief dangerous?" a passenger called out.

"Extremely," Zac answered, and turned his attention directly on Prudence.

"Apprehend him before he steals from us," yelled a woman.

Zac stopped a few seats in front of Prudence. "You have nothing to fear, ma'am. This thief steals but one thing and only from men."

"What's that?"

Prudence's brow raised considerably upon recognizing her father's voice.

Zac smiled and sent James an appreciative nod. "This thief stole a heart. Left it bruised and broken."

Granger stood up as though to protect Prudence when Zac stopped in front of their seat.

Zac shook his head over his petty demonstration of strength and shoved Granger back down into his seat, dismissing him without a second thought. He addressed Prudence in a voice that all could hear. "You have two choices, Prudence Agatha. You can serve a punishment or make amends."

"See here!" Granger tried again to defend.

"Shut up," Zac warned and poked Granger's chest roughly, pushing him back against the seat. The man stilled instantly.

Prudence's voice was strong, though it took much will-power to control the quiver that hid beneath. "What would be the punishment and what of the amends?"

He held her stare for a minute, and it was clear to Prudence that these terms would offer her only chance.

"Return to Boston alone, or stand up here now and declare your love for me."

Prudence felt the icy shiver down to the tips of her toes. She had placed herself in this position. There was no one

375

to blame. She had forced the issue. He had come after her . . . had proven his love beyond a doubt. Now it was her turn . . . and the only one she would get.

She dropped her head a moment, closing her eyes and taking a deep breath. It was now or never. She tugged on her gloves, adjusted her bonnet — Zac's favorite one — and stood up prim and proper before him.

Every eye on the train was focused on her. Her father and mother were turned around in their seats with smiles brightening their faces.

This wasn't how she had envisioned it. Zac would state his love for her and then she would do the same. She felt the sob lodge in her throat and cut off her voice. Her eyelids fluttered and tears tickled at her lashes.

"Damn!" Zac said, and his hand was instantly at her face, wiping the watery beads from her cheeks. "I love you, Prudence Agatha."

Prudence's eyes popped open wide, and she half sobbed, half cried out for all to hear, "I love you, Zac Stewart."

The train car burst into a loud and approving round of applause.

Zac grabbed Prudence around the waist and pulled her past Granger to stand in the aisle before him. He bent down and, with a broad smile, kissed her soundly.

Another loud burst of applause carried throughout the car.

"Let's go home, Pru," Zac said, resting his forehead against hers to catch the breath that her kiss had robbed from him.

"Yes, let's go home," she agreed. Her voice was a shaky whisper.

She gave her mother and father a quick hug and kiss and told them to hurry back *home*. Zac and she were walking toward the door of the train car when she suddenly stopped.

"What's wrong?" he asked.

Prudence patted his arm. "I forgot something."

Zac looked her up and down appreciatively. "Looks as though you've got everything to me."

She kissed him on the cheek. "I'll be right back."

Granger stood as she approached. "Thank God you've come to your senses. For a moment I actually thought you were stupid enough to go with him."

Prudence smiled kindly and shook her head. "No, Granger. Stupid I'm not." And with that, she pulled her right arm back, made a tight fist, and threw it with full force at his nose.

Granger stumbled back. His hand grabbed at his face, catching the blood that poured from his nostrils.

"That's for the pain your father brought my family and for what you tried to do to me." Prudence gave her mother and father another quick kiss and told them to enjoy their second honeymoon.

She ran down the aisle to Zac and threw herself into his outstretched arms. "I love you, Zac Stewart. I love you."

Chapter Thirty

Prudence found herself standing beside the bed in their room at the Hotel Lillian, nervous and apprehensive. After they had exited the train, Zac had insisted that they find a decent preacher and get married all over again.

They had stood before Preacher Handel in the small church of Plattsmouth and willingly repeated the vows that they had once before recited. Granny Hayes had stood beside Prudence as witness and Mr. Lewis of the mercantile had stood beside Zac. Afterward, it seemed as if the whole town had shown up at the local saloon to help celebrate their union. There was singing and dancing and rabble-rousing, in which Granny happily took part.

Now that Prudence stood before her husband in their hotel room she felt the shyness of a newlywed bride. This night would be different from all the others. Today they had declared their love readily before God and friends. And tonight they would share their love with no restraints or bounds, almost as if it were their first time together.

Zac walked up to her. He had already shed his jacket and shirt. His chest was bare and mighty appealing. "Shall I help you undress?"

Prudence recalled the night at the fort and how he had undressed her then. She shivered from the erotic memory.

"I'll take that as a yes," he said, and lifted her mouth up to meet his lips. He kissed her thoroughly, sampling every nook and cranny of her delectable mouth. She was breathless by the time he released her.

His fingers worked quickly, divesting her of her clothes. "I do so love undressing you. Seeing your warm naked flesh come into view piece by sensuous piece excites the devil in me."

She stood in her chemise, bloomers, and gloves. He caught her cautious look and smiled wickedly. He raised her arms above her head and sternly ordered her to keep them there. He then lifted her cotton chemise slowly, easing the soft material up and over her breasts while his mouth feasted at her hard nipples.

He moaned when she brought her hands down around his back. The feel of her white cotton gloves against his hot skin was torturous.

The moan heightened her own passion, as she felt his breath tingle across her nipples. She didn't think they could harden any farther, but they did, aching from her need for him.

He didn't disappoint her. He eased and intensified her condition all with the skillful lick of his tongue.

His hands moved to her bloomer band and his mouth traveled up to rest next to her ear. "I have a confession, honey."

"What, Zac?" Her breath was heavy with passion.

"It's wicked, awfully wicked."

"I like when you're wicked, *Mr. Stewart*."

"Good, honey, because tonight I'm going to be *real* wicked."

He took a moment then to slip out of the remainder of his clothes, discarding them to the side.

Prudence was about to rid herself of her gloves, when his hands stopped her. She looked at him strangely.

"That's the wicked part, honey. I want you naked, except for your gloves. I want you to leave them on."

His sensual suggestion heightened her eagerness by leaps and bounds. Then she smiled a playful smile of her own and slowly ran her hand down his chest, circling his nipples with the tip of her glove-covered hand.

Zac sucked in his breath.

Prudence laughed.

"Sinful hussy," he whispered, though it sounded more like a choke.

"But you do like it, don't you, Mr. Stewart?" she said, running her hand down lower and lower until she found him and gently took him in her hand.

"Damn," he cried as she stroked him languidly.

"Your language, Mr. Stewart."

"Your actions, Mrs. Stewart."

"Shall I stop?" Her hand stilled.

His hands rested on her bloomer band. "Only if you want *me* to."

She gave a naughty laugh and resumed her stroking.

He removed her last piece of clothing.

They stood naked before each other except for the gloves.

He rested his forehead against hers while she continued to touch and caress him. "Fantasies do come true, honey."

"Don't I know," she murmured, capturing his lips with hers.

Zac took her in his arms, deepened the kiss, and picked her up to place her on the bed. He covered her with the length of him. Their touches were urgent, their kisses hungry. They needed each other with a desperate fury that spun out of control.

He spread her legs with his, wasting no more time, his

need for her ferocious, unrelenting. He had to have her and now.

They became one in an instant. Their moves were exact, their tempo perfect. Their bodies blended together like a perfect tune, their release timed to the second. Together they cried out their love for each other.

Prudence's arms remained wrapped around him. She stroked his back as he lay exhausted on top of her, his breathing heavy and labored as though he had run miles and miles.

Her own breathing came in short grasps and she relished in it. She had missed intimacy with her husband much more than she had ever imagined she would. Zac was her life. She loved him beyond reason.

"You keep touching me like that with those gloves, Mrs. Stewart, and you'll find yourself in this position for the entire evening."

Zac's breath was hot against her cooling skin, and it sent shivers through her body.

Zac pushed himself up to look down at her. "Cold?"

Her hands rubbed at the sides of his arms. "I have the perfect blanket."

He laughed and slipped off her, taking her with him. She was settled without fuss or trouble on top of him. "Now I have the perfect blanket."

"I'll keep you warm." Her soft tone promised his temperature would remain constant. Constantly hot.

He laughed. "You've changed, Prudence Agatha, and I like it."

"You mean, I'm not stiff and proper any longer?"

Zac ran his finger slowly along her lips. "You've matured into a radiant beauty in more ways than one."

Prudence sighed and accepted his compliment without doubt. "You mean, I'm not the same woman you met back in Boston?"

"Let me think about that," Zac paused, and received a

swat to the arm from Prudence for his teasing. "You are definitely not the same woman, honey. You're *my* woman now."

Prudence didn't mind his suggestion of ownership of her. She understood that Zac didn't actually want to own her and that he never could. She was too free in her thoughts and opinions, and no restraints could be placed on a woman with such tenacity. No, Zac spoke of a different type of ownership. One they both shared in equally.

"I love you, Zac," she whispered, and nuzzled her head in the crook of his neck.

Zac shivered and hugged her to him. "You have no idea how wonderful that sounds to me. I thought it would take . . . oh, say, until our tenth wedding anniversary to hear it."

Prudence nipped playfully at his neck.

"Careful," he warned. "I bite back."

"Promise?" she teased.

He swatted her bottom lightly. "There's no need for promises, Pru. I'll love you until my dying day and even afterwards. "You're everything I ever wanted. I don't need any more."

Prudence pushed herself up, resting her hands on his chest for support. "But I can give you much, Zac."

"You already have," he said, winking.

Prudence shook her head. "No, no. I mean I have money that will help our ranch grow and prosper. There's also more than enough to help the town grow."

Zac looked her straight in the eye. "I don't want, nor do I need, your money."

Prudence's pout was obvious. "But there must be something I can give you. Something you've wanted but perhaps put off."

"Can't think of a thing."

Prudence sighed her disappointment. "But I wanted to give you something special. Something nobody else has.

Something you'll cherish forever and ever." She realized she was being overly dramatic, but for some reason it was important to her. He had given her so much, had taught her so much about life, real life, that she felt this imperative to their relationship.

"What I want your money can't buy me."

Excitement instantly filled Prudence. "But it can. It can. What is it you want? I'll get it for you immediately."

Zac shook his head slowly. "There are some things money just can't buy."

Prudence was about to argue but stopped when she realized he was right. Her money couldn't have bought his love for her. Her father's hadn't even bought his services to come after her.

She touched his chin tentatively. "If it's in my power to give you what you want, then I will give it freely and most willingly."

Zac smiled contentedly. She had learned and grown so much since that first day he had met her. She was like the last blossom on the vine, late in maturing but the most beautiful.

"Will you tell me what it is?" she asked anxiously.

He cupped her face in his hands and drew her to him. He whispered in her ear. "I want you to give me a son or a daughter."

Tears threatened to spill as she looked down at him. "Mr. Stewart, I'll gladly fulfill your request. Actually, I could fulfill it many times."

"Promise?" he teased with that disarming smile she loved so much.

"I promise on one condition."

"Which is?"

"We begin immediately."

Zac's answer was a long, intoxicating kiss that left her weak and wanting for more.

She raised her hand to his lips after he had released her

mouth, placing the tips of her white gloves near his teeth. "I want to feel you when I touch you this time."

Zac took the gloved tip of each finger between his teeth, one by one, and pulled the gloves off, letting them fall to the side. "All the barriers have been removed, honey. There's only you and me."

He was right. All the barriers were gone. Nothing stood in their way.

Prudence Agatha lowered her head with a smile and captured her husband's waiting lips.